The Sacred Ten

A Philosophical and Historical Novel spiced with advanced Spiritual Science.

The Sacred Ten

BOOK 1
The Quest for Truth
&
BOOK 2
Quantum Leaps to Paradise

SIMHA SERAYA *and* ALBERT HALDANE

THE SACRED TEN –THE QUEST FOR TRUTH -QUANTUM LEAPS TO PARADISE
Copyrights © 2000-2012 by Simha Seraya and Albert Haldane. All rights reserved.
No part of this book may be used or reproduced in any manner whatsoever without written permission, except for brief quotations in books and critical review.

For information contact Publishing Management: and Authors
MANAKAEL MASTERWORKS INC
E-mail: archangel7997@gmail.com

Visionary, Metaphysical.
Categories: Keywords
Philosophical novel, Linguistics, Universal Language.
Adventure, Time Travel, Cosmic Travel.
Kabala, Hebrew, Christian Cabala.
Old Testament, New Testament,
Ten Commandments, Exodus, Genesis.
Angels. Archangels. Celestial visitors.
History of Humanity, Egypt, Mesopotamia,
Israel, Judea, India, China, Japan.
Adam, Yohanan Ben Zakai, Benjamin Franklin, Beruriah,
Buddha, Eve, Lao Tzu, Moses.
Philosophy, Religion, Spirituality, Mythology, History.

First Edition
ISBN 10: 0-98371-020-1
ISBN 13: 978-0-9837102-0-2

LCCN 2011933056

Printed in the United States of America

The scanning, uploading and distribution of this book via the internet or via any other means without the permission of the publisher is illegal and punishable by law. Please purchase only authorized electronic editions, and do not participate in or encourage electronic piracy of copyrighted materials. Your support of the authors' rights is appreciated.

Novel - This is a work of fiction. The characters, incidents, and dialogues are drawn from the authors' imagination and are not to be construed as real. Any resemblance to actual events or persons, living or dead, is entirely coincidental.

Also by Simha Seraya *and* Albert Haldane

ANGEL SIGNS

A Celestial Guide to the Powers of Your Own Guardian Angel

SIGNOS DOS ANJOS

Brazilian Portuguese Version

Translations from French and Commentaries

MISSION OF THE JEWS

Alexandre Saint-Yves d'Alveydre

THE GOLDEN THREAD OF WORLD HISTORY

Advanced Civilizations as far as 30,000 Years Ago.

Alexandre Saint-Yves d'Alveydre

By Albert Haldane

L'Ethique de Giordano Bruno

Les Mémoires du Futur

Alpha Song

DEDICATION

To all our mothers, to all our fathers,
to all our ancestors,
on Earth and in the Heavens.

FOREWORD

In regard with the destiny of this literary work we can only be sure of this: *you* are reading the first lines of the foreword to "The Sacred Ten", and we, the authors, hereby extend our warmest greetings to you! We assume, with delight, neither the word SACRED nor the genre "PHILOSOPHICAL NOVEL" are repellent to your curious mind.

Now we sincerely hope you shall continue reading this short introduction, and then reach the *Table of Contents*, the *Prologue* and the page listing the *Protagonists of this cosmic saga*.

At this point you shall be aware the book is a complete narration of our prodigious voyage "on the wings of Angels". And (quote) "*reminiscence of our recent cosmic adventures, for the purpose of writing this journal, we expect to be, for us and for you as well, excellent cerebral calisthenics, a betterment of mental and spiritual capacities to the effect of traveling farther in space, deeper in time.*"

You will also have read the words Angels, Celestial humans, Kabalah, Ten Commandments fully alive, their true meaning decrypted, unveiled and revealed, Archae Lingua, Universal Language, mother of all tongues.

You will have pondered on familiar or unfamiliar personal names such as Moses, Yohanan Ben Zakai, Lao Tzu, Eve, Adam, Buddha, Beruriah, Benjamin Franklin.

You will have mused on space-time locations such as Manhattan USA 2001 AD, Lo-Yang China 6th century BC, Brur Hayl Galilee Israel 1st century BC, Paris France 2001 AD, Edenia Zumaria Constellation Eternity, Chartres cathedral Ile de France Off Time, Philadelphia USA 1782 AD, Santiago de Compostella Galicia Spain Off Time, Rajagriba India 6th century BC, and last but not least, The Corridors of Paradise, on the edge of Infinity.

When you reach this point, beyond the appearance of perusing a series of preambles you shall have in fact already started reading the novel, and, furthermore, through your own inner questioning, you shall have yourself become an active protagonist of this philosophical spiritual exploration, the Quest for Truth!

Soon, after reading one or two chapters of "The Sacred Ten" you too shall be able to provide your own answers to the questions often asked:

Is it a novel? Is it a book of deep spiritual teaching and practice? Is it a daring philosophy book? Is it an enlightening account of humankind's origin and evolution, encompassing millions of years? Is it a book of intelligent Faith? Is it a book of advanced Science? Is it a book of personal betterment and growth? Is it a book of true Kabalah? Is it about religion and religionists? Is it an easy to read "no-brainer" book? Is it a book who offers deep answers to one who questions nothing?

Does "The Sacred Ten" chart new continents of the mind and open new paths linking mind and spirit, human and divine? Yes.

Does "The Sacred Ten" clearly and fully decipher the hidden messages MOSES has linguistically encrypted in the biblical Ten Commandments? Yes.

Does "The Sacred Ten" reveal and expound the true nature and universal import of the Exodus? Yes.

Does "The Sacred Ten" demonstrate the existence and fundamental role, past, present and future, of a core Universal Language, valid for communicating all around planet Earth and beyond? Yes.

Does "The Sacred Ten", revisiting biblical scriptures, ancient myths and legends, give them a new life and meaning under the light of today's and tomorrow's science and technology? Yes.

Does “The Sacred Ten” resolve the mysteries of Death, Life and Soul immortality? Yes.

Is “The Sacred Ten”? Does “The Sacred Ten”? One Thousand and One more questions could not encompass the uncountable facets of this work!

That is why, dear reader, we must set you free, immediately, for you to start reading “The Sacred Ten” and commence your own discovery journey, seeking for Truth, through time and space.

Farewell!

SIMHA SERAYA & ALBERT HALDANE

The Sacred Ten

BOOK 1
The Quest for Truth
&
BOOK 2
Quantum Leaps to Paradise

TABLE OF CONTENTS

PROLOGUE

For *you* we are penning the complete narration of our prodigious voyage “on the wings of Angels”. For those who will, sooner or later undertake a similar journey, we are relating in great details the events, emotions, thoughts and revelations emerged during our recent voyage through time and space. We have no doubt that travels on the “wings of an Angel” will become widespread, and many men and women will certainly appreciate finding those amazing charts and astonishing reports we are presenting here to the attention of the seekers of Truth.

The next lap of our impending exploratory expedition will soon commence, and it is only to record our discoveries electronically and on paper that we came back to Manhattan NY, our home base on Earth. Year 2001 has just begun; we expect commencing soon the second phase of the voyage.

Reminiscence of our recent cosmic adventures, for the purpose of writing this journal, we expect to be, for us and for you as well, excellent cerebral calisthenics, a betterment of mental and spiritual capacities to the effect of traveling farther in space, deeper in time.

When you read those lines, chances are we shall not be around to answer your questions. And that is why we are endeavoring to be clear and thorough, for your benefit, for your enjoyment and, if need be, for your inspiration.

Simha Albert
Manhattan, March 26, 2001

PROTAGONISTS OF THIS COSMIC SAGA

Humans

SIMHA: truth seeker, time-space traveler, kabalist. Principal Narrator.
ALBERT: truth seeker, time-space traveler, philosopher. Second Narrator.
MARIE TANIA: friend, on planet Earth.

Angels

YELIYAEL: Seraph Angel, time-space navigator and celestial archives keeper.
YEZALAEL: Seraph Angel, beyond time-space navigator, special messenger.
GABRIEL: Archangel.

Celestial Humans

YOHANAN BEN ZAKAI: Rabbi in the 1st Century BC, Academy Founder.
MOSES: Prophet and civilization founder, 1492 BC.
JOSUAH BEN NOUN: war and peace strategist, successor to Moses.
MANOUSH: tribe leader and Gypsy singer.
LAO TZU: Chinese sage and poet, 6th Century BC.
LADY BERURIAH: Talmud and Kabalah teacher, 2nd Century AD.
EVE AND ADAM: on Edenia sphere, Eternity.
BUDDHA: the Enlightened One, 6th Century BC.
BENJAMIN FRANKLIN: Founding Father of USA, 1782 AD.

Locations

MANHATTAN, NY.
MOUNT NEBO, Judea.
BRUR HAYL, village in Galilee.
PARIS, France.
LO-YANG, Duchy of Chou Capital, Cathay, China.
CAPHERNAUM, on Tiberias Lake, Israel.
RAJAGRIBA FOREST, on the Ganges' Delta, India.
PHILADELPHIA, Pennsylvania, America.
EDENIA: capital of Zumaria constellation.
CHARTRES, cathedral, Ile de France.
SANTIAGO DE COMPOSTELLA cathedral, Galicia, Spain.
CORRIDORS OF PARADISE, Center of Everywhere.

The Sacred Ten

MOSES' 10 COMMANDMENTS fully alive, their true meaning decrypted, unveiled and revealed.
ARCHAE LINGUA, Universal Language, Mother of all tongues.
KABALAH, SEPHER TORAH & THE ARK OF COVENANT.

Book 1

The Quest for Truth

Chapter One

Eccoci Luna!

1. Manhattan, June 28, 2000 AD, 12:01 p.m.

YES TODAY, SOMETIME TODAY, WE SHALL TAKE OFF "on the wings of an Angel". For the past 20 years, Albert and I have made careful and extensive preparation for that flight, and it is today that seraph Angel YELIYAEL will, once again, emerge from invisibility, in front of us, here in our Manhattan apartment, giving us the signal to embark. We are ready, well trained, as much as we think possible for our voyage through space-time multiple layers.

Once in flight, surely we shall rely on the immense expertise of Angel YELIYAEL.

Here, on Earth, we have gained much knowledge on trans-dimensional travel through multitudinous books reading, followed by vigorous discussions and commentaries. We have prepared our minds[1], exploring texts, directly or through translations, ancient and modern, in French, Hebrew, Latin, English, Italian, Greek, Chinese, Japanese, Hindu. We have also researched works and books focusing on linking and synthesizing different topics, all

[1] Main directions of research preliminary to this cosmic journey: Philosophy, Psychology, Metaphysics, Natural Science, Classical Physics, Quantum Physics, Alchemy, Hermeneutics, Linguistics, Astronomy, Poetry, Logics and Axiomatics, Theology, Angelology, Arts, Painting, Sculpture, Architecture.

providing us with a new glimpse on facts, new hints, new clues, signaling new trails leading successfully to the kingdom of Truth.

Today we shall commence our journey through time and space. Our goal: puncture the veils of terrestrial ignorance and discover universal Truth.

With similar purposes, there are many examples of such voyages having occurred in the remote and recent past. In modern times the radiant joy raised in the hearts of millions by the televised first step of one man on the Moon[2] is still blazing in our memory. On front page, large print ECCOCI LUNA! HERE WE COME, MOON! heralded a major Italian newspaper, clamoring the wonder on behalf of all humanity.

Albert and I, then students at the Sorbonne University, were spending vacation time at our friends' house in Brindisi, and we have experienced first hand, at home and in the buzzing streets, the gigantic popular enthusiasm, irrepressible sense of intense liberation generated by the event. Man had conquered gravity, man could travel in space; humanity was freed! ECCOCI LUNA, fresh echoes of ECCE HOMO, Here Comes the New Free Human, proclaimed by Erasmus of Rotterdam[3], five centuries earlier, at the dawn of Europe's Renaissance.

We have now reached year 2000, at the edge of 21st century, far away from the Sixties. But we have not forgotten our dear friends in Italy, Sylvano, Melissa, Rocco, Dante, our companion witnesses of the first moon landing. The present "carnet de voyage", we are launching like a bottle in the ocean, hoping that it will reach their shores and bring to them the expression of our love.

In a few hours, we shall start our very first travel for distant worlds, through the folds of Time and Space, whole, body and mind, our entire persons leaving the planet as *enseraphed*[4] space-time travelers. On Earth there will be no witnesses, no media, no audience, no cheers, no encouragements coming from other hu-

---

[2] Official date of human first step on the Moon: July 20, 1969

[3] Erasmus of Rotterdam, 1466-1536.

[4] Enseraphed: we created the verb "to enseraph" to succinctly describe the way humans may travel within the fold of a seraphic Angel.

mans. Our journey will start in total silence; however, I know, our giant leap will be observed by a vast celestial host, of immense number and intense quality. Real sentiments of joy, anticipation, excitement emanating from those friendly celestial beings are expressed noiselessly but with immeasurable strength.

From the bottomless cosmic depth, continually surge harmonic murmurs conveying intelligence, sapience, conscience, prescience. Touching our senses they transmute into crystalline melodies, delicate fragrant breezes, silky caresses, long luminous streaks, following solitary messengers hasting through interstellar spaces.

The Angel with whom our mental waves are finely attuned, in view of our first body-mind cosmic travel is a brilliant celestial Seraph named YELIYAEL.

The phone rings, interrupting my reverie.

"Hello!"

"Hi Simha!" (It's the voice of my friend Marie Tania)."I am on lunch break. I would like to speak to you before you go, before the big jump!"

"Come over, Albert too will be here in a moment."

"See you!"

Marie Tania is currently the only person aware of our imminent adventure. We befriended her a short time before the publication of our book *Angel Signs, A Celestial Guide to the Powers of Your Own Guardian Angel*, at a time the work was a mere unpublished manuscript. Our other friends and acquaintances mostly preferred to take no notice of our interest in Angels and Guardian Angels. Conversely, Marie Tania provided us with constant emotional and intellectual support while we were finalizing our research work. Now she is encouraging us any way she can, never doubting the earnestness of our new enterprise.

And she is the only person cognizant of our project, as we told nobody else. In fact, nobody we know *wants* to hear of us leaving Earth traveling "on the wings of a seraph Angel". Unwillingly, but not too sadly, we share a similar experience with medieval poet

Ruteboeuf who wrote:

"Those were friends by wind moved
so as winds blew
by door mine,
away they flew."

"Ce sont amis que vent emporte,
or il ventait
devant ma porte,
sont envolés."

By the door and inside our Manhattan apartment, Marie Tania alone stood firm.

2. Manhattan, June 28, 2000 AD. 12:15 p.m.

TIME OF OUR DEPARTURE IS NEARING. I am looking through the wide-open window, still daydreaming. My sight embraces the floral garden below, classical designs offering an elegant association of antique Greek austerity with the vegetal profusion of an atrium in a Roman villa.

The tiled large interior plaza is circumscribed by twelve high columns, topped with blooming flowers and vines. The circular central fountain spurting fresh water from a sculptured giant fish, reminds 17th Century Versailles. Nature is still wearing its spring colors. Seven wooden benches judiciously placed under the columns are demurely awaiting visitors. I love this quiet garden at the heart of frantic Manhattan. Peace reigns here, the mind is free to wander, imagination flourishes, spirit soars. But I am leaving soon, very soon. Shall I ever come back?

Leaning on the windowsill, lulled by the soft music pouring

from the fountain, I let my mind freely drift through time, present past and future. I remember of another garden, tiny, very far from here, far away in time and space.

Riding memory flashes of my childhood I now fly toward Morocco, landing in the antique city of Fez. I meander into the old narrow streets, built at the start of the 16th century, when Andalusia collapsed at the hands of tyrannical and fanatical Isabella of Spain, misnamed "the Catholic"[5]. Defeated, crushed all the noble cities, one after another, torn apart Toledo, Cordoba, Malaga, and finally erudite Granada, the last of the lost battles marking the end of any hope of uniting the peoples of the Book.

My ancestors became then the "boat people" of their time. By the thousands they drifted from Spain towards the shores of Africa, to Tetuan, Ceuta, Melilla, Tangier; then they journeyed deeper inland into the Sous valley, reaching the foot of the majestic mountains and water canyons of the middle Atlas.

Here is Fez[6] the beautiful, its intellectual radiance, its "Medressa Universities" buzzing with the voices of chanting students; Fez, the medieval city filled with refined artisans and savant teachers. My ancestors entered the city peacefully but passionately, like amorous embracing lovers. United by Catholic Spain's violent rejection, Jews and Mohammedans exiles built a mysterious labyrinth of narrow streets and small bridges, open fountains, stained glass covered terraces, wrought iron balconies, and sculpted cedar moucharabiehs. Here is Fez on African land recreating Iberic Andalusia, its soft colored mosaics, its tranquil Judeo-Muslim alliance.

Small water cascades, sensual shaded street atmosphere, filled with warm spicy fragrances, everything expressed tolerance and

[5] Catholic: from Latin "catholicus", derived from Greek adjective "katholikos", meaning universal, inclusive, all embracing. Queen Isabella betrayed that grand spiritual goal by violently expelling from Spain all those human beings who did not embrace the religion of her choice, namely the Roman Christian doctrine.

[6] Fez: Moroccan town, founded in the 8th century AD, remained a small settlement until Jews and Mohammedans, expelled from Andalusia, settled in large numbers, fleeing the murderous fanaticism of "Catholics" Spaniards, from early 13th to late 15th century (1492 AD).

love of life under the same radiant sun. I remember you, the Muslim in your mysterious medina, I the Jew in my dark mellah[7]; you, in your mosque, as ornate and superb as God's palace, and I, the Jew in my synagogue, as simple and austere as the authentic tent of a nomadic Bedouin, designed to disappear at any moment, body and soul, with all its people, at the first announcement that oh miracle, oh fulfilled prophecy, "the flying carpet has just arrived from Jerusalem!"

Footsteps in the corridor, key turning in the door lock. Albert and Marie Tania enter. I interrupt my reverie to greet them. All three standing in the small entrance foyer, we tensely look at each other, silent, uncertain. Albert bears his serious look; Marie Tania's face is a bit pale, displaying concern. I am feeling very nervous. Although Marie Tania doesn't speak, I am hearing her burning questions; they are also my questions:

What will happen to us? Surely similar extreme experiences have met with success in ancient times, but shall I and Albert be able to accomplish the same deed in modern times? Shall we come back on Earth? If we come back, under which form and appearance? Maybe transmuted into luminous eggs, by the magic wand of a Fairy, or transfigured into mischievous frogs by malevolent witches? And if we return in our same human forms, what about our minds, our psyche, our souls? Shall we reappear as obsessive mystics, arrogant cunning cultists, or unbalanced inadequate schizophrenics?

I utter a few words of reassurance: "Your concern is justified, Marie Tania. But, be assured, I am very confident in the value of our undertaking, thanks to the powers and knowledge of our Angel-guide YELIYAEL. I am sure this journey will bring positive results, because…I believe in the indomitable power of Life!"

Marie Tania has now settled into her favorite seat, quietly ensconced, ready once more for a friendly and passionate conversation, before we leave Earth. Albert is pensive, apparently ponder-

---

[7] Mellah: name of Jewish neighborhood in Fez, and all large cities in Morocco.

ing his future in the palm of his open hands. He appears very serene now. Since I met him in Paris three decades ago, he has always affirmed he was "living on Earth by an accident purely accidental". The prospect of "unearthing" himself is perfectly acceptable to him, our plan to explore the cosmic vastness fascinates him.

I step back for an instant toward the window, looking beyond the inner garden, continuing my daydream. In the cool shade of my parents' house, in Fez where I was born, I am looking through a narrow window, out of which comes an extraordinary pure, white light, full of misty solar fragrances, as one would imagine ether filled with divine essences. I am four years old. Under my sight, a modest garden, paved with smooth bright colored tiles. On the left, stands a sculptured cast iron fountain engraved with bas-reliefs representing birds carrying olive branches.

In the middle, at the very center of the garden, surges a frail tree, its branches ornate with scarce green leaves. As a little girl I know without the shadow of a doubt that, in front of me, lays the Garden of Eden, and the tree standing at its center is certainly the Tree of Life. I remember that I have never shared this secret with anyone, not even with my older sister. To know essential and burning truths I dare not tell anyone, is a dilemma that has often tormented me throughout my life.

In the course of the centuries which followed the fall of Granada in 1492 AD, in the land of Spain, the descendants of the old Andalusia people were joined in North Africa by many new immigrants, exiled by force from Holland or England, or deliberate adventurers, coming from all four corners of the world.

I am fourteen now. At present the streets of the Mellah-Jewish quarters are almost empty. The call has been heard in all the synagogues, shops and homes:

"To all families, announcing the imminent exodus toward Sinai, Galilee and Jerusalem."

Thus, the Jewish people have, sadness mixing with joy, abandoned beautiful, savant, hospitable Fez. Its members scattered, and resettled in all the Jerusalems of all promised lands, on all continents: France, Canada, Australia, Americas, Istanbul, and sometimes also in the old Jerusalem of Israel.

Now I am an adult, in 20th century Manhattan, meditating, glancing over an American garden, bigger, richer than the courtyard of my childhood home in Fez. However it doesn't have a discernable Tree of Life in its center, and thus I know for sure that I am not looking at the Garden of Eden.

Emerging slowly from my dreaming stance, I hear Marie Tania asking softly:

"This is it, Simha, Albert! In a few hours, a few minutes perhaps, you will be taking off on the wings of an Angel. Tell me your very last thoughts now, about your goal..."

I gladly enter into details:

"What I find exciting is the prospect of meeting *face to face*, several ancient masters, truth seekers, founders of our civilization, whose giant thoughts, clear visions and grand intellectual deeds are incompletely recorded in human history. For me, after so many years of solitary reading, so many uncertain interpretations of ancient texts, how wonderful will it be to meet with those who actually conceived and wrote those texts, and hear their voice directly expounding on their teachings!"

ALBERT intervenes: "Frankly, I hope they will remove for us the multitudinous veils they have placed to hide so many aspects of their knowledge. We will ask them to elucidate their metaphors, allegories, symbols. At last we shall get closer to Truth!"

I agree, and continue: "Angel YELIYAEL told us our first encounter will be with Prophet MOSES, and our first destination is Mount Nebo, nowadays located in Jordan, the old country of Moab, across from Judea's wilderness. We shall be transported there by Angel YELIYAEL, landing on the very day the prophet addresses the assembled twelve tribes, giving his last recommendations, pronouncing his final testament, and announcing his imminent departure into sidereal space."

Albert adds: "As stated in the Old Testament, MOSES also took off from planet Earth on the wings of a celestial being. However, according to witnesses, his vessel was not a seraph Angel, for no Angel could embrace him totally. The chronicle reports that he has been taken away by an ELOHA[8], a giant of the heavens, a GABAR[9], an eminent Archangel. It may have been GABRIEL[10] himself, the famous celestial hero, known to humans as a frequent visitor of Earth, the friendly announcer of great news!"

Once again, a peaceful silence settles among us. My friends continue their quiet inmost journey. Marie Tania, Albert and I are sitting, like meditative Buddhist monks, in the small living room enlivened by a variety of red colors, the fire tones I have always loved to surround myself with. We are intensely enjoying the slightest sound and minutest scent, the subtlest light reflection, our thoughts and emotions quietly swirling.

Marie Tania leans comfortably on a soft tapestry pillow, one among the many I designed during the last fifteen years. Pensive, her face glowing, her blue-green eyes shining with curiosity, she probes:

"You both are more than ever determined to "take off", I feel it. And you are well prepared, I know. Your research work *Angels Signs* certainly put you in personal touch with Angels, as it did for me and all your readers. Your book is also a marvelous source of knowledge regarding the "celestial language" underlying all languages spoken on Earth…"

"In our book we refer to it as "Universal Resonance", adds Albert. Each letter-sound is endowed with a specific core meaning, and the same meaning is conveyed by those sounds composing any word, in any tongue or dialect all around the planet."

"Yes, says Marie Tania, thanks to the Archaeo-Linguistic

---

[8] Eloha: Hebrew word meaning an ELevated (el) Spirit (ha). More often found in the Old Testament as Elohim, plural form of Eloha.

[9] Gabar: means "hero of unique stature" in Hebrew, Aramaic, classical Arabic (kabar or kabir).

[10] Gabriel=gabar-iyel= meaning a Celestial Being of unique and high stature. The Y (Hebrew letter Yod) adds the meaning: Action perfectly guided by an Ideal Goal.

method that you are also presenting in your *Angel Signs* book, the profound meaning of each Angel's name can be revealed. Do you intend to make use of the same analytical method during your upcoming exploration?"

SIMHA: "Preparing for this journey Albert and I have mulled at length over that particular issue. We also discussed it with Angel YELIYAEL, who, during our voyage, will be our vessel, our master navigator, and our spiritual guide. On several occasions our celestial friend has communicated his view on the subject. Here are extracts from the Angel's enlightening teachings:

"In the past, everywhere on Earth, said YELIYAEL, *men and women have been familiar with Angels. Humans have come into contact with Angels and Angels in contact with humans. At times, a great number of people were able to achieve harmony with angelic personalities, for they knew to invoke them by their personal names.*

Presently, for most humans, simple logic and commonplace reason prevail over all other mental abilities. Men and women today, being only sensitive to the physical components of the firmament, perceive, identify and encounter less and less living celestial creatures. Humans have turned the heavens into a desert, made only of blazing gazes, burning rocks, and ashes floating in lifeless emptiness."

YELIYAEL went on: "*Nowadays, humans speak and prattle abundantly, but in tongues we Angels can barely empathize with. Now and again one can catch a glimpse, in the human mind, through tales and legends, of the scattered remains of an era when the Heavens, the promised and beloved Highland, was also known as a world streaming with divine essential milk and honey, so sweet to the senses, so nourishing to the body, so inspiring to the mind.*

However, in spite of pervasive ignorance, the firmament is permanently above your heads keeping alive the signs and symbols of your celestial origin, and starlights recount myths and legends to rekindle your faded memories.

Observe the signs that have been deliberately planted in your expanding self-inflicted desert. Watch the flickering stars telling you, like a wide-open book, of the promise of your return to heaven. Listen; listen to the music of the spheres."

Pause. Silence.

My eyes are closed. I am listening intently as Albert recalls aloud for Marie Tania what my memory whispers to me. It is so rare to hear about divine origin, return to heaven in such a casual, natural tone. I am overjoyed.

YELIYAEL: "*And on the surface of Earth, inserted into the human languages and dialects, you can hear the melodic resonance of the Celestial Language. Scattered all over the planet, and beyond, those magical sounds are, in your earthy abode, signs and clues of the existence of living celestial kingdoms, intermingling with your terrestrial world. They are messages the Angels are spreading for all humans to decipher..."*

Marie Tania, presses her inquiry: "Do you think Angel YELIYAEL was alluding to the Archaeo-Linguistic method you have been unfolding in the past twenty years?"

"Yes, the Angel was referring to our method, says Albert. You know YELIYAEL is one of the 72 Angels who inspired our book *Angels Signs*. YELIYAEL, among other Angels, introduced us to the revealing powers of the Archaeo-Linguistic decoding system."

I add: "Thanks to that method, all human languages deliver their concealed meanings and preserved spiritual treasures. And the method clearly shows that each particular language on Earth is an offspring of this unique Universal Language. Which Universal Language is...well...is a Celestial Language, valid universally, including for communication with Angels!"

But YELIYAEL told us more: "*During our journey, you are not going to seek only traces, or remnants of a rich and active universal language. You shall quench your thirst for knowledge at the very source of the divine Verb, reach the high mountain peaks touching the heavens.*

As soon as your minds will firmly reconnect with the dormant basic archetypes underlying your human existence, the Archaeo-

Linguistic approach, so useful to map out the natural structure of life's history, will become insufficient.

You shall walk the routes leading to discovering and exploring the true mountains, the vivid rapids, the majestic rivers, and the open valleys of your divine origins.

Together, we will take over the fortress of our common legends. And, as in fairy tales, we shall raise all decayed drawbridges, open corroded gates and obscured windows. We shall call and invite gifted architects and builders, and transform that medieval castle, custodian of our immense wisdom, our rich and eternal memories, into a free and joyous Renaissance château.

"Then, whispered YELIYAEL, *you shall invoke more Angels and together we shall awake the Sleeping Princess."*

ALBERT: "And what is the Princess's name?"

"*ARCHAE LINGUA is her name*" answered YELIYAEL.

SIMHA: "Where are we going to find beautiful Sleeping Princess ARCHAE LINGUA?"

"*The answer to this question will soon become evident to you,* said YELIYAEL. *You shall find her asleep, walled into a seemingly impenetrable prison, with no doors or windows, in the midst of a dense forest, fenced by intertwined thorny bushes and tall trees fearlessly erected towards the sky.*

Princess ARCHAE LINGUA is asleep there, surrounded by the Ten columns of MOSES' Commandments."

ALBERT recounts: "Our tension suddenly released by this stunning finale, pure joy burst into our hearts, and we laughed and laughed endlessly, and clapped our hands, chortling without control. Finding MOSES' austere Commandments at the end of a fairy tale, what a surprise!

During our exploration journey, we were ready to tackle the enigma of those mysterious stern Commandments, expecting rather serious explanations by the wisest men of the past about the true meaning of these impenetrable verses. But, just now, we had been told by our companion Angel that the way to the truth was also imagination and poetry, not necessarily ponderous reasoning."

SIMHA: "However, we must admit, Marie Tania that, as our

mirth was receding, panic was powerfully taking over. We realized we would find ourselves trekking across vast deserts, climbing steep mountains, entering deep perilous forests to find and get through the walls of a possibly unconquerable fortress, aiming at uncovering the magic formula that will wake up Princess ARCHAE LINGUA! None of those formidable obstacles had we anticipated!

The Angel showered us with soft harmonious music, a virginal and crystalline song, a soothing spiraling melody, pristine like a little cascade, murmuring to our souls:

"*To each day its burden, to each moment its joy.*"

And we felt deeply at peace. We knew our intentions to be as pure and translucent as diamonds emerging to the surface after thousands of years of love and patience, of suffering and happiness, of fears and hopes. This living diamond of pure intentions, no murky or thorny obstacle would fault it; no fire from hell could ever smolder it."

Hearing that story for the first time, Marie Tania appears puzzled and even more curious: "I see now what made you vow to undertake the deciphering of the Ten Commandments, converting yourselves into explorers of the celestial realms, finding in past epochs wise men who could help you open a safe that has been locked for 3,500 years. I have admired your honest and persistent effort to free the meaning of these ancient and obscure biblical words. I often heard you explain how much those famed scriptures are ambiguous, each alternatively telling "more than" or "less than" it appears."

ALBERT: "Those ambiguities being due to incomplete, abusive, or even deliberate misleading translations."

SIMHA: "Or ambiguity caused by the ignorance of the actual language in which those texts have been originally written."

3. Manhattan June 28, 2000 AD, 3 p.m. Calling upon the Angel.

MARIE TANIA'S FAREWELL ENDED IN A prolonged silence. Her eyes glossy with contained tears, she was making a huge effort not to cry. And so did we. Those last moments, filled with feelings of sadness mixed with hopes of discovery of a better world, reminded me of the heartbreaking times we all experienced in Morocco in the fifties, when from one day to the next, a loving grand-mother, a sister or brother, a cousin who had been our childhood playmate, our best friend at school, were leaving for Israel, to ascend[11] toward the mysterious land of our ancestors.

Now alone, Albert and I are sprawling on a sofa, listening to polyphonic medieval chants, ethereal voices and profound silences purifying and uplifting our mental energies.

While on the outside everything is ready for our flight, on the inside, we are, as much as we can, attuning our individual mind projections with the subtle vibrating streams of the Cosmic Mind, focusing our thoughts on the ideals of wholeness and unity. In unison we call upon the Angel:

((((((YE LI YA EL YE LI YA EL))))

O Angel YELIYAEL
Your Name twirls in the heavens,
Forming arches of light,
Your flowing gesture, white and lucid,
Gives and gives hopes freed of fears,
Ultimate knowledge and supreme faith.[12]

((((((YE LI YA EL))))

At first, the water droplets in our living room fountain glitter

---

[11] Ascend= Aliyah, Hebrew word for" ascension". All emigration to Israel, in ancient and modern times, is described as Aliyah, an "ascent".

[12] Poem-Invocation to Angel Yeliyael: excerpt from book *Angel Signs.*

and twinkle joyfully, announcing the presence of a friend from the Heavens. Then slowly, gradually appears the characteristic shape of the Angel, both well defined and subtly fluid, with ever changing dimensions.

Today YELIYAEL's bloom is a mix of brushed opalescent crystal with artistically streaked translucent alabaster. Here and there colorful sparkling and iridescent bubbles appear and adjust themselves to the emotions of the moment. Something pure and beautiful emanates from his large dark green eyes, reminiscent of a mountain lake under a blue-gray sky.

YELIYAEL, our celestial conversant, humorously acknowledges our presence, symmetrically waving his large veils of light in the shape of flapping edgeless wings.

The apparition of the celestial Angel, his very presence in our familiar surroundings is the clear signal that we cannot reverse our decision to leave this time-space location. We now have no choice but go forward with our adventure. My throat tightens up, my thoughts spinning in my head. By contrast, Albert looks peaceful and meditative. I am trying to draw reassurance from his inexhaustible inner confidence, to no avail.

To be "enseraphed" and travel "on the wings of the Angel" still feels awfully mysterious and frightening, even though YELIYAEL has already given us cautiously worded information on such method of transportation by which he is, from our point of view, both the Ship and its Captain.

Borrowing from human archives, Angel YELIYAEL expounded:

"S*hamans spoke of "journeys on the wings of the Eagle", other ancient sages refer to it as the "Messenger's Flights", Hebrew, Babylonian and Phoenician prophets evoked celestial voyages on "Chariots of Fire".*[13]

[13] Chariot of Fire: the word Cha-ri-yot indicates that one moves forward by neutralizing "the cosmic energy stocked" (Cha) in the micro molecules, comparable to macro structures called suns, (Ri) by using them as "fuel"(Yo), that is to say burning them by means of a higher power integrated into the celestial organization of the "Seraph". The final T of the word Chariot indicates that the Seraph transforms the Time into Energy. In Akadian-Hebrew, the word seraph, ha saraph, means "burning" "torching", the one who burns and fires the ether.

I am silently arguing with myself: "OK, OK, the shamans did it, the ancient prophets did it. But now, today, in 21st century America, I have to do it..."

Angel YELIYAEL's voice, softly, gently, cautions me that "*strong vibrations of deleterious fear and anxiety emanate from your aura. Worries and doubts, murky emotions, shadowing the clarity of your mind...*"

Again asking myself: What if, during the journey, the Angel follows the wrong coordinates? Shall we find ourselves going astray, forever lost in space and time?

"*Such an error is impossible* YELIYAEL soothingly, but firmly, responds, *a Seraph Angel cannot wander off the intended path.*"

At this point of tension and anticipation, neither Albert nor I wish to ask Angel YELIYAEL why he can never be lost. We know our quest for truth will be an arduous journey; and, as we go along, personal experience will surely enable us to understand what Angel YELIYAEL precisely means by "error impossible".

Moreover, isn't it to find at last knowledge and truth "without error" Albert and I have planned this whole journey on the wings of an Angel? Tired we are of hearsay and second-guessing, endless approximate comments about truth, manifold uncertainties and reservations regarding facts, events and thoughts.

This time we shall immerse ourselves in truth and knowledge, and Angel YELIYAEL will take us behind all veils, curtains and cloaks! If we can keep close to our angelic companion, that is, be with him and him with us.

4. Manhattan, June 28, 2000 AD. 3:30 p.m. Departure Time: Delayed.

SITTING IN OUR DIMLY LIT LIVING ROOM, patiently waiting, silently meditating, I watch YELIYAEL who is quietly floating about the room. Whatever object he focuses on becomes surrounded by a soft and pulsating aura. By "looking", he is also "touching", and we can see and feel in tune with his spirit.

All is quiet in our small apartment decorated with antique fabrics and damask drapes. A grand beautiful tapestry figuring a pastoral scene is reflected in the mirror stretching across the entire back wall.

YELIYAEL scrutinizes carefully the colorful woven rendition of that renowned Renaissance painting. The artwork displays cheerful Angels, mischievous Cherubs frolicking around a huge central Edenic tree. Men here are represented muscular, strong, and commanding; women dressed in pastel colored togas, picking blooming flowers, carrying fruits, watching over sheep, and surrounded by playful children.

Our companion Angel lingers in contemplation of this rural idyllic scene, and a responding opalescent light emanates from the tapestry. YELIYAEL is apparently amused by the fancy of human artists attempting to represent celestial Cherub Angels as plump, cheerful baby bodied mischievous creatures.

The atmosphere is now relaxed. Albert softly asks YELIYAEL:

"We can clearly see what you see, we can even feel the emotions and colored messages filtering through your eyes. How is that possible?"

YELIYAEL answers: "*You can perceive those signals because, presently, I hold you in my visibility tract.*"

Minutely audible, melodic notes cascade through the room,

shaping into a multicolored stream of lights. Gradually we attune to the soft and crystalline sounds, increasingly feeling their beneficial and elevating virtues.

Now that I am sure the three of us, future traveling companions, are calm and confident, I address YELIYAEL:

"You and I agreed that before leaving for Mount Nebo to meet MOSES, we would at first examine together, one of the Ten Commandments. You selected the Fifth Commandment yourself."

Albert frowns, mouth open in surprise, annoyed by the prospect of a delayed departure.

"Do you mean we're not taking off yet? We do have first to investigate, in depth, one complete Commandment before leaving Manhattan? And Angel YELIYAEL agreed?"

"Yes. Isn't it better to have Angel YELIYAEL help us clarify at least one of the 10 Commandments in preparation for our encounter with MOSES? Thus we shall not appear too naïve or ignorant in front of the Master. I see you are disappointed. But, you must admit, there is no valid excuse for departing unprepared."

"All right" agrees ALBERT. "Let's begin! Anyway I can't wait to know more about the genuine content and real meaning of the Commandments. The Fifth Commandment, right in the middle of the list, will be first to reveal its secrets!"

Albert, wasting no time, eagerly reaches for our familiar thick green leather covered book, opens up the Old Testament with the Hebrew text on one page, facing the English translation on the other, and starts reading aloud:

> HONOUR THY FATHER AND THY MOTHER THAT THY DAYS MAY BE LONG UPON THE LAND WHICH THE LORD THY GOD GIVETH THEE.

Barely masking his ennui, ALBERT sighs deeply, and, disputatively utters:

"Frankly, now as before, and in spite of the inspiring presence of the Angel, this text to me appears bland, banal. Am I mentally obtuse and spiritually insensitive? Given the historical notoriety of these words, I am a bit ashamed not to feel immediately how particularly valuable they are."

Judging by the unusual antagonistic tone of his voice, I understand Albert is still upset by the delayed departure.

The Angel turns into a compact shape, indicating a sitting position and a close attention to what is being said.

YELIYAEL resembles now an ancient master teacher, ready to answer questions from his assembled students. Softly, the Angel starts speaking:

"The first law of the Universe is the Sphere. This means..."

We are instantly and completely communicating with the Angel, we fully understand him, we are precisely conversing with him. Not only has he integrated us into his visibility tract, but also into his sensitivity field. Neither inner nor outer voice, the angelic sounds reach us like perfectly and immediately meaningful waves gently stroking our psyche.

It is as if the words are vibrating modulations, touching not only our ears, but our entire body and surrounding aura, and we interpret his words with all our senses as a whole.

YELIYAEL initiates our quest for truth by expressing an intense, bright and powerful joy. Swirls of enthusiasm permeate our hearts; warm fluids and very light electric vibrations ripple like snippets of energy throughout our bodies. We feel we could levitate and rise above ground! YELIYAEL notices our wonderment, his nodules of light turning pink as a sign of excitement.

Now shielded by a transparent angelic aura, no city background noise reaching us, in absolute silence, we listen to Angel YELIYAEL:

"The first law of the Universe is the Sphere. This means Truth is multifaceted and extensive in many dimensions. In order to actually comprehend that multifaceted reality, one has to be, in essence, all at once mathematician, musician, poet, linguist, engineer, naturalist, architect, lover, parent, child, man, and woman. One must be able to multiply points of view, angles, launch exami-

nation from within, above, here now, and thereafter. To progress further, and deeper, one must be able to obtain the assistance of Angels.

The second law of the Universe concerns Life. Principally Life manifests as neutralization of Death by boldly merging "opposites" in the ocean of cosmic Love. This process does not eliminate conflicts and contrasts, but it controls and masters implosions, deflagrations and dissolutions. Opposites complement like Black and White, Red and Green, Blue and Orange, Yellow and Violet, and engender Harmony, Truth, Beauty, Goodness."

Albert and I are listening attentively to this lecture, while becoming aware of how perfectly extraordinary this situation is. A situation many of our contemporaries would declare "unreal" and totally "impossible". We are back at school, taught by an Angel, understanding everything, and it feels good. What the Angel is saying is true, and his multi-sensory display, permeated with music, fragrances and colors is beautiful and enchanting. We experience enlightening enlivening synaesthesia!

Angel YELIYAEL continues:

"When you deeply recognize this simple founding principle, base of all laws of Harmony, there are very few realities you will not understand, comprehend, concerning the creation and evolution of the Universe and all creatures, be they celestial, human, animal, vegetal or mineral..."

YELIYAEL is now manifesting his feelings by displaying happy, intense colors and shapes, in the simple style of an artistically gifted child. Then the Angel invites:

"Let us examine the complete text of the 5th Commandment as it is ordinarily translated and presented in English language."

This time I do the reading:

HONOUR THY FATHER AND THY MOTHER THAT THY DAYS MAY BE LONG UPON THE LAND WHICH THE LORD THY GOD GIVETH THEE.

Addressing Albert, YELIYAEL asks softly, gently:

"What are now the thoughts coming to your mind concerning

this Commandment?"

ALBERT ventures a second opinion, a little less antagonistic that his first: "Awkward style set aside, the words seem simple and do not appear to hold any obscure or mysterious meaning. The sentence is built in the usual way parental precepts are, including the typical conditional reward: "If you do this, then, and only then, you shall get that!"

"*And you,* Simha, *what are your thoughts?"* probes YELIYAEL

I hesitate a little, and reply: "Contrary to Albert, I think the words are very obscure, and I can assert they contain various hermetic meanings on many levels."

"*Which ones?"* asks YELIYAEL, his curiosity obviously piqued.

SIMHA: "First of all, the sentence starts with the word "honor", not "respect", as popular belief usually states. Our present-day education tends to convince us to principally "respect", therefore "not to hurt" the feelings of our father, mother, or neighbor, "not to demean" anybody. It seems to me that the injunction of "*honoring*" demands that beyond simple respect we supply special feelings, emotions, and love.

My conclusion is that this Commandment, as it is translated, presents us with a first challenge. It prompts us to do a more careful reading of it, one that goes beyond vague and careless interpretations of the type that says "respect your father and mother".

"Thank you!" says ALBERT. Then I continue: "Besides, if the first part of the Commandment, "Honour thy father and thy mother" seems to make good sense as a necessary "civilizing" founding principle, the second part leaves me rather perplexed. Why am I being promised that, by honoring my parents, "my days that God gives me" will be "prolonged on a land that will be given to me"? What does it mean, truly? Is it about implanting in me basic moral precepts? Teaching me social discipline while promising me a longer life as an incentive? And on top of the incentive to live longer, I am offered a bribe, in the form of a piece of land that is promised and will be given to me if I behave properly.

Oh YELIYAEL, such words and notions cannot originate from

either the Divine messengers or MOSES himself!"

YELIYAEL rejoins: "*Therefore we must now examine the Fifth Commandment in Hebrew, the tongue nearest to the universal language enshrined and preserved by Princess ARCHAE LINGUA, as it has been originally pronounced and engraved in stones by the celestial messenger.*"

The Angel's pressing request to revisit the original biblical text rekindles the flames of a haunting crucial question, hampering my ability for appropriately thinking. Casting a silvery pearly shine above his widely open eyes, the Angel indicates he welcomes the mental detour. Thus, abruptly, I start a lengthy digression.

SIMHA: "All right, why did MOSES notoriously pronounce these ten fundamental Commandments in a language unknown[14] to the people? Even the keys to this language were concealed in the Ark of Covenant, the documents and legacy Abraham, the patriarch from Mesopotamia, had brought to Egypt 400 years before MOSES' birth. However, the Egyptian people did not know that language; in the Goshen valley the tribes' leaders were unaware of it, even their priests barely knew it existed."

Albert looks at me, taken aback, but remains silent.

YELIYAEL then interjects: "*Why this query, Simha? I know you could answer precisely your own question.*"

The air all around us becomes warm and vibrant. I start laughing freely and joyously. I relish YELIYAEL's humor. I know the answer to my own question, but the Angel also knows the answer to the question he has just asked me!

Relieved by YELIYAEL's approval, smiling, I resume:

"I trust it is up to you, Angel YELIYAEL, to disclose why MOSES has wished to pronounce his testament in a language incomprehensible to his intended audience, a medley, a mosaic[15] of multiple races composing the 12 tribes exiting from Egypt?

If the answer to the question issues directly from a celestial

---

[14] The Archae Lingua, later denominated Sumero-Akadian, then Hebrew language.

[15] Mosaic: this word draws its meaning "medley, assortment, variety, montage, mixture" from the fact that the 12 tribes led by Moses out of Egypt, were a medley of origins, races and colors.

Angel of YELIYAEL's spiritual stature and rank, second in the Seraphic hierarchy, it will hold considerable uncontroversial value.

For, who am I to speak of and assess the intents of Prophet MOSES? What legitimacy, what authority, what credibility would I offer facing great numbers of erudite men, theologians, priests, imams, rabbis, all of them men backed by influential religious and long-established social institutions?

What can I convincingly say, I, Simha, a Sephardic Jew, born of the "black" Jewish tribes of North Africa, a Jew honoring all together the words of Buddha, Lao Tseu, Moses, Jesus, and Mahomet? A Jew who doesn't veil her love and admiration for the thoughts of Socrates, Plato, and German philosopher Hegel and Christian theologian Teilhard de Chardin.

Worse even, my most avowed detractors will irately clamor: she shamelessly acknowledges and values as enlightening the "idolatrous" myths of gods and half gods whose active presence is ascertained by the ancient Greek, Egyptian, Toltec, Maya, Hindu, Chinese and Japanese traditions!"

Taking a deep breath, I pursue:

"And to top it all, will whine the modern scientist critics, she wide opened doors to the countless celestial armies that our sound logical and reasonable minds had finally successfully expelled from our technological house. And now she boldly claims she is customarily conversing with "angels"!

You see, YELIYAEL, humans are very sectarian, often saddled with deep-seated prejudices, especially males…"

5. Hova! Love!

YELIYAEL CLOSES HIS EYES. He is presently chortling, as we can perceive from the cadenced undulations of his coloring. Light green and muted red waves, rippled with iridescent vibrations, swirl around his pulsing shape. The Angel is clearly signaling he will answer the crucial question himself, and I feel grateful for it.

"Listen carefully. Each of the original Ten Commandments was given a title, as one would name a book's chapter or a part of a libretto. The title of the Fifth Commandment is HOVA[16]*. Now, when those two universal sounds HO-VA are cast together in space, they deliver all the core ideas present in that Commandment, as it was created in eternity and for eternity.*

The title HOVA in itself is a complete meaningful song. It tells us how the universal mother-spirit (HO) connects, through an eternal act of love, with the ultimate living principle of all development and evolution (VA)."

YELIYAEL pauses, to let us absorb in silence what he just said, then resumes: "*This Commandment enfolds a complete cosmic, universal symphony, and HOVA is the key which opens both the magic vessel and all the messages contained in the 5th Commandment."*

ALBERT: "Then why enunciate a long sentence, compounding so many words:

HONOUR THY FATHER AND THY MOTHER: THAT THY DAYS MAY BE LONG UPON THE LAND WHICH THE LORD THY GOD GIVETH THEE?

Why not just simply proclaim: HOVA, LOVE!?"

---

[16] In all Mesopotamian languages, and present Hebrew, Hova is the root of all the words expressing Love.
hova=hava=eve=love and fecundity (ova=egg). ahava=love. ahova=lover. lo-hov= to love. The Hebrew word-sound Lo-hov is clearly the root of the English word-sound Love.

YELIYAEL: "*Within the celestial universal choir, humans have very specific characteristics that must be taken into account.*

All minerals react to perennial cosmic radiations, all plants follow the cyclical energizing sun rays, animals obey the organic forces of instincts, celestial beings have almost perfectly achieved sacred alliance between their wishes and the will of the Creator, and, higher up, divine beings, Deities, are wholly united with the totality of the Creator.

However humans, ah humans! They are living the most exciting experience of the Universe: they aim at balancing a maximum of individualistic Freedom with a maximum of unifying Higher Authority, be it manifesting as Nature, Ancestors, Parents or God.

Humans are the remotest beloved creation of the Divine, destined to come back to their Creator from a considerable cosmic distance, following the most extended time path that leads from mortality to immortality, to finally reach "eternality".

Now and again, in a true act of free will and faith, an exceptional man or woman will make the journey in one full sweep, and achieve instantly a perfect fusion of his or her free substance with a spark of the Divine Being's persona."

"Try it! Pronounce, vocalize the sounds HOVA! *Several times in succession..."*

"HOVA! HOVA!" exclaims ALBERT.

I follow in chorus: "HOVA! HOVA! HOVA!"

Our voices resonate in the room, now alone, now in unison, and YELIYAEL swirls and dances slowly, seizing and releasing our spherical sounds in the air like a juggler.

"*Now stop and listen!*" intimates YELIYAEL.

At that very moment, Albert and I are struck by a powerful intuition. Words are dancing in our minds, sounds are echoing harmoniously within and around us. The obfuscated text of the Fifth Commandment has become clear without having been thoroughly and painstakingly investigated.

HOVA! LOVE!

HONOUR
ALL THY FATHERS
AND *ALL* THY MOTHERS
THAT THY DAYS
MAY BE LONG
UPON A LAND
WHICH I GIVETH THEE

We now realize this formulation is not a simple promise of longer life to be fulfilled only on the condition that we respect and honor our own parents.

"I understand! says ALBERT. This law does not solely apply to parent-child relationships on this Earth. This law, given to MOSES by a divine messenger, also refers to the relationship of humans with celestial ancestors in the Heavens!"

YELIYAEL adds: *"This divine song enlightens the cosmic mind of humans, directs them towards the paths leading to ultimate survival, in the sacred heavenly abodes ever ready to receive them."*

ALBERT: "I now comprehend the meaning of that strange promise:

THAT THY DAYS MAY BE LONG
UPON A LAND
WHICH I GIVETH THEE

"Longer days" stand for Eternal life, and "land" stands for Infinite Cosmos!"

The Angel continues his teaching: "*This formula expresses an absolute cosmic law. Each word is a clear sign, a precise indication for every evolving human to find the nearly undetectable ascending "narrow path" of spiritual survival, immortality, and eternal life; a method for surely reaching the divine Promised Land, the center of the Infinite Cosmos."*

ALBERT, pensively: "I appreciate now why some words of these Commandments have not been modernized in their form. The original translators from the old tongue have included the "TH", like in THY, THEE, GIVETH, everywhere they could, to remind the readers of THEOS[17], the Divine presence. And their successors maintained in print the old-fashioned style, accepting humbly all criticisms, and mockery, over centuries, to preserve, as much as possible, the kernel of truth."

Says YELIYAEl: "*Albert, your lucid understanding of the ancient translators' intents is the best defense ever made to counter modern critics and the only apology the noble language scholars are truly cherishing.*"

Nevertheless I keep questioning YELIYAEL, persevering in my desire to solve the enigma of ARCHAE LINGUA, and I ask:

"Why didn't MOSES formulate the Ten Commandments clearly, in a language that everyone could understand?"

Angel YELIYAEL doesn't move for a long time, doesn't ripple, swirl, or turn colors. Then he begins:

"*MOSES had to absolutely pronounce them specifically in ARCHAE LINGUA. He had no choice.*"

ALBERT, ever an ardent Socratic philosopher, reacts:

"No choice! He had no choice! MOSES the genius, the human giant was not free?"

YELIYAEL responds without hesitation:

"*MOSES was in his time the freest human being on Earth. He was a High Priest at the Supreme Temple-University of Egypt, High Priest of the most civilized nation on the planet, a potential Pharaoh. All the wealth of this world was within his reach, and yet he renounced everything. Beauty was not enough to fulfill his ideals. Divine Truth, and social justice based on Goodness were just as important to him. Even a lost lamb in the mountains of the Sinai desert attracted his compassion.*

MOSES, free, intelligent, royal man, humbly chose to renounce everything, forsook his personal will and obeyed the supreme principle, acting solely in accordance with the will of the Creator of all Principles."

---

[17] Theos: in Greek means Deity, God, hence the derived words theology, theocracy. The word therapy thus conveys the notion that any effective cure occurs primarily through divine intervention.

I interrupt, resolute:

"So MOSES was free and chose to put his freedom at the complete service of the Divine Will, as YEHOSHUA's words later expressed "*Our Father who is in Heaven, thy will be done,*" or as in the words of Mahomet "IN SHA A ALLAH", "according to God's profound design". Angel YELIYAEL, will you let us know why the Universal Father's messenger transmitted the Commandments in ARCHAE LINGUA, instructing MOSES not to translate them and forever keep them in this "coded" language?"

Following is YELIYAEL's complete answer to my question:

"There are many reasons for this careful ciphering. First and foremost MOSES' highest intelligence complied freely with the all-knowing all loving and supreme Will of the Universal Father.

Second, ARCHAE LINGUA is the language of the BERITH[18]*, the original ancestral Covenant between Heaven and Earth.*

All celestial creatures in essence understand and communicate thoughts in ARCHAE LINGUA, as implied by MOSES in his last testament on Mount Nebo.

In fact, evolving humans also ended up learning and understanding part of this celestial language, starting with a few gifted individuals, until more and more did so. First transported by missionaries, like a rare and precious water poured out of a jar, ARCHAE LINGUA was then spread more and more widely, akin small irrigating canals during MOSES' Keltic tribes' civilizing influence. Then later, their successors Christian monks brought it to all peoples, through the larger rivers of spiritual knowledge.

Today, ARCHAE LINGUA is an integral part of all languages and dialects on your planet, in the form of small droplets that, though isolated in appearance, may nevertheless be assembled back together into a strong and fertile stream.

Over time ARCHAE LINGUA spread everywhere. Its purpose was, and is, to seed, nurture and enhance men's and women's unconscious minds, and then develop their intellects, until a profound

[18] Berith is translated in Hebrew as Alliance, Covenant. In fact, in Akadian and Hebrew that word means: New Birth through acquirement of cosmic consciousness.. Hence the English common word birth which in fact designates a Re-birth.

union between Heaven and Earth is established."

"And of course, added YELIYAEL, *there is the MYSTERY effect..."*

"The MYSTERY effect!?" echoes ALBERT, for whom the word conjures up fiery feelings of a passionate hermeneutist.[19]

YELIYAEL explains: *"Human beings are the freest beings of the universe and their curiosity knows no limit. Anything that resists their understanding they will study again and again until they finally break the secret code."*

And the Angel adds: "*All of the preceding divine revelations enclosed in the Ark of the Covenant were also pronounced in pure ARCHAE LINGUA, as it was and remains absolutely necessary to maintain a consistent unfailing unified code. This pure Akadian Mesopotamian language, later to become Hebrew, remained over many millenniums strange and anachronistic, thus sheltered from erosion caused by ordinary usage and time distortion.*

All of us in the heavens, continues YELIYAEL, *are grateful to the Israelites, then the Jews and Christians who, since the beginning of their Mosaic history until the 19th century, have maintained alive the Archae Lingua, allowing it to be pronounced only in prayers, studies, by legal authorities, rabbis, educated monks, erudite men and religious followers.*"

"What a wonderful destiny for a Universal Language, says ALBERT. However, nowadays Israelis speak Hebrew in their everyday lives! Does that mean secrecy is no longer necessary, and different new times are approaching for humanity concerning its primeval Covenant with the Heavens?"

YELIYAEL suddenly freezes. All his colors and musical tones fade away. The Angel has turned into a barely visible white ghost.

Meanwhile something is now happening we have never observed before: his large eyes literally vanish, instantaneously. The message is clear: *"Burning topic. Do not trespass!"*

---

[19] Hermeneutics: art of interpretation. Origin of this word: the Greek deity Hermes, known for veiling his messages.

Thus YELIYAEL discourages any incursion and exploration into what we understand to be forbidden territory, namely prophecy.

I took a deep consoling breath; Albert and I observed a long moment of meditating silence. As we finally indicated our firm intent to sincerely comply and obey the law of secrecy on that important issue, Angel YELIYAEL became visible again.

6. Kabed. All your Ancestors…

NOW, SAYS ALBERT, DREADING EVEN MORE preliminaries and digressions:

"I think it is time for us to examine the words of the Fifth Commandment in ARCHAE LINGUA, the language in which it was first given to MOSES and to all humanity, past, present and future."

Albert opens up the book of the Old Testament at the page signaled by a tasseled tapestry bookmark, and starts reading the Fifth Commandment in Hebrew.

Deliberately, he pronounces each syllable separately, clearly vocalizing each consonant. Always caring, YELIYAEL is still preventing all city noises from entering the room. The antique words are reaching me, pure, crystal clear. Beneficent refreshing sounds caress my ears and touch my entire body. Centuries condense into a single present moment. Beautiful ARCHAE LINGUA echoes, reverberates in my mind, in my heart…

> KABED ET AVEYKHA VE ET AMEYKHA LE MAÂN
> YE ÂRKHOUN YAMEYKHA ÂL HA ADAMAH
> ASHER ADONAI ELOHEYKHA NOTEN LEKHA.

I close my eyes. The words resound over and over again in my mind:

((((KABED)))) (((((ET)))))

(((((((AVEYKHA)))))
((((VE ET)))))) (((((AMEYKHA))))

I feel my heart pounding with joy. I am home! My true home! This is my mother language! Each word opens up like a rose bud, as each consonant sends out its distinctive note, fragrance, color, casting unique mind-spirit powers: Ka Be D E T

The inbuilt meanings of each consonant, each word, penetrate my whole being, discreetly re-acquainting me with fundamental truth. Each word previously settled in the vastness of my memory, awakens when evoked, and revives my cosmic consciousness.

I know that Albert and YELIYAEL are receiving those waves of knowledge simultaneously and are interpreting them each in their own ways, the former intellectually, the latter spiritually.

"Superb sounds" whispers ALBERT, calm on the surface, but deep down very moved.

SIMHA: "Each word by itself delivers the full meaning of the sentence in which it is contained. As YELIYAEL taught us "*The first law of the universe is the Sphere"*. In ARCHAE LINGUA each word is a holographic sphere on which are reflected all the words and meanings that compose the sentence in which it is included."

Then, abruptly, I burst into tears, overwhelmed by despair and anguish; suddenly blackened, my soul gives up all hopes. How complex the task at hand! While hearing Albert assiduously read the 15 Hebrew words of the Fifth Commandment, one law among Ten, reason has been wearying down my enthusiasm, insistently pointing to all the difficulties and obstacles that will interfere with our mission.

How can we possibly come up with a refined, yet intelligible, translation of these antique words and pass it on to others? Isn't it presumptuous of me, of us, in this room, to claim that common interpretations of the biblical texts are to be revised; that a more precise, exact, true translation is possible, even necessary? After all, everyone around us, ignorant or savant, seems content, nobody is asking for such a revision! Am I not piling up the stones that shall be thrown at me?

Through my tears I can see YELIYAEL has now changed his appearance from compact cloud into an immense effervescent sphere composed of myriad luminescent balls, all rotating at various speeds, reflecting colorful dazzling lights. Multiple fragrances drizzle from the ceiling; swirling harmonious melodies traverse the room. Then the fluidic outer limits of YELIYAEL's multifaceted shape expand, beyond the garden, into the city streets, high into the Manhattan sky, encompassing the moon, the sun and all orbiting planets. The small illuminated spinning balls are everywhere around us, but I cannot discern the periphery or the center of this immense field of spiraling floral scents, colors and notes.

Filled with surprise and wonder, now standing up, arms raised like children pointing to balloons in the sky, we extend our fingers, attempting to touch the colored singing fragrant spheres flying above our heads. Then YELIYAEL's smiling radiant wide-open eyes appear in front of me. I turn towards Albert, who is looking in a different direction, and I see YELIYAEL's eyes again, staring at him; the Angel's eyes are looking at both of us at the same time from every direction.

SIMHA: "Thank you for the luminous metaphor, O YELIYAEL!"

ALBERT: "Each word is like a blooming sphere, consistently, constantly, releasing the multiple senses and meanings enclosed in each syllable. Everybody can feel, see, touch, smell, hear, and understand the living notions enclosed."

YELIYAEL's voice soothes me, gently dissolving the invading black cloud:

"Do not despair! Not you Simha! Not you Albert! Just go ahead, accomplish your mission. I am here, everywhere, before, after, and hereafter, to help you."

Enthused by those heart-warming words I am elatedly singing and laughing, almost dancing.

"Thank you, thank you YELIYAEL, thank you for the beauty of the lesson!"

"Thank you, thank you, said Albert, thank you for enlightening us with truth!"

"Thank you, O YELIYAEL, I have regained my enthusiasm!"

With renewed determination I then commence the deciphering work.

SIMHA: "The Fifth Commandment starts with the word KABED. I will now translate it making use of the Archaeo-Linguistic analytical method, complemented by my personal knowledge of ARCHAE LINGUA."[20]

ALBERT: "And, as the first word KABED is in itself a holographic sphere reflecting multiple meanings, your translation of the word will also reveal the meanings of the whole Fifth Commandment!"

SIMHA: "Here is a translation and spherical interpretation of the word KABED, offering an alternative to the common "Honor thy father and thy mother":

It is good to be inserted, body and mind,
into your family, social and natural fabric,
in order to experience and know of your sources
and clearly identify your personal purposes.

On another facet of the sphere, the same word KABED can also be understood as follows:

You may not detach yourself
from the fabric in which your birth
included you,
without honoring and paying tribute to it,
so that you repair the damage
caused by your detachment.
Thus you shall repay
your debt of honor and love.

---

[20] Archaeo-Linguistic analytical method=a method revealing the core meaning of every sound consonants composing a word, in any language. Example: Ka-Be-D. The sound-letter K stands for cohesion/ Be stands for Basis/ D stands for Discovery.
Archae Lingua expresses multifaceted meanings of a word in its totality. By example the single word KaBeD conveys at the same time: 1/ Honor 2/ Heaviness 3/ A word of endearment: "my sweet heart" "honey" 4/ A tight fabric (materially or figuratively) 5/ Attachment, as in being restrained or held down, through physical or emotional means.

Let's observe other reflections amidst the many facets of the "spherical" word KABED."

If you are constrained by a powerful, cohesive,
restrictive force, which intimidates you,
or by an emotional
and sentimental force you cherish,
I authorize you, in the name of the divine law,
to detach, to free and to distance yourself
so that you may empower your own body,
your own mind, your own soul
and create and style your own personal world.

"Now dare I offer yet another translation of the Fifth Commandment's first word KABED?"

"Dare, dare!" says Albert, tirelessly encouraging me. "I could listen to you till the end of my life on Earth!"

I continue decoding the elements composing the word KABED, catching more echoes of ARCHAE LINGUA sonorities:

The powerful, cohesive force (KA),
that may even feel oppressive (KABED),
which chains the physical and mental body (KABA)
to the divine spirit (DA),
is by nature detachable and releasable (DA),
even if the spirit is anchored in fixed form (BA).
Thus, through exploring and discovering
the universe's spherical and circular law,
when you use your ability to uncover
and open doors (DA),
you shall release a true creative force (KA),
in the universe,
and this creative force will allow your mind
to adopt a new, more mutable spiritual form (BA).

However, always keep in mind
that you shall die-transit again
and release this new form

so that you may again detach from it
in order to walk through other gates
and explore other worlds;
and this will repeat itself
until you have walked through
the ultimate gate
of ultimate finality.

"Bravo! Brava! Brava!" exults Albert, clapping and laughing like an Italian opera lover at the Scala of Milan.

"*More, more!*" whispers YELIYAEL .

SIMHA: "Alas, as you know, my contemporaries like to have fun while learning, and if we continue to explain the meaning of the Fifth Commandment word by word, they will all leave the amphitheater of knowledge."

YELIYAEL stares at me, transfixed, and in his wide jade-green eyes I can read astonishment and bewilderment for the first time. Did he not know that humans would willingly abandon the sphere of knowledge and choose to have fun instead?

The Angel, once recovered from his surprise, looks insistently at us; an extraordinary aura of kindness emanates from his wide deep liquid eyes. Multicolored pastel-toned phosphorescent lights are floating around him, forming a moving wheel of fluttering butterflies, recreating the scene of a lively enchanted garden. Fresh virginal water and unknown exotic flowers are springing all around us.

In full agreement with me YELIYAEL admits it would be wiser and sensible to avoid a series of detailed, word for word, syllable-by-syllable explanations.

7. Manhattan, June 28, 2000 AD. 6:30 p.m. More revelations.

"*I HAVE IDEO-SCANNED THE BOOK you are going to write and publish about our shared cosmic adventure,* says the Angel. *Often truths are clearly and courageously expressed. Overall the work is rather engaging and has a nice lively rhythm. Other celestial attentive witnesses of our saga are of the same opinion.*"

SIMHA: "You've read our book when it hasn't been written yet? This is the first day of our quest, we haven't even left Manhattan! We have barely evoked the subject of the Ten Commandments!!! And you've read the book!?"

"What is the title of the book?" asks ALBERT, who can be practical, at times.

"*THE SACRED TEN!*" proclaims the Angel.

"Voilà! Very interesting"! exclaims ALBERT. "Then will you tell us how we coped with the prickly situation? How did we get out of the ambush, cornered by a throng of rationalist scientists on one side, religious traditionalists on the other? Thus venturing, at the beginning of the 3rd millennium, to single handedly provide a "truer" translation of MOSES' Commandments, pronounced 3,500 years ago, in a language utterly archaic and almost impenetrable!"

YELIYAEL: "*Let's uncover the four versions of the Fifth Commandment to be published in your book. This original version is, naturally, scripted in Archae Lingua:*

KABED ET AVEYKHA VE ET AMEYKHA
LE MAÂN YEÂRKHOUN YAMEYKHA ÂL HA ADAMAH
ASHER ADONAI ELOHEYKHA NOTEN LEKHA.

Reading directly from the book's virtual version which I am now projecting in her mind, Simha shall voice for us an interpretation at Level 1, expression of a Basic Human Moral Law."

I immediately place my hands on my closed eyes and patiently wait for white letters to appear on the dark walls of my inner eyelids. To my surprise, I cannot see anything but the natural filamentous creations of my retina. However, suddenly I HEAR something sounding like a voice pronouncing a series of words I can understand but cannot translate. Then the voice becomes stronger, seems to return to the beginning of the same sentence, and my mouth reproduces the words as they emerge, one after the other, into my psyche:

"If you ignore the *sources* of your own being,
and cannot recognize them,
you shall always be disoriented,
lost in the universe and your life
shall be valueless.
It is important and good to be inserted
within the social and family fabric
which reflects the whole presence
of *all your fathers*, your paternal origins
as well as the whole presence
of *all your mothers*,
your maternal origins.
Thus you shall perceive the value
of your unfolding life on this earth
that the Lord of Grace
has given you,
He who has brought you up
uniting you to Him
through the Universal Spirit
so that you may
consciously explore,
question, discover and understand.

Without giving us a moment to contemplate those new revelations, YELIYAEL intervenes:

"In your book the second exact interpretation of the Fifth Commandment is presented like a divination, a recommendation

from the Deity to men and women of this Earth willing to listen. Here it is as printed":

If you find yourself constrained
by a *restrictive righteous force*
to which you must obey,
such as by one of your *fathers*,
and if you find yourself
locked into a *loving situation*,
such as by one of your *mothers*,
invoke the Divinity and connect yourself
to the miraculous Source,
your utmost *Ultimate Ancestor*,
for His presence is in you,
in your own life,
He who is closest to you,
and resides within you,
is also the one who dwells above the earth,
beyond space.
He is also the *Father* who judges
the clarity of your *intentions*
when you go through
the purifying fire of death-transition;
also there dwells the *Mother*,
that you shall find by traveling beyond
the country of the Elohim, the Angels,
when at last you shall take the road leading
to the Promised Land, the Eternity
that has been granted to you.

Now it is Albert's turn to cover with his hands his tightly closed eyelids. I hear him recite:

"Third version of MOSES' Fifth Commandment, extracted from original ARCHAE LINGUA, another angle, another facet of the same diamond. This transcription reveals the pledge and commitment humans engage into with their Divine Creator:

When attempting to liberate myself
from the crushing weight of the past,
when I am about to disengage
from my roots,
thus leaving behind my *father, my mother*,
my family, my country, my race,
I first shall attempt
to identify perfectly my origins,
research thoroughly
how they manifest themselves within me,
study their chronicity and historical sequences.
Thus through such exact knowledge
I shall reach the source of mental fluidity
that will allow me to survive
in my new environment, whether it be air, earth,
water, or ethereal fire,
on the way to the Supreme Celestial world.

Developing well founded acknowledgement
of what binds me to my sources,
sharpening the perception
of my individual identity in the midst
of the woven social fabric of my origins,
shall also be my way of paying my tribute
and my debt of honor to *all my ancestors*,
for the powers they have given me,
and to repay them back a hundred fold
for protecting me and nourishing me
at the very risk of weighing me down
with their attentive care.

Then yes, shall I be worthy of rising to Eternity
beyond Space and Time
and shall be united with the Ultimate Deity
by a spiritual and *personal bond*.

"Now, says YELIYAEL, *Simha you shall have the honor of de-*

ciphering the Fifth Commandment, titled HOVA, and uncover the scientific cosmic law it contains.

Earlier you expressed your fears to fail in this difficult task, to be criticized and condemned by a throng of learned institutional scholars. Now, read for us, Simha, the new deciphering as published under interpretation number 4, which unveils the absolute universal value of the Fifth Commandment."

This time I hear the melodic whisper of an inner voice. My whole body vibrates, shaken by the meanings unfolding in my mind, opening up like supple and scented floral corollas. Listening to those intimate sounds, I modulate as best I can the words that carry the celestial message:

Mental identity and spiritual personality,
are, at time of death-transition,
detachable one from the other,
if one has attained
in the course of one's life
a complete knowledge
of human celestial origin,
the source of the vital energies
bestowed by the Universal Father,
and one has also acquired
the understanding
of human earthly roots,
source of maternal loving nourishments.

However, those two foundations
of life on Earth,
all fathers and *all mothers*,
have two common driving forces:
one, the ultimate cosmic life energy,
substratum of all existence,
the other, the absolute spiritual substance,
substratum of all consciousness.
These two forces join and unite

in the same universal flow
of the spiritual network
manifesting itself into several forms:
at first the material earth,
then, the burning purifying ether,
and beyond,
the celestial kingdoms,
where living souls are enlightened
by the knowledge
of the Universal Creator,
then, finally,
the eternal paths leading
to the ultimateness
of the Supreme Being,
bestower of total personality
and ultimate freedom.

It took us a while before regaining consciousness of our present space-time position. YELIYAEL's enlightening teaching had projected us "elsewhere", beyond here and now, and we had received knowledge in a totally unfamiliar way.

Hyperdream? Ultracounsciousness? A mix of both, and more.

We profusely thanked YELIYAEL for the magnificent present he had just given us. Not only were we now certain that our work on the Ten Commandments would be recorded in a book, but we also knew that Angel YELIYAEL will undeniably help us write it. With his angelic guidance, we will be able to dare generate the most courageous translations and deciphering, the closest to truth.

I now feel I am truly ready to take off "on the wings of the Angel".

A question concerning the "published book yet to be written" came to my mind:

"Oh YELIYAEL, shall we, while composing the SACRED TEN manuscript, finally write a formula concise, easy to understand and to memorize, clear enough to illume the obscurities of the Fifth Commandment current common translation?"

Replies Angel YELIYAEL: *"Here is the end of the first chapter of The Sacred Ten."*

This time YELIYAEL said nothing. I didn't hear any voice echoing in my mind, but on the mirror at the far end of the living room, in luminous letters, as if projected from behind a tainted glass, this statement appeared:

HONOR YOUR DEBT TOWARD ALL YOUR ENGENDERERS
HOWEVER, LIBERATE YOURSELF FROM THE PAST,
THUS CREATING YOUR OWN IDENTITY.
BY SO DOING YOU SHALL FULFILL THE TRUE PURPOSE OF
YOUR PERSONAL BIRTH AND PAY BACK TO YOUR PARENTS,
ANCESTORS, YOUR DEBT OF HONOR AND LOVE.
THEREFORE YOU SHALL LIVE FULLY
AND SURVIVE IN ETERNITY.

And on the large tapestry facing the mirror, glimmering words surging amongst clouds, mountains, brooks, trees, rocks, ferns, animals, birds and cherubs, lively flashed this celestial recommendation:

HONOR *ALL* YOUR MOTHERS,
ALL YOUR FATHERS,
ALL YOUR ANCESTORS,
ON THIS EARTH AND IN THE HEAVENS,

THEREFORE
YOUR SOUL SHALL SOAR
AND EXPAND
BELOW AND ABOVE,
WITHIN THE COSMIC TOTALITY,
FREE OF DEATH.

Chapter Two

Elation

8. Manhattan June 28, 2000 AD. 8 p.m.

THE DAY IS COMING TO AN END. Mixed blue gray and warm purplish shadows take over the sky above the city, signaling the approaching calm of a starlit night. Having now deciphered the glyphs composing the 5th Commandment, we are enjoying our last nightly rest on Earth, before soaring into the cosmic abyss. Had we asked Angel YELIYAEL to wing us away, we could have left immediately. But, so be it, we shall relax here in our Manhattan home, thus allowing our curious minds time to absorb the stirring knowledge our Angel friend kindly offered in the afternoon.

Sitting on the sill by the open window, my face caressed by a vesper soft breeze, I am thinking, questioning myself. Have we really completed our deciphering work on the 5th Commandment? Have we released its essential, fundamental, crucial meanings? Anyway, is there an end to such an endeavor? Am I, is Albert, are we both, up to the formidable task remaining before us? There are now nine more Commandments to examine and research. Can we, mere humans, measure with such a gigantic enterprise?

I let my thoughts wander. And what is a HUMAN being? Who can say, truly? Of course by applying our Archaeo-Linguistic analytical method, drawing from the generous Universal Language reservoir, we can analyze the word "HUMAN" itself. Open it like a nut, uncovering the specific role of each component: protective shell outside, kernel seed inside.

I let my mind follow its analytical course, separating the blocks composing the whole word. At first glance HU plus MAN. Here the Hebrew language, which allows vowels swapping, offers valuable help:

Hu=He, sounding like Hey
MaN=MiN, pronounced like MiN-ister.

OK, it is easier now to reveal a core meaning for the word He-MiN. The letter He universally connotes "spiritual connection", and the word "MiN" in ancient Hebrew means: species, a class, a type.

Et voilà! Here emerges a primary sense for the word HU-MAN: the species (Man)[21] with the ability to hear, perceive spiritual calls and connect with divine entities! (Hu)

Ever since we are regularly communicating with him, Angel YELIYAEL repeatedly reminded us that, in the past, and for ages, millenniums ago, humans knew to elevate themselves to a point where celestial beings could easily contact them.

Can we achieve the same feat now? Aren't our modern minds almost exclusively logical and rational preventing us from even attempting a genuine spiritual call?

Will we ever know which words to utter to contact those beings so they may come down to us?

How far should we rise up?

And where is Up?

Are we real HU-MANS? I earnestly wonder.

Suddenly I feel dizzy…anxious…I realize that today we did not follow our plan as designed; we did not "take off" after having elucidated the Fifth Commandment with YELIYAEL's assistance. We are still here, on Earth!

---

[21] Man: the word Man here doesn't refer to a gender (male or female), but to global hu-Man-ity. Notice the word Wo-man contains the word Man. The prefix Wo, also present in the word Womb is an indicator that a Woman, is a generic HuMan with an added womb.

The approaching darkness of the night was no valid excuse for delaying further our skyward departure, on the contrary!

What happened? YELIYAEL left us stranded…did not invite us to embark…and neither Albert nor I did positively ask the Angel to take us aboard.

Did we miss our flight?

Calming down, my mind continues to wander, associating ideas freely. Yes indeed, as Angel YELIYAEL often reminds us, we should pay more attention to myths, tales and legends so they may unfold and reveal to us their deepest mysteries, thus using our human consciousness to transmute metaphors into clear knowledge.

If we understood legends truly reflect our real history, we would see they hold precious enlightening truth in regard with our past, our origins, and our future.

This evening, without advance warning, Angel YELIYAEL has progressively dissolved before our eyes, allowing us to enter into the realm of sleep and dreams, where humans may expand their souls toward the centers of universal gravity and discover unlimited horizons.

Wishing us "Good Night! Golden dreams!" YELIYAEL has left behind a trail of melodic whispers, bordered by absolute silence.

Albert is relaxing on the living room sofa, asleep, apparently no more troubled by our delayed departure.

I continue my solitary meditation, my thoughts taking on a different route. *"Error impossible*", YELIYAEL has proclaimed.

Why is it impossible for Seraph YELIYAEL to go astray? How could he affirm that he can't possibly err in choosing his course?

At this point, unexpectedly surging from all directions, chanting voices mixed with resounding plucked strings, resonate in and around my head like a thousand harps all played in unison, together with innumerable Seraphic voices singing in chorus.

((((ELEH GODA))))

((((EL)))) ((((EH)))) ((((GO)))) ((((DA))))

Are celestial Seraphs answering my question?

(((((ELEH GODA)))))

EL HE GO DA

Then, all sounds fade slowly, gradually, leaving behind a vibrant transparent stillness.

Albert opens his eyes, raises his head. Fully awake, he asks:

"Did you hear that amazing chant?"

"Yes I did. Maybe it is an answer to my question about the coordinates of our future journey, on the wings of the Angel."

"I heard the sounds ELEGODA, ELEGODA, says Albert. What about you?"

"Same sounds, first contracted then expanding: E L H E G O D A

"It surely means something! exclaims ALBERT. Let us decode this word."

And, as we always do, and have been doing for decades, we begin a new discussion on linguistics, etymology and beyond, hermeneutics, aiming at unveiling the "hidden" meanings of letters and words-sounds composing every language of the world.

Resolute, I unfold the first layer of my Archaeo-Linguistic reasoning: "As a whole, the word ELEGODA resembles the French word TÉLÉ-GUIDÉ, to be translated as TELE-GUIDED, which literally means guidance (guide) from afar (tele)[22], a sort of remote control. Same construction as TELE-VISION, meaning "vision from afar"."

"However, argues ALBERT, the Angels were distinctly chanting ELE-GODA, not TELE-GODA."

"As a matter of fact, they rather were singing the melody:

EL……*HE*…..GO……..DA……..

Let's go ahead and translate the word EL HE GODA, letter by letter, sound by sound, as it unfolds like marigold petals."

"All right, here we go:

EL = directional elevating linking motion,
spiraling ELevation, connecting with the luminous synapses forming the eternal circuits of the universe,
He = spiritual life force, link with the Highest spiritual level,

[22] Tele= Greek for "afar" from a distance, like in Tele-pathy, influence from afar.

GO = intentional move directed and attracted by central Gravitation,
DA = the Door, threshold, passage, from one world into another; Discovery, and Dissolution of all obstacles."

"Thank you Archaeo-Linguistic method! ALBERT comments. Now we may convert the results of our linguistic analysis of the apparently obscure word ELHEGODA into a clear sentence. As Angel YELIYAEL asserted that a book will be published to report on our adventures, we have the extra responsibility to make our explanation understood by others as well, not only ourselves."

Exchanging ideas back and forth, correcting each other in a common concern for precision and clarity, we come up with a transcription we feel would provide an inquiring reader with a good basis for understanding the word EL-HE-GO-DA:

EL:
The celestial messenger,
by Elevating motion,
HE:
connects his/her directional intention
with the Highest spiritual life forces,
GO:
harmonizes his/her intended course
with the path opened by the Universal Guidance Center,
DA:
and each successive threshold
lifts its veil before the approaching Angel, and opens the proper Door.

"So, our guide YELIYAEL is right. For an Angel of his rank, no navigational error is possible! As we are traveling on the wings of the Angel, we are sure to reach our goal without error, because we will be ELHE-GUIDED, guided by the Angel, who is guided by the highest spiritual forces, the Highest Divine Spirit…"

"But, says ALBERT, there is a But! Angel YELIYAEL will also follow our will, our human Free Will, and we shall be ELHE-

GUIDED only if our own intentions are precisely adjusted to the universal circuits. How can we be assured of that?"

Albert has a point, and I ponder with him our true capacity to generate and maintain clear and pure intents. If we don't, the Angel will not take us anywhere…

ALBERT picks up my line of reasoning, as if he was reading my thoughts: "If the Angel takes us along, it will be because our intentions are in harmony with universal values. However, if our intents are flawed, then we shall not take off with the Angel. Meaning more delays, and possibly, flight cancellation!

Therefore, if any error is possible, it cannot be made during our journey, but only BEFORE WE LEAVE!"

Rushing disturbing emotions.

Is that the cause of us being grounded yet? On the very day we had planned to fly off we are still lingering here, in Manhattan! YELIYAEL has been mute on the subject of our intents, as he doesn't want to apply on us any direct influence. He let us free to devise and refine our personal goals. We are as free to err as free to succeed…By leaving us tonight YELIYAEL led us to understand there can be no mind-spirit journey without guiding universal values. Otherwise it would be similar to radio remote control, with inherent risks of inaccuracy and error. Or worse, our journey would be more akin to abduction, a deportation camouflaged as a voluntary voyage.

Pensive, prolonged silence. Then we continue our dialogue.

ALBERT: "Surely YELIYAEL gave us all of the necessary hints while we were studying the Fifth Commandment, in order to help us project and refine our Intent. We have to remember the words he pronounced, those evoking broader horizons and higher values. Those special words, enlightening our thoughts and feelings, will guide us flawlessly."

SIMHA: "Prominently the Angel mentioned TRUTH, BEAUTY, GOODNESS, the major fundamental triad, foundation of Universal Harmony."

ALBERT: "By staying with us, by manifesting himself to our

senses, the Angel indicated we were on the right track. Otherwise neither you nor I would have perceived his presence. YELIYAEL and all of his angelic brothers and sisters are aware of and feel our sincere effort to understand and act according to Truth, Beauty, and Goodness. Yes, we stumble a lot on the way, for dark shadows often hide inner and outer obstacles, but we are honestly trying to hurdle beyond capricious desires in order to reach the heights of pure Intent."

Sighs of relief. Smiles. Nascent elation.

"Now, let's go to sleep and dream. When we are ready, truly ready, Angel YELIYAEL will surely reappear."

9. Mount Nebo, Land of Moab, at first light.

"YOU HAVE LANDED. THE LOCAL YEAR is 1492 BC. Right time, right place. Angel's YELIYAEL voice resonates softly in our mind. *Today MOSES shall appear nearby on Mount Nebo and pronounce his farewell to the people he has led and instructed during 40 years. The effulgent and courageous members of the twelve tribes are now standing at the threshold of the home they will inhabit for more than 15 centuries to come. MOSES will not enter this land. Achieved is his mission on Earth."*

Angel YELIYAEL, Albert and I are now slowly walking down towards one of the rocky terraces surrounding majestic Mount Nebo. Peachy rosy dawn has just taken its leave and a friendly sun illumes the scenery.

We are sliding down the hill at the top of which we just "ele-landed". A few green short bushes offer lively contrast to the ocher, reddish, semi-barren soil. Interspersed sand-colored family tents have been raised on the hillsides; here and there a few shepherds are sitting under knotted twisted olive trees, watching their skinny flocks nibbling at sporadic grass.

Further to my right I discern an ancient well partially covered with flat stones, encircled by small rocks smoothed and polished by countless centuries of use.

This morning at dawn, in Manhattan, YELIYAEL joined us, vibrant with opalescent light, announcing our imminent departure. The Angel quietly shaped himself into a glistening iridescent flattened sphere, topped with a raised alabaster dome on which his translucent green and golden eyes looked like two elliptical windows.

Albert had burst into a sonorous laughter, responding to the humorous Angel who had chosen to appear in the form of a typical E.T. spaceship.

"This hilly landscape, at the end of MOSES' journey in the year 1492 BC, comments YELIYAEL *is in many aspects similar to the land JOHN PAUL II will contemplate, has contemplated, during his visit here on March 20, 2000 Anno Domini."*

Twisting immense time-space spans back and forth with ease and grandeur, Angel YELIYAEL suddenly projects in our minds a gigantic multidimensional, multisensory vivid representation of the Papal pilgrimage.

We actually see the Pope standing at the top of a dry and rocky platform, the natural rostrum on which MOSES is going to appear in a few hours. John Paul II is gazing at the rich green valleys of Judea, agricultural villages surrounded by rich orchards and century-old olive trees.

Side by side, at time holding hands in the antic custom, both MOSES and JOHN PAUL II wonder at the mysterious fog hovering above the Dead Sea. They ponder the import of the legend of Sodom and Gomorrah, the sea waters suddenly solidified; Lot, Abraham's nephew, fleeing disheveled with wife, daughters, and flock. Were those two cities really destroyed as punishment for the iniquity of their inhabitants?

From these heights the Pope departs to visit the sacred places of the Holy Land he could see from the top of the barren mount.

On that very day, March 20, 2000, JOHN PAUL II praying in the company of Christian monks nearby the 400-year-old Mount's Nebo monastery, the Pope proclaims: *"Here I am, looking at the very city of Jericho. I also see the foggy stretches of the Dead Sea on which hover the mysteries of a legendary past. My brothers, let us pray to the Lord and ask that all of the people of the Promised Land — Israelites, Christians, Muslims — be united."*

Then, kneeling on a stone bench, he adds: *"Here I am today in Jordan, close to the river where John the Baptist initiated the apostolic journey of Christ, a familiar land for the travelers of the holy scriptures, a land sanctified by the presence of Jesus Christ himself, by Moses', and the prophet's Ely."*[23].

Continuing his pilgrimage, JOHN PAUL II visits Hebron the city dedicated to Adam and Eve[24], then Bethlehem, and finally, enters the city of Jerusalem.

As we approach a populated area at the foot of mount Nebo, Angel YELIYAEL is judiciously extending towards us his aura of invisibility and I feel on my face and skin the caress of a fresh delicately scented mist. *"You are now invisible,* announces our protector, *like Angels, beyond reach of human eyes.*"

"Simha, I can see you, can you see me?" asks Albert, excited.

"Perfectly! Even better than before! And I can see all around me, wide and far."

"And there is more, much more! I can fly! Can you?"

Borrowing YELIYAEL's extensive levitation powers, I jump immediately, and reach in one wide single arc, the antique well on the east side of the hill.

I am now, unbeknown to all, standing near a young woman sitting on a rock, her head gracefully covered with a brightly embroidered scarf; slender and composed, eyes light brown speckled with gold. Her dark smooth complexion, long narrow neck, gracious position, is reminiscent of the Ethiopian women from Nubia, as seen on Egyptians frescoes. Patiently she is waiting her turn to fill

---

[23] Papal address: see New York Times March 21st, 2000.
[24] Hebron is also known for hosting the tombs of the Patriarchs and Matriarchs.

a long necked perfectly rounded terracotta jug now resting at her feet. A dozen young boys and girls are playfully running and jumping all around.

I am watching attentively the Nubian maiden filling her jug with precise and coordinated elegant hands and arms movements. Albert is sitting on the opposite side of the well, reflecting on the many wondrous aspects of the present circumstances.

YELIYAEL is now floating high in the air, way over us, under the guise of an elongated white vaporous puff, slightly whiter amongst small clouds drifting in the azure sky.

We are all savoring these serene morning moments, immersing ourselves in that magically quiet ambiance.

Time flies. The rapidly rising sun is now warming our faces. YELIYAEL is back on our side and we eagerly resume our advance toward the foot of the mountain.

More of little rocky slopes, more of quiet sunny landscape.

Together we are effortlessly ambling a few inches above ground, following a large and dusty trail. Curving around a stony hill the path widely opens on a huge amphitheatric valley.

And surging from the valley, the shock!

We are stunned with the unexpected spectacle of a large, colorful population, an unruly, dense crowd redolent of sweat, pungent spices, burning incense mixed with streams of fragrant unguents.

Like waves on the ocean racing to the shore, thousands and thousands men and women are purposefully moving towards a precise, urgent, and important destination. On the edges of the crowd, some people linger seemingly unconcerned; in the midst, mischievous children meander their way among adults, running around, playing games only they know the rules.

"I thought I had seen the most colorful, multi-ethnic crowds in the world, says Albert, just by living in New York City in the years 2000! But here, what a surprise! What a sight!"

YELIYAEL comments:

"These men and women are eagerly preparing for a unique

unprecedented event: the farewell to MOSES, their king, mentor and educator for decades; their last farewell to MOSES, a dauntingly valiant loyal leader, providentially endowed with unmatched spiritual powers."

Assiduous reading of ancient biblical texts and study of modern historical reports has not prepared us at all for the mix and contrasts now surrounding us.

All skin colors are represented: milky white, copper red, curry yellow, jet-black, warm brown, pale olive. In the midst of this ocean of exotic humanity, we are invisible.

Men looking as fierce as Caucasian horsemen, ancestors of the future Medic people precede their women proud, haughty, long mahogany curls floating freely around their faces, foreheads decorated with delicate dotted drawings, their wide skirts twirling with every step conjuring up passions and dances.

Sitting calmly and meditatively around their elders, a large Bedouin family from Sinai, faces wrinkled by life experience, eyes creased by exposure to severe desert winds.

Everywhere domesticated animals roam freely: donkeys ridden by young boys, skinny but lively milk cows, small roes wearing tinkling bells around their necks, and dreamy-looking goats.

Alongside us, for a moment walking in concert, strides a beautiful, elegantly slender, dark-skinned woman with sparkling emerald-green eyes and African-style curly Irish-red hair.

About thirty members of an Ethiopian tribe are streaming together toward the end of the valley, men wearing embroidered bright silky clothes, women sumptuously covered with jingling bracelets and wrapped in shimmering togas. Just behind, young boys looking like nomadic Bedouins, dense and wavy hair hiding partially their inquisitive bright eyes.

Farther away Thracian giant Caucasian blond men mingle with families of short people, whose ancestors came from the heart of Africa, the far away land of abundant rivers and immense lakes.

Audacious looking Gypsylike musicians, holding harps and lutes, play nostalgic tunes reminding those of the Kelts of today's Galicia, Brittany, and Ireland. And close by, several majestically dressed Levite priests are marching slowly, conspicuously displaying their self-importance, eager to be noticed.

I already knew we would find at the foot of Mount Nebo a whole array of tribes representing the most daring and adventurous among all the populations known at the time. And yet, this lively, energetic, ebullient, spontaneous choreography astonishes me.

Even more astounding, they all speak one common language, *"a dialect,* comments YELIYAEL, *of the Egyptian working classes and craftsmen in the Goshen valley".*

I notice that, in this vast plain, at the very base of the mountain, no tents are raised. Carriers of fresh water meander in the increasingly dense crowd, shouldering goatskins animated with dozens of ringing little bells, sounding exactly like those of my childhood, in the Moroccan city of Fez.

The contrast is striking between adults, evidently worried, and the young people, bursting with hope and laughter, in anticipation of new adventures and discoveries.

Angel YELIYAEL continues to envelop our bodies with his aura of perfect invisibility, enlightening our intellects while we make our way, side by side, toward the center of the gathering place:

YELIYAEL*: "After MOSES' farewell, the tribes will know which lands, near, far away, or even very far away, will be conferred to them. The eldest and wisest of each tribe expect the conflicts with the current inhabitants of those lands will be minor and battles only slight skirmishes. For Yoshua and the assembly of the leaders are sensible diplomats. Parleys have been going on for 40 years with the Plishtim, the Caftorim, the Bivlim, the Koushim, the Shkittim, the remote Arapim, and the even more remote Asian people of Mithania and Bactria.*[25]*Parleys and negotiations have almost always produced peaceful agreements and comprehensive treaties. Reciprocal exchanges of men, women, metals, flocks, arts and crafts, agricultural techniques, astronomy, mathematics, water management and architecture have already taken place."*

---

[25] Plishtim=Philistines, Caftorim=Cypriots, Bivlim=Babylonians, Koushim=Africans, Shkittim- Scotts; Arapim=Europeans, Mithania-Bactria=Persians and Hindus.

YELIYAEL continues:

"During the past 40 wandering years in the Sinai desert, the twelve tribes have experienced together the exhilarating and trying adventure of a new spiritual utopia. Coming from all racial horizons, purposefully gathered in the Nile delta valley of Goshen for almost four centuries since the time of Joseph, son of Patriarch Jacob, these men and women have acquired a common culture, a common language, and a unique vision of the world: one cosmic guiding Principle, one Law, one People.

They are united by their ancestry, the legendary Adam and Eve, Cain and Abel, Seth, Noah, Shem, and Japheth. Now a new and different multiracial people with an increased knowledge of ethics, has sprung into human history from the Egyptian melting pot. This people, at the call of MOSES, is about to renew today the ancient alliance with the heavens, the Covenant that has been established 35,000 years ago in Gan Eden, the Garden of Eden, the delta between Tigris and Euphrates."

10. The Tent. Mount Nebo, year 1492 BC. Mid-Afternoon.

SUDDEN PERFECT STILLNESS, SWIRLING BALMY air brushing my face; wind puffing my hair, my long dress closely clings to my knees. Then, gradual stop, my feet touch terra firma. In a huge and unexpected leap, Angel YELIYAEL has transported us onto a rocky hill at the opposite edge of the valley.

In front of us stands an imposing sand-colored tent. Above the temple-like entrance, 12 elongated banners are floating elegantly, their creamy yellow background matching perfectly the sandy-beige tone of the tent.

Each pennant bears an emblem, embroidered with bright shiny

purple threads, almost crimson.

I recognize the familiar symbols. I am thrilled to find them here, in the real world, flags floating in the wind, and not only embossed on the metal cover of a Jewish prayer book. I can't refrain from profusely sharing my elation with Albert.

I enounce for him:

"Superb Lion of JUDAH"
"High seafaring Sail Ship, ZEBULON"
"Peaceful, Graceful Gazelle, NAPHTALI"
"Majestic Oak Tree, ASHER"
"Luxuriant Grapes and Vine leaves, EPHRAIM"
"Fruitful Palm Tree, MANASHE "
"Jug and the Sword, SIMON & LEVI"
"REUBEN's Rising Sun"
"ISSAKHAR's Resilient Donkey trotting along"
"DAN's Daunting Cobra"
"GAD's Impressive Tents"
"BENYAMIN's Ominous She-Wolf"

"Look, look, how magnificent! All twelve tribes of Israel are represented here!"

Protected by the Angel's aura Albert and I step into the tent, timidly, frightened by our own audacity.

The inside textile walls are covered with artistically hand painted drapes, depicting Nile delta[26] live scenes: houses on the water built on stilts, young couples' romantic encounters behind bushes of intertwined reeds; fishing boats sailing amidst innumerable profusely irrigated small islands covered with abundant luscious green tropical bushes and trees, and in the background, fleets of impressively huge sail ships entering the delta, or leaving it for high-sea adventures.

The effect is superb, the ambiance in complete contrast with the barren rocky landscape surrounding the tent. On the reed-covered floor, rush braided celadon baskets are filled with a variety

---

[26] Nile Delta: In Ancient Egypt, also called the Valley of Goshen

of fruits.

An imposing old man is sitting on a finely sculpted ebony throne, his bearded face surrounded with gray long hair. Around him, comfortably settled on foldable wooden chairs, around a large circular table, twelve men and a woman are conferencing. Six scribes, seated cross-legged on comfortable pillows, feverishly record down every word.

Laying on the large round table, a wide open scroll, covered with colorful drawings, lines and graphs, is the unmistakable focal point of the meeting.

"*Get closer to the center,* says YELIYAEL, *you are invisible, untouchable, inaudible. Go and look at the scroll on the table, quench your curiosity*!"

Guardedly, still unsure, we both move a few steps forward.

"It's a map of the world, exclaims ALBERT, a complete map of Earth, an exact rendition of the planet, as we know it today, including all continents and oceans!"

My heart is pounding fast, my vision blurred, I dare not speak out loud, I merely whisper:

"Albert, we have entered "The" Tent of Assignations, the house of the famed tabernacle described in the Old Testament!"

ALBERT, excitedly, apparently not grasping the import of my previous declaration:

"This really looks like a high-level meeting. These participants seem to know each other well. Surely it is not the first time they assemble. And who is that young lively woman sitting nearest to the leader?"

"*ISHTARIT the prophetess, MYRIAM's disciple, is sitting nearest to the leader*, says YELIYAEL. And he adds: *The leader YOSHUA BEN NOUN is speaking.*"

YOSHUA: The Oak Tree, emblem of KOHAELET *Coalition*[27] *of the People of the Spirit,* seals all the treaties our emissaries have come back with. The majestic Oak Tree embroidered on Asher's

[27] Kohelet in Hebrew means "assembly". Ko=Cohesion/ He=spiritual covenant/ Elet=elect people. Thus the word Co-al-ition.

tribal pennants, connoting peace, cooperation, and prosperity is now worldwide symbolizing the same intents and goals shared by the new Federation's numerous peoples."

The voice tone, the physical composure, the rhythm of the sentences, even the poise of each listener, all indicate that YOSHUA BEN NOUN is now wrapping up collected facts and thoughts already discussed during previous similar conferences.

ALBERT: "Maybe this is the last summit of the kind. It feels like YOSHUA is mostly speaking for the scribes, faithful recorders of important events and resolutions."

SIMHA: "Or, maybe, perceptive YOSHUA aware we space-time travelers are now present in their midst, is condensing information for our edification. O YELIYAEL, please, is that so?"

YELIYAEL remains silent. In fact, I cannot see him around! The Angel has disappeared! That bluish ray of light floating just under the ceiling tent, is that you, YELIYAEL?

YOSHUA BEN NOUN continues, evidently unperturbed by my erratic emotions:

"Now forty years have fully elapsed, during which took place countless explorations, embassies, meetings, surveys and preparations. Many groups, tribes and nations are impatiently awaiting the famed Egyptian colonists, expecting our imminent arrival, in accordance with the prophecies and predictions of their wise men and insightful leaders.

We shall bring with us and share all the benefits of the Nile valley civilization, which they know of by frequent direct contact or commercial trade.

Several communities have wished to receive proof of our good will, and their observers still live among us, studying the art of digging wells and irrigation, carpentry to build better houses and seafaring ships; practicing advanced social laws and disciplines of mind-spirit synergy, sciences until now safely preserved within the vaults of major Egyptian Temples-Universities."

YOSHUA pauses, fleetingly turns his head in my direction…or is he staring at YELIYAEL now standing between me and Albert?

Taking a deep breath YOSHUA resumes his oration:

"Following the instructions of our Master MOSES, we have, prudently, not mentioned to the peoples of the world either the Ten Commandments or the commitments and Covenant we have ourselves avowed to the powers of the Heavens. However, many of their leaders are awaiting recommendations relative to social, ethical, and spiritual wisdom, particularly the Shamans who are keeping alive the fabulous legends of human history.

Everywhere, thanks to the color of the pennant of our great Federation, we are called the "purple people",[28] or "liberators"[29]. From all horizons, rumors of our impending arrival are buzzing.

And our code name *KO-HA-ELET* resounds in all languages and dialects, locally accented: KO-ALTA, KO-ELTIKA, KELTIKA, KELTIC, GO-ALLA, GAEL-LICA, GALLITA, even OLMEKA.

To this day, all of our ambassadors have been successful, with very few exceptions. Some specific situations need adaptations and adjustments. This is the topic of our meeting today.

A young scribe now points his reed pen to a formidable looking man, with a dark eagle face, and solid, virile features. The man stands up, getting ready to intervene.

YELIYAEL: *"This is MATOSIS, charismatic member of the ASHER tribe, coordinator of all KO-ALTA[30]embassies. MATOSIS, whose parents are both Nubians, was born on the Elephantine Island in the far South of Egypt. One of his ancestors is an ancient black KUSHA Pharaoh, from the original founding lineage of the early Egyptian civilization."*

"What means KUSHA?" inquires ALBERT.

YELIYAEL: *"KUSH is the ancient name for the African area expanding from Ethiopia on the shores of the Indian Ocean to Senegal on the Atlantic Ocean, including the Sahara desert and the actual country of Mauritania."*

---

[28] Purple: People: am segoula in Hebrew.

[29] In Archae Lingua the word segoula means both "purple" and "liberator."

[30] The word Coalta, sourced in Archae Lingua Ko-helet, means Federation, commonly rendered by the words Coalition and Kelt.

For a moment MATOSIS contemplates the assembly, a regal woman[31] and all men like him, experienced, devoted, and highly motivated leaders, aware their mission leaves no room for political tension or personal power conflicts. His warm and vigorous voice, grave, stentorian, is typical of the men of Afrikiya:

MATOSIS: "Before any of the tribes leave the countries of Plishtim, Canaan, Edom, Moab, for farther worldwide destinations, their first duty is to help the designated groups of families settle around SALEM, in the valley of Jezreel, around Hatzor in the highlands of GALILEE, in the YARDEN Valley, in GHAZA, and all along the seashore, from YAFFO to the CARMEL Hills in the North and beyond."

Pause. Scribes scratching on their tablets are devotedly working on their reports.

MATOSIS: "Ten years from now all caravans will have departed for their long-range journeys."

Pause. More feverish scratching and scripting.

MATOSIS: "Our beloved leader YOSHUA himself, shall reside at the permanent center of the Federation, with headquarters in the old settlement of SALEM. Here too shall reside selected families representative of each of the twelve traveling tribes. Thus the emblematic gravity center of the KOALTA, pulsing heart of our civilizing expansion, shall be the city of SALEM."

"MATOSIS is designating the future land of Israel and Judea, as well as the future capital city Jerusalem" comments YELIYAEL.

"Why two names for the same land? asks ALBERT. Does this mean the Federation will have two distinct central states?"

"Correct, confirms YELIYAEL, *two foundations of equal strength: JUDEA will impeccably keep the archives of the past, the total memories of humanity since Adam and Eve's times till the Exodus from Egypt; while ISRAEL will permanently act as the proficient coordinator of the new thrust of civilization, the founder of*

[31] The woman present during this important meeting is Ishtarit, disciple of prophetess Myriam, and leader, in the desert, of the large group of women, dedicated to psychurgy, divination, music, dance. Myriam herself, sister of Moses' and Aaron, passed away long before the 12 tribes reached Mount Nebo.

progressive human Universality and Unity."

MATOSIS now calls the assembly's attention, designating successively six tribal leaders:

DAN	JUDAH	SIMEON-LEVI
GAD	ASHER	ISSAKHAR.

"Within the next 10 years, as planned, your tribes shall divide into equal parts and head towards each of the agreed directions, traveling with the settlers to reinforce their scientific and technical skills."

YELIYAEL provides more details: "*MATOSIS is now about to instruct NEFERHOTEP, also called ELIDANA, leader of the DAN*[32] *tribe.*"

MATOSIS: "I have assigned six large DAN families to each traveling group. Their members possess the necessary knowledge and skills for implanting successfully the seeds of Justice and the principles of harmonious Social Law. Their ensuing mission will be to start schools of law and ethics to instruct future leaders, similar to those soon to be established in ISRAEL and JUDEA, at the center of the Federation."

"The SIMEON-LEVI tribe, continues MATOSIS, shall leave a quarter of its current combined population in Israel and Judea. This arrangement will maintain an adequate number of Levi priests for liturgical ceremonies and intra-universe communications, as well as a suitable number of Simeonite metallurgical and military engineers, to further the training of the families staying in the land of the Federation, from Salem to the mountains of Levanon."

Now speaks NATHANYAHU BEN YOSEPH, a stocky and quiet man, representing the Simeonite elite warriors:

"We must anticipate some troubles around the cities of JERICHO and AIA. However the main effort of our diplomatic action will take place in Ghaza, the Plishtim's fortified center, which recently received a massive immigration from KAPTOR[33]Island.

---

[32] Dan-Din (Dayan) in Hebrew means "judicial power and skills"

[33] Kaptor: Ancient name given to the island of Crete in the Aegean Sea.

Among those new immigrants may be found the best metalworkers, descendants of the old maritime power of Minos. They are said to be the offspring of dreaded Hephaestos[34]."

AVIDOROS, leader of GAD is now addressing the committee:

"We are secretly keeping observers in GHAZA. Recent reports indicate that, in order to obtain cooperation from those adroit metallurgists, weapon makers and warriors, it could be sufficient to remind them of our common Egyptian origin.

However, they will have to be fully assured the Federation will not attempt to imperil significantly their local manufacturing and trading armament monopoly. We could even use their skills to better arm our soon to be traveling tribes before they leave for faraway destinations. This would guarantee the PLISHTIM's good will towards us."

YOSHUA BEN NOUN signals he wants to speak again, and a respectful silence falls on the assembly.

Voice soft and calm YOSHUA reminds everyone "the success of the federated co-allied colonists, regardless of their destination, will not primarily depend on weapons, but mainly on the contents of their numerous transport carts."

He goes on explaining:

"These iron wheeled carts[35] filled with textiles, jewelry, useful tools for agriculture, technical and scientific papyruses, will allow the settlers to demonstrate their competence in cultivating the land, mining and working with metals, improving the security and comfort of men and women in all territories they will enter peacefully.

Bringers of prosperity, sciences of health and life, nutrition and body care practiced since ages in the lands of Egypt and Mesopotamia, they will be welcomed with open arms.

And later they shall be able to introduce a new social and mor-

---

[34] Hephaestos , known as the God Goldsmith, in the ancient Cretan writings.

[35] Carts: recent archeologists and historian researchers have uncovered that, during decades in the 15th century BC, mysterious groups of civilizing peoples driving hundreds upon hundreds carts have brought textiles, metal instruments for agriculture and monuments building. The territories of that immigration, cover the Black sea and Balkans roads, through Europe up to England.

al order based on the sacred 10 Commandments.

Thus the program our beloved MOSES received from EL ELYON's messengers[36] shall come into fruition in the future centuries."

With great respect, all the present military leaders ponder the words of YOSHUA BEN NOUN, the genius strategist, fully aware of his devotion to the cause of ascending human evolution.

YELIYAEL kindly informs us:

"YOSHUA is getting older, and preoccupied with the well-being of the entire KO-HA-ELET, Coalition of the People of the Spirit, his people, the universal people. At the same time, he is anxious at the thought of the always-possible hostility and violence that may be awaiting this energetic and audacious mosaic of new tribes when they reach far away lands and unfold their new spiritual message. YOSHUA dreads confrontations and conflicts. He intends to muster his strategic skills and ambassadorial talents to avoid shocks, traumas and bloodsheds."

After a short silence, YOSHUA BEN NOUN concludes:

"Always and persistently all our colonists must implement the basic rule contained in the 6th Commandment:

"MASTER YOUR STRENGTH,
THEREFORE YOU SHALL WIN WITHOUT KILLING
AND CONQUER WITHOUT WARRING."

MATOSIS now continues his presentation of the marching orders and addresses ELIOSIS, leader of the JUDAH tribe:

"ELIOSIS, your tribe shall provide three large families, well trained in the sciences of clan management and governance, to join with each of the twelve departing groups of colonists. It is also agreed that JUDAH's other families shall split into two equal parts.

The SALEM group shall be in charge of building the future state of JUDEA between HEBRON and BETH LEHEM.

The other half shall travel North, in concert with DAN and EPHRAIM groups, way beyond the mountains of LEVANON, towards

---

[36] El Elyon: the High Above, name given to God by the Bedouins of the Sinai

the obscure and wild regions of northern EREBA[37]."

MATOSIS frowns worried; a secret inner thought is haunting him; he picks up a clay jug in front of him, pours himself a generous portion of refreshing bitter Egyptian beer; he stares pointedly at another leader, as dark skinned as himself.

"MATOSIS is about to address AMTESH, comments YELIYAEL, *ASHER's leader, his great Nubian friend, born of an Ethiopian family, beyond ASWAN, near the Nile River source."*

MATOSIS: "ASHER's instructions are as follows: select twelve families for settlement in Galilee, at the core of the Federation. Divide the remaining large number into twelve equal parts to accompany each traveling group of settlers, so providing each colony with the indispensable science and vital expertise in constructive dialogue, negotiation, diplomacy and preservation of peace. In the whole new world we are building, the people of ASHER will be responsible for embassies and treaties. Their mission will be a difficult one, as they will have to introduce social order in the midst of barbaric cannibals still swarming all over EREBA to the north, in AFRIKIYA to the south of the Equator, as well as in the vast separated continent on the other side of the great Atlantean ocean.[38] But the tree of ASHER, emblem of our universal Federation, shall constantly inspire those missionaries of peace."

YELIYAEL: "*They are the ancestors of the Keltic and Gaelic Druids of Europe, men of the robe who, sitting under century-old oak trees, shall act as wise compassionate judges, quick to iron out conflicts in order to avoid deadly battles and fratricidal wars."*

MATOSIS pauses, catching his breath, and YOSHUA BEN NOUN,

---

[37] Ereba: sometimes pronounced Erepa or Arapa. It is the ancient name given to Europe. Ereba means "sunset," or occident, therefore this word has come to designate the Western countries.The word Ereb, to this day, in Hebrew means the "sunset". This word may be found in Genesis, chapter one: Va Yehi Ereb, "and there was a sunset. In Greek mythology Ereba designates the land of "darkness", alluding to the wilderness and cannibalistic peoples of Europe.

[38] Atlantean: the root-word ATL is in use since ages to designate the Greek god Atlas, from which is named the Atlas chain of mountains in Morocco and the Atlantic ocean. The Atztec people record that their founding tribes, originated from the south of north America, were named Atalantes; the Aztecs broadly use the root atl in thousands upon thousands of their words; the ATLatl a cutlass, was their preferred weapon. The US city Atlanta was named after the Atalant tribe.

with an inspired prophetic tone, intervenes:

"The GAD people do not embroider protective tents on their banner in vain. These men, besides their gift for the science of measurements, calculations and mathematics, possess the genius of great architects and planners, which the whole world needs in equal parts. GAD shall leave twelve families in the Central Land; the others shall divide equally and travel in every direction of the upcoming worldwide exodus.

May these men and women succeed everywhere in giving fame and prestige to the God of Unity, the GODAI, the One Divine Guide."

MATOSIS' voice continues to pronounce the assignments. I suddenly feel dizzy. Names and their meanings incessantly echo in my head. Now I can only understand fragments of the speech:

...ISSAKHAR,....trade experts ...

...shall go in every direction

...towards EREBA...shall land in AFRIKIYA...

...shall traverse GABAR-AL-TARA [39].......

...reaching the HESPERIDES[40]......

I am fascinated. Awed by what I am hearing I confide my questioning to our companion Angel YELIYAEL:

SIMHA: "Thus the members of six tribes possessing a special expertise shall accompany equally each of the others. ASHER the great negotiators, DAN the law makers, JUDAH experts in state affairs and politics, SIMEON-LEVI combining the art of war with the science of liturgy and exo-communication, GAD the geniuses of logistics and construction, the unrivaled planners, ISSAKHAR the tireless merchants trading all over the world."

YELIYAEL calming my excitement with a soft and steady voice, kindly completes the interpretation of the puzzling words I just

---

[39] Gabar el tara : ancient name given to the Straits of Gibraltar.

[40] Hesperides: original name of the Iberian Peninsula that includes today Spain and Portugal. Hesperides is a contraction of two words Ha and Separades which, in Modern Hebrew, is translated by the "separated". This expresses the geologic break that happened, about 12,000 years ago, in that part of the world, creating the Straits of Gibraltar. Still today, Spain is called in Hebrew Sepharada, and the Jews who long ago exited Spain are called Sephardim.

heard, reviews these men's past and their descendants' future, explains the consequences of the actions that are being decided inside this tent of assignations.

HANONESH leader of ZEBULON, red haired, freckled face, a man of solitary and almost shy demeanor, is now addressing his brothers. The destinations and the names echo once again in my head.: "My crews shall use the remaining ten years to build a gigantic seafaring fleet with the help of the JEBUSITES, EDOMITES, and MOABITES. The bay of YAFFO north of GHAZA is strategically the best point of departure in the midst of a peaceful and friendly population, a deep natural port, well protected from storms.

Cedar wood timber shall be shipped down along the coast from the mountains of LEBANON loaded in TYR, the port facing the island of KAFARASH[41]. From there, my ships shall head in two major directions: One to AEGEA[42], KAFTOR, KAFARASH, the other heading toward the Straits of GABAR-AL-TAR will navigate up along the HESPERIDES to reach the bay of SOFATAR[43] in EREBA.

And we shall build a third flotilla at AILAT, with the intent to reach east AFRIKIYA, and further, the fabled Asian coasts."

"The ZEBULON seafarers, says YELIYAEL, *will be joined by parts of each of the traveling DAN, GAD and NAPHTALI tribes. They will then form the DA-GANA people, in the very center of the AFRIKIYA continent..."*

I burst out, amazed:

"The future empire of GANA! Its greatness will last through 15th century AD! The famous DOGON people!!!"

"That is correct" says YELIYAEL

Memories of books I have read spring in my mind. The questions anthropologists and ethnologists have forever asked, find

---

[41] Kapharash: Ancient name of the island of Cyprus.

[42] Aegea: present day Greece.

[43] Sofatar in Hebrew means: End of the Earth and indicates here the ultimate western point of Galicia in Spain, called Finisterra; site of the port of Santiago de Compostella, a holy place of pilgrimage from immemorial times Its symbol is a sea scallop shell, a sure sign that high sea navigation is part of that pilgrimage's history.

here a rather humorous answer[44].

HANONESH the high sea navigator continues to evoke all the oceans ZEBULON's fleet will sail, pointing at the hostile or peaceful continents they will be landing on:
.....ATLANTIKA........ARMORIKA..........*AMHARIKA*.......

This time I dare not believe what I am hearing! Under shock, I close my eyes, bewildered. I need a witness, a friend to reassure me. I open my eyes, but Albert is no longer nearby me.
He has stealthily moved to the center of the assembly and is now standing to the right of YOSHUA. The map is widely spread out on the central table, and I see him lift one edge of the scroll, looking concentrated and preoccupied. YOSHUA slowly and seemingly absent-mindedly moves a crystal rock to the corner, thus allowing the roll to stay open.

Albert ascends quickly to the top of the tent, drops slowly to the floor, settles nearby YOSHUA's right shoulder, pores over the central document. Then, flying back to my side, he whispers haltingly in my ear:

"This map is complete. Not only are all of the continents there, all of them, but they are named as we know them in our times!"

SIMHA: "Even the American continent? This would mean I really heard the name AMHARIKA!!!?"

ALBERT: "Yes, Simha, you did, you did!! You heard perfectly! The leader of the Zebulon seafarers actually pronounced the name AMHARIKA, a land to be reached beyond the ATLANTIKA Ocean.

And I discovered something else!...This map is thick, it has several layers. I slid my fingernail under the top map and the next, and I clearly saw the second layer. This scroll lies on top of several superimposed maps, slightly glued together."

SIMHA: "I think we have a few more questions to ask Angel YELIYAEL..."

"This set of maps is the work of MOSES *himself,* answers YELIYAEL. *Only YOSHUA knows the secrets it holds. Each layer of*

[44] Dogon peoples are highly knowledgeable in astronomy, with emphasis on Sirius, a star particularly studied by the ancient Egyptian astronomers.

the map defines a specific era. What is inscribed on those large glued pages is the future of the civilizing missions. When a cycle is over, the next page is uncovered.

SIMHA: "How does one know when a cycle is over? When is it time to reveal the next layer?"

YELIYAEL: "*After 250 years, the map is examined to check on the progress of each mission. And every 500 years the top map is unglued, and the new assignments are uncovered.*"

ALBERT: "And where is this scroll nowadays? I mean now, year 2000 AD…"

YELIYAEL: "*Where it has always been, in the Ark of the Covenant.*"

SIMHA: "But if the Ark is lost, so are the maps!"

YELIYAEL: "*Everything is a Sepher, a Sphere, Simha, you know that; everything in the universe is spherical. If the map is lost here, it will be found somewhere else. If the edges of the continents are erased, their names continue to exist in human memory.*"

SIMHA: "ARCHAE LINGUA! It is our ultimate recourse!"

YELIYAEL: "*Names and words inscribed on monuments, ancient manuscripts and bards' memory, allow the sharp-minded investigator to track the tribes' movements, confirm their progress, check where they have established settlements. Do you want an example? Let us follow DAN 's main path, along the river DAN-UBE, to the land of DANE-MARK, where the settlers were joined by a group of the JUDAH tribe, in the peninsula of JUDE-LAND. Hear the tales of the Tuatha de DANAAN, early settlers in Ireland. Or listen to the Greek poets, praising the high merits of their ancestor founders, the famous DANAENS evoked by the poet Homer…*"

"Descendants of DAN the DANAENS princes and princesses who founded Athens during the heroic times" whispers ALBERT.

SIMHA: "I heard the seafarer leader of ZEBULON utter the word AMARICA. Was he really referring to a journey by sea to our America? We are taught this continent was named after AMERIGO Vespucci in the 15th century AD. Who named America? Where is the truth?"

YELIYAEL: "*Everything is a Sphere, everything that is true is providentially synchronized. The word AMHARIKA*[45]*, meaning "the land of the red faces" has been used to designate that continent way before the 15th century AD, and even way before MOSES' times.*

It also designated a star that many navigators would follow in their adventurous journeys across the Atlantean ocean.

ARCHAE LINGUA will tell you everything, reveal absolutely every move, every direction of human peregrinations on the planet.

"But, asks ALBERT, the map, or rather the multiple maps now on the table, also describe the evolution, the future of humanity. This means that MOSES inscribed not only what he knew, but his prophecies! An act of divination!?"

"Everything is a Sphere, says YELIYAEL. *On the circle of time, present, past and future are barely separated."*

"Synchronicity…"

YELIYAEL: *"Now pay attention to the words of SOSTRIS, the leader of EPHRAIM tribe*."

Meaningful words and emblematic names resound again in the tent, their momentous vibrations uniting even more the courageous members of the assembly, committed to undertake this formidable and endless mission for the benefit of all humans, present and future: "EPHRAIM shall carry the symbol of the vine and the grape to the EREBA lands, mixing with the local tribes, GARMANS and FRANAKS. They shall travel northwest, cross the sea channel, and establish themselves as the people of the BERITH-AIN[46], on the vast islands recently[47] separated from the continent."

YELIYAEL explains:

"On the EREBA continent the descendants of EPHRAIM will be GERMANS, GAULS, and FRANKS. In the BERITH-AIN, the British Isles, their offspring are named WELSH, SCYTHES, and SAKSONS. Adept in agriculture, EPHRAIM's colonists will introduce the love of fer-

---

45 Amharika: Hebrew Am=people / Harika=burnt red

46 Berith-ain: Archaic name of Britania. The expression Berith-ain in Hebrew means "original alliance" or "the source of the covenant"."

47 Recently: event "recent" only on geological time scale. The British channel break occurred about 10,000 BC, during one of the planetary upheavals, called the "big flood" caused by the thaw of the last "mini" ice age.

mented beverages, wines and beers everywhere they go."

"And, adds YELIYAEL, with a large humorous smile, *you may retrace the journeys of Ephraim's people by spotting enthusiastic beer and wine makers and drinkers."*

YOSHUA's voice resounds again in the tent: "I shall now speak to REUBEN's tribe, named after the beloved first son of Leah and Jacob, the tribe bearing the Rising Sun emblem. These men and women have so many talents they can embrace and comprehend the whole universe. They shall leave half of their numerous families in the land of Israel, be the only ones to settle in such great numbers on the hills of GALILEA. Their name and emblem clearly identify them to the Prophecy of Jacob: they are the seed from which shall spring the Peace Loving, the eternal son, the savior. From the RE-OV-BEN[48] tribe shall rise the shining sun of the eternal son. The other half of the REUBEN people shall take the same route as the NAPTALI tribe, marching east and spreading out on the lands of the MEDES, toward the vast horizons of Persia.

As for the families of NAPTALI they shall extend their journey much further to the east, all the way to CATHAY[49], and, leaving behind them a large contingent they shall then journey north, to NEPALI, and later, heading south, reach the land of the future BEN-GALILI[50]."

"Now listen to BEN-YAMINA", announces SOSTRIS, laying down the jug of purple liquid he has just drunk from, provoking an explosion of carefree laughter shared by everyone present in the tent of assignations.

"Speak up now, LOUVSAIS, leader of BEN-YAMINA, whose pennant bears the fierce she-wolf emblem. Let us know of your decision."

"Let me remind you, declares LOUVSAIS, with a calm but reso-

---

[48] Re-ov-ben, means in Archae Lingua, the Prince, the shining leader, the King (Re), born of the egg (OVa), of eternal substance (Ben). Re-ov-ben in short can be translated as: the "Son of the First Creative Principle".

[49] Cathay: The future China

[50] Nepali – Ben Galili: Two countries known today as Nepal (from the Naptali tribe), and Bengal meaning the descendants (Ben) of the Galileans. Word Galil is rooted in Hebrew GAL meaning "exile", "exodus".

lute baritone voice, that our proud and powerful tribe shall dutifully leave the required twelve families on the land of Canaan, at the core of the Federation.

Let me also point out clearly that our families are very wary to do so, in spite of their respect for our master MOSES and the leaders of the coalition.

As you all know, the BEN-YAMINA people, virile tempered conquerors, dislike the CANAAN settlers whom they see as soft spirited and lacking passion for adventure. They equally dislike that new notion of living in the midst of such a heterogeneous mix of races and customs. We the BEN-YAMINA above all aim at the racial purity of the HYKSOS, first ancestors of the HITTITES, and of the THRACIANS, race of warrior Gods, who conceived us. We do not favor the mosaic mix of ethnic groups encouraged by MOSES and YOSHUA."

LOUVSAIS pauses briefly, then continues:

"Therefore, all the BEN-YAMINA families who are not compelled by lawful assignments to settle here in the vicinity, shall travel north and head back to the original country of our divine Hyksos ancestors."

LOUVSAIS abruptly stops. A heavy and anxious silence weighs on the assembly…

"So shall it be done!" sternly declares YOSHUA, with a firm authoritative voice tone. "In the centuries to come, the people of the wolf shall receive the salary of the wolf!"

YELIYAEL elucidates this enigmatic statement:

"The direct descendants of BEN-YAMINA, will be major cofounders of the Roman Empire[51], which as much as bringing law and order, will at times spread racism and violence in the world, until the she-wolf people meets its fate by the swords of the Gothic barbaric invaders. After their secession from the Exodus Coalition the BEN-YAMINA at first built the prestigious and proud city-state of Troy, to see it destroyed, burned and razed to the ground by the

[51] The she-wolf remained the emblem of Rome from foundation until the fall of the Empire.

Achaeans from Greece. Totally vanquished the scattered survivors will flee toward the Latium, in the Italian peninsula, and seek refuge among the Etruscans, compassionate descendants of EPHRAIM, DAN , JUDAH and ZEBULON. After the foundation of Rome the Ben Yamina colonists will ferociously eliminate their benefactors."

11. The Secession.

A BURLY MAN, WHO ANSWERS TO THE NAME MANOUSH is now addressing the assembly. Voice soft and melodious; features clearly Hindu. His tribe MANASHE features a graceful and resilient palm tree on its pennant.

"MANASHE, comments YELIYAEL, *is by design a nomadic tribe whose origins go back to the plains of the Ganges River, at the foot of the Himalayas. Their dialect is filled with Sanskrit words, the sacred language of India; their tribal mores remind those of the DRAVIDIAN peoples who have been living in India for more than 35,000 years. Their current leader is MANOUSH namesake of their hero and founding ancestor."*

Says MANOUSH firmly: "We do not wish to participate *AT ALL* in this civilizing choreography. The sedentary Edenic utopia of the descendants of ADAM and EVE does not appeal to us. We are and shall remain an independent nomadic people.

Of course, we are nomads always roaming in countries of sunny and temperate climates on the warm side!" he adds with a large carefree smile, giving his face an extraordinary powerful aura that illuminates the whole place.

The audience bursts into a candid warm general laughter. The atmosphere in the tent has become friendly, cheery, relaxed. I myself feel enchanted and charmed.

For our eyes only Angel YELIYAEL materializes a large straw hat, from which dozens of multicolored silky scarves escape swirling toward the ceiling of the tent.

The general laughter quiets down, and MANOUSH resumes his stunning address:

"We are nomads, but we are also artists, singers, dancers, poets, and musicians. We live by tales and legends, we tell EVEN-TORAH[52], people's good fortune.

Here is our plan. We shall separate into two groups. One shall travel up to the inner sea of ANTALIA[53], on a parallel road albeit far away from the Federation tribes heading toward the Black Sea.

For purpose of identification this first group shall be code named TZI-GANAS, meaning those who seceded from the coalition. Others have chosen to be called RO-MANOUSH, as a reminder that they will establish a central albeit ever renewed colony and travel and roam from and back to their base."

"That central base of the MANASHE tribe is known as the nation of RO-MANIA" whispers YELIYAEL for our ears only.

Meanwhile MANOUSH continues:

"The second group shall head south, to the palm groves of the Sahara desert, where they shall travel dressed in blue. Then crossing the GABAR-AL-TAR channel, make their way into the HESPERIDES, under the name GAETANOS and EGYPSOS[54].

We shall roam everywhere, often crossing paths with our brothers, but settling nowhere."

MANOUSH has now stopped his fortune telling address. His

---

52 Hebrew Even-Torah means the Rock of the Torah, which Moses was holding on Mount Horeb while God's messenger beamed the fire glyphs of the Commandments. This event has become a legend, told to our days on the roaming treks of the gypsy tribes, giving birth to the idea of telling the "good fortune", Aven-tura in Italian, Spanish, French, Romanian etc, in English Adven-ture; Avana-tara in Hindu Sanskrit designates an "auspicious happening".

53 Antalia=currently Anatolia in Turkey, on the sea now called the Black Sea. Modern archeologists and historians have clearly found evidence of a civilized population, with very dark skin and curly hair that lived there about 3,000 years ago.

54 Gaetanos becoming Gitans in French, Gaetanos in Spanish. Egypsos, becoming Gypsies, meaning of Egyptian origin.

strange speech clearly announces the unambiguous secession of the MANASHE people. He raises his head to confront the gaze of the twelve implacable judges, and what he sees pleases his soul and spirit. All the leaders staring at him, no one appears to be angry, distraught, or even slightly discontented.

"By JEHOVE! he exclaims. Then, smiling, he corrects himself: by YAHWEH!!!"

The CO-HA-ELET's coalition leaders understand his people's decision and they do not judge it to be wrong. Obviously relieved, MANOUSH valiantly continues his speech.

"I shall now sing a ballad composed for you by GAETANOSH, our stars inspired cantor."

Taking a small harpsichord handed to him by musician prophetess ISHTARIT, MANOUSCH launches into the first chords of a melodious chant:

We the people of MANOUSH
shall remain forever
on human history border.
Dark people with pale skin, we shall be.
White people with olive skin, we shall be.
Yellow people with bronzed skin, we shall be.
Red people with dark skin, we shall be.

Dressed as Princes of the desert
or covered with the rags of Gypsies,
forming circles around rising flames,
we shall honor the soul of music,
and the spirit of art around the world.
Always wandering, never still,
we shall inspire troubadours,
minstrels and bards of all nations.
Without priests, temples or pontiffs,
our worship and devotion shall rise,
filling the world with rhythmic melodies
up to God the Supreme, directly.
In the privacy of their heart

every King, every Queen,
rulers and lords glued to their land
will dream of joining our itinerant dance.
Dear brothers in Galilee,
holy source of a universal people you shall be,
and your rebel brothers we shall be,
villainous thieves and tricksters,
infamous freedom seekers.
But through us you will remember forever,
that all utopias eventually pass away,
stone houses crack and vanish under the sun,
but on human heads
the firmament never falls,
and starry lamps never wane.
The Sixth Commandment we honor,
We shall not kill only we pledge,
to keep that oath untouched and safe,
avoiding fratricidal wars,
inevitable amongst sedentary peoples,
drifting constantly we will.

Brothers, Sisters under the stars,
Never forget to chant and dance!
Sisters, Brothers, see you around.

MANOUSH stops reciting. The twelve men, and prophetess Ishtarit, toughened by decades of hardship, suffering, and patient hope, remain silent for a long time, their eyes hazed and watery from holding back tears. They just heard the final farewell from their beloved brother. The black sheep is leaving the flock. A company of Angels, like transparent giant doves expanding their majestic wings envelop the assembly, caressing minds and spirits with waves of celestial compassion.

12. Moses, Hermes and Orpheus.

AFTER MANOUSH'S MOVING CHANT ENDED, Albert, YELIYAEL and I left the tent of assignations and assignments, in which the leaders of the twelve tribes have just asserted the fate of the men and women who, outside, are preparing for what they know to be Prophet MOSES last testament.

I remember Albert asking to remain alone for a while, and we left him sitting, pensive, in the cool shade under a small pale blue-green olive tree.

Meanwhile, YELIYAEL answers my as yet unvoiced question:

"Long before this final meeting MOSES and YOSHUA sent families representing each of the ten tribes, excluding BEN-YAMINA and MANASHE, to settle in the country of DILMUN, in the Arabic peninsula. Those settlers have already spread the new message under the code name BENI-ISRAEL.

For centuries to come those colonists will be the proficient and prominent teachers on this vast territory. They will establish, further southeast, the Israelite settlements of INDIA and YE-MEN[55], then, crossing the red sea to the west will soon expand the Federation to the far confines of ABYSSINIA-ETHIOPIA. Those are the famous BENI-ISRAEL, descendants of the federated twelve tribes, the future fiercest defenders and first followers of Prophet MAHOMET."

Another sign that MOSES spread his universal message way beyond JERICHO, JERUSALEM and GALILEE, in order to sow the seed of a people of God without frontiers in a promised land which encompasses all of the lands in this world.

Many strange, paradoxical, and contradictory statements in the Old and New Testament suddenly came to light. I promised myself to attentively re-examine the three sacred books in order to better appreciate their science, their memory, and their prophecies: The

---

55 In Hebrew Ye-Men means Men of God; also means "righteous people". And by extension the "right" as opposed to "left".

book of MOSES, the NEW GOSPEL OF JESUS, as well as the KORAN of MAHOMET.

A recurring thought has been hovering in my mind during the extraordinary session we have just witnessed. I address YELIYAEL:

"If MOSES is a universal founder of civilization, why is the Old Testament practically the only ancient document to prominently mention his name? All modern historians notice that even ancient Egypt legacy doesn't show any trace of his existence."

YELIYAEL answers:

"In fact, Simha, that is not the case at all. MOSES has made his mark on all of the peoples of this Earth. However he is called by different names."

This remark startles me. It surely addresses my perplexity. Obviously, in all the antique hieroglyphic documents that have been abundantly unearthed by Egyptologists, there is no trace of the Hebrew exile, no hint of the leader MOSES, no clue about AARON, or MYRIAM. This is a serious enigma I cannot explain.

However, a very vague recollection manages to painfully make its way at the edge of my usually impeccable memory. It is as if a small wavy snake is wriggling on my forehead, but I can't put my finger on it. Then suddenly, I catch it! YELIYAEL just projected clear images on my mind, as if on a screen. There, in that intimate corner of my brain, I am reading the translation of a travel account written by Diodorus of Sicily, who lived in the first century BC:

"For the priests of Egypt recount from the records of their sacred books that they were visited in early times by ORPHEUS, MUSAEUS, MELAMPUS, DAEDALUS, also by the poet HOMER and LYCURGUS of Sparta."

"Excellent! approves YELIYAEL. *This is one of the major traces I was pointing at. ORPHEUS, who civilized Greece, received his education and initiation in the temples of Egypt at the same time as the MUSAEUS mentioned in this Diodorus' text*."

This new perspective totally shatters the historical vision of our time, as taught officially by the 20th century scholars. I hear Angel YELIYAEL telling me:

"The gap, the conflict is even more profound than you imagine...From the word MUSAEUS found in the ancient text, derives the word MUSES, to designate "poetic" inspiration and creation, which, at the time, was synonymous with MUSIC. The word MUSIC also borrows its root from the same name MUSAEUS. The MUSEUM, temple of the arts in modern western countries, draws from the same linguistic reservoir."

Enthusiastically YELIYAEL offers more details concerning the inextricable network of mysteries weaving this ancient historical fabric. However, I have decided not to divulge them.

Says YELIYAEL: "*You see, MOSES-MUSAEUS was not his birth name in the house of Ramses the Pharaoh. His real name has never been disclosed. MOSES-MUSAEUS was his initiate's name as High Priest; it was composed to evoke his genius for measuring "vibratory rhythms, wave frequencies and resonances" by which humans conceive and construct instruments of long distance communication*[56] *and musical instruments as well. It is as if someone nowadays was called TELEO, ELECTRONA, or SILICONEX, to evoke his or her skills for high-level telecommunications, electronics, or computer sciences.*

In those days, people were named after their most essential talents. Thus OR-PHEUS was a genius in the sciences of Light (AURA-OR), and Fire (PHEUS). HOMER was a "Master of Words", and in every one of the Sumerian / Akadian / Hebrew / Aramaic languages, the word HA-OMER is clearly translating into "the storyteller". You know this, Simha, for you understand these ancient languages. Story telling, this is exactly what Homer has done in the tales ILIAD and ODYSSEE.

We could go on and far on this path, adds YELIYAEL. *One could write and rewrite most of human history simply by founding one's understanding upon the words and names used by diverse*

---

[56] In Exodus:25-27 one may read the detailed instructions Moses gives to his people for constructing apparatuses, designated as "the ark of testimony"," the tabernacle", "the table of offering", "the lamp stand with knobs", "the ephod", breast plate with its "precious stone knobs". Every Hebrew word designating those "appliances" may be translated in the "religious" lingo and in technological lingo as well.

peoples on all the lands of this planet. In your time, this linguistic science is still in infancy. Only a few historians and archeologists suspect that language will give them the whole and living knowledge they so much want to acquire when digging the ground, and finding a few broken clay jars buried under tons of dust."

When finished with the above linguistic detour, YELIYAEL continues his story.

"MOSES is indeed very present in ancient history, under the name HERMES, known by the Greeks as a great initiator to the mysteries of Eleusis[57]*, set around 1,500 BC, and of Egyptian inspiration. They associate HER-MES with the coming of the DANAENS, colonizers from Egypt. The Egyptian historian MANETHON writes about a high-ranking personality called HER-MAIS, who lived at that time. This becomes much clearer when we know that in ancient Egypt, HER*[58] *is the ceremonial title given to the great initiates of the temples-universities. In ARCHAE LINGUA, the term HER literally means "the one high up", "the awakened" "the bright one", "the enlightened", and, on another dimension, the "quickener"."*

SIMHA: "Therefore HER-MAIS / HER-MES / MAISA / MOSES / MOSHE / MUSAEUS / MUSSA, are the same and unique person?"

"*Yes,* says the Angel, *confirmed.*"

SIMHA: "So the word MAIS-TER that led to the word MASTER and the word MYS-TERY are all related to the "musical and rhythmic" talents, skills and techniques used to communicate with far away receptors-emitters on Earth and beyond, including celestial beings?"

"Yes, answers YELIYAEL, *exactly!"*

Unexpectedly, like cold rain falling from a clear sunny sky, sadness invades my heart. I suddenly feel miserable and hopeless.

"You see, YELIYAEL, here we are evoking the past, we are explaining how men and women of the ancient times were MAIS-TER,

---

[57] Eleusis means El-Isis, meaning the Celestial Isis, goddess from the original Egyptian pantheon.

[58] Her: this word is still in use by German speaking people as Herr, a title and expression of respect, by example Herr Doctor, Herr Professor.

MASTERS of MYSTERIES, but our contemporaries, reading our book, will they perceive the intricate links those skills, talents, and mysterious rituals and exact procedures have woven into our present? And most importantly will modern minds recognize the extraordinary insights such knowledge harvested in the past could provide to the future manifestation and growth of Universal Human, the upcoming Homo Spiritualis?"

YELIYAEL, reassuringly, in a friendly tone, comforts me:

"This broken vision is only temporary. Soon, many physicists, biologists, astronomers, archeologists, historians, philosophers, and artists, musicians, painters and writers shall reestablish links with the science of Universal Harmony.

They will then understand the techniques of human-celestial interweaving. The science of quantum physics has taken the first step. It has already driven the human mind beyond a linear, mechanical, causal vision of the perceived reality... the rest will follow naturally, or rather, divinely..."

I feel better, a little better...However, I cannot dissolve entirely all that shadowy sadness stealthily permeating my heart.

14. Moses' Testament.
Mount Nebo 1492 BC, at dusk.

FOLLOWING THE TRAIL LEADING to the deep valley, we are winding our way through the flowing multitude now more and more enthralled by the upcoming imminent farewell of their charismatic leader. Angel YELIYAEL protectively surrounds us with a slightly perfumed translucent aura. We are totally invisible; yet, a few among the more sensitive children are gazing insistently towards us, sensing our presence in spite of our shield of invisibility.

And, as we pass by them, she-goats become nervous, as if spooked, frantically shaking their little bells.

We move along; YELIYAEL's voice informs us that *"15,723 invisible sentient beings are now positioned to attend MOSES' last allocution, among them many space-time travelers from Earth, such as you are, but the majority originating from inhabited planets which have been celestialized since centuries, millenniums, and more. Each cosmic traveler is accompanied by one or two luminous colorful Guardian Angels."*

YELIYAEL also points out that *"celestial broadcasting circuits are just being opened; the universal archiving channels are on standby, ready to receive and encrypt. Seven Master-Archangels are focusing their reflective communication beams towards the land of Moab. Superb GABRIEL and Glorious MICHAEL, both loving and attentive, float on thrones of light."*

Suddenly, at the highest point of Mount Nebo, standing on a narrow rocky platform, MOSES appears. Slender waisted, shoulders wide, thick curly brown hair barely peppered with gray. His face is luminous and smooth, with no wrinkles, no traces of wariness that could indicate old age. A company of Angels surround him, slowly moving like a harmonious ballet of small vaporous clouds. Giving to the Master an extraordinary aura of glory, the sun forms a large expanded discus of orange fire behind his face, contrasting with the shimmering lavender blue veil of the firmament.

The whole crowd roars with passion and joy, hundreds young girls play their sistra-tambourines; children whistle crystalline tunes on small shepherd's flutes. Thousands feet in chorus stomp on the ground, thousands hands raise to the sky; the accompanying roar is giant, colossal, expanding from the valley, shaking every rock on the mountain.

Majestically MOSES raises his right hand, palm open toward the crowd, and stillness descends cascading from terrace to terrace.

The sea of humanity progressively quiets down. MOSES, immobile, waits. Then there is absolute peace.

Now MOSES' voice alone thunders and echoes in the valley, his resonant words flying from the top of Mount Nebo in concentric circles towards all horizons and to the edges of the Heavens.

> "You stand this day all of you before Yehovah Elohekhem your Eternal Guide; so do the captains of your tribes, your elders, and your officers, representing all of Israel, your little ones, your wives, and the strangers residing in your camps, the apprentice wood hewers and wells diggers.
>
> You stand this day so that you shall enter into covenant with Yehovah your Guide in Eternity, and enter into the pledge of spiritual elevation, which your Attractor Yehovah today promises to you to be ineffaceable.
>
> You stand that He may establish you today in the consciousness of being a people under His protection, and that He may be to you a Divine Guide unifying all deities, all divine entities, as he has said to you, and as He has sworn unto your fathers, Abraham, Isaac, and Jacob.
>
> Not only with you standing do I carve this covenant and this promise of celestial elevation, but with ALL ethereal beings that hover here with us this day before Yehovah, and also with ALL ethereal beings that are not here with us this day."

Yes, MOSES is clearly announcing the universal alliance of all humans on Earth, as well as the universal alliance between all humans and all celestial hosts! MOSES himself is proclaiming in front of all the tribes assembled before him that the Lord, Supreme Master of our local universe, and his celestial cohorts, are here, now, present with us!

Men and women are deeply moved, entranced by MOSES' mighty words. We all look up at the sky, beyond the mount, shadowed with hues of turquoise blue and muted pink-orange. A shiver of intense mystery runs through the fascinated crowd.

Gradually an immense undulating cloud of white doves appears in the sky, silent, pure, virginal flight. A cool fragrant drizzle, as thin as a fleeting translucent veil, gently falls on heads, faces and hands of the multitude.

The white doves slowly disappear flying upwards; the whole assembly is in awe, while silence remains total.

MOSES continues his address…

"I understand everything MOSES says, whispers Albert, and yet I don't know the language he is speaking."

YELIYAEL answers: "*Presently you and Simha are still partially enseraphed, imbued with angelic substance. You have perceived MOSES' words through the angelic filter, and the sounds you heard were relayed by archangelic circuits. In fact, what you have perceived is a translation of MOSES' words into the Universal Language.*"

"ARCHAE LINGUA!!! exclaims ALBERT. Every word, every sentence is immediately clear to my mind!"

"It is the famous MOSES special effect, says YELIYAEL mischievously, *associated with angelic intervention, enhanced by archangelic intercession."*

I address the Angel:

"Then, in what language is MOSES actually addressing the 12 tribes?"

YELIYAEL: "*The Master is using an Egyptian dialect, a tongue the twelve tribes all understand. He will soon, in private, transcribe his allocution into Akadian-Hebrew for the human archives, which is now to be found in the book of the Old Testament, post Daniel's Hebrew Version, Deuteronomy Chapter 29 to 31.*"

MOSES about to conclude his farewell is enouncing for the last time on Earth, the Ten Commandments again, as offered to humanity on Mount Horeb decades ago.

Now, shifting from Egyptian dialect to the pure sounds of unadulterated ARCHAE LINGUA, he pronounces each syllable slowly and intensely:

(((ANO KHI))) (((YE HO VAH)) (((ELO HE KHA)))

Simultaneously, with a perfect intonation, a chanting voice from the Heavens is translating MOSES' words into a beautiful classical Egyptian language, using simple, evocative, and poetic rhythms.

All in the host, above and below, repeat MOSES' sound-words, as the Master allows silence after each word.

LOA TA CHAMOD ... LE RE Ê KHA

The miraculous celestial vibrancies of ARCHAE LINGUA penetrate and divinely transform all men and women, children and elders, Angels and Archangels above, all humans on the planet, now and "thenafter".

Finally MOSES declares the moment has come for him to leave, his mission as human among humans on Earth is complete. The eternal Lord has called him, he will soon join Him, body and soul united.

YELIYAEL comments:

"The rumor of his soon-to-occur disappearance from Earth has already circulated around the tribes; however the imminence of his lonesome exodus is deeply upsetting to them."

But the fate is sealed. Men, women, and children suddenly realize they shall be orphaned, missing the father they all loved and feared so much. In his absence, would the Lord of Hosts, ADONAI TZEVA-OT, assist them as much as He has done in MOSES' presence? Would the new leader YOSHUA BEN NOUN have the necessary spiritual poise to attract divine favors on the wandering people who soon will start a new human adventure?

MOSES is now leaving the high platform. Carried by invisible Angels, he seems to glide with great speed on the steep slope of Mount Nebo, his arms widely spread, his blue robe floating in the wind. Men, women, and children, worried, preoccupied, somberly leave the valley, and slowly head towards the neighboring hills, everyone to his camp. Tonight, they are walking to their tents pensive and solemn. Tonight there will be no campfires, and no moonlight dances at the sound of tambourines played by the disciples of prophetess MYRIAM.

Tonight the children will not gather around the storytellers, triple rows of wide-open eyes, brightened by the wonders of the time and again recounted exodus from Egypt. No resounding tales recollecting the old times when their grandparents were living in the fertile Goshen Valley. Under the stars, no epic recital will be staged to replay the exile, the miracles, the pains and joys of the life in the wilderness. Tonight a new legend is born, the mosaic tribes are again at the core of the planetary action, contemplating an uncertain future.

"The Exodus stories have been told, recited, sung, replayed a thousand times, and, for this new people, they have become founding legends. For the young skeptical logical minds, they have become fairy tales, entertaining myths and fables, good for dreamers only." explains YELIYAEL.

15. Manhattan, March 18, 1996 AD, nighttime. Paris, dreamtime.

Un rêve me serais-je doutée qu'un rêve introduit dans mon cœur un désir qui m'inspire, partout il me suit, partout je le poursuis.

I AM STANDING ON A VAST beautiful piazza. I can identify it perfectly as the Trocadero esplanade in Paris; in the background, the Eiffel Tower majestically soaring up, standing on its giant four legs like a triumphant warrior on the Champs de Mars. Presently I am a little elf-woman following three vibrant, powerful looking handsome men, their hair floating in the wind, one with a ponytail in the manner of 18th century gentlemen. I see them and identify them clearly as three 20th century businessmen, fashion gurus, moguls of art and entertainment industry. They are walking fast, assertively, and I, the elf little woman, am hovering behind them observing every detail of the scene.

To them, I feel, I am nothing but a mere fly buzzing around. I can see them, but, in no way can they take notice of me. They are powerful producers, big budget film promoters. They just exited a small movie theater located on the side of the Trocadero esplanade, its obscure and mysterious aura still visible through the half open doors. The theater is yet empty, waiting for the "go ahead" these men are about to give.

They now reach the edge where the piazza narrows into a terrace balconied with majestic columns overlooking the slopes. Steep stairs and floral gardens elegantly drop all the way to the Seine River, the sightseeing boats, and the green Champs de Mars. When I myself get to the edge, I can perceive what they see: a huge crowd is lining up along the side of the hill, all the way to the other bank of the Seine River, even across the bridge.

The three "conquerors" raise their hands firmly at the same

time,, a signal to the patient and disciplined crowd the movie they have been eagerly awaiting is about to begin. Immediately, the first people in line start moving with much anticipation, eager to finally see THE great new masterpiece…

Watching this multitude, I become perplexed.

This question is filling my mind: considering the size of the crowd, how did some people manage to be *first* in line? At what time did these men, women, and teenagers had to be there in order to be first in line? In the middle of the starless night? In the cold and desolate early morning?

How can one be first in such competition? And to watch a movie, of all things! What powerful inner desire, tension, and interest motivate them to put up with such abnegation?

My second question is purely arithmetical: how can that very small theater accommodate this large crowd?

As an answer to my first question, a telepathic message impresses my mind: "*the people of that waiting mass didn't come here spontaneously on their own free will or stirred by the desire to be here.*"

I then understand this crowd is somewhat artificial, the same way modern food is composed of chemical substitutes and artificial flavors. These obedient peoples have been collected in their suburban residences and carried here in buses chartered by the movie promoters. The first ones in line are there because they were dropped off first, and so on. They have accepted the destination, the time and the place the conquerors have chosen for them. It's very simple: this is a "pre-fabricated" crowd. After fast foods, we have now "fast crowds". I feel an intense urge to understand better this phenomenon.

Therefore I decide to try and enter into the theater and watch this latest "big budget" film.

For a fleeting moment I am skeptical. What chances do I have to get in? But if people at the end of the line still expect to enter the theater I might as well try also. A simple act of faith. So I am running down the stairs.

No longer am I an elf, but now displaying my own visible and physical identity. Bravely I position myself behind the last person in the line, and wait, while my psyche wanders.

The day is pleasantly cool; the sky tinted with the milky gray mist that seems to be forever hanging above Paris at dawn.

To my astonishment, the line moving up very fast becomes quickly diluted, thinned, and very stretched out. Half way up the hill, a small group of noisy demonstrators is watching the upward procession of those 'idiots' who want to see the new movie. For reasons I cannot fathom, they think this film does not deserve such adulation, and loudly revile those about to see it by shouting "Fascists! Bastards!" At the bottom of my heart, I disapprove of such display of intolerance and lack of minimal courtesy.

As I continue to move forward, midway to the top, I am reaching a terrace which appearance triggers my curiosity. That terrace seems to be built differently, with more ancient materials than the esplanade at the top. I can see narrow winding streets, arcades, small hanging balconies, all built in white and pale ocher chiseled large heavy stones. I recognize some areas of the ancient city of Jerusalem. I decide to meander there, thinking that among those narrow winding steps, some are bound to lead me up to the esplanade and the movie theater, if I ever still want to go there. I now have a feeling the theater is too big for the crowd, so I am not worried, I will certainly find a seat.

Meanwhile, I am indulging in a little off track distraction, and truly enjoying it. The movie can wait!

Coming out of a narrow ascending street I am facing a monumental amber colored gate made out of solid oak wood, time weathered. Entering the wide open door, I realize I am now standing in an old cathedral. Nothing gothic here, all is of the roman style. On each side of the stone-paved nave several rows of seats are positioned obliquely, like in a small quaint Parisian theater. I see most of the seats are occupied, and I count a dozen people, looking straight in front of them, towards a beautiful, very ancient and vast courtyard, spreading out on either side into deep corners the audience cannot see.

An exceptional, surreal bright, but soft white light sprinkled with gold is glowing out of the courtyard. As it is easy to gaze straight at that white golden light, my exploring eyes broadly open without strain.

I decidedly advance towards one of the old wooden benches and I sit down. A priest in a gray cassock immediately approaches me. To my surprise, with a commanding gesture, he says:

"One may stay here and watch only after having received a Hebrew name."

"Here is something weird, I tell myself, I have never heard anything like that."

Quietly I address the priest: "I do have a Hebrew name anyway, and I bear it since I was born."

The priest then orders: "Say it loud and clear!"

I comply: "My name is SIMHA."

A few people in the audience turn their head, wondering about such a strange first name. It doesn't sound biblically familiar! Neither is it Miriam, nor Sarah, nor Rachel, or Leah!

"SIMHA? What does it mean?"

I inform them it translates as "spiritual joy," just as Simha Torah translates as "happiness one feels holding the scroll of the divine law while singing and dancing." It signals also, in Hebrew, the mark of a rabbi, who getting the SMIHA, will be authorized to minister a religious community."

Apparently fully reassured by that short explanation, they turn their attention back to the fascinating spectacle taking place in the surreally bright courtyard.

The priest, on the other hand, appears to be inwardly troubled. He is anticipating something that could be a cause for worry. I read his thoughts:

"If she is, by birth and education, an expert in Jewish history, perhaps she will find faults and errors in what she is seeing in the courtyard. She knows so well how to perceive with her intellect, will she also perceive with her heart?"

At the same time he is interested and enthusiastic at the prospect that someone who "knows more" is participating in an event of great emotional import to him. Silently, he tells me: "This courtyard is the heart of the Passion of Christ." Such information seems obvious to me. I sense he now leans towards his second thought, the positive anticipation, and, courteously invites me to stay seated as long as I wish.

Suddenly, I am no longer part of the audience, as I find myself standing in the courtyard itself.

It is a vast space, a special place in the old city of Jerusalem, covered with large, uneven paving stones. People are moving about on donkeys or walking. This ancient courtyard is surrounded by low walls interspersed here and there with open arched high gates. Through those gates one can see the classic landscape of the old city. It was still there decades ago when I visited for the first time, wandering, asking for directions on the rocky, semi-grassy hills, where scattered houses barely emerged out of the lush vineyards among gnarled century-old olive trees, wizened by the winds of time.

I feel I am definitely in the midst of what Christian worshippers call the Passion of Christ, and the scene permeates and penetrates my whole being. I notice also that Jesus is not here. A warm breeze caresses every cell in my body; I hear myself think *"Jesus Yehoshua is not here because he is of divine essence, and therefore cannot be seen here",* and his absence becomes the very presence of an intense fire of faith burning inside me, as I am attempting to unite with the presence of his absence.

I meet MYRIAM, his mother; she is warmly consoling a woman dressed in a fine see-through black negligee, revealing titillating under-garments. This woman stricken with grief is crying, for her beloved is gone. I know and I see: it is MARY MAGDALENA, the lover, the woman who achieved the sacred union. So very feminine and attractive, she is desperately crying.

Walking along among men and women riding donkeys, I am now facing a shop entrance, redolent of powerful smell of olives and fresh sour cheese, a scent perceptible around the Mediterranean countries since thousands years.

Moving forward, I breathe in the dense slightly acrid fragrance of pure olive oil. The inside of the windowless shop is kept cool by a deep permanent shade. Standing under the arched entrance, three magnificent men all dressed in white. All wearing an immaculately clean light blue linen headgear, faded by repeated sun exposure, similar to the classic Egyptian headdress, pleated and folding back on each side of the face, covering the ears. The headgear of the Sphinx and Pharaohs! The three men are wearing it with both majesty and humility.

I feel deep inward I have known these three masters for a long time, and they tell me who they are. One of them is Rabbi YOHANAN BEN ZAKAI, a great scholar of Judaic studies, a contemporary of the early Christian saga, he lived at the beginning of our era. I am moved by their humbleness and the profound beauty of their faces, the strength and compassion in their eyes.

Their modest appearance impresses me with a message of wisdom, of self-imposed discipline, simple and unobtrusive, just like the olive oil shop filled with terra-cotta jars and jugs, like those one can still find nowadays in the old Arab neighborhoods of North Africa and the Middle East. Their headgear tells their wealth of knowledge streams from a tradition passed on to them straight from ancient Egypt. Could it be the headgear of the kings and princes from the celestial kingdom Jesus talks about?

I ask them with my eyes, and they, likewise, answer without words or gestures.

"Where is YEHOSHUA?"

"He is not here, but for us, celestial men, he is, because he is EL-ELYON, the Higher One."

"What are you doing in this courtyard, under the arch of an olive shop?"

Their large wide-open black eyes radiate ageless wisdom. The three rabbis' souls speak to my spirit in harmony. I hear them say:

"Go, explore everything, experience and contemplate beauty, with your own eyes, listen with your ears and heart to the voice of Truth."

Something in me is set in motion, bringing me to the edge of conscious clarity, like the light filling this courtyard, miraculously isolated from the rest of the city, the light from the Heavens, the light of grace. A hidden part of me is reciting a simple prayer, as simple and rustic as the stones of this ancient courtyard, enduring witness of passing events and ideas, polished and curved by centuries of stomping pervasive uncertainties, bearing the marks of intermittent blazing certitudes and the signs of flaring immense faith…

I feel like standing on a miraculously protected island in the center of an unfaltering sandstorm.

"Go, see and become" silently say the three rabbis, together.

And suddenly another soft voice from an invisible source proclaims: "Go and believe!"

That is my dream. When I recounted it to Albert for the first time, in our Manhattan residence, my eyes filled with tears.

Will I ever know why I cried? Memories of my exile, perhaps?

Three years later, events unfolding, we started to understand the meaning of this dream. It was neither a symbol, nor a parable, it was a prophecy. And it became reality.

So be it: VA YEHI KHEN. I will keep going, continue the journey, reaching as high and deep inside as I can, because the dream says that I can…

Chapter Three

The Rabbi from Heavens

16. Galilee, Brur Hayl. Universal Time. Transient temporal coordinates.

WE HAVE ARRIVED! COOL EARLY MORNING, clear sky lavender pink and nascent turquoise. I feel rested and relaxed. Moments ago Albert and I ele-landed on undulating terrain covered with short grass; alert, springy, agile, we are now strolling towards a sparkling murmuring brook, virginal water streaming down the hillside. Literally light-footed we are meandering around surfacing rocks and scattered deep green bushes. Cloudy rosy filaments lazily hovering high above in an otherwise azure blue sky, add a peaceful touch to the scenery.

Sliding ahead above ground Angel YELIYAEL swiftly unfurls wide open before us a large white veil, like a semi transparent mirror, and we can see the reflection of our physical shapes as we quietly continue our walk down the hill.

Albert is wearing a white Hindu style short tunic on wide floating sand-colored pants, tied to the waist with a light lavender braided cord.

As for myself I have also given special attention to my appearance, emulating the traditional dress of a Yemenite Bedouin woman. My ankle length ample and gracious yellow gown is slightly embroidered with violet flowers, enhanced with bright tiny fuchsia dots. A thin belt around my waist drops on my left hip into a long, elegant cascade of tasseled fringes, intertwining shiny golden and indigo blue threads. Midway to the valley, a man is sitting at the edge of a small vineyard, on a patch of fresh tender grass, under the soothing shade of a time weathered olive tree.

Sudden pang in the heart! Flashback vision! That man looks exactly like one of the three wise men I met in one of my most striking dreams, origin of our current quest!

"Rabbi Yohanan BEN ZAKAI is waiting for us" says YELIYAEL.

"Who is he? asks softly ALBERT. I surely have heard his name mentioned sometimes by Simha, then recently by MOSES, but his name sums up my knowledge of Rabbi Yohanan BEN ZAKAI."

"*You may find in human chronicles,* reports Angel YELIYAEL, *that Yohanan BEN ZAKAI was born in Galilee around year 6 BC, during a period marked by the birth of both YEHOSHUA-Jesus, son of Myriam-Mary, and, Yohanan BEN ZAKARIA, John the Baptist, born three months earlier, son of Elisabeth"*

YELIYAEL's concise information reminds me that, during several months following my singular dream, I wondered whether Yohanan BEN ZAKAI and Yohanan BEN ZAKARIA could be the same person. However too many documented historical data contradict such a peculiar assertion.

YELIYAEL asks:

"Simha, will you activate your precise memory, and tell us about both Yohanan *BEN ZAKARIA and Yohanan BEN ZAKAI?"*

I comply willingly:

"Yohanan BEN ZAKARIA, surnamed John the Baptist, son of the high priest Zakaria and Elizabeth, cousin of Mary-Myriam, is known for baptizing "repentant" men and women in the living waters of the Jordan River, enticing many followers to open their hearts to the new spiritual message of that time. He had a mission: to ceaselessly prepare the way for the coming Messiah, which coming he was compellingly heralding, unafraid of political and religious reprisals."

We all pause. Albert leans on a large rock, listening intensely, fascinated by the chronicle.

Standing facing the valley, I continue:

"Yohanan BEN ZAKARIA died decapitated on King's Herod Antipas order."

"How reliable are the historical records on that matter?" inquires ALBERT.

SIMHA: "Those facts seem undeniable, historically confirmed by all available concurring documents. The decapitation of Yohanan BEN ZAKARIA is thought to have occurred around 30 AD.

Now, regarding Yohanan BEN ZAKAI whom we are about to meet soon: That wise man had the privilege to lie down twice in a coffin, years apart. The first time, he stepped by himself in a casket, alive and well, and he so exited besieged Jerusalem, the Roman guards at the gate assuming the funeral procession was carrying a corpse for urgent burial beyond the city walls. "

YELIYAEL offers new information:

"I shall open for you a copy of old documents, to be found later by your historians. The escape took place not long before the sack of Jerusalem and the destruction of the Temple in 70 AD.

As soon as the destructive fires and mass executions tapered down, Yohanan BEN ZAKAI entered in negotiation with General Vespasian, leader of the Roman legions in the land of Israel and thus Yohanan obtained permission to start an academy at Yavne.

Hence he created a new charismatic center for study and spiritual development which quickly replaced the Temple-Academy of beleaguered Jerusalem."

SIMHA: "This is a confirmation of what can be found, scattered, in scholarly books. However, for reasons remaining mysterious to this day, Rabbi Yohanan BEN ZAKAI vanished from the school he had himself founded. Before leaving he handed to Rabbi Gamliel the leadership of the flourishing Yavne Academy.

Why did Yohanan BEN ZAKAI leave so suddenly? And why did he choose a blatant religious conservative traditionalist successor? Apparently, no one knows. One can suspect that, even if the real reasons have been identified, they have been buried, or suppressed by sectarian dissidence, amid turmoil, chaos and violent quarrels erupting at that time."

"*Essenes, Sadducees, Pharisees, and Christian Minims, among many others*" YELIYAEL enumerates.

I continue: "And yet, later, unbeknownst to all other official schools and academies, sitting under a proverbial olive tree, in the Galilean village of Brur-Hayl, Rabbi Yohanan BEN ZAKAI attracted the greatest minds of his time: Judeans, Israelites, as well as a large number of very recently converted proselytes from neighboring countries. In that new "plein air" school he instructed most of the future Talmudic and Kabalists luminaries. His teachings bear an uncanny resemblance with the message of the Christian-Minims[59]."

"However, I guess, he never openly divulged the true source of his beliefs and teachings" comments ALBERT.

SIMHA: "And consequently he was able to continue his mission without interference. His devotion and abnegation did not waver until his death. And it is said he lived a very long life, perhaps up to 120 years."

ALBERT, elaborates: "In view of those historical accounts, it is evident the life story of the two Yohanans indicates without the shadow of a doubt that no personal tie ever existed between Rabbi BEN ZAKAI and Rabbi BEN ZAKARIA."

I cannot disagree with Albert's reasonable conclusion. Yet, in a mysterious, subtle way, I deeply sense that some kind of link is connecting those two lives, in the same way they both connect to the life of the illustrious Rabbi, YEHOSHUA ben Myriam, Jesus the Christ.

SIMHA: "Consider this, Albert. The names ZAKARIA and ZAKAI are identical, but for the last consonant letter R. When you remove the letter R out of the name ZAKARIA, the remaining letters form the name ZAKAI."

---

[59] Minim=followers of Jesus' apostles, to be named Christians much later. In Greek Kristos=anointed

"The letter R, Hebrew Resh, means "radiant head", as reflected by the Arabic word Rais chief of state, the French Roy head of kingdom, or English Rich, being at the top (RI) like a Radiant sun (CH)!

Yohanan BEN ZAKARIA died untimely decapitated, had his "Rosh=head" slashed. Thus, missing the R, Resh[60], his soul later reconnected with the spirit of Yohanan BEN ZAKAI, therefore continuing his mission of enlightenment, spreading the new spiritual message brought to humankind by YEHOSHUA the Messiah."

"Wow! murmurs ALBERT, an Israelite was spreading the words of Christ! Surely the lengthy Council of Nicea[61] has been tackling that subject too, finding there one more alleged heresy to slash, suppress and bury!"

Resuming our walk down the hill, we are now approaching the Rabbi, and I focus on the here and now. Was Yohanan BEN ZAKAI secretly listening to our conversation?

An inviting albeit slightly amused smile enlivens Yohanan's beautiful, rested, unwrinkled old man's face. Fair complexion, eyes intensely blue, aquiline nose authentically Mesopotamian. His enigmatic smile appears to hold and conceal a secret. My curiosity is aroused.

Although I sense the Rabbi is well determined not to easily reveal his mysterious thoughts, the encounter is promising. I feel energized, eager like a child on a first day back to school.

Rabbi BEN ZAKAI, nimbly stands up, body perfectly straight. He is wearing the Israelite traditional caftan, aged and discolored by repeated hand washing. The fabric's original soft lavender blue has turned into a very pleasant pinkish gray. I am gazing at his blue linen headdress, similar to that the three wise men wore in my

[60] R-Resh. In Hebrew, like in Greek, every letter of the alphabet is enounced as a complete meaningful word. By example: A=Aleph (Hebrew), A=Alpha (Greek).etc. The letter R, in Hebrew enounced Resh, means "Head" symbolizing leadership, chieftainship, the charisma of a bright mind.

[61] The First Council of Nicea was a council of Christian bishops convened in Nicea in Bithynia (present-day Iznik in Turkey) by the Roman Emperor Constantine I in AD 325. The Council was the first effort to attain doctrinal consensus in the church through an assembly representing all of early Judeo-Christendom.

dream about the Passion of Christ, the dream that struck so strongly my imagination.

The headdress smartly surrounds his heavenly face, falling into two flawless symmetrical folds over his ears, firmly tied to his head by a braided cord encircling his forehead. The braid, ocher yellow, is enhanced with vibrant purple threads. His face conjures up ancient Egypt figures eternized by the Sphinx's emblematic statue forever standing guard at the foot of the Giseh pyramids. The Rabbi's whole countenance radiates unpretentious majesty.

We now form a semi circle facing the Rabbi, Angel YELIYAEL hovering slightly behind us.

"Shalom Rabbi YOHANAN BEN ZAKAI" intones ALBERT.

"Shalom, ALBER-TOV!"

"Thank you, Rabbi! I promise you I shall do my best to deserve the TOV quality you are generously adding to my name. Alber-TOV[62], Albert the GOOD!"

Acknowledging Albertov's expression of thankfulness Rabbi Yohanan BEN ZAKAI starts translating the alchemical formula of Albert's novel name, letter by letter, in accordance with the celestial harmonies: "AL-BE-R-TOV,

he who elevates himself (AL),
he who begins and bases his life (B)
on constant renewal (R).
He who reaches beyond the fence of Time (T)
driven by primordial original energies (O)
offering to the Divine Creator
the fruits of his Vigor and Vitality (V).

"Shalom, ALBERTOV!" [63]

---

[62] Hebrew Tov= good. Also used to express "best wishes" like Mazel Tov

[63] In Hebrew, every "block" in a word, noun, verb or name -single syllable, double syllable- holds a meaning by itself. By example, the word Shalom, which is commonly used to express a salute, peace, or something that is complete, may be split into significant "blocks", each participating to the overall meaning of the word: Sha=sun / Al = raising up / Shal= envelops / Om= all life.
The whole word Shalom means: the sun from above covers all living beings. Thus it becomes clear why the word Shalom is used to express a heartfelt salutation, a wish for peace, and completeness.

I chuckle both amused and deeply moved. I feel elated by the true beauty of this deciphering of the ancient melodic language. Aided by Archaeo-Linguistic analysis, one could easily formulate other translations for the same name "Albertov"; the meanings would appear different, but, made with the same letters, their vocalization would direct towards the same space-time coordinates in the living spirit. And from every melody would emerge a celestial "persona" perfectly matching Albert's multifaceted personality.

"Greetings to you YOHANAN, answers Albert, greetings to you, YO-HA-NAN:

He who unfolds the mystery of the divine Verb (YO)
and reveals to all spiritual beings and humans (HA)
the essence and substance of eternity (NAN)."

Yohanan BEN ZAKAI, quietly nodding, signals approval.
Then it is my turn to greet the Rabbi:
"Greetings to you YO-HAN-ANA,
greetings to you,
he who transmutes (ANA)
the divine Verb (YO)
into compassion (HAN)."[64]

In a muffled voice, I add:

"Shalom Yohanan, Yohanan BEN ZAKARIA's alter ego, spiritual twin of the Jordan River Baptist."

At that very moment, Angel YELIYAEL surrounds our group with a white purplish aura, and the four of us, Rabbi, Albert, YELIYAEL and I, feel the scented vibration and melodious quiver of Yohanan BEN ZAKARIA, *John the Baptist's* presence…

Silence. Immobility. Peacefulness. Security.

A host of Angels appears, V shaped escadrille swirling and spiraling, up, down and around, exuding a fragrant wavy breeze,

---

[64] In all languages on Earth, every name -of a person, city, nation- is composed of several "blocks", and each block constitutes a sub-meaning of the overall meaning of the name. This linguistic reality is more easily perceived in Hebrew because that language has not been used as a vernacular tongue for millenniums before the 20th century. Without the erosion due to common use the ancient Archae Lingua has been best preserved in the Hebrew language.

even as we hear and feel the caress of a long rhythmic silence. Trees, flowers, rocks, mica dust and birds keep melodiously quiet as well, communing with us in the wake of this ineffable majestic procession. We are experiencing profound union, unity, and uniqueness. Then, our combined emotions receding progressively, each of us reintegrates his separate and encapsulated self, "body-mind-soul", aware of our own enclosed personality, individuality, identity.

Yohanan BEN ZAKAI: "It is my turn to greet you, SHI-MA-HA:

She who exudes and generously dispenses
passionate shining intelligence (SHI)
weaving together the threads of material (MA)
and spiritual (HA) dimensions."

The Rabbi continues deciphering my name:
"Shalom, SHIMA-HA, she whose name is Spirit.

Or more completely, I shall decode your name, sound by sound, by syllabic units:

SHI: Shining Solar sparkle,
MA: enclosed in living Mother-Matter,
HA: heart burning with divine spirit."

Yohanan BEN ZAKAI turns out to be a great master of Universal Language! I feel like a small child facing a giant, like an ordinary gymnast in front of an Olympic champion, a little girl on a swing watched by the greatest tightrope walker on Earth.

I like the feeling. It challenges me. Thanks to the Rabbi a corner of the veil will lift at last, revealing vast continents of knowledge we have yet to discover and explore.

However, something, a small detail, a glitch, lightly troubles me. Reading my thoughts, Yohanan BEN ZAKAI, interjects:

"Yes, SHIMAHA, you are wondering why I pronounced your name with the warm SHI sound, instead of the whistling SI."

SIMHA: "This is true, Rabbi. Whenever my friends have called me *SHI*MAHA, I have always corrected them, forcefully, perhaps too forcefully, and I insisted they pronounce exactly SIMHA."

Yohanan BEN ZAKAI's answer is paternal and reassuring:

"You were absolutely right, until now, to firmly preserve the sound vibrancy of the syllable SI at the start of your name. It has enabled you to receive and reflect knowledge in a Structured, Stable, and Scientific form. This is an absolute necessity throughout your present life and time, during which rational analytic science is the ruling power.

However, know that we, in the eternal heavens, always we call you SHIMAHA."

I would love to inquire deeper, continue this cabalistic foray, learning more of the conversations taking place about me in the heavens. But the Rabbi curtly interjects:

"Why are things the way they are? You know it, and it shall remain a private and secret conversation between you and the heavens."

I know that during my remaining time on this Earth I will continue to be called SIMHA; the harmonic formula of that name vibrates with the forces and energies appropriate with the spirit of my time. The Rabbi again has read my mind, and approves.

Then Rabbi YOHANAN proffers a mysterious comment:

"At the very time of your death transition, your name SIMHA will transmute into SHIMAHA.

And ALBERT, you will enter the world of your future existence with the name-frequency ALBERTOV, until you reach a new spiritual position where you will be known as ALBARTEN. Then, later on, at the final stage of your cosmic pilgrimage, your name shall be ALBARDAN."

Albert frowns pensively, visibly pondering the interpretation of his new given names, thus taking a glimpse at his future lives after this present life on Earth.

I then hear myself asking: "Rav, do you know why we came to see you? Why did we land at this exact place, where you are now, standing by this vineyard under an olive tree near the village of BRUR HAYL in the land of Israel? Are we the only ones you are expecting? Are we the only ones to have come to see you? Are we the only ones to be with you at this very moment?"

YOHANAN: "You are shooting at once many complex questions. I shall duly answer them, in the ancient style, one by one. Have patience!

Yes, I know *why* you have come to *see* me. However you will refine that question, re-formulate the phrase by which you ask me to download answers from the cosmic database.[65] Your choice of words, the way you pronounce them, the intonations of your voice, shall enlighten me concerning the intent underlying this question. Only then can I truly answer."

Silence. Silence.

"And now, let's consider the second question. You are asking me why *you* are here with me, in this place. But there is a parallel question, lurking behind, that is: "Why am *I* here, Rabbi Yohanan BEN ZAKAI, and how is it possible that I am here?"

"You are right" I say.

RABBI YOHANAN: "After my transition through death, ending my sojourn on Earth in Galilee, I first lived in the seven heavens as an apprentice time-space traveler; then I became a full-fledged pilgrim on the roads to immortality.

But, in truth, I remain sentimentally attached to this earthly place, origin of unique life experiences and feelings, now indelibly engraved in my immortal memory.

Your special singular relationship with the Hebrew language, and your awareness of its celestial origins, clearly reflect your own fondness and attraction for this land, the land of Israel. Therefore it is wonderfully appropriate that we, you and I, meet here. This answers to the "why" of your question.

Now let us tackle the "how" part of your query. How do we, travelers of immortality, live?

After death, in deep slumber, shrouded in an angelic aura, with

---

[65] Data: this word in English refers to "Information, facts, knowledge", complete and reliable on a defined subject. This root-word-sonority is similar to the Hebrew word Daat, often pronounced during every Friday night prayer, in the following sentence: "Daato le olamim le zulato", which translates literally as: "the factual knowledge, He (the Supreme One) revealed to us, involves all Universes for all Times".

or without our body depending of how we passed away, we are carried unconscious through immense transitional intervals, to wake up on the new land of our future eternal life.

That is, if we have made the right choice beforehand, when the option was offered…"

YOHANAN pauses, for a fleeting moment, then pursues:

"During our corporeal life, we may have or have not shown or signaled our choice for spiritual survival, by our life style, our thoughts, the music of our hearts, the celestial harmonies we have received and projected.

However, whatever the choice we made during our life on Earth, at the very moment of what is commonly called death, we find ourselves facing several paths wide open in front of us.

The ultimate test of free will!

We may have earlier during our life on Earth chosen to go right, and, at the instant of our death transition, choose to go left, thus reversing our previous choice. We can change course…"

ALBERT exclaims: "Change course at the last moment?!"

YOHANAN: "Yes, at the precise instant we go unconscious, we can decide which option to seize: Dissolution? Return? Sleep? Survival?

One only of those options shall be our last "call."[66] And that call shall resonate forever in the Universe, for all concerned deities and celestial beings to hear and act upon…"

"Then what happens? expounds YOHANAN. How does the living Universe answer our last "call" for survival?

Understand that for every individual soul-spirit who opts for survival and consequently gets it, begins a long journey from Earth to the Heavens, with successive stages on seven transitional mansions. Like a newborn child, the survivor clothed in a unique shape of light, is raised, fed, and educated, experiencing many lives, experiencing many deaths and many rebirths in the realm of the seven heavens.

---

[66] Call: in Hebrew Kol = "Voice". In Archae Lingua Kol means "Coherent vibration-sound (Ko) directed by and linked to a higher elevated Force field (oL). Hence, a Call, according to Archae Lingua, always implies a Higher Calling.

After many "life-death-rebirth" cycles, we are finally ready to leave the seven heavens maternal womb. From then on, we are born again into a "*timeless essence of being*", clearly intuited by the Hindu master of your time, Krishnamurti.

Once you reach this new sphere of the Universe, laws are no longer those you are accustomed to. Some advanced thinkers, scientists and mathematicians of your era are already beginning to hint at some of those laws. Proceeding by daring intellectual "leaps", they outline and structure new ideas for the unfolding of a new science, so paving the royal way for humankind's brilliant future in the vast cosmos.

Albert Einstein has uncovered the first link; and quantum physics science, which in truth should be called quantum *metaphysics*, has taken over the journey's lead of humanity's advancement of knowledge and enlightenment.

In the past, the master keepers of the spiritual branch of science, be they Hindu, Greek, Egyptian, Sufi or Jewish and Christian Cabalist, have already apprehended the Super-Universe essence and foundation, by exploring the direct and luminous road of Just Intent.

The science of Kavanah[67], science of Intent, teaches, since thousands of years, how to live, exist, will, act, and move forward in harmony with our final intentions, our higher goals, and not to operate exclusively through analysis of fractional causes and partial effects. There is much for you to learn about the science of Intents…"

At this prospect, my eyes fire up like live embers, Albert's hands join into the human gesture of fervent supplication; Angel YELIYAEL empathically quivers with supra-luminous iridescent flares.

The Rabbi continues, unmoved by our demonstration of fervor and passionate curiosity:

"However, I shall not teach you more today. It is enough to

---

[67] Kavanah: a major aspect of the Kabalah science. The Hebrew word Kavanah means: Intent of high focus and perfect coherence, like a laser beam.

know Shimeha's two first questions have been rightly answered.

Now as for how I did land here, today, to encounter you?

By the law of Intent! There is no material, technical, logistical, reason that *causally* explains my presence here and now.

The quantum Law of Intents, divine Law of Purposefulness, the Cabalistic Kavanah Principle, explain my presence here, and nothing else. Master Hillel[68], my contemporary at the time the New Message was announced, at the beginning of the new era, often said, to whomever wanted to hear him: "Wherever I will to go, my legs take me." And I am telling you: Wherever I will to go, the Divine power takes me."

I feel immensely dizzy, Albert is exulting with joy. A bright purple flare escapes from Angel YELIYAEL's sinuous artistic shape, traveling through space to reach the high spheres of the galaxy.

Unperturbed, the Rabbi continues:

"Are you the only ones I was expecting? Are you the only ones to be with me at this very moment? Yes, you were the only ones I was expecting here and now. No, you are not the only ones to be with me at this very moment."

Amused by our dismayed expressions, the Rabbi exclaims:

"Oi Dai! Enough!" (a Hebrew interjection signaling that his answer is to remain enigmatic).

"Now, Shimeha, Albertov, back to your very first question. Go ahead. Upload and I shall decipher!"

[68] Rabbi Hillel: a famous teacher in Judea 1rst century AD.

17. Yohanan is having Fun.

YOHANAN BEN ZAKAI WHO HAS BEEN standing since the beginning of our dialog, now moves back two steps and slowly takes a Buddha position; emulating him I sit cross-legged, the way my Sephardic grand-mothers showed me, on the grass next to him. Albert takes position nearby on a small flat rock, softened by rain, wind and generations of men, women, and children, a natural platform to rest, converse, play, star gaze or daydream.

I sum up: "Rabbi, you know why we have come to see you, the reasons why this encounter with you is taking place, and yet we must express our purposes with our own words, and our own voice. Only then shall you be able to provide the most precise answer?"

RABBI YOHANAN: "Yes, your present situation, here and now, may require new words, and new intonations, different from those you were using before meeting me. Since your departure from Manhattan, your position on the sphere of knowledge has significantly changed."

Albert takes it upon himself to explicate our reasons for coming here. As usual, whenever the subject matter is important to him, his introduction is both poetic and metaphysical:

"Master, as YELIYAEL's presence here attests, we are customarily communicating with Angels, and Archangels, though less directly. And we know the vast universe we live in is populated with and traveled by countless living elemental, physical and spiritual beings, so numerous and diverse that listing them would take not years, not centuries, but millenniums by time standard on Earth.

Beyond human common perception, past the first layers of appearance, Life develops into multitudinous dimensions. There, Truth can be found. And it is with enthusiasm that we have entered the Quest for Truth.

"A Quest, huh?" murmurs BEN ZAKAI, with a gentle skeptical tone.

And the Rabbi bursts into a jolly, vigorous, sonorous laughter, the force of which tips him over, his back lying on the tender green grass densely dotted with wild yellow and white flowers. Then, swiftly, at lightning speed he is sitting up again, holding in his right hand a beautiful daisy flower, surreally white petals surrounding a yellow center resembling an intense flaring sun.

At that moment, in his hand, zooming at us, almost touching our eyes, we are privileged to glimpse at the heart of an immense pulsing star, luminescent fiery lava encircled by staggeringly bright orbs.

Pure delight shimmering through his slightly squinting eyes, Rabbi YOHANAN explains:

"I have traveled through galaxies and embraced universes filled with indescribable wonders. However, I have a special fondness for the grapes lazily wrapped around this vine, the daisies growing freely in this humble and simple meadow, for this centuries-old olive tree, and that unique soil subtle fragrance, as wild as a man's burning desire, as sweet and fine as a woman's curvaceous breast. I have a particular liking for this brook cascading over rocks and pebbles, water so fresh, alive, always in motion, and yet so serene..."

OK, I thought humorously, our Rabbi is going bucolic on us, turning into a sensitive, romantic, and nostalgic poet. Furthermore, his energetic laughter is intoxicating, and a relaxed, friendly, warm atmosphere has settled between us.

Upon Angel YELIYAEL's announcement *"Rabbi Yohanan BEN ZAKAI is waiting for us"* we had mentally prepared to confront a serious, even pompous Rabbi, and, by contrast, we find ourselves in the company of a charming, kindly mischievous personage.

We all join him again in a burst of carefree, invigorating laughter.

Now, I try to refocus everybody's attention on the object of the search that brought us here:

"Rav, as Albert said, we are currently on a Quest...With your help we hope to shed light on MOSES' Ten Commandments."

"Yes, yes, it's coming back to my mind, says YOHANAN, the Ten Commandments! Why 10? he adds whimsically, there might have been only 9, or 8, or 7; even One would suffice!"

"Only One would be enough? I said, stunned by such a strange statement."

ALBERT: "Are you saying that only One Commandment is the true one, and that all the other 9 on the list are useless and redundant?"

RABBI YOHANAN, barely able to control his mirth, says:

"There could even be none. Not 10 or not 1. Zero, and that would be it!"

Here he goes again, being ironic and enigmatic.

"This means, I snap back, the world could very well do without MOSES' Commandments? Rabbi, we saw and heard MOSES when he pronounced his last testament on Mount Nebo, facing the blue horizon of the Judean hills. The twelve tribes, men, women, children, and foreign apprentices, were gathered for his final farewell.

MOSES unmistakably enunciated the Ten Laws, prescriptions, and Commandments. He addressed the crowd facing him, as well as the beings listening in the heavens and the peoples who, on Earth, will hear and study them in times to come.

In front of all those witnesses he declared, maintained, and confirmed that each precept, each law, each Commandment is sacrosanct, essential, and that nothing could be added to or removed from the formulation, lest maledictions ineluctably fall on humankind, generations upon generations."

Says the Rabbi: "True, MOSES made that declaration at that time."

Silence. Eyelids down, YOHANAN seems to review in his head the verbatim of MOSES' speech. Smirk. More silence.

"Now, continues the Rabbi, before we start discussing the Commandments, I wish you to recount *in details* your conversation with Moishe Rabbenou[69], our Master MOSES, after he completed his final public address, and called for you at the entrance of the Tent of Assignations."

Albert turns towards Angel YELIYAEL, and asks him if it would be appropriate to go back into time and space to face MOSES again, taking along Rabbi Yohanan BEN ZAKAI, who could thus be present himself, invisible or visible, at the meeting.

In lieu of a clear positive response, YELIYAEL progressively dissolves into a light mist, like a morning fog quietly evaporating under the rising sun.

We plainly understand: no time-space shortcut allowed!

18. Face to Face with Moses.

ENCOURAGED BY THE RABBI'S REQUEST to tell all, *in details*, Albert inhales deeply and embarks on recounting our story. RABBI YOHANAN comfortably leans back against his familiar olive tree; I close my eyes and offer my face to the light sunrays piercing through the top of the green foliage.

Albert, standing, starts his narrative:

"In front of the tent of assignations MOSES was resting on a beautifully ornate wooden high seat. He could see us, but our encounter remained totally secret and non-visible, non-audible to other humans, for Angel YELIYAEL was enveloping the three of us in his shielding aura.

Picture the scene: YELIYAEL swinging slowly like a spherical light wrapped in a tenuous pearly veil; facing the throne, Simha and I, dressed Egyptian style, sitting on small round-shaped artily

[69] Moshe Rabenou: in Hebrew "Our Master Moses". A familiar expression of affection and love.

engraved stools, set here and there with turquoise lapis lazuli and scintillating precious stones; MOSES' head and eyes radiating beauty, mastery and serenity.

I was expecting to hear Simha first address MOSES, but she was holding her head low, keeping obviously still, apparently silenced by multiple restricting precepts, and taboos impressed on women in her native Sephardic community, traditional rules allegedly derived from MOSES' Ten Commandments. She looked ill at ease, inert as an earthenware jug tucked away in a remote corner.

Unprepared, I swiftly improvised an introduction, which, in retrospective, I find to be utterly ridiculous. So, I used a formal style, appropriate, I thought, for addressing someone of such high spiritual nobility, authority, and fame."

I thus addressed MOSES:

"I am asking permission to enter the Quest about the Ten Commandments, not just for myself, but in the name of all men and women of my world and of my time."

MOSES, silent, nodded.

Thus, gaining confidence, looking at MOSES, straight at his formidable radiant eyes, I continued my introduction:

"We have come here to hear from you the indispensable explanations and enlightenment that will clarify and resolve the enigmas we all have been faced with for centuries while reading your Ten Commandments. Those Commandments you gave to humanity, after receiving them on Mount Horeb in the midst of thunderous blazes.

O MOSES, will you explicit those Commandments for us, one by one, so that, by understanding each thoroughly, we confidently communicate their essence and founding principles, their letter and spirit to all, men and women, young and old, poor and rich, biblically educated or uneducated?"

Conscious of the pomposity of the convoluted discourse he had proffered when facing MOSES, Albert interrupts his narrative, staring apprehensively at the Rabbi, dreading a sarcastic reaction.

Then, assured Rabbi Yohanan BEN ZAKAI is not about to burst into ironic laughter, ALBERT resumes his account:

"MOSES remained pensive for a moment, then reasserted the Ten Commandments were of capital and vital importance for the future of humankind, as long as it inhabits its earthly abode."

Yohanan BEN ZAKAI bows his approval, all off-hand manners and derision gone. He appears sincerely captivated by Albert's report on the progress of our Quest.

ALBERT: "MOSES added the following: "To understand the Ten Commandments' full meaning will be a difficult and arduous task for you and those who will listen to your interpretations and deciphering. However, yours is a Sacred Quest, your discoveries are absolutely necessary to the good and future life of humankind."

In a lyrical and vigorous tone, though speaking with a soft quiet quasi-maternal voice, MOSES indeed insisted there are exactly Ten Commandments, nothing should be taken away or added, not one single letter, not one tiny dot, at the risk of malediction for all transgressors, without exception, with endless catastrophic consequences for humanity.

Conspicuously Simha hadn't moved or uttered a word since the beginning of the conversation. At this stage of the reunion, I respectfully asked MOSES if a woman, more specifically my dear companion sitting next to him, would also have his permission to speak, to express herself and freely converse with him.

A humorous smile briefly shone on the Master's face. MOSES surprised us by his simple and energetic answer, and immediately, the atmosphere became stress-free, amicable."

MOSES: "I recall fondly my sister's Myriam feminine impetuous behaviors, her pleasantly brazen, enjoyably rebellious, and artistically charming outbursts. And I fully enjoy my Ethiopian wife's Tsiporah sharp and soothing intelligence; she delights me day after day with her soft, melodious, divine tsipor-bird chant."[70]

Now, sharing in the protective shade of the antique olive tree, Albert sits nearby the Rabbi and pursues his detailed narration:

"Slowly turning his face towards Simha, MOSES gazed into her

---

[70] Tsiporah, Hebrew word, feminine form of the word tsipor, which means bird, particularly agile (tse) and melodiously singing (por).

dark brown eyes. A cosmic communication began between them, expressing their deep and eternal love of Life, in and beyond time, in all worlds and beyond all spaces.

MOSES then addressed Simha directly: "Naturally you may speak, Simha. Tell me, ask me!"

SIMHA, casting a large thankful smile at MOSES, said:

"Here are the words I have been preparing for so long in my mind and in the sanctuary of my heart. O MOSES, high initiate of the savant Temples-Universities of Egypt, attentive disciple of the great Ethiopian priest Jethro, you are the son of Amram, son of Abraham, son of Akad, offspring of Adam. You know that I come from an era blooming thirty-five centuries after you presented humanity with two stone tablets engraved with the sacred Ten Commandments. I come from a continent called America, from a special place called New York City."

"Ken Yes, I know" said MOSES.

SIMHA: "O MOSES, in your time, you have known about Adam's descendants, resilient traveling Mesopotamian early missionaries[71], teaching their science and spreading their skills around the world. Their persistent efforts are bringing fruits. The grand unity you and them sought for all the world's peoples is now about to be accomplished. On Earth all countries and peoples are physically connected by roads, ground, sea and air.

In year 2000 AD peoples even living in remote territories are reached by radio and television airwaves. Greek shepherds may know about customs of Alaskan Eskimos, athletes of all nations compete in Beijing or London, and so on. However, at the same time, bloody murderous conflicts are erupting here and there, incessantly spouting misery and violent death. Obviously, the pursuit of human unity is at standoff.

Clearly, one thing is missing, a tenuous thread, a subtle and indestructible link which would insure attainment of Unity.

We have come to you, O MOSES, to uncover that thread. We

---

[71] Missionaries, descendants of Seth, third direct offspring of Eve and Adam. Seth organized, 30,000 years ago, a large "Peace Corp" of competent instructors who traveled all continents on earth, for centuries.

think we shall find it at the Source, your source."

Simha paused, waiting for MOSES to respond. And MOSES answered, his voice calm and firm:

"I cannot yet reach the Source, nor can I myself discern the thread you are evoking. Therefore, I definitely cannot provide it to you…"

SIMHA, trying to hold back a threatening panic:

"Maybe "source" and "thread" are not the appropriate words? When we initiated this quest to discover the truths you have encrypted in the Ten Commandments, we first interviewed many people on the subject, in the country we live in, America.

As you know, America is a human "melting pot", as was Egypt in your time coordinates, particularly in the Goshen Valley which you describe in your Testament.

Through centuries, men and women of all races, coming from various populations and lands: black Nubians and Saharans, brown immigrants from India and Mesopotamia, whites from the remote western lands close by the Atlantic ocean, blond haired Hyksos-Hittites from Caucasus, and Tuscans from Latium, all gathered in the valley of Goshen.

You have organized their descendants into tribes and led them out of Egypt so they would carry to the whole world the message of Unity of all Races, the goal of achieving harmony through contrasts and differences.

In America, our own Goshen Valley is called New York City. On a small rocky island and adjacent four large boroughs live the descendants of immigrants of all origins. So much so that, in case of planetary disaster, such as in Noah's time, if one wanted to rebuild humanity in its entirety, without losing its rich diversity, one could gather in New York at least one couple for each race and each culture to take root and insure the permanence of human genetic and cultural treasures."

ALBERT: "I discreetly waved my hand. Simha understood I wanted to intervene, and I said:

"Actually, the name New York, or NEV-Y-ARK as pronounced in Hebrew, indicates that NEW YORK is meant to be "the New Ship

(NAVY) of the Ark", the "new *rescue ship*" to embark in case of colossal catastrophe."

Said MOSES, with a conniving blink:

"And I am aware of the high destination and destiny of those new pilgrims! Anyone who, like you, dares decrypt words and symbols, will uncover the significance of the famous acronym: U.S.- Up to the Stars! The new pilgrims' exodus shall aim at the stars, as is unmistakably reflected on America's STAR spangled banner."

"U.S.A! Upwards to the Stars America!" exclaimed SIMHA.

ALBERT: "Your remark, O MOSES, gives a renewed significance to the US national Anthem[72]. Its lyrics, based on past heroic events on Earth, now deliver a prophetic message, destined to future interstellar travelers:

Then conquer we must, when our cause it is just,
And this be our motto: In God is our trust
And the Star Spangled Banner
in triumph shall wave
O'er the land of the free and the home of the brave!

SIMHA confirmed:

"In ARCHAE LINGUA, the universal language, the name NEW YORK translates as such:

The center of growth and expansion (NeV)
from which humans who align
themselves with divine principles (Yo),
shall produce a renewal (R),
both in quality and in quantity (K)."

ALBERT: "I saw Simha giving me a suggestive nod, in response to which I winked at her discreetly. Our minds were on the same wavelength; we were determined to signal to MOSES our eagerness to interpret the Ten Commandments by drawing from ARCHAE LINGUA's bottomless well. So we conveyed to him we are ready,

---

[72] "The Star-Spangled Banner" was recognized for official use by the Navy in 1889 and by the US President in 1916. It was legally voted to be the National Anthem by a congressional resolution on March 3, 1931 (46 Stat. 1508, codified at 36 U.S.C. § 301), which was signed by President Herbert Hoover.

eager even, to follow him should he wish to dig below the surface of ordinary translations, and propose us deeper levels of elucidation of his Commandments."

MOSES said nothing, remained still, and Simha continued:

"In preparation for our meeting with you, before our travel on the wings of Angel YELIYAEL, we asked men and women of diverse origins and cultures about your Ten Commandments. To your credit, O MOSES, all peoples know you, whether they name you Moise, Moyse, Moshe, Moishe, Moussa, Moses, or Mosse, and they associate you with the origin of the Ten Commandments.

However, when it comes to reciting the Commandments, things are quite different; unanimity dissolves entirely. Many peoples recall one, two, or three, but fewer and fewer prove able to recite four or five.

Thou shall not kill, thou shall not steal, thou shall not lie, thou shall not desire your neighbor's wife: those Commandments emerge from the lot. Some individuals who attempt to stand up on the podium of morality remember: thou shall not commit adultery or you shall respect your father and your mother.

As for the other Commandments! Nothing! Blank! Pensive hair scratching, embarrassment, unproductive brain storming! The fateful Sacred Ten are never remembered by a single ordinary person. Of course, we did not include professional religionists in that investigation.

Consequently, O MOSES, we have to admit the fact that after 35 centuries of uninterrupted fame, millions of discourses, speeches, debates, missives, dissertations and sermons, millions of books published and sold, sometimes distributed for free, especially in America, in spite of genuine efforts by rabbis, imams, priests, pastors, ecumenical missionaries, and benevolent laymen, yes, we have to admit that, at the beginning of the third millennium, only fragments of your message are memorized."

ALBERT: "Well determined to precisely update MOSES, Simha continued providing details:

"In recent times, in the twentieth century, programs after programs are broadcast on radio and television, on top of big budget

Hollywood films, the most famous being precisely titled "The Ten Commandments". Yet, nothing has changed: individual knowledge of your Commandments seems to have come to a halt: we can report no progress beyond the count of five."

Up until then, MOSES had remained impassive, listening attentively. However, at this point, straightening his back, he said:

"Are you evoking this strange film in which I am portrayed by the handsome Hollywoodian actor, Charlton Heston?"

Simha nods silently.

MOSES*:* "That depiction of a dramatic exit from Egypt, motivated by an alleged liberation from ignoble slavery is boldly straying from the truth. The ancestors of the people I led to Canaan through the Sinai desert had entered Egypt *voluntarily*, under contract, an indenture for a long albeit limited time: 430 years.

The original sworn contract initially agreed to by Pharaoh was fair and equitable: the new residents were allocated a fertile land to live on, the Goshen valley; the peoples were to learn superior crafts and techniques, sophisticated science, higher theology and metaphysics, from the more advanced Egyptians, while providing in turn a necessary work force, physical and mental, to sustain the Egyptian civilization.

Then after 430 years of learning and practicing, they would, as originally planned, exit the Goshen Valley, leave Egypt, to discover new horizons. But the film shamelessly reproduces a pseudo historical cliché, hinting in no way at the true purpose embodied in the mutually bonding agreement between noble Egypt and patriarch Abraham, then representing the descendants of Adam and Eve at the time scattered almost everywhere on the planet!"

MOSES smiling broadly: "However, the Title of the motion picture, and the talent of Master Charlton Heston, both provide great publicity for my work! What tremendous fame it brought to the Ten Commandments!"

MOSES pauses, sighs, and adds: "Alas, this same wondrous handsome actor was later chosen to impersonate the fictitious Ben Hur character, hero of an imaginary story, taking place in Judea

1,500 years after my departure from Mount Nebo. That blunder has neutralized, and at times destroyed in the minds of millions, the very notion of my authentic existence on Earth."

ALBERT: "Then, MOSES encouraging Simha, said: "Go on, I am listening, I hear you."

SIMHA: "In short, ignorance seems pervasive. After 35 centuries, we have yet to penetrate the core meanings of your message. Will you enlighten us, O MOSES? Why are modern-day peoples so ignorant, so ill-informed?"

MOSES looks perfectly at ease. The question interests him, and his answer is swift:

"Serious reasons and perfectly identified motives explain such imperfect knowledge."

"All right", rejoins SIMHA, with the fiery passion of a Socratic Athenian philosopher practicing dialectic on the agora, getting closer to the heart of a heated debate:

"Then what are those reasons and motives?"

MOSES, curtly, tantalizingly:

"I don't know!"

"You don't know!?" echoes SIMHA, stunned.

"I don't know" MOSES insists.

Deeply troubled, Simha and I temporarily coped with this strange situation. Angel YELIYAEL reinforced his protection, insuring that MOSES' astounding confession of ignorance remains undisclosed to others in the camp.

MOSES turning his attention to me:

"Albert, will you express the same question differently? I shall answer you with integrity, as I just have, responding to Simha's questing."

ALBERT: "So, you state, there are serious reasons and well-identified motives explaining the near total ignorance of five Commandments out of ten, and you, MOSES, do not know what those causes and motives are. Let's look at the enigma from another angle.

We know that men and women of the third millennium have a

good enough awareness of four to five Commandments. This means they possess knowledge of half of your legacy. Better than a third, or a quarter, or a tenth, or nothing, surely!"

Short pause.

"Then why is it so many men and women in our society and all around the planet do not put their knowledge to practice? Why do they steal, lie, covet their neighbor's wife, or house, and less and less honor their father and mother?"

MOSES doesn't wait long to rejoin:

"That is because they do not yet know the contents of the other five Commandments."

"Great Systemic thinking, again proving more effective than common linear reasoning! Very sound answer. We should have reached such simple, enlightening conclusion ourselves!" I said.

Simha takes the opportunity offered by MOSES' explanation, and swiftly questions:

"Then, why, O MOSES, why do humans know only these particular four or five Commandments and ignore the other five or six? Why these and not those? Why?"

MOSES' terse answer flows like a music box leitmotiv, an unavoidable ritornello: "There are, he says, serious reasons and perfectly identified motives explaining this very partial knowledge."

Simha, in a last desperate attempt to get a direct answer before MOSES pulls himself together again, charges on quickly:

"What are those reasons? What are those motives?"

"I do not know them" responds MOSES, in a distinctly final tone.

And yet, for a fleeting moment, a barely discernible inner smile filtered through his immortal eyes, and his face took on a Mona Lisa expression, forever unfathomable.

We had reached a dead end. MOSES had been a profound enigma for 35 centuries and appeared decided to keep his secrets.

SIMHA, serious: "So, definitely, there is a mystery surrounding the Ten Commandments?"

"Not just one mystery, replies MOSES, thousands!"

ALBERT: "The legend of the Sphinx surged into my mind. MOSES was staring at us, his face conjuring up a vision of the mysterious statue he had himself so often contemplated during his stay in Egypt, the country of the Nile River.

I addressed him again, calmly, intending to show MOSES we were not giving up:

We came to meet and speak with you, because we think and trust that you, MOSES, are most competent to clarify enigmas and mysteries, to enlighten deeply obfuscated passages in the Sacred Ten Commandments as we read them in our times. You are the source of their propagation. For sure you must possess the secret thread which will lead us to an accurate and truthful interpretation!"

Softly, kindly, MOSES answered:

"Verily, I am not the one meant to answer your question. I personally received the Commandments and transmitted them exactly as I received them, omitting or adding nothing.

Before the exodus I have always lived in Egypt; in fact, I am an authentic Egyptian Prince. In spite of persistent rumors that, born from a Hebrew mother, left as a baby floating down the Nile in a wicker basket picked up by an Egyptian princess, the truth is that I am the son of AMRAM, an Egyptian nobleman, member of Pharaoh's court. True, Amram is himself a direct descendant of a son of YOSEPH, himself descendant of ABRAM, who became the patriarch ABRAHAM after his spiritual initiation by celestial Melchizedek. When you read and decode carefully the ancient texts you shall find confirmation of this fact.

As a Prince of Egypt, I have been mostly instructed in military and administrative disciplines, to become an efficient and wise leader of a nation or a people. In the university temples of my country, then the center of the world's knowledge and wisdom, I have learned the fundamental principles indispensable to federate tribes of different racial and cultural origins.

Such unification made Egypt most powerful, and insured its enduring civilizing influence.

I also ascended all the steps of spiritual initiation, reaching the upper ranks opening the doors to all secret crypts, and to ancestral, human, and celestial knowledge."

MOSES clarified even more:

"Examining history, you will notice that when ABRAM[73] left the city-state of UR KASHDIM in Mesopotomia-Akadia, formerly inhabited and blessed by the Gods, fleeing savage attacks of wild tribesmen descended from the Caucasian mountains, he traveled directly to Egypt, pausing only in Salem. For only in Egypt could he safely deposit the treasures of advanced science and art, the precious gems of astronomy, mathematics, irrigation, high precision craftsmanship, as well as advanced techniques for conceptualization and expression of thoughts; he also brought momentous historic Akad-Sumerian[74] records of terrestrial and celestial relationships, thus saved from destruction and neglect.

Reading my testament, you will notice that ABRAM brought to Egypt, a very long time before I was born, the legendary Ark of Covenant that contained all the living knowledge gathered and preserved in Mesopotamia-Akadia.[75] It specifically included codes for reading, speaking, and writing in the Universal Language, the Stars' Language, as well as systems and methods to communicate with celestial and divine beings."

"KEROUBIM![76]CAPTORIM![77] excitedly exclaims Simha. Those

---

[73] Abram: when leaving Ur Kashdim for Egypt, his name had not been changed into AbraHam, for he had not yet become Melkitzedek's disciple and initiate.

[74] Sumerian or Shumerian: in Hebrew the word Shomer conveys two core meanings: 1/ shem = science relating to celestial realities (shamaim). 2/ shomer= preserving and safeguarding the integrity of celestial sciences.

[75] Akadia: in Hebrew Ikhoud means unity. Therefore Akad, the other name of Sumer, indicates the harmonic union the Mesopotamian civilization has accomplished in merging Human and Celestial legacies.

[76] Kerubim: Simha's exclamation refers to the 2 open winged Angels (Cherubs) statues placed on the lid of the Ark of the Covenant. Exodus 25:18-22.In Archae Lingua the word Kerub indicates the activity of "broadcasting" messages. In Hebrew, the verb Kerob (or Kerov) means to reduce or cancel the distance that separates two objects in space or time.

[77] Captorim: Simha's exclamation refers to the "knobs" inlaid in the gold Lampstand Exodus 25:31-40. In Archae Lingua the word Captor (or Caphtor) indicates the action of "reception" of messages. In Medieval French. a "caphteur" is a person who transmits a message which should have remained hidden. In English the root "Capt" is used in the words "captor" "capture", and "captivate".

are the legendary powerful "Emitters" and "Receivers" of angelic and archangelic streams of messages! And means of reciprocal communication with all kinds of exo-terrestrial visitors!"

ALBERT, almost screaming: "ARCHAE LINGUA!"

"OI DAI, humorously says MOSES. So, I am an Egyptian, not quite the Highest Priest, nor quite a governing king. And I know the essentials of the "unifying" language from Sumer and Akad.

However, the Egyptian hieroglyphic language is far removed from the Stars' Language. At the time of my birth, 400 years after ABRAM brought the Ark to Egypt, few of the Memphis temples superior initiates were fully mastering the 35,000 year-old mysterious and legend-filled obscure Mesopotamian language of Sumer and Akad. Understanding perfectly the Sumerian language, source-code of all human tongues, has always been the goal of every great priest-scholar in my country, but, for many, that goal had yet to be achieved."

MOSES, quiet for a moment, appeared to wander away from his throne, far from Mount Nebo, far from us, conversing secretly, perhaps, with Angel YELIYAEL. Then he continued:

"It is now your mission, along men and women of the third millennium after Christ, to rediscover "SUMER", the Sum of celestial legacies", and "AKAD", the supreme unity connecting God, humans, Angels, and all of the heavens' inhabitants."

ALBERT: "You can empathize, O RABBI YOHANAN, the shock, the mental explosion we have experienced at that moment! MOSES had spoken softly, and yet his compelling words echoed in our minds like a prolonged scream in an empty crypt.

Here we are, given an awesome, overwhelming mission, handed by MOSES himself! We had hoped a genuine face-to-face conversation with Master MOSES, bringing about precious first hand information, would surely solve most of the major riddles encrypted in the Ten Commandments. Thus we would have easily restored the original brilliance and clarity of that wonderful masterwork, now faded and discolored by the passing of time.

Alas, we then realized, it was not meant to happen as we had anticipated. We understood clearly, albeit painfully, we would have to face the inevitable frightening situation with much courage. We had been taught a bitter lesson:

There is no instant relief to Ignorance!

Constant personal involvement, commitment, devotion will be necessary to even reach the outskirts of wisdom…

Then, it was almost time for us to part, for we could already distinguish white star rays cutting across the Angel's virtual dome, and hear muffled whispers, the voices of peoples preparing for their nightly rest. Simha asked the Master permission to question him a little more before taking leave. MOSES encouraged her with a gentle movement of the head."

SIMHA: "All translations of the Old Testament state that Commandment number 7, which reads "LOA TIN AF," means: THOU SHALT NOT COMMIT ADULTERY. O MOSES, is this a correct rendition?"

"No, it is not correct. Although I cannot provide you now with a "spherical" revelation, I can tell you the common translation is a hideous perversion of my message, one of the saddest and most oppressive errors impressed on human intelligence.

You shall find the truth yourselves, by going over the original text, word by word, sentence by sentence, with your magnificent "Archaeo-Linguistic" method. You shall uncover the secret!"

ALBERT pursues: "Reminded of his 3,500 years old message fallacious deterioration, MOSES appeared profoundly distraught, his handsome face suddenly invaded by dark sorrow.

At this point, Simha was visibly hesitant to impose another ordeal on the great Master, and I was ready to refrain from further questioning. However, I thought, if we don't insist for answers now, will we ever find another opportunity for such a dialogue?

Consequently, I stayed put and listened to Simha thrusting another question, one that has been prepared ahead of time for this encounter with MOSES."

SIMHA: "The Sixth Commandment, LOA TIRTSAH, is commonly translated and understood as meaning: Thou shalt not kill. Is it the right translation from the original Hebrew transcript?"

MOSES replies:

"The general idea of "not killing" is definitely there. It would be preferable, if we must stick to the basic understanding, to say: "Thou shalt not commit homicide". However, there is more, much more in that Commandment. Look for it, look for it, it is urgent!"

SIMHA: "And what about the Fifth Commandment "Honor thy father and thy mother"?"

MOSES: "This translation is also incorrect, not blatantly false but insufficient. However, I listened to the archangelic recording of your entire dialogue with Angel YELIYAEL, or rather your lively debate concerning the Fifth Commandment, at the start of your journey. I was very pleased by what I heard, and so were many other celestials at my side."

ALBERT: "I recall MOSES adding this mysterious sentence:

"The egg of knowledge that was given to you both is hatching just on time. You have shown no impatience, and no indolence. Your thinking mode, neither exclusively rational nor excessively mystical, is in harmony with your mission: to unearth antic wisdom and reveal its value for the nourishment of modern third millennium science. Now the shell of ignorance may crumble down, soon Truth will appear in the light, grow in beauty, kindness, and grace."

ALBERT: "By now Simha was addressing MOSES as if he were an old friend, perceiving the Master was intimately certain of our profound integrity, and aware of the crystalline pristine purity of our intentions towards him and towards our quest."

SIMHA: "And what about Commandments number 1 and 2? Their translations leave us perplexed, and wanting!

Let's consider Commandment number 1. Here is what we read in the common language of our time: "I am the Lord thy God, which has brought thee out of the land of Egypt, out of the house of bondage."

It is not even expressed in the form of a command. Is it a genuine Commandment, a law?

And number 2: "Thou shalt have no other gods before me. Thou shalt not make unto thee any graven image or any likeness of any thing that is in heaven above, or that is in the earth beneath".

How can humans manifest their humanness if they are, by imperative command, forbidden any representation of their earthly abode or the surrounding cosmos?"

MOSES: "Yes, I know these transcriptions, that long ranting series of misrepresentations. If I lived in your times, may God in his infinite compassion preserve me from that ordeal, and I came across those two Commandments, I would try not to memorize them, and even less let my emotions be penetrated by these commonly accepted feeble meanings."

SIMHA: "Do you mean, O MOSES, that this imperfect partial knowledge, this *amnesia* that has been hampering minds for 3,500 years is good for humanity, a godsend gift from the Heavens?"

ALBERT: "Startled, MOSES raised his right hand slightly above the armrest. Could we have hit one of the enigma's sensitive points?

Was the Sphinx finally about to speak?

Alas, the great Master put down his hand, smiled, remaining silent and impassive.

We still had so many questions to ask MOSES, and we were getting used to his peculiar frank way of shedding light while not answering directly.

Disturbed, we could not find the strength or the right words to express a proper farewell. We felt like pieces of metal energized by a powerful magnetic field, or like two orbiting planets illuminated by a brilliant sun. So close to the Master, our hearts and minds are continually imbued with truth, beauty and goodness. All we could do was to let our tears express our feelings."

MOSES offered a brief conclusion: "In order to continue your Quest, you are going to meet a little known, highly spiritual man, a truly powerful enhancer of Jewish, Christian, and universal spirituality. His name is Rabbi Yohanan BEN ZAKAI."

ALBERT: "Hearing that name, Simha paled. Rabbi Yohanan BEN ZAKAI has visited one of her dreams four years ago. She often told me how well she remembered his ancient Egyptian style headgear, the gentle though firm character transpiring through his inspirited eyes. In her vision he was standing in front of her, with two other ancient wise men, in an inner courtyard she identified as the scene of "the Passion of Jesus"…

"But, said Simha, Rabbi Yohanan BEN ZAKAI has been dead for almost 2,000 years!"

MOSES: "And I have been dead for 3,500 years, yet I am here, you are here, and we are conversing together!"

SIMHA: "Well, O MOSES, you never died! It is said you were lifted up directly to the Heavens, "body and soul," by a Celestial Being."

"This is true, replied MOSES, I did not die the way most humans depart. Thus there is no memorial tomb to be visited and fanatically idolized. And Rabbi BEN ZAKAI also lives on in the Heavens, with even more intensity than many people treading on Earth, and you are going soon to encounter him."

ALBERT, addressing YOHANAN, concludes his lengthy detailed report:

"And MOSES slowly turned towards the narrow pale yellow beam YELIYAEL had just extended; moving his right hand fingers in a subtle and fluid gesture, he gave to the Angel, silently, your virtual cosmic coordinates, defining the exact time-space location, where you, Rabbi Yohanan BEN ZAKAI were expecting to meet with us."

19. The First Divine Commandment. Galilee, Brur Hayl, Universal Time.

"THAT'S IT, RABBI, FINALLY SAYS ALBERT. So MOSES provided navigational instructions to Angel YELIYAEL who flew us here, and, with your help, we surely shall unravel the mysteries of the Ten Commandments."

SIMHA, passionately: "Naturally you will first explain Commandment number 1, probably the most important of all, as it is, since centuries, presented at the top of the list of the Sacred Ten. However, it is difficult to understand why it is not expressed as a law. Here is how it is written in our Bible:

I AM THE LORD THY GOD,
WHO BROUGHT THEE
OUT OF THE LAND OF EGYPT,
OUT OF THE HOUSE OF BONDAGE.

Rabbi Yohanan BEN ZAKAI pauses for a long moment, Albert and I sitting on supple grass, enjoying the cool Galilean morning. Feeling happy, we are waiting, peacefully, patiently.

YELIYAEL's familiar angelic soothing aura pulses above, its subtle sky blue undulations rippling on the edges. With long luminous curved beams, multicolored iridescent filaments, colored like rainbows, Angel YELIYAEL gently touches an olive branch here, smells a buttercup there, and our small patch of rustic nature empathically responds to the message conveyed by each caressing stroke. Animals, insects, flowers, rocks and trees feel the celestial messenger's presence and rejoice. Butterflies and dragonflies appear to be the most sensitive, some fraternal connection uniting them to the Angel's aura.

After a long, harmonious, fragrant, and musical silence, the Rabbi looks as if he had just come out of a trance. His expression is resolute and firm.

"First of all, he reflects, we have to clarify the matter of the order in which the Ten Commandments were presented to us by MOSES. When, on Mount Horeb, the celestial messenger handed MOSES the Ten Commandments tablets, he did it with a powerful incommensurable celestial energy, out of proportion with human perceptive abilities.

Actually, the crowd assembled in the valley was utterly terrorized. That vivid event is picturesquely reported in the Old Testament, Book of Exodus, Chapter 20, verses 18-19 as follows:

"And all the people witnessed the thundering, the fires and the sounds of trumpets, and the smoking mountain: and as the people saw it, shaking they moved away, and stood afar off. And they said unto MOSES: Speak thou with us, and we will hear, but let not God speak with us, lest we die."

Pause. Silence.

RABBI YOHANAN resumes: "The first divine words cast by the celestial messenger as a burning flash, fell down on the stony slat like a blazing beam, inadvertently covering most of the carved letters with smoldering cosmic lava making it inaccessible for many centuries to come. That message is still aflame today; few men and women dare approach it to receive the burning living Word of God.

SIMHA: "Do you mean, Rabbi, the light surrounding the First Commandment being so bright and blinding, the "divine Word" is locked into the darkness of neglect and incomprehension?"

"And yet, offers ALBERT, this first Commandment as presented in the Bible appears to be so simple and easy to memorize. It is not demanding either: unlike the 9 others, it contains no categorical imperative, no imposed direction, not a bit of prohibition. "*I am the Lord thy God,*" is a clear affirmative pronouncement, followed by "*which have brought thee out of the land of Egypt, out of the house of bondage.*"

SIMHA: "Had we not personally met MOSES at Mount Nebo, had we not seen the extraordinary variety of peoples composing the 12 tribes, we could be led astray and interpret that pronouncement as the election of a special people particularly cherished by

God, brought out from Egypt. But MOSES himself, and YOSHUA BEN NOUN, and Angel YELIYAEL led us to understand clearly the fundamental Intent was totally universal, involving all humanity, all races."

Rabbi Yohanan BEN ZAKAI, who has been waiting for a pause, asserts:

"The First Commandment is the crown of the Ten Laws. It is important, not only to the whole of humanity on Earth, but also to all humanities in the Universe, and even to all other creatures, the extra-ordinary multitude of supra human celestial cohorts.

Of all proffered opinions reducing the outlook on the First Commandment to a plain innocuous easy simple statement, I demand you: FREE YOURSELF! "

The Rabbi's tone, though filled with kindness, is commanding, like that of a loving authoritative father firmly transmitting a rule vital for his child's future.

This "Free yourself!" striking injunction, amplified by Angel YELIYAEL's spirit, resounds in our minds like a powerful gong.

Refreshing winds twirl around our bodies and heads, ruffle our clothes and hair. A gray cloud of malevolence suddenly spirals out and dissolves into the atmosphere. Strangely, we feel immediately purified, surrounded by a soft, subdued light. First thoughts to cross our psyche are lucid, pristine and serene.

YOHANAN resumes his welcomed lecture:

"God's messenger tendered to MOSES the blazing First Commandment, which he then transcribed in the book of TANAKH[78], a code name for the Old Testament in Hebrew. The word TANA-KH in Hebrew means: GIVEN TO YOU."

"As simple as that?" exclaims ALBERT.

"Yes, says YOHANAN, but, what has been given to MOSES by Divine Decree has not been fully *received* yet! Thus, the particular significance of the word KABALAH[79], meaning OK WELL RECEIVED, has still to be clarified and understood."

---

[78] Tanakh=-in Hebrew literally means «that was given to you». Root Tan=give, and root Akh=you.

[79] Kabalah= in Hebrew derives from verb Kabel, meaning "to receive and accept".

SIMHA: "Then, the major aim of a disciple in the science of KABALAH is to learn laws, paths and keys allowing attainment of a state of impeccable LISTENING and faultless RECEIVING?"

"*Correct*, swiftly intervenes Angel YELIYAEL. *MOSES first endeavored to become perfect Receiver of the ineffable messages of Truth, perfect disciple of KABALAH. Then he set himself up to become equally perfect Giver, Master of TANAKH, giver of the five books of Torah, in which are included the Ten Commandments.*"

"Is it why the Old Testament, the TORAH, is frequently referred to as TANAKH by the Talmudic scholars?" ponders Albert.

Says YOHANAN: "The luminous enlightening science of KABALAH-TANAKH has still to be unearthed, to fully emerge out of the shadows. Before pretending to access the profound contents of celestial knowledge, men and women must learn the basic laws of perfect mental and spiritual "receiving mode"."

SIMHA: "Obviously there have been in the past and there are now in the present time, men and women nurturing their capacity for listening and therefore receiving the celestial gifts: Jew Kabalists, Christian Cabalists, Sufis, Native American and African Shamans, Taoist sages, enlightened Buddhists, gifted musicians, poets or individuals who simply consult their own inner voice-master, and maintain their spirit in a state of KABALAH–OK WELL RECEIVED."

Says YOHANAN: "All humans must honestly attempt to receive the message enclosed in the First Commandment: I AM THE LORD THY GOD. Start by giving attention to the very beginning "I AM" "ANOKHI", pointing to the wonder of self-awareness, the supreme consciousness of "being".

To RECEIVE the consciousness of "being", one must aim at GIVING back immediately that gift of supreme awareness. The key to perfect Receiving is the unwavering intention of Giving!

Take heed, the First Commandment is the unifying law of the supreme creation, the brightest purest multifaceted diamond of the universe of all universes, encompassing all centers, all peripheries, in the past, present, and future.

SIMHA: "OI VE! Rav YOHANAN, if this jewel is surrounded with such searing fire that no one can touch or even approach it, never shall we find someone on Earth to help us. We might have to journey deeper and deeper into the universe, far into the celestial expanses, to meet the "Majestic Master" who, burning with the same fire, shall guide us, help us catch a glimpse at this diamond's facets, and unveil its truths and beauties."

"Yes Simha, answers the Rav, your conclusion is correct."

Angel YELIYAEL, reinforcing his focus, indicates he perceives and understands our intention. He is quick to kindly inform us:

"When it is time for you to leave and travel through the recesses of space and time in search of the one shining star revealing the magnificent enlightening First Law, I shall no longer be transporting you, and you shall have to find another navigator."

I acquiesce silently. Albert, habitually so reluctant to giving trust, and yet eternally loyal to his chosen friends, is already worrying about our angelic companion's future absence.

But I am confident Angel YELIYAEL shall not leave us "lost in space-time" without providing the mental energies necessary to leap over interstellar synapses, to meet ethical challenges and approach the spiritual meaning of that First and Ultimate Universal Law. Optimistic as always, I reassure Albert:

"For the moment, YELIYAEL is with us. When the time comes, the new messenger will certainly appear!"

20. Creation of the Tenth Commandment.

ADDRESSING RABBI YOHANAN, I SAY: "So, you shall not teach us more about the First Commandment?"

YOHANAN: "No, it is neither possible nor even desirable. As for the Second Commandment, it may be less unapproachable, but still blazing with too much strength for your current level of mental energy. I propose to introduce you to the secret and sacred meanings of the Tenth Commandment…"

ALBERT: "Jumping right away to the last on the list!"

YOHANAN: "It is the last from Divine point of view, but for humans on Earth the Last is actually the First.

For Homo Sapiens progressively and painfully emerging out of mineral stiffness, vegetal rooted immobility, animal impulsiveness, aiming at suddenly entering and exploring the elevated realm of spiritual consciousness, the 10th Commandment is the necessary solid foundation. For the newborn voyager in the heavenly kingdoms, the Tenth Commandment is truly and definitely the First."

Intensely focused like two attentive students fascinated by a new teacher, Albert and I remain deeply silent.

Rav YOHANAN elaborates: "The Tenth Commandment is the first humans are able to comprehend, accept, and understand. It is the starting point for humanity emerging from animality, the point 0 of its evolution towards the first level of spirituality, and for that very reason it is given the number 10, namely 1 + 0."

"What an elegant illustration of heavenly mathematics!" I exclaim.

The Master continues: "To those who can hear, I may reveal this: Unlike the other 9 laws, the 10th Commandment THOU SHALL NOT COVET was not formulated by the divine messenger. MOSES himself provided the content. *Listening* keenly he received the idea, the form, the rhythm, the inspiration, although he was left completely free to select the essential sound syllables and assemble the words into phrases fitting the divine melody, known to all of us as the 10th law."

Very animated and anticipating a rain of questions on the subject, the Rav changes course:

"Before any further discussion, I would like to be updated on the progress you have made in your "Quest", your investigation on the Ten Commandments. So, where do you both stand now? What did you find within that gigantic monument of human history?"

Teasing him, I say: "Just a few moments ago, you were telling us very casually: "*There could even be none, neither 10, nor 1, simply Zero*"!" Now you are presenting those ten verses as the most exciting and valuable treasure ever handed to humanity!

Yohanan BEN ZAKAI smiles gently, humorously, and says:

"Note, Shimeha, my exact statement was: "There could even be none, neither 10, nor 1, simply Zero!" I didn't say that there could be none *in the history of humanity on planet Earth!*

In truth, each of the Ten Commandments is indispensable for each individual willing to unfold completely and harmoniously his transient life on Earth. Furthermore each one of these Ten Laws provides a path for positive evolution, and cosmic survival."

For the first time since we met, the Rabbi's tone is really serious, bordering on pomposity:

"When humanity as a whole will cross the threshold of its earthly natural sphere, expanding its aura beyond what it considers to be its physical, mental and spiritual boundaries, when humans will evolve as supra-humans, exploring the new dimensions of spirituality and "meta-spirituality", then men and women will no longer need any Commandment.[80] Humanity will then have landed on the shores of its true kingdom, that of the Father, the Creator who is in Heaven. It was said, announced, promised, and it is true."

With an elegant graceful brush stroke, Rabbi BEN ZAKAI had just painted a wonderful utopia, a truly accessible utopia! At the sound of his voice, our imagination took off, and we could easily see, even travel and explore this new celestial vastness.

"I understand, Rabbi, I say, I understand perfectly!"

Watching Albert I see his face and entire body are glowing, basking in happiness. To be where we are now, talking about progressive humanity, the Divine, the Cosmos, the Future, there is nothing he loves best. At this moment, he is exactly where he always wanted to be.

"So, Master, Albert interjects, you wish us to succinctly pre-

---

[80] Evocation of the ideal of "Self Governance" when all fundamental ethical values are internalized by all individuals. The Founding Fathers of the USA emphasized the notion of political self-governance as a basic tenet of Ideal Democracy.

sent you with our previous discoveries?"

"Yes, acquiesces the Rabbi, but not succinctly, please! I like explanations to be extensive and detailed." He wets his lips with anticipation, and continues:

"I want to be presented with every detail, detour and contour, every curb and spiral of your thoughts, because only with exact words, exact syllables and consonants, shall we build vast cosmic landscapes and majestic heavenly temples and cathedrals."

Albert proposes to communicate all the details through mental projections "compacted and zipped" by Angel YELIYAEL, however YOHANAN disapproves with a swift gesture of the hand, and commands:

"Download everything, every detail! Vocalize! Recite! Intone!"

ALBERT: "Everything started, I trust, with Simha's dream."[81]

Albert glances at me, encouraging me to intervene. Thus, for the benefit of the Rabbi, I recount my dream about "what is competence", the empowerment it provided, leading us to writing the book *Angel Signs*. I also describe my second dream, "the passion of Christ"[82] in which Yohanan BEN ZAKAI appeared to me for the first time.

As I stand now on this Galilean hill, my face upturned to the blue sky, images of my dreams surge in my memory, and I see them taking on a new life, as Angel YELIYAEL projects moving scenes, personages, thoughts and emotions on a high and large spherical ethereal veil. Surrounding our little group the delicate screen reflects precisely all the dimensions of my dreams.

Now convinced he has no time limit, Albert explains step by step how we started on our Quest, our determination to decipher the Sacred Ten Commandments' enigma and bring light to their obscure albeit apparent simple formulation. For YOHANAN's benefit he retraces the thoughts and synchronic events which provided opportunities for starting this investigation, this Quest, our project

---

[81] Simha's dream 1:see the Foreword in *Angel Signs'* , by the authors of present book

[82] Simha's dream 2: see end of Chapter II in the present book.

to encounter the greatest personalities of human history by traveling through time and space on the wings of benevolent and proficient trans-dimensional navigator Angel YELIYAEL.

Then Albert adopts a silent mode, closes his eyes and looks as if immersed in a deep hypnotic stasis, hand under his chin, his elbow leaning on his right knee.

We remain quiet, patiently waiting. A soft breeze caresses our faces, our hands, and our bare feet. YOHANAN's eyelids are semi-closed. I see him turn his head slowly towards the higher branches of the olive tree.

ALBERT resumes telling our most recent adventures:

"Before taking off from our Manhattan living quarters Angel YELIYAEL pointed at the central position of the 5th Commandment, at the equilibrium point on the list of the fiery revelations received by MOSES. He also provided us with the necessary insights, energy and courage to undertake the Archaeo-Linguistic analysis of the 5th divine law, titled HOVA, LOVE!"

YOHANAN shows his enthusiasm: "Remarkable, he interjects, wonderful!"

Angel YELIYAEL intervenes in this heated passionate debate, projecting a flight of musical high pitched notes, mixed iridescent flashes of light, and various pungent fragrances, evoking in his own way all of the discoveries towards which he has led us during the deciphering of the vocal formula HOVA! LOVE! title of the 5th Commandment.

Satisfied with our explanations and recollections, YOHANAN finally accepts to tackle the subject for which we have come to meet him.

"So, I shall now recount the origin of the Tenth Commandment. Remember, it is the tenth from divine point of view, but the first for humans who are beginning their ascension towards the realm of Deity. Please enounce it the way it is written in America, at your epoch."

SIMHA: "I will quote the exact text, as it appears in the English Version of the Old Testament:

Thou shalt not covet thy neighbor's house,
Thou shalt not covet thy neighbor's wife,
Nor his manservant nor his maiden servant,
Nor his ox, nor his donkey,
Nor anything that is thy neighbor's.[83]

THE RABBI: "Shimeha, what are your first thoughts?"

SIMHA: "Rav, I must avow that women particularly are shocked by these assertions designating them as mere material property, equaled to houses, slaves, oxen, donkeys and things!"

"Yes, rejoins YOHANAN, nothing's new under the sun! In my own time during my sojourn on Earth also, this Commandment, taken literally, profoundly displeased women, and a great number of them rebelled against the outrageous male domination this Commandment appeared to encourage. Many intelligent educated women found relief, comfort and dignity in the midst of Christian sects, called "Minim," which means, as you well know, "the two genders equal". In these new sects, men and women could study together, participate in every dialogue or debate, without gender discrimination. The Minims of course could pray together, without the women having to hide in the shadows behind thick drapes, wooden and metal lattices.

But tell me, you, personally, Shimeha, what do you think of this Commandment?"

SIMHA: "Setting aside houses, women, slaves, donkeys, as mere illustrations of current objects of property at the time of the exit from Egypt, one may sum up the Commandment as:

DO NOT COVET ANYTHING THAT BELONGS TO YOUR NEIGHBOR.

Of course, at first reading, this may seem very simple, even simplistic. But, Rabbi, you just asserted this Commandment is the tenth from the divine point of view, but the first for humans who are beginning their ascension towards the Divine Realms.

Therefore one may not lightly dismiss this Commandment.

My impression is that this law is meant to be a basic principle, a foundation for a primary social order. This Commandment appears

[83] Exodus 20:1-17

to be the origin of a plain moral code in order to minimize conflicts between individuals, with some sort of social peace in view.

Moreover, as you have just informed us, this Commandment was not planned to be scripted as such in the first place, the Divine messenger did not formulate it, and it is MOSES who composed it for the purpose of elevating his people's moral standards…"

YOHANAN looks at me, amused by the casual and detached tone of my turn of phrase.

"I know you have more to say. Now, Shimeha, tell us what's really in your mind?"

SIMHA: "To you Rabbi, I shall dare say what, until this very moment, I could share only with Albert. I have conferred many times with Angel YELIYAEL, and several celestial beings regarding all Commandments, including the 10th. The angelic records confirm your disclosure. It is true that the Divine messenger expected MOSES to add this Tenth Commandment on his own volition.

Within the stream of divine vibrations transmitted sequentially, repetitively to MOSES, the celestial envoy always left a minute silent time-space, apparently empty. Nine melodies followed by a void in which a tenth melody could fit perfectly as soon as MOSES would compose it. Everything was ready for this "man made" work of art that is now the Tenth Commandment, tenth for the Divine, but first for humans.

This sublime human creation, like a last verse enhancing a meaningful epic poem, was absolutely essential to complete the tower on whose summit the spiritual pyramid would be erected, an arrowhead pointing to an ultimate objective, aiming at the center of the Eternal and Infinite Universe."

"And MOSES, says the Rabbi, was totally free to accept or decline to play a part in building that tower. Such is the force of Free Will, divine gift granted to every human being."

Now, YOHANAN suddenly turns to Albert and flings a volley of questions at him, in rapid succession, at the speed of a skilled archer: "Was the Tenth Commandment necessary? Is it a foundation for eternity? What would have happened if MOSES hadn't decided to add a tenth Commandment to the nine others? What if the

Commandment MOSES composed hadn't enounced: "Do not covet any thing that belongs to your neighbor", tell us, Albertov, what would have happened?"

Albert, who does not consider himself an expert in biblical exegesis, is surprised to be the one chosen for such a difficult task. He frowns, stays put, frowns again, then declares:

"Rabbi, those are the questions my mind was burning to ask you! I feel I have no competence to answer them. I am a student of Aristotle, Plato, and Socrates, who never mentioned directly the Ten Commandments in their writings. On the other hand, Simha is perfectly knowledgeable and well trained in discussing all biblical topics..."

RABBI YOHANAN: "For the moment I do not want to question your companion Shimeha, for she is constantly connected to celestial messengers with whom she easily communicates in ARCHAE LINGUA. Everything Shimeha apprehends and says comes directly from the heavens. So intuitive she is, receiving the most blazing messages without being burnt herself!

However you, Albertov, a philosopher born in a world and epoch where and when few understand the aims and usefulness of philosophy, poet in a world in which most inhabitants take pride in disregarding poetry, I know you will answer those questions through clear logical reasoning. How wonderful it is for the celestial assemblies to observe a pure human mind rising like a flamboyant LAMED[84], an ascending spiral of fire and gold!

Albert, blushing noticeably, deeply moved by the Rabbi's compliment, remains silent, intimidated.

YOHANAN: "Shall you answer my first question, Albertov? Was the Tenth Commandment necessary?"

Calm and silent, Albert reaches out and grabs a small dry branch under the olive tree. Kneeling, he prepares a flat surface on

---

[84] Lamed: Hebraic alphabet letter L. The common meaning of the word Lamed is Learning-teaching. The Archeao Linguistic deciphering of this consonant-sonority reveals the sense of: to Link, to eLevate the Mind, the enLightened inteLLect, Knowledge iLLumination acquired by Logical as well as intuitive Links with the Cosmic inteLLigence.

the sandy ground in the middle of our attentive circle, and carefully starts drawing and writing on the dust:

DIVINE

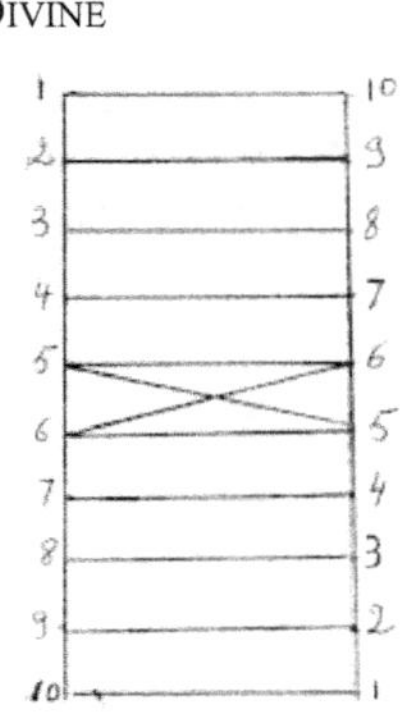

HUMAN

Albert now whispers words and numbers, and, in order to hear, we have to lean towards him.

"To build a structure capable of connecting humans to the heavens and the heavens to humans, a base has to be established, a stable supporting base. And the center of that structure has to reflect the nature of the purposed reciprocal connection. Such support must also be the symmetrical center between the two worlds; otherwise the structure will not be stable. A series of 10 numbers does answer both requirements. See how balanced, symmetrical, and elegant the diagram's center is, when 10 laws are positioned on the structure:

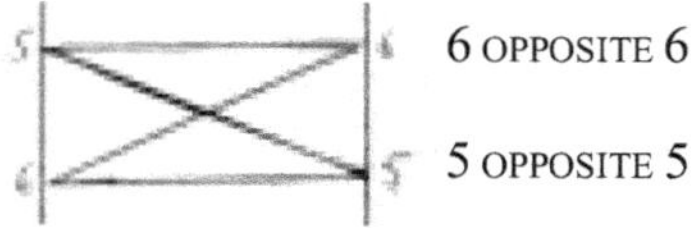

All other numbers, positioned in reverse, order themselves in a similar graceful manner, reflecting each other in a harmonious and elegant ascending and descending movement.

However, look at what happens when the diagram is built with only nine numbers:

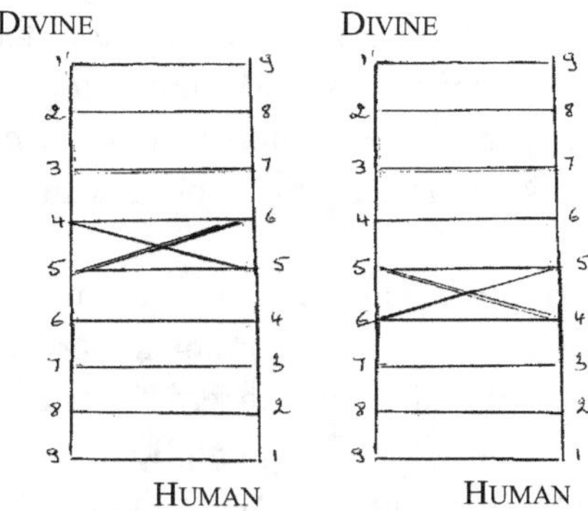

On a ladder displaying only 9 laws, wherever we position the base of the future structure, one can find neither reciprocity nor symmetry. Here there is no elegance; only fractures, irregular jumps, abrupt movements, steep slopes. The structure displays no true center foundation; everything is asymmetrical, arrhythmic, unbalanced.

The pattern is even more chaotic when we imagine diagrams in space, in three dimensions, the way architects and builders do.

You see one structure is rickety, unbalanced, unsound...the other is balanced, stable and harmonious.

9 COMMANDMENTS

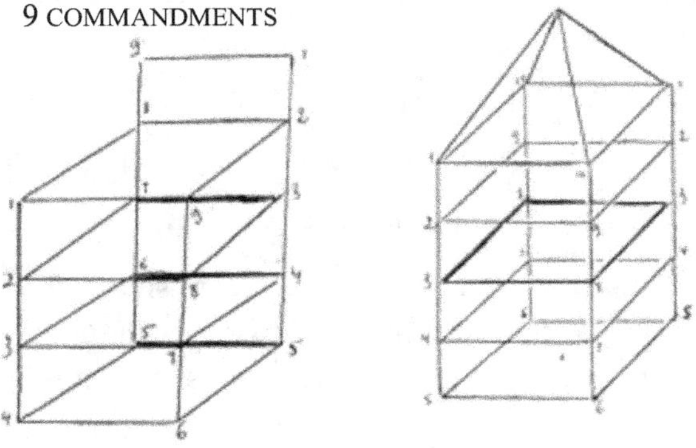

10 COMMANDMENTS

In short, 10 Commandments, not 9, build a coherent, complete, and reliable trustworthy structure. And this is GOOD."

"TOV![85]confirms Rabbi YOHANAN. One may admire the symmetric and harmonious correspondences emerging at every level of the structure, when constructed with 10 units, each symbolizing one of the 10 laws. And, as well as Goodness this Harmony provides Beauty."

"Moreover, continues ALBERT, looking at the architectural drawing, one may observe the 10 Commandments provide, at the upper level, four additional pillars to erect and firmly support a new construction, a pyramid, an ideal temple from the top of which humans may rise higher up to reach even higher levels, therefore uncovering more layers of Truth."

YOHANAN: "But, still, my second question remains unanswered. Is this Tenth Commandment a foundation for eternity?"

ALBERT: "I shall take a little detour to answer that question. May I proceed on a curved line of thought, O YOHANAN?"

YOHANAN: "Please proceed! Curves, Arches, Circles, Spheres, in motion all revolve along a straight line, the line of symmetry…"

ALBERT: "I shall then utilize our Archaeo-Linguistic tool."

YOHANAN: "I am curious!"

ALBERT: "Each letter of the alphabet, when vocalized, activates a vibration-sound, and each letter-sound activates a number-vibration-shape rippling in the whole universe, in its totality and integrality.

Look at this set of correspondences:[86]

1= Aleph 2= Beth 3= Gimel 4= Daleth 5 = He

6= Vav 7= Zain 8= Chet 9= Tet 10 = YOD

Letters and corresponding numbers are positioned according to their order in the Hebrew alphabet. Aleph, Beth, Guimel, etc. The Greek alphabet as well provides the exact same set of correspond-

[85] In vernacular Hebrew Tov means Good.

[86] Alphabet: unlike Latin letters designated by simple sounds Ae-Bee-Cee-Dee, all ancient languages designate each letter-sound by a word name. i.e. Hebrew: Aleph-Beth etc . Moreover, every letter represents a number used for calculation. Aleph= 1 Yod=10 Koph=100 etc

ences, Alpha, Beta, Gamma etc.[87] and so does the Arabic alphabet Alif, Bit, Gamal, etc.

In that 1 to 9 numerical series, each letter, from Aleph to Tet, produces a unique and singular sound resonating in the universal mind as a specific concept, a fundamental "idea", essential to understand our world, and to act within it.

By example the letter Vav signifies, and pulses essential Vigor and Vitality; letter Tet connotes motion and cyclical repetition of Time.

Furthermore the letter YOD, associated to the number 10, has a particular and exceptional function: *it activates the operative spiritual energies of the Universe,* so providing a super value and significance to all other letters in the series[88]. The resonance of YOD elevates the frequencies of all other letter-sounds, therefore lifting their effect from the material to the spiritual level. By elevation it transforms *ideas* into *ideals*.

Therefore, Rabbi, to your third momentous question: "Is the 10th Commandment a foundation for eternity?" The answer is: The number 10, and its associated letter YOD, elevate all substance to the realm of "ideality" and "eternity".

"Now, continues ALBERT, to answer the third question: If MOSES had *not* created a 10th Commandment in response to divine wish and expectation, what would have happened? I need more time and insight to think about that....

Would have humankind on Earth disappeared? By his decision, did MOSES save humanity from annihilation?"

"No, says YOHANAN, no destruction would have occurred. However, a sound base for humanity's evolution towards suprahumanity would have been missing. The path to immortality would not be wide open for human species. For ages, human creatures would have been dominated by local natural material laws, thus

---

[87] Alphabet: Latin language simplification has eliminated the name of the letters, and specialized a few to compose numbers (X=10, V=5 etc..)

[88] In the Hebrew Bible, the letter Y, with any added vowel, represent the Verb-Vibration through which the Creator activates the Creation. Genesis 1-3 va-Yo-mar adonai-Ye-hi-aur va Ye-hi-aur = then God said let there be light and there was light. Moreover Hebraic Tradition writes YY to represent Adonai, Yahweh, God.

subjected to the constraint of entropy[89], the apparently unavoidable continuous flow of decline. Men and women would not have had direct access to the powers of Divine Providence."

SIMHA: "So, Rabbi, humans would be nothing more than a force of nature among many others. Without supra-natural powers, that is to say dreadfully lacking cosmic awareness and afferent capacity of communication with elevated invisible spiritual beings, without the help of Providence, humanity cannot survive in the universal arena."

Says ALBERT: "Unaware of their spiritual origin, not voluntarily trekking the higher paths leading towards immortality, humans, individually and collectively, are *actually mortals*."

The Rabbi comments: "That's right! MOSES, put to the test by the Divine messengers, successfully reacted to their ultimate challenge. By using the most elevated thoughts and deepest intuition to rise up to the peaks of "cosmic receptivity", kabalist MOSES paved a high way towards immortality for each man and woman, then, now and forever."

SIMHA: "Great responsibility, exciting mission!"

I now call Albert's attention to the Rabbi's fourth question:

"MOSES definitely decided to add a tenth Commandment. Such decision in itself was necessary for building a sound structure based on Goodness, Beauty and Truth, a structure aiming at supporting humans on their way to immortality and eternalness. However, what would have happened if MOSES had proposed different contents, inscribed different words?"

ALBERT: "This is a difficult question. Can logic alone solve this enigma?"

Silence. I wait patiently. I know Albert will find a coherent answer to the riddle. Rabbi YOHANAN is waiting too, smiling gently.

We hear Albert's whisper, calling on his guardian Angel, presently imperceptible:

"O Angel HE-AA-YAH, help me!

---

[89] Entropy: gradual energy loss from use and time in a closed system, unless new energy input is being "provided" from outside the system.

Enlighten my mind,
Stimulate the creative jump that,
At the extreme boundaries of my logical mind,
Will lead my intelligence to the blooming gardens
Where the spirit of Truth rules."

Albert sighs deeply, closes his eyes for a long moment, then with a voice filled with new energy, says:

"After consultation with Angel YELIYAEL and my personal guide HEAAYAH, I feel authorized to draw the conclusion that nothing extreme would have happened. Regarding humanity's progress and future, the Tenth Commandment's *contents* were absolutely interchangeable."

The import of this statement shocks and alarms me. I feel confused and surprised by this paradox, not ready to accept or comprehend what it really means.

YOHANAN's eyes flash with delectation.

ALBERT continues: "Nothing dramatic would have happened. The contents of Commandments 1 to 9 have been dictated by the Divine envoy, but MOSES was free to enounce the 10th in many different ways, with totally different contents. Fundamentally the intent and goal of the 10th was *to exist*, establish equilibrium and create harmony. MOSES was an extraordinary statesman, a brilliant adept in social engineering as well as an Egyptian spiritual master, an enlightened cosmic communicator. He was a great leader and proved it later by governing for 40 years over a heterogeneous turbulent mosaic[90] of families and tribes, leading them, united, to the Promised Land. So, on Mount Horeb, he made a truly intelligent choice. He gave as a cornerstone to his monument the simplest formulation most apt to receive general approval, securing the consensus of all peoples.

Truly, at all times, in any circumstance, everyone possesses something, a something he or she does not want to be coveted and stolen; everyone wishes to be duly protected against his or her neighbor's envy and greed. MOSES thus chose to build the most

[90] Mosaic: word built on the word root Moses, synonym to medley.

solid fortress to protect *personal property*. And, consequently, by aiming at defending resolutely personal property, he installed extremely efficient strong fences against all depredations, deteriorations and, lastly, destruction of the spiritual monument he was contributing to erect, at the Divine's request."

YELIYAEL: "*As above so below! On the sphere of total reality, private property on Earth, as in Heaven, is a manifestation, and a symbol activating the endowment of uniqueness, individuality and personality for each created being.*"

ALBERT: "Enacting a Commandment to the effect of protecting the most common commodity, MOSES made everyone who owns anything become a vigilant protector and defender of that law.

Social delinquents, criminals, thieves, wrongdoers of all kinds ineluctably would encounter the owners' multitude high and powerful defensive walls, their law, and their strength. MOSES decreed the 10th Commandment *"Do not covet…other peoples possessions*", and the most formidable army took up arms immediately to defend that law.

Consequently, owners of women, servants, donkeys, oxen, and houses and things, gladly joined the "popular defense force" making the social law unshakable and indestructible."

Albert pauses for a moment, expecting remarks or comments. Neither I nor YOHANAN attempting to intervene, he continues:

"Intuitive MOSES knew that even before grabbing and hoarding someone else's possessions one has first to bring to mind and nurture *covetousness*, the morally impure *intent* of malicious appropriation. He thus did not choose to simply edict "Do not steal your neighbor's possessions", but, raising the stakes, he wisely stated: Do not COVET, a command to potential "coveters" to pause before acting rashly, and to reflect on the ethicality of appropriating someone else's property.

Astutely Master MOSES intertwined two laws into one, as the newly formulated Commandment wisely holds a puissant *ethical* imperative inseparably linked to a *judicial* law."

"A rare occurrence, indeed!" comments Rabbi YOHANAN, both

serious and sarcastic.

ALBERT: "Mostly, judicial rulings rely on tangible evidence and witnesses, involving physical senses only. By contrast, ethical judgments are founded on invisible, intangible notions of justice, authenticated by higher authority than man's."

SIMHA: "As illustrated by the TH = THeos=God composing the word eTHics."

ALBERT: "By choosing to insert a key ethical component in the 10th Commandment, MOSES offered humankind a firm spiritual rung at the base of the ladder of divine ascension. A first step indeed, at the beginning of a long journey.

And, although it stands at the bottom of the list, the 10th Commandment really deserves to be ranked first, from humanity's point of view.

Q.E.D! Quod Erat Demonstrandum!"

YOHANAN: "Your thoughts regarding the Tenth Commandment are remarkable, profoundly philosophical, highly ethical, brilliantly sociological. Albertov, you are well versed in genuine classical Greek and Roman culture, and you honor the masters who taught you, in Athens, Rome and Paris! The celestial assemblies are just now telling me how much they enjoyed the fireworks of your intelligence, exemplary illustration of the beauty and elegance at the origin of the prestige and fame of the land of France."

ALBERT: "French "esprit" is well perceived and beloved even on the celestial spheres?!"

"Mostly on the celestial spheres!" wittily exclaims the Rabbi.

YOHANAN now turns to me and requests my attention.

"Albertov charmed our minds, and to do so he reflected on the Tenth Commandment's common translation as well as the new information he had just received: this Commandment is at the same time ranked Ten and First, and its contents are of MOSES' conception.

Now, Shimeha, what would you like to add? By which blazing embers gathered from passing fiery comets will you illume the elegance and classic beauty of Albertov's argument?"

At this point I feel somehow uneasy, quite embarrassed. I understand Rabbi BEN ZAKAI is endorsing, through MOSES' 10th Commandment, the law protecting private property as a divine command.

I enter into the debate decisively:

"If this reasoning is published in our book, we have to expect, caustic and somewhat deserved criticisms from many modern readers! I ask permission from the Rabbi to present our defense case now, before it's too late."

"Go ahead! encourages YOHANAN. We are looking for truth, not unanimity! I agree with you that it is preferable to respond as soon as possible to inevitable objections."

SIMHA: "First expected criticism, a "political" disapproval: You are concluding that MOSES favors owners, at the expense of the economically disadvantaged.

Ah! The pushy modern social activists! I can already hear them screaming: Shame! Shame! Shame on you!"

RABBI YOHANAN: "And yet, there is neither shame nor guilt in protecting in good faith legitimate wealth and lawful ownership. Every individual is owner of something, starting with his/her own body; owners exist in great numbers, and the 10th moral injunction keeps away the strong-armed rulers, who are constantly tempted to covet almost everything, ready to take what they desire by sheer physical force. Protection of private property leads to more balance in the wealth and health of a society, and makes it less vulnerable to tyranny. To prevent the emergence of a "government by force" it is first essential to progressively weaken arbitrary measures and tyranny. Liberation and freedom then happen on their own.

MOSES created a true army of eternal defense, an unassailable fortress against tyranny, arbitrary measures, and dictatorship, thus opening a natural, progressive, subtle, underground pathway to all freedoms and liberations that shall forever be guided by the same moral principles that generated them.

SIMHA: "And there is a second criticism we must consider, this time from the "feminist" side: "You are exalting the value of a Commandment that portrays women as mere men's property, just like houses, oxen, donkeys, servants, and things!"

RABBI YOHANAN: "However one can justly argue that no "liberation" may happen by denying the spirit of the time. If at a particular period of human history, 3,500 years ago, women and servants were owned in the same way houses and donkeys, they had therefore to be equally protected by the same law. Had MOSES omitted the women on his list, he would have opened a loophole, with even more terrible consequences than those created by inscribing womankind in the law."

"We are, continues YOHANAN, drifting on an ever-stormy lake of opinions and shortsighted judgments. Socio-political activists are similar to business lobbyists: they mostly try to heavily tip the scale strongly to their advantage, never considering the necessity of general balance and global harmony. So much suffering could have been avoided at the beginning of the 20th century if the "Marxist activists" of your time had understood the Tenth Commandment is the First for humanity, the moral foundation of all organized societies. Each private property has to be protected not for its own intrinsic value, money and material wealth, which is relative and in constant flux, but in order to make everyone aware of the power of ethics, and the restraint it imposes on the many tyrants and criminals, the perpetual "coveters of power", cleverly dissimulated behind "abusive liberators". The defense of private property liberates humans from the "covetousness of coveters." That is its foundation and its *raison d'être*.

One can progressively and adaptively modify the "contents" related to property, and that is the role of evolution, but one can never allow shaking the principle itself by arbitrarily declaring a "revolution" against it. For, in this same principle is deeply ingrained the protection of *intellectual and spiritual freedom*, itself founded on the undeniable birthright to develop a unique identity and personality, the true *real personal property*.

Dramatic recent national tragedies on your planet have amply demonstrated that one cannot suppress personal property without simultaneously destroying the empowerment of personal identity.

Again, I firmly assert that, although the contents and items regarded as "personal property" surely must evolve in time, the fundamental underlying principle is a Universal Eternal Ideal."

Now Yohanan BEN ZAKAI, still and silent, is dreamily staring at the horizon, softly silhouetted by Mount Carmel's cascading blue hills. Tenderly embraced in his vision and ancient memories, we accompany him on his imaginary peregrination in gorges filled with countless majestic fragrant cedars, interspersed with giant eucalyptuses, their leaves shivering at the minutest wind breezing from the beautiful blue sea, called "mare nostrum" by the ancient Romans.

I myself let my imagination wander, freely sailing on famous Mare Nostrum in the company of Sumerians, Akkadians, Phoenicians, Greeks, Etruscans, Romans who shared the same feeling of liberty, all those sailors and explorers who, for thousands of years, have been blithely riding the waves of "Mare Nostrum", Our Sea, the Mediterranean. And we, celestial space-time navigators presently ashore in Galilee, welcome and enjoy the respite. After a long dreamy moment, the Rabbi now turns to me and requests my attention.

"SHIMEHA, what more do YOU have to say?"

21. The Cedar wood Tablets.

"O RABBI, I WISH TO ASK A FAVOR of you, a great one..."

"Only one?" he rejoins, both skeptical and amused.

"Would you tell us how MOSES went about adding a new Commandment, he who was so punctilious in obeying all divine instructions?"

"I noticed, says YOHANAN, that during your encounter, MOSES remained the secretive and humble man he always was. He did not tell you anything regarding the events that took place on Mount Horeb...Albeit all is recorded in the archangelic archives...So much happened there…"

We sense the Rabbi is going to give a long answer. Angel YELIYAEL is back hovering above us; Albert and I are spirit-united in anticipation of the revelation soon to emerge.

A childhood memory blooms in my mind: I am sitting next to my grand mother Rebecca; she is about to tell me a story from ancient times, when resilient donkeys carrying dried fragrant lavender flowers, roamed the narrow meandering medieval streets of Fez. Stories of rich palaces and mysterious harems, of young women forced to marry ferocious and cruel princes…and I, a five years old child, protected and feeling secure in the shady, quiet ancestral stone house, know those fears, troubles, and dangers are lurking somewhere else, and in another time, a long, long time ago…

Now the Rabbi begins his narrative: "Enthused MOSES, infused by the divine Word, received from the celestial choir each Commandment as a complete song, with singular title, theme, melody, and intonations. Each unique song-Commandment MOSES could hear with his heart and decipher with his mind.

The First title is Aa-Yo,
the Second Bo-Ta,
the Third Go-Cha,
the Fourth Do-Za,
the Fifth Ho-Va,
the Sixth Vo-Ha,
the Seventh Zo-Da,
the Eighth Cho-Ga,
and the Ninth To-Ba.

At first, MOSES was entranced by the magnificence of each song, its rhythm, and its melody and by the incomparable grandeur of each chorus. The chants were continually repeated for 40 days and 40 nights. MOSES never tired of them, and, completely distracted, missed the appointment he had with his brother Aaron who, along with his people waited in vain for his return, down in the valley.

Deeply charmed by the celestial uninterrupted chant, MOSES

was immersed in a powerful ocean of words and rhythms whose regular recurring movement was exciting and stimulating his human senses, with caresses, sounds, colors, smells, tastes. He also noticed other sensations, until then unknown to him, coming from the celestial world, permeating his heart and spirit. At first MOSES, concentrated his attention on each melodic command, separately.

Then, little by little, he began to intuit synchronizations and accords were forming. He noticed recurrences, similarities in style, outlines of a musical architecture; he progressively felt and became aware he was receiving in his heart and mind enough corresponding elements to identify a complete and unified symphony. Now, every time he inwardly relived each Commandment's melody, it seemed perfect. But if he paid attention to the overall polyphony, he no longer sensed and enjoyed the same wholeness and perfection.

Of course he was extremely happy, even ecstatic, but in the depth of his spirit, a tiny, indefinite oddity was taunting him.

Then suddenly, on the 40th night, a burst of light, a spiraling fire emerged from the sky, a fire dotted with LAMED[91] shaped diamonds. The intellectual and emotional bonds linking the nine Commandments flared up, and MOSES suddenly saw, by the grace of this illumination, there was a "gap" in the rhythmic flow.

The musical pattern was incomplete; the system was out of balance, since day one. The hiatus had been in front of him, around him, within him, since the beginning.

MOSES, infuriated, vigorously slapped his forehead, cursing himself with common Egyptian words edging on profanity. He had suddenly understood that no harmony was possible between the nine songs, because a tenth was necessary for the whole symphony to express the most perfect contrasting diversity as well as the most coherent unity."

"Observe, says YOHANAN, the song titles related to the nine

---

91 Hebrew Lamed=Latin L. Archaeo-Linguistic analysis reveals Lamed connotes Links-Lights-inteLLect. In current Hebrew the verb LAMED means Learning and Teaching. The design of the Hebrew letter Lamed evokes eLevation of the mind reaching out for the Heavens.

Commandments: the 2nd BoTa mirrors the 9th ToBa; the 3rd title Go-Cha, reverses as the 8th ChoGa, the 4th song DoZa reflects the 7th Zo-Da, the 5th HoVa is the harmonic companion of VoHa the title of the sixth Commandment. And here we see that the 1st Commandment AaYo, the creation's supreme song, the ultimate melody of all origins, had no contrasting companion!!! AaYo, the ultimate Verb of God, had no alter ego. AaYo called for YoAa to exist!

Thus MOSES understood! Tradition tells us he was the only man who faced the Divinity, because he heard God's messenger chant AaYo: "I AM THE LORD, THY GOD".

MOSES, feverishly, passionately, intensely endeavored to compose the song that was to become the 10th Commandment, titled YoAa, which really proclaims: I AM THE CELESTIALIZED MAN.

So, in the whole universe, the messengers of the divine and myriads celestial beings rejoiced in anticipation, eager to hear a human voice chanting a hymn, in tune with the harmonic music of the spheres, with lyrics aiming at projecting and elevating divinely endowed humanity.

MOSES, adept at all Muses' arts, composer, musician, linguist, poet, architect, and mathematician, was casting a melodious chant into the universal chorus. MOSES' ebullient mind imagined in a swirling vision the song, music and lyrics, rhythms and rhymes which would complete the divine symphony he had heard resonate for 40 days and 40 nights.

Human MOSES was to fashion the unbreakable link binding forever humankind to their Supreme Creator.

But, as the blazing flow of inspiration progressively recessed, MOSES gradually went back to being a humble, apprehensive man.

He wanted to tell the celestial messenger he wished to add a law. Forgetting the stimulating bursts of light and enlightening flashes of knowledge, even loosing conscience the composition of this song was commanded by the law of cosmic Harmony, a categorical imperative necessity, MOSES shied from his own audacity.

He wanted but did not dare inform the messenger that he was ready to add a song to the symphony. On Mount Horeb, on the 40th night, MOSES' body was trembling, his mind was vacillating, his intent was wavering. And, uncontrollably, MOSES was stuttering[92].

Stutter, indeed, but only temporarily!

So, stuttering MOSES informed the celestial messenger that he had had the boldness to compose a song of his own, in the name and for the benefit of all humans, present and future; as the messenger resumed beaming gigantic lightning flares and massive thunderous detonations that further terrified the peoples assembled in the valley, MOSES himself thought his last moments on Earth had come!

Then realizing the celestial hosts were powerfully expressing their own relief and joy, MOSES started to dance, twirling and stomping between rocks, blissfully."[93]

YOHANAN suspends his story telling for a moment, looks at his entranced audience. I am captivated by the tale, my mind traveling through the multiple recesses of time and space, catching ricocheting echoes of the celestial harmonies which, centuries ago, filled MOSES' heart and mind with wonder.

YOHANAN: "Finally, after forty nights spent on Mount Horeb, MOSES pulls out of his memory 9 + 1 songs, and artistically carves them on two tablets, in ARCHAE LINGUA [94], punctiliously obeying the celestial messenger's instructions."

SIMHA: "O Rabbi, could you explain why, as related in the Old Testament, MOSES climbed back Mount Horeb *a second time* to effectively collect all the Commandments he passed on to his people?"

YOHANAN: "OI VE, OI VE! You did perceive that gap in my recounting. Your memory of the ancient texts is flawless. You see, Shimeha, you are asking me to reveal a *sealed* secret. YEHOSHUA ben Myriam himself, Jesus, knew that secret very well, and out of compassion, he never revealed it. Or, more precisely, he revealed it to only two among his disciples, themselves sworn to secrecy,

---

[92] Stutter: popular tradition, and common biblical records mention Moses' stuttering bouts.

[93] Moses' dance on Mount Horeb emulated by King David and later by the Hassids, a Jewish group emphasizing joy and mystical ecstasy.

[94] Archae Lingua= well preserved in the Hebrew language.

whom he privately taught, each separately, before he began his public teachings."

THE RABBI then pronounces the words Albert and I feared to hear:

"My lips are sealed. I cannot answer your query."

"However, he adds, you, Shimeha, are fully cognizant of this particular concealed event, as I am sure you have picked up its reflection in the course of a celestial conversation, or perhaps in a dream, because everything essential happening on Earth is recorded in the spiritual and eternal archives."

SIMHA: "But do I have your authorization to unveil this event and disclose the truth?"

YOHANAN remains silent for a long moment. Angel YELIYAEL playing with the fluid early morning breeze softly moves his delicate waving veils, the sensitive leaves of the olive tree responding with a quiet rustle. And Albert, arms raised, eyes closed, seems to be requesting help from the skies. I am worried, fearing YOHANAN's approval as much as his refusal.

"Yes, Shimeha, I authorize you to unveil the hidden event; *your* lips were never sealed on the subject."

Feeling relieved, invigorated, I begin disclosing the secret.

22. Even Torah! Event Orah!

SIMHA: "AS REPORTED IN THE OLD TESTAMENT, after 40 days and 40 nights spent on top of Mount Horeb, MOSES trod down back to his people. Only, at that time, contrarily to what you reported in your story, O YOHANAN, he was carrying, with love and care, two tablets engraved with *9*, not 10, heavenly Commandments!

Down from the mountaintop, standing on a plateau offering a

panoramic view on the valley, a horrid tumultuous spectacle struck and stunned MOSES' sight, ears, heart and mind. Chaos, noisy drunkenness, boisterous general orgy, deafening exhortations to return to Egypt, lascivious hordes dancing around a golden Calf divinized statue, sad reminder of the Egyptian Apis bull symbol of deity.

In his absence, guideless and wary of the difficult life looming ahead, thousands upon thousands men and women were hiding their fright of an uncertain future awaiting them in the East behind this bacchanal celebration of the past good living they had recently forsaken in the West. Thus MOSES' peoples were, en masse, indulging in material sensuality, reliving, in their camps lying in scorching desert, the pleasures and ecstasies modeled from the rich, depraved blasé Egyptian materialists.

MOSES, enraged, lost control of his shattered emotions, and, smashed on a rock the *cedar wood* tablets he was carrying, making them forever unreadable.

But MOSES understood immediately the extent and depth of the loss created by his brusque, uncontrolled destructive act.

Thus, overwhelmed by the deepest compassion for humankind, present and future, MOSES resolutely climbed up again to the top of Mount Horeb. The next day at dawn, when MOSES rushed down back to the valley, he was carrying two hard *stone* tablets, carved by divine fire. And this time, the 10th Commandment had not been omitted!"

YOHANAN: "Even Torah[95]! Divine TORAH laws carved in stone!"

ALBERT: "Eventora" sounds like the Italian word Aventura, meaning adventure! Based on what you revealed so far, surely the advent of Even Torah unfolds like a real adventure, at the same time a journey, a venture, an exploration, a quest and an exploit."

YOHANAN: "So Shimeha, please continue, what happened that second time, on top of Mount Horeb. What did really happen?"

---

[95] Even Torah. Hebrew Even= Stone. Hebrew Torah=Law and wisdom. In Sanskrit= avantara means: unexpected happy event coming from the heavens.

SIMHA: "Here are more details reflected from the archangelic archives: *"The first time on the mountain MOSES was intensely entranced by the ideal beauty of each chant, its rhythm, and its melody, by the incomparable harmony of each chorus.*

Nine songs were continually repeated for 40 days and 40 nights. MOSES was utterly penetrated by the exquisiteness of each chant, at each recurrence immersing himself more profoundly in its beauty, craving the cyclical return of each enchanting melody."

"But, on that first sojourn on the mountain, in contrast with your narrative, O Rabbi, MOSES did not discern a structure, he did not distinguish a pattern, he did not perceive incompleteness, he did not sense a gap. To MOSES' exalted mind, supreme Beauty was hiding the supremacy of Truth.

Down from the mountain, faced with the abominable spectacle of degradation of goals and ideals presented by those same men and women he was to offer nine divinely inspired laws to guide them towards an elevated future, MOSES destroyed the message he was carrying.

Then, turning his back, walking away, MOSES suddenly, understood! It dawned on him as an epiphany: the origin of such degradation was simply the ecstasy overwhelming these men and women enraptured by the enchanting beauty of this Earth!

Artistically molded gold statues, jewels inlaid with the rarest, most beautiful shimmering stones and turquoises, colorful floating long veils, exquisite aroma of rich foods, exciting tastes of wines, golden and intoxicating beers, passionate beats on gongs and tambourines and rhythmic music accompanying the erotic dances of young virgins, had utterly bedazzled those men's and women's intellect, engulfed their senses into a massive delusive mirage.

Beauty had driven the peoples to meaningless and absurd pleasures, sexual orgies, fantasy inducing drugs, and excessive covetousness.

MOSES understood these peoples, craving for beauty mirroring Egypt, recreating times past and places recently abandoned, were enjoying goods, feelings, and emotions that belonged to others, and thereby were betraying their own identity, their new goals and ideals, at that time and at that place.

Coveting beauties that did not belong to them, these peoples were hopelessly losing themselves through their dependency on others. They had alienated themselves by absorbing foods that did not suit them. They had called on deities that could not guide them. These newly exiled peoples had forgotten they had assembled to finally be led to the promised land of Revelation and Truth. Only later, much later, would they find, and manifest their own Beauty, born of new long matured Ideals.

And MOSES, reminiscing his most recent personal experience on the top of Mount Horeb, relived his feelings of extreme ecstasy engendered by the beautiful celestial polyphonic songs delightfully swirling in his mind and heart. His own soul, intoxicated by Beauty had been blind to the Truth flickering in front of him.

He realized he had been himself seduced by the recurring entrancing rhythms of nine celestial chants, had wanted their repetition, their perpetual return, their comforting symphony. He knew then his soul had coveted the supreme spiritual nourishment his humanity was unable to absorb at that time.

MOSES then understood the tablets he had held in his hands were illuminated with celestial Beauty, but that he, MOSES, had not engraved them with all the Truth the Heavens wanted to reveal to humankind. He washed away any regret for having broken the cedar-wood tablets that carried an incomplete message.

Reflecting on the whole sequence of events, MOSES saw his people were not guilty, at least not more than himself. The peoples in the valley were exalting earthly beauty, celebrating the wonders of the *material world* only, while he, on the mountain, had been ecstatically engulfed in the irresistible splendor of the *spiritual world* only.

Neither himself nor the peoples had perceived the unbreakable eternal cosmic link bonding those two worlds.

Raising his hands, eyes moistened with tears, MOSES called upon the heavens to get a second chance. He received no answer! Admitting his guilt to the heavens, he set out to climb up, a second time, to the top of Mount Horeb.

The messenger from above was waiting for him, and MOSES humbly said: "I have come back. I wish to begin anew."

The celestial envoy gazed at him with skepticism. Was he coming back because he could not live without the resonating beauty of the divine melodies, or was he coming back because he had at last seen the Truth?

O Rabbi, we all know what happened next. MOSES went back to his people no longer with 9 Commandments, but with 10. This time it was the right number, and the Tenth Commandment, added by MOSES as harmonic human covenant, gift offered in exchange for the divine promise contained in the other nine.

And the message reads as such:

(((LOA TA CHAMOD))) (((BAYT RE ÊKHA)))
(((LOA TA CHAMOD)))
(((ESHET RE ÊKHA)))
(((VE ÂVADO VE AMATO)))
(((VE SHORO VE CHAMORO)))
(((VE KHOL ASHER)))
(((LE RE ÊKHA)))

Written in ARCHAE LINGUA this 10th Commandment may be transcribed as follows:

DO NOT *COVET* WHAT BELONGS TO YOUR NEIGHBOR,
DO NOT DESTROY *YOUR IDENTITY* AND AUTHENTICITY,
DO NOT DAMAGE YOUR *SOUL'S* EXTRAORDINARY POTENTIALS
BY ALIENATING IT THROUGH COVETOUSNESS,
LEADING TO BLINDING PLEASURES
AND EGOTISTICAL SATISFACTIONS.

YOHANAN: "Thus, through this human poem added to the 9 divine songs, MOSES declares firmly for the benefit of everyone, everywhere: *"I am a man representing the Universal Spirit in the material world of Earth. In the name of humanity, I pledge to renounce covetousness, satisfaction of my mortal ego, and start now my spiritual journey towards You, O Supreme Creator."*

"Now, continues YOHANAN, has come the precious moment I was waiting for! It is the reason I came here with joy to meet you,

O Albertov and Shimeha. Together, we shall translate and uncover hidden facets of the 10th Commandment, archived by the Archangels under the title: YoAa – I AM THE CELESTIALIZED MAN.

YOHANAN settles more comfortably at the foot of the attentive olive tree, arms around his knees, eyes sparkling with anticipation.

I feel nervous, although I try to appear calm and relaxed by controlling my inner tensions. During our encounter, MOSES had been very warm and friendly but mysterious, totally enigmatic. However, YOHANAN now appears determined to help us unveil the deeper meanings of the Tenth Commandment.

Meanwhile, Angel YELIYAEL follows with his dreamy eyes all the winged creatures flying around him, those close by, as well as those farther away: an eagle circling high on the warm air streams, a robin hopping from branch to branch, bees buzzing by, silent vibrating dragonflies…

YOHANAN: "As Angel YELIYAEL predicted at the beginning of your journey through deep time-space, Princess ARCHAE LINGUA is expecting our visit. Shimeha, look! The Princess is opening her treasure chest before us: like precious stones on purple velvet, brilliant flamed letters scintillate multifaceted essential meanings; Hebrew words embroidered on silky ribbons are profusely flowing over the rim, eager to free their limpid messages…

Shimeha, please, with your own voice, let ARCHAE LINGUA's accents resonate in the cosmos…"

SIMHA: "In Hebrew, the language nearest to the Stars' Language, the 10th Commandment begins by: LOA TA CHAMOD.

ARCHAE LINGUA's sound "LOA TA" is reflected in Old English as "LAW (for) THY". And the key word CHAMOD means, even in today's conversational Hebrew: to be utterly delighted, thrilled, enchanted, charmed.

Truly captivated was MOSES on Mount Horeb. He was so "entranced" by the beauty of the celestial chorus he had deserted both his people's expectations and his own human reasoning ability. Just as men and women in the valley were enslaving themselves under the attractive dominance of earthly pleasures, MOSES on the summit was succumbing under the relentless radiant charm of divine Beauty. His mind powers so weakened, MOSES had no science or conscience he could justly call his own. Thus MOSES started his Commandment by the admonition: LOA TA CHAMOD!

Do not submit your own self to enchantment!

Charmed, ecstatically covetous for more celestial Beauty, eager to continue drinking at the divine source, human MOSES had lost conscience of the necessity to express gratitude.

Overwhelmed by his desire to *receive,* MOSES had forgotten the cosmic law of balance and harmony: he had nothing to *give* in exchange for the abundant treasures he was *receiving*.

ALBERT: "If I understand correctly, covetousness is a state of unbalance, when one receives a present, even a gift from heavens, and responds to generosity with envy and greed. Instead of being thankful for what is given, one demands more, more often, one never stops coveting, constantly exacerbating one's desires."

SIMHA: "Yes, and this is a diabolical temptation, because a human being, generously surrounded by an aura of kindness and beauty, can use that radiance as an instrument of absolute power with the intent to covet, possess, capture, hoard, and take pleasure in what is not "him," nor "his," nor "for him."

ALBERT: "Or not "her", not "hers" and not "for her"."

YOHANAN: "This is why the Tenth Commandment says not to covet one's neighbor's *wife*, which symbolizes the abduction of beauty by vile kings; not to covet someone else's *home*, a place where one can securely rest and restore strength."

SIMHA: "Moreover, all types and forms of covetousness lead to dependency and alienation. Covetousness for too much safety leads to indolence and stagnation. Beauty's adulation can lead to blindness, almost always blocking awareness of other important essential ideals such as Goodness, Justice and Truth.

An excessive desire to procreate can destroy social equilibrium and engender immoral behaviors. Greed for earthly pleasures can become a source of corruption and extortion. Total dependence upon an instrument or a machine restricts access to authentic science and Truth. The uncontrolled drive to acquire and possess leads to tyranny, cruelty and fraud."

We pause, taking time to reflect on and examine the notions, ideas and wisdom emerged from our dialog.

Then YOHANAN addresses our Angel-navigator directly:

"O Angel YELIYAEL, I hereby thank you for the wonderful encounter you have made possible! Guiding Shimeha and Albertov from New York through time and space, you have brought them before me, under my familiar olive tree, on Israel's sacred land, and now I am indeed as happy as a wheat stalk watching its own grains germinating, maturing and goldening under the summer sun! O Angel YELIYAEL, I know that you patiently and brilliantly contribute to the reawakening of the celestial language, the Stars' Language, revitalizing ARCHAE LINGUA, throughout the inhabited worlds. Will you now decode for us more facets of the Tenth Commandment?"

Signaling his acquiescence, the undulating forms and colors of Angel YELIYAEL's perpetual movements progressively slow down; a few bright spirals of coherent orange light surround his aura.

Silence. Immobility.

Then YELIYAEL's soft and subtle resonances impress directly our minds, evolving into a brisk rhythmic medieval song.

In a slightly ironical, monotone baritone voice, YELIYAEL chants, simultaneously, in ARCHAE LINGUA as deposited by MOSES in the Ark of Covenant and in current translations: English, French, Latin:

Thou shalt not covet
Ne convoite pas   Non concupisces

thy neighbor's house,
la maison de ton prochain   domum proximi tui.

though shalt not covet
ne convoite pas   non desiderabis

thy neighbor's wife,
la femme de ton prochain   uxorem eius,

nor his manservant, nor his maidservant,
son esclave et sa servante non servum, non ancillam

nor his ox, nor his ass,
son bœuf ni son âne non bovem, non asinum

nor any thing that is
ni rien de tout ce qui est nec omnia,

thy neighbor's.
à ton prochain. quae illius sunt.

Suddenly changing tone, his voice becoming deeper, the melody opening up and amplifying akin to a Gregorian chant, YELIYAEL deciphers the 10th Commandment:

LOA: *Oh human, here is your LAW!*
CHAMOD: *when endowed with divine empowerment*
TA: *and divine grace attuned to your personal time cycle,*
BAYT RE ÊKHA: *you shall not use these supra-natural powers to impede your neighbor, by seizing his protective home and thus alienate him.*
ESHET RE ÊKHA: *You shall not use your power to seduce and take away his companion, light of his home on this Earth,*
VE ÂVADO: *nor take hold of his means of economic survival, his helper servant,*
VE AMATO: *neither separate him from the AMMA, the mother who raises his children, thus perpetuating his lineage,*
VE SHORO: *nor snatch his cow-ox which feeds him and labors for him.*
VE CHAMORO: *nor seize his donkey by which means he travels and explores the world,*
VE KHOL ASHER: *nor deprive him of his specific identity*
LE RE ÊKHA: *not meant to be yours, for what is meant to belong to another cannot belong to you at the same time.*

YELIYAEL's voice is progressively fading away, his chant now whispers a compassionate crucial advice: (((VE KHOL ASHER LE RE ÊKHA))

"Know that the powers you have received are powers you may not misuse by seducing, abusing, corrupting, or hoarding, for you would gravely disrupt and certainly impede the course of your own survival journey towards immortality."

RABBI YOHANAN: "YELIYAEL just offered us an enlightening interpretation focusing on the *moral-ethical* facets of the 10th Commandment. And, furthermore, the Angel elevates the message to *metaphysical* understanding."

SIMHA: "Adding to the value of the moral version, YELIYAEL is inviting us to broaden our field of awareness, hinting that the 10th Commandment's language contains precise knowledge regarding the highest aspects of Life, even immortal Life."

RABBI YOHANAN: "TOV! Now, Albertov, will you read and enlighten another facet of this wonderful Commandment?"

Hesitant, unsure about his ability to decipher such a long text, Albert opens the faithful scroll traveling with us since the beginning of our hermeneutic journey. Shy and modest in front of YOHANAN, we hear him call mezzo voce on Angel YELIYAEL, then on Angel HEAAYAH, his personal guardian Angel, asking them for help and inspiration in this Quest for Truth:

"Oh Angel HEAAYAH
My soul yearns to soar
Oh HEAAYAH
To the eternal Source of the Angels' Love.
Activate my will, inspire my knowledge
In the eternal thrust of the divine whirlwinds.
Oh Angel HEAAYAH
Ignite my courage,
Enlighten my freedom,
Illuminate for me the sublime ways
That rise from the Earth and join in the Heavens."

Once more Albert vocalizes the text in the ancient language:
LOA TA CHAMOD...VE KHOL ASHER LE RE ÊKHA.
Progressively we are experiencing a deeper and deeper state of

enlightened concentration, ARCHAE LINGUA's magical resonances rippling through space, preparing all open minds to receive the radiant fruits harvested in the celestial orchards.

Then ALBERT slowly begins:

"Wondrous divine wisdom is locked and sealed within the 10th Commandment, titled YoAa, as revealed by Rabbi YOHANAN, and translated with the help of Princess ARCHAE LINGUA as:

I AM THE HUMAN IMAGE OF THE ORIGINAL DIVINE CREATOR.

ALBERT sighs deeply, and continues:

"This tenth Commandment expresses a divinely clear, patent, fatherly advice, intended for each human being:

Do not give in to the temptation to go back to your HAMA[96], the warmth of your familiar HOME, once you have decided to exit through the gate that opens to new unfamiliar worlds.

Do not covet the person you were in the past, do not remain enthralled by your old material possessions whereas you have embarked on the path leading you to transcendental existence: LOA TA CHAMOD.

Soar, open your mind's wings and fly high, thrust into new worlds and rise, guided by the renewed awareness of your true primeval sources (LOA).

Do gracefully abandon your false certainties regarding your sources, inadequate beliefs, illusions that you only originate from TA CHAMA, delusions of being only an offspring of an earthly territory, a sweet home akin to fertile ancient Egypt CHAMA[97], believing you come only from the nourishing womb of your terrestrial mother (MA), replicated by your temporal HOME, warm shelter of your transient existence (TA).

---

[96] Hama or Homa is the root for many Hebrew words. Although apparently diverse they all indicate the same meaning, namely hom=Heat-Warmth; homa= native neighborhood, like home in English and Heim in German. Hebrew Re-hem=womb. re-hama=compassion. Almost identical words in Akadian, Aramaic and classical Arabic, deliver the same meaning.

[97] In ancient times, Egypt was called "the country of Chama", named after the people who lived there, the Chama people. Cham was one of Noah's three sons.

NO, (LOA)[98] that is not true, that is not the Law (LOA), for your real source is not only where you come from, not only earth, matter, animality and temporality (TA CHAMA), but your true origin resides also where you are heading to, the celestial transcendent dimensions to be attained by the high way of DA[99], entering through the cosmic threshold wide open before you, calling on you.

How to detach yourself from earthly ties? The same energies used to say NO (LOA), you can transmute into supreme YES, so responding to the appeal of the fundamental LAW (LOA).

Fired by a firm Intent, the forces of attraction will change direction. This is the LAW (LO-A): *do not covet, evolve*!

Do not regret what you leave behind while leaving the familiar old world, because you are heading to your new home (BAYT RE ÊKHA)[100], bonding in a new union, knowing a new spouse, the true heart and flaming hearth of your next home (ESHET RE ÊKHA).

Thus your former existence as a human-animal (CHAMA) will transform into divine-human (HA MADA).

However, when you step through the gate of Death (DA), I, the Divine Ultimate Diviner, advise you to take along with you, carefully engraved in your mind, the essential memories of your former existence: your distinctive physical forms and traits (BA), the structure and arrangements of the emotional and mindal house you inhabited (BAYT), your personal worthy actions and deeds (YA), and all details allowing to identify you as a valuable unique Human being (HAMA), a mortal pilgrim hovering on the edge of Time (TA).

Yet, responding to divine pull, your new self shall detach from your prior reality and become "other"; an alter ego who is partly yourself though different, like a familiar neighbor (RE ÊKHA).

Beware! Resist temptations! Do not covet the beauty, charm and safety of your past identity, now belonging to your "neighbor-

---

[98] Loa: In spoken Hebrew this word is used to say no. Fundamental Archae Lingua transcribes Loa into Law. Consequently, each Commandment commencing by Loa, simultaneously states what should not be done and what should be done.

[99] Da is the Greek letter Delta, the Hebrew letter Daleth, representing the doorway, the threshold, the world of transition.

[100] Bayt=Hebrew for home. re-ekha in popular Hebrew means '"your neighbor". In Archae Lingua re-ekha indicates all aspects of "Alterity", for good as for bad.

self"; do not claim your terrestrial origin as the *only* source of your being, lest you destroy all your capacities to rise, evolve, and raise a new, more expansive, eternal personality.

Yes! Know thyself, identify all your former possessions, the material and mindal wealth you have used and enjoyed during your sojourn on Earth, but I recommend that you freely detach from the past, according to the universal LAW-LOA of cosmic Harmony, the NO converting into YES, a conscious positive statement:

YES I WELL KNOW WHAT I AM LEAVING BEHIND, AND WHAT IS LEAVING ME, BECAUSE I KNOW TOWARDS WHOM I AM RISING UP.

That LOA-LAW is ever perpetual and cyclical. On the path to eternity, as you have passed a threshold and successfully entered a new world, whenever you transcend your obsolete forms, detach from your old habits and inclinations, I beseech you, O Novice, not to relinquish the powers of your individual intelligence, not to disperse the distinctive essences composing and texturing your true self, unique irreplaceable being in the entire universe.

At each stage of your everlasting evolution you shall gather new joys, new treasures, new feelings, new ideas and new ideals: those acquisitions are yours and no one else's.

On your way towards ME (LOA), during your cosmic voyage, do not covet the fiery beauty (ESHET) and wondrous brilliance (RE) of myriads other beings you shall encounter, do not envy their advanced knowledge (RE ÊKHA), do not covet their higher celestial station or the range of their spiritual influence, nor the distinctive properties owned by each of your heavenly neighbors, lest the spiritual structure of your own Self sways, and swings and bends, and finally disintegrates (VE KHOL ASHER LE RE ÊKHA).

The LOA-LAW commanding the eternal oscillations of NO-Death and YES-Birth, provides the everlasting energies necessary to elevate your true unique Self, your Soul, at each phase of your wondrous transcendental journey, experiencing recurring death and re-birth even as you are constantly drinking at the Sources of Immortality.

And, as you reach the gate of your ultimate human transience, as you approach the inner circles of divinity, boundaries of your future home, readying to receive the ultimate gift of Eternal Life, then, BEWARE!

Do not covet, even do not regret, your former and diverse states of existence, (VE ÂVADO VE AMATO VE SHORO VE CHAMORO), all forms by which you have been experimenting human terrestrial life and mortality."

Albert pauses, and very slowly sits down, signaling he has completed his interpretation, assisted by the inspiring vibrancies of ARCHAE LINGUA. Angel YELIYAEL's ethereal veils gently flutter in front of us, multiple pastel colors pulsing from the opalescence of his fluctuating shape. Rabbi Yohanan BEN ZAKAI remains immobile as a statue, his eyes sparkling, expressing extreme happiness.

I am intensely focused, my mind reviewing the bright paths of knowledge and consciousness generously opened by the Tenth Commandment, LOA TA CHAMOD.

I hear YOHANAN's subdued voice calling on me:

"Shimeha, I know you are a Master in the kingdom of YES, and Princess ARCHAE LINGUA is a good friend of yours! Surely together, acting as a team, you shall clearly enlighten new facets of the 10th Commandment!"

Fighting both stage fright and excitement, I take a deep breath and begin: "This Commandment, formulated by MOSES to the benefit of all humankind, reveals the covenant and pledge made by each individual with their Divine Creator:

At the time I leave the purely animal stage of my existence (TA CHAMA), transiting to enter a new supra-human habitat (BAYT), my new house, new temple protecting my Soul, to my self it feels as much foreign as familiar (BAYT RE ÊKHA).

I promise that, whenever I shall experience death-transience, becoming more and more fluid, flowing and malleable, my mind acquiring energy at the sparkling links of the universal mind (LOA), I shall not covet an abode that is not mine; I shall not covet any enchanting and beautiful tempting form glimmering in front of me, attracting me by divine fiery brilliance (ESHET RE ÊKHA), lest I burn and melt and my identity be lost forever (RE ÊKHA).

And I shall not covet all the privileges eternally conferred to Divinities: such as being utterly protected (BAYT), intensely loved (ESHET), immensely enriched (ÂVADO), lovingly served (AMATO), profoundly nourished (SHORO), limitlessly transported (CHAMORO).

On the contrary I shall act only in accordance with my current form and capacities, and with the language made available to me when I pronounced the sacred vow sealing my holy union with YOU (VE KHOL).

I vow to always present myself in front of YOU with my own coherent light, the ineffable link uniting my human experience with your Ultimate Radiance (ASHER).

Only then, shall YOU recognize my specific, albeit ever changing, personality, past, present, and future (RE ÊKHA).

And because Prophet MOSES' formulation commands me to constantly repeat my commitment at all levels of the expanding Universal Sphere, I assert once more the following:

I pledge, on my way to YOU, not to blindly impassionate with my other self (LOA TA CHAMOD ET RE ÊKHA). Which other self? The arrogant fake prince (RE), the impostor in me claiming to be the only source of Life (E) and only master of my destiny, Satan-like mutinous (LE RE ÊKHA).

I commit myself to preserving the flowing power of perpetual renewal YOU endowed me with from the Beginning (LOA TA CHAMOD), not to ever covet nor my former time conscious existences (TA), nor my oldest animal existence (CHA), nor my future Self, discoverer of immense divine worlds (DA).

And, fulfilling MOSES' prophecy, I repeat and reiterate again, my vow:

I promise to BE without envying (CHAMA), to LOVE without possessing (ESHET), to PRODUCE without destroying (ÂVADO), to LIVE without exploiting (ÂVADO), to NOURISH without killing (SHORO), to USE without corrupting (CHAMORO), to ADMIRE without degrading (VE-KHOL), so BEING ENLIGHTENED by blazing Beauty and PURIFIED by universal fires without being altered (ASHER LE RE ÊKHA).

Reaffirming my vow, I shall learn through honorable means to navigate the ever-pulsing cosmic circuits of universal fluids without ever renouncing the constancy of BEING (LOA) and I am committed to preserve and safeguard within me the Divine Light, spark of your Eternal Presence, without forsaking the irreplaceable value of my flowing human transience (LO-A)."

Silence.

I stop, because I have to eventually stop. However, I know this declaration of faith could surge indefinitely, like a river running by new shores while maintaining its essential unity, deeply conscious of being both unique and ever changing.

Silence.

I feel like dematerialized, my physical body replaced by a tenuous ethereal veiling, as virtual as Rabbi YOHANAN's presence here in front of me. Albert now appears to me like a pulsing multicolored aura, alternatively entering in and exiting from the ancient millenarian olive tree…

More silence.

Then Angel YELIYAEL casts a lavender-colored triple beam that ends crackling gently on YOHANAN's chest; and in my mind I distinctly perceive the Angel addressing him:

"*O Rabbi, we shall be grateful to hear you decipher and reveal the scientific Law of LIFE and DEATH encrypted in the 10th Commandment.*"

YOHANAN: "I am greatly honored by your request, YELIYAEL. And by now Princess ARCHAE LINGUA, awakened by our dialogs, is ready to deliver more secrets, unveil more knowledge, reveal more truth. Let's uncover another layer of the Universal Sphere:

"Although seemingly starting at the bottom of the evolutionary ladder, all human beings receive the gift of intelligence (LO) from their remotest, most ancient, and therefore most divine origin (AA); they so begin their ascending journey towards their own source of life, and this source becomes their ultimate purpose.

And now here is the law (LOA) unveiling and governing the essential stages of transience and journey towards the ultimate source of existence (LOA).

First, every human being shall transit through space, akin to an unconscious substance, carried by the orbs of cyclical time (TA).

Then after, the human being enters within the dimensions of conscious motions and emotions (CHA), expressed by actions and reactions within the maternal material matrix (MA), a necessary phase on the return journey to the original divine source (DA).

At this stage, under protection of the material envelop (BAYT), reborn human beings may appear to themselves as radiating princely inhabitants of their newly built personal palace (BAYT RE). Limited awareness convincing them they are the perpetual source of their own enjoyments, they become inebriated by self contentment, blinded by hubris, and inevitably fall into mental poverty and emotional destitution (Ê), the thrust of their mental quest weakened then suffocated by lack of aspiration for the original spiritual goal (KHA).

Enjoying more material delights, they covet more material possessions, cause of more material pleasure, enjoyment and bliss. Of course, living in a sphere where matter reigns, humans feel like princes and princesses, enriched by material wealth, basing value solely on abundance and profusion.

At this stage, humans are in the greatest danger of destruction and annihilation (LOA). Unaware of their true elevated goal, they seek material perpetuity, in vain, because their means of self-reproduction on Earth (TAMA) only produce the same by the same, leading to the most degrading desire and love (TA CHAMA), self-love, by oneself, and for oneself.

However, thinking and acting in accordance with universal law (LOA) it is possible to twirl and detach from this destructive cycle, and discover the apparently hidden channel leading to sudden *transmutation*. Thus material human nature, spiraling in the whirlwinds of infinite spiritual forces, releases density and reaches the magnetic moment allowing each soul to attract and internalize the divine science, the total intelligence of the Divine Law (MADA).

Then they can cross the threshold (DA) the Supreme Creator has always kept available to them, within them, eternally open yet temporally invisible.

By opening the door themselves, humans then experience the ultimate cosmic drama (DA):

They discover that their BAYT, their own house which, more than enveloping them, gives shape to their existence, belongs to the Universal Union of all living beings (LE RE ÊKHA).

And that in each new house they shall inhabit, they can enjoy everything, but take possession of nothing.

Experiencing that, at the time of their physical, mental, and intellectual death transition (LOA), when finally they decide to abandon the illusion of indestructibility (LOA) and free (LO) their Soul (AA), they discover that true fluidity of being (LOA) is not acquired by one's body abolition (MATA).

Every human being then experiences the universal drama, or darama, the fact that, in truth, dissolution of the material body (MATA), the womb and physical form in which the Soul, the celestial newborn child, has grown (MADA), does not guarantee immediate and eternal enjoyment of blissful satisfactions, heavenly pleasures and ineffable happiness."

LOA TA CHAMOD BAYT RE ÊKHA ESHET RE ÊKHA, VE ÂVADO VE AMATO VE SHORO VE CHAMORO VE KHOL ASHER LE RE ÊKHA.

"Therefore, continues the Rabbi, death is neither the appeasing and lethargic dissolution some people expect, nor, as other dream of, the doorway to a land of constant happiness and eternal bliss."

ALBERT: "So, what is Death? Does the Tenth Commandment reveal its secret?"

YOHANAN: "Yes, and for many temporal beings, for many humans who are now going through their earthly stage of life, that revelation may be disappointing, because apparently too obvious.

Actually, *Death is,* simply and wholly, *Pure Life.*

Death is ultimate continuity of all continuities. It is continuity through intelligence, not through matter; through unifying and sharing, not through selfish, divisive acquisitions. Death does not change us into anything different, it does not alter or adulterate us.

Death leads to total integrity and integrality of Self."

YOHANAN continues to translate from ARCHAE LINGUA, resuming his celestial meditation: LOA TA CHAMOD

"What a marvelous resonance! It signals that when the extraordinary transience towards a renewed Life begins after material Death, every human free will is confronted with a fundamental choice.

Individual human can either quietly forget everything and let dissolve the identity experienced during the course of physical, psychological, and intellectual life (MATA), or fight on vigorously and energetically to open up new supra-physical, supra-mental and meta-physical senses that connect the soul to the souls of many living beings in the limitless eternal universe (CHAMOD).

This latter choice projects humans towards a new life, livelier than their former life, in which divisive time (TA) is changed into unifying time (DA)."

SIMHA: "Does MOSES describe the passage and transfiguration from mortal creature (TA) to divine creature (DA)?"

YOHANAN: "Yes, MOSES describes that passage clearly with the word CHAMOD. The true home of the soul emerges from the emotional life, feelings, sensations experienced in the enveloping, protective, warm, affectionate womb, combined with the structural force of the mind, supernal ideas and universal ideals.

Pristine emotions and crucial thoughts produced during an unfolding lifetime constitute the rich living experience transmuting matter's spirit into mind's spirit (CHAMO-HAMO)."

YOHANAN adds: "On the way from mortality to the worlds of immortality, and then towards the spheres of eternal essences, there are many traps, dangers, and obstacles. Not because the Creator felt like setting up obstacles there, but because of the very nature of the universe's creation, as corollaries to universal existence."

I feel Albert is, as I am, enthralled, fascinated. To follow YOHANAN's description is like rehearsing one's own future passages from Life to Death to Life.

"What are those dangers?" I ask.

The Rabbi resumes his scientific decoding:

"If along the road, on this pilgrimage to the supreme sources of being (LOA) we were to regret, covet and take along our past habits, our materialistic urges, our bygone secure houses, our companion's attractive loveliness, our helpers' kindness, our assistant's loyalty, our instruments' performance, the colors, savors and fragrances of the foods we loved, and if we also were to covet, therefore carry along with us only scientific certainties, or only mystical ecstasies, enormous, then, insurmountable would be the temptation to stay put on the way, overpowering would be the lure to abandon all intent to move up, migrate, and transmigrate.

In short, we would reach the dead end of *stagnation.*

This Commandment, "do not covet", is valid for all acquired experience and knowledge in all dimensions: human development and progress, collective history on Earth, unique personal legends, including survival adventure in the Quest for Eternal Life.

Hampered by utter stagnation in a single existential dimension, humans would remain mortal, and yet they would maintain the illusion of being immortal, deceptive self-idolaters.

However, whenever humans become aware of the Law (LOA), recognize the powers of universal values and do not indulge in self-adoration, or in adoration of self as reflected in others, then shall they successfully, safely, traverse the ultimate fire of purification, the Acheron[101], the ever-flowing stream of mutation, transformation, transmutation, and transfiguration (ASHER).

Beyond the purifying river, transported and elevated by celestial messengers, the triumphant Soul becomes a spiritual essence, attracted by perfect and total differentiation, (LE RE ÊKHA), the true Other, the authentic Neighbor, the King Father of the Universe, the Unique Creator of Life, who engenders and sources everything in His own neither similar nor comparable image, the One who does

---

[101] Ascheron: Greek mythology: river of Hades on which the dead humans flow in the underworld. Note similitude with Hebrew word asch-er meaning fire, transformative power, trans-mutative energies.

not covet anything or anybody, and that nothing or no one can covet.

Thus those human mortals who opt for survival on immortal worlds (LOA), not burdened but clearly identified by their unique emotions, distinctive thoughts and spiritual insights composing and integrating the totality of their temporal experiences (TA), turn their Soul's eye towards the abode of the Supreme Deity, and rejoice at the prospect of entering into the house of the Ultimate Other, the Extreme I AM (CHAMOD BAYT RE ÊKHA).

Therefore, being ever conscious of the universal principles underlying the 10th Commandment, the High Path pilgrims shall reach the threshold of the Highest Abode. Each splendid personality now adorned with all fundamental knowledge and cognitions, insights, foresights developed during their trans-universes peregrinations, constantly gaining energy by questing, questioning, loving, enjoying life multiple experiences, freed from the alienation of "coveting", which would dissolve their personal coherence and mastery. Living fully but consciously forsaking *covetousness*, each human being intentionally preserves his personal liberty unscathed, intact, integral.

Knowingly renouncing covetousness every ascending human shall be truly independent, inalienable, non-exploitable, shall no longer be limited to being a hearth confined to an earthly home (ESHET), to the role of protector (BAYT), a pure instrument of reproduction (AMA) of the same by the same (MAMA), nor shall he be reduced to being a functioning automaton (ÂVADO), made of expendable substance (SHORO), limited to the role of a subservient servant (CHAMORO).

Eternally aware of the 10th Commandment's significance, at all levels of cosmic progression, the new human attains the rank of King and Queen, equal in science and nobility to all other divine beings engendered by the Universal Father (LE RE ÊKHA), forever the eternal source of coherence and intelligence.

(((LOA TA CHAMOD)))
(((BAYT RE ÊKHA)))

(((LOA TA CHAMOD)))
(((ESHET RE ÊKHA)))
(((VE ÂVADO VE AMATO)))
(((VE SHORO VE CHAMORO)))
(((VE KHOL ASHER)))
(((LE RE ÊKHA)))

Enlightened and guided by the 10th Commandment, humans may finally reach the true Promised Land, the land promised by the Divine Higher One, EL ELYON, to their ancestors, to be theirs forever. Then, and only then, will they be freed from Egypt[102], the land of bondage."

And the RABBI adds, smiling broadly:
"As likewise proclaimed by the 5h and the 1st Commandments."

23. The Farewell Song.

YOHANAN BEN ZAKAI IS SITTING STILL, meditative. Albert and I remain silent, both continuing our inner voyage on the path traced by YOHANAN and MOSES. The meaningful sounds of ARCHAE LINGUA echoing in our open minds, continuously deliver more enlightening messages, unveil more helpful knowledge, offer more caring guidance. LOA TA CHAMOD…VE KHOL ASHER…
Each letter, each syllable, each word a signal, a beacon, a guiding light, a compassionate encouragement on our ascending cosmic journey beyond time and space.

[102] In the Old Testament, Egypt is named Mitzrayim. Archae Lingua reveals this word means: the maternal enclosing egg-womb from which one must exit using great physical power. It also evokes the pain felt at leaving the comfort of enveloping waters: mi=waters / tzar=constricting shell one must break to exit/ yam=maternal comfort. Egypt Mitzrayim is justly symbolizing "extrication from bondage and stagnation".

I look around me. The day has gone by ineluctably, the soft and subtly scented spring sun is disappearing behind the horizon. Grasses and plants are fluttering, happily awakened from their afternoon languor by the fresh evening breeze. Trees rustle songs towards celestial heights. Rocks lean comfortably on their dark shadows, preparing for a peaceful night.

More silence.

Angel YELIYAEL is nowhere to be seen. The Rabbi and Albert stand up. I become aware my friends are expecting something from me, a simple word of farewell perhaps, before we part.

It is then I realize something remains to be said, not on the Tenth Commandment, wonderful poem MOSES composed, but regarding Master MOSES himself.

Taking a deep inspiration, I commence:

"MOSES represents the very essence of the new man. On Earth he was a Prince guided only by universal principles, a High Priest, initiated to all sciences of Egypt's temple-universities, who dedicated his terrestrial life to humbly serve the Divine by serving His creatures in the universe He has created.

Therefore MOSES composed the Tenth Commandment with specific sounds, letters and words, choosing those signaling the way of the pilgrim who willingly renounces everything in order to freely adhere to the universal Father's will.

MOSES relinquished social and religious power, and freely submitted to his Creator's absolute supremacy, following to the letter the message and teachings of the Messiah who would come 15 centuries later to make the humblest creatures witnesses of the glorious presence of the Divine amongst them on Earth.

And this is why MOSES, perfect human, reached the worlds of immortality without experiencing common Death, neither physical dissolution, nor corporeal degradation, thus reflecting and embodying the hymn to ultimate freedom he composed and sang on Mount Horeb. The Supreme Divine Judge has found that nothing of transiting human MOSES was to be taken away or added."

Carried away by my own emotions, I had not realized that

YOHANAN was weeping, and Albert sobbing. Sideways I looked at YELIYAEL's white vaporous shape; his wide-open liquid eyes turned towards the darkening horizon, the Angel was throwing thousands of purple beams, some illuminating the fiery orange-yellow hilltops. He too was deeply moved.

We are totally engulfed by an immense melancholic cloud. To be here, apparently separated from the Creator by the limitless Time-Space oceans of cosmic evolution, and at the same time so intimately united to Him by the unbreakable link of Love!
After several minutes of total silence, I say to YOHANAN:

"O Rabbi, we are going to part soon. Will you accept to instruct us just a little more? For you lived on our planet at a crucial time, a period of great revelations, passions, fervor, zeal and corresponding fanaticisms.

You were born around 6 BC, in an era that witnessed two other important births: JESUS-YEHOSHUA ben Myriam, and John the Baptist –Yohanan BEN ZAKARIA.

You lived on Earth during an extraordinary vibrant apostolic epoch, an era thriving with amazing promises. You witnessed Jerusalem Temple destruction, sacked and burned by order of Roman Emperor Vespasian, in 70 AD.

Prudent and resilient, you survived this tragedy and insured the continuity of Jewish science and wisdom, creating the first "post-temple-destruction" great Talmudic academy, the school of Yavne. After you, through you, Israel's Judaism was transformed. It abandoned its degraded priesthood, senseless animal sacrifices and religious corruption.

You allowed the Jewish people to recover the very essence of its original purity of purpose that was brought to the Promised Land by MOSES and his pioneering peoples.

Thus you purified and enhanced Israel's spirituality, ridding it of its historical plague represented by fanatical Judean sicariim and Zealots, and all sorts of extremists who first and foremost covet only political power.

You also peacefully destroyed the influence of the Tsadokkim, inheritors of the oppressive religious hierarchy. You neutralized the bigot and hypocrite orthodox Pharisees.

The school of Yavne you founded in a time of reigning pain and terror, taught and enlightened for three centuries, generation upon generation of learned students and Rabbis who consistently promoted justice, knowledge, tolerance. They became the bearers of intellectual faith, which combines unhampered intellectual freedom with unhindered intuition of the divine presence and consciousness of cosmic human destiny.

At the Brur Hayl school, your second academic foundation, the first modern Universal Judaic Academy, you became the teacher of the future famed masters of Kabalah and ancient primordial theology, reconnecting thus with the antique knowledge of Mesopotamia, Jerusalem, Memphis, Delphi, reviving all purposes that had been forgotten by peoples' failing memories and dishonest historians, most of them servants of oppressive powers.

And paradoxically, the transformed new Judaism you revealed embodies almost perfectly the core of YEHOSHUA ben Myriam's teachings…"

YOHANAN lifts his beautiful and compassionate left hand with authority, stops my impetuous verbal flow before I openly reveal the underlying currents of my thoughts. Then he says, his voice even and soft:

"I understand perfectly what you are saying, Shimeha, and I can see where you wish to lead this conversation. I approve of it, but I cannot authorize it.

To you Shimeha, and to you Albertov, I can avow the visions filling your hearts are truthful, coming from unadulterated sources.

However, for your own protection on Earth, your respective Guardian Angels firmly instruct me to close all discussion on the subject. Your planet is as yet deeply permeated with intolerance. Fundamentalists from all sides are more insidious and sinister than you may perceive. Universal unification is barely a whisper, often nothing more than hypocritical wishes, half-heartedly uttered by numerous men and women harboring hateful, divisive and aggressive intents.

The good way of the heart is still narrow and constricted; the luminous beam of cosmic awareness does not have yet the density, intensity, or openness necessary for a reversal of attitudes and emotions. Later, I know, you shall come back to me.

Profound changes are occurring on your planet, and the New Age dream is not an empty ideal. Judaism, Christianity, and Islam, a Trinitarian revelation is in the process of unification.

Taoism and Buddhism, American and African Shamanism, scientific spiritualism, all are going to open up to everyone's understanding.

However, you shall have to wait patiently for the burning inferno of base instincts to lose its momentum. Then Truth shall take root on your planet, Isolation will end, Unification with all other worlds will start."

Stillness.

We are prolonging the silent pause in a vain attempt to indefinitely delay the ineluctable parting.

Finally we embrace, YOHANAN, YELIYAEL, Albert and I, the way celestial beings do: our auras intermingle and fuse, a soft and crystalline melody fills the air, musical notes emanating subtle floral fragrances, densely saturated with orange blossom aromas.

We all silently give thanks to the land of Israel, the beloved land of recurring revelations, our generous and glorious host for that munificent encounter with Masters Yohanan BEN ZAKAI and MOSES.

In the mist of our reverie, the harmonic sounds of two Keltic harps tenderly permeate our senses, and note after note, as the melody unfolds, myriads speckles of light materialize above us, drawing progressively the shape of a simple golden crown.

And from above, the male voices of King David and King Salomon, in full accord with the high-pitched thrills of Prophetess Myriam, now sing for us:

BOHI BE	*Farewell in peace*

SHALOM[103]	*Vessel of Revelation.*
ÂTERET	*Listen, O my beloved,*
BA ÂLLAH	*Come, O come back to me.*
GAM BE	*This joyous chant*
SIMEHA	*transports our souls*
BERINA OU BE TSA	*To the kingdom of*
HALLAH	*sacred wisdom.*
TOKH AYMOUNE	*Among your faithful followers,*
ÂM SEGOULAH	*O Liberator,*
BOHI KALLAH	*Unveil your purple heart,*
BOHI SHABAT	*Resplendent lys of light,*
MALKETAH.	*Shining in the immense*
	celestial heights.

[103] Bohi be shalom: last verse of the Poem Prayer lekha dodi ("to you o my beloved), always chanted at the beginning of Friday night prayers.

Chapter Four

In the Void

24. A Star Named Yoella.

BROKEN HEARTED WE PARTED. Earlier Rabbi YOHANAN let us know his soul and our souls were offspring of the same spirit matrix; he promised we would reconnect with his "presence" later, perhaps before our final departure from Earth, and we felt comforted. He whispered those words while Angel's YELIYAEL subtle rays of love decisively pulled us toward his crystalline dome, as we were entering into the cosmic journey's trance.

We enjoyed a long last melancholic look at the small Galilean vineyard, miraculously shielded from the frenzy of modern buzzyness at least for the time of our meeting. Then, all of a sudden, before we could express more of our sincere gratitude, the Rabbi was gone. No one was keeping company to the centuries-old olive tree, the vines recording no human voices, the grass blades already bending under the thrust of nightfall.

Before the Rabbi vanished, I asked if he would provide Angel YELIYAEL with the precise coordinates of our next celestial interlocutor. As MOSES did, I was certain YOHANAN would move his hands and fingers, in coded motions our Angel navigator-vessel would instantly decipher.

YOHANAN, surprised: "What coordinates?" said he.

I remained speechless. And yet, on second thought, why would he provide us with our next interlocutor's time-space position?

Just because MOSES did it?

"Could you at least suggest whom we should visit next to decipher the 9th Commandment?"

"The detours of your voyage do not concern me" answered YOHANAN. Noticing our disappointment, empathizing, the Rabbi patiently explained:

"In the celestial forum, I study, conceive and polish mind's diamonds on a virtual sphere whose lights are perceived as far as the central Isle of Paradise. This sphere represents, in the universe, the First human Commandment, which is the Tenth on MOSES' tablets."

"Do you mean, O Rabbi, that your sphere is named LOA TA CHAMOD- DO NOT COVET?"

"No, my sphere is called YOELLA. And any human soul rising from Earth, or elsewhere in the Universe, may at will attain this sphere by an instantaneous, unique and gigantic leap. YOELLA can be reached by a living man or woman, without passing through carnal death transition, if during physical life (CHAYIM) that being is capable to penetrate the deep true meaning of the Commandment DO NOT COVET."

The Rabbi continued: "MOSES was and is a super mind, a GENius, GiaNt in the celestial forum, a GENeral, a GENeric personality, a GENotype founder, who went straight from Earth to the garden of eternal genes.

In ARCHAE LINGUA this Garden is called GAN ADAYIN[104], literally translated as: "the GENes of eternity", genes which release the faculty for eternal soul survival. Because of his GENerality, MOSES is forever concerned by the Ten Commandments in their totality, including the actual and potential forces as well as any real and virtual presences springing from them. MOSES is the genotype of each element composing the global phenomenon of the Ten Com-

104 Gan Adayin, commonly known by Hebrew speaking people as Gan Eden, and English speaking people as Garden of Eden.

mandments. I, Yohanan BEN ZAKAI, am a specific celestial being, inhabitant of, as well as inhabited by, the sphere YOELLA. And my current name is actually YOHANAN BAR YOELLA, YOHANAN MASTER AND CREATOR OF YOELLA."

Those were the Rabbi's last cryptic phrases. Tears yet flood my eyes and cheeks whenever those words resurge in my memory. Far from Rabbi BEN ZAKAI and from Galilee, an immense regret came over me, which I shared with Albert:

"Had we been informed beforehand of MOSES' GEniality, we might have asked him to provide YELIYAEL with the coordinates of each sphere corresponding to each Commandment! Therefore we would have known in advance whom celestial inhabitant we would be visiting next!"

Silently, I prayed Angel YELIYAEL to reconnect us, through the celestial mindal network, directly with MOSHE RABBENOU, MOSES, for a new round of questions-answers.

Tiny ruby red sparks flashed on my retina, sure sign that no providential road would open up for us toward this "goal–kavanah"[105].

So, alone, we were now launched onto the cosmic scene, like circus acrobats with no safety net. Our projected journey was supposed to evolve in the correct direction, using the right energies, with a perfectly calculated force. However, no one was here to provide us with accurate space-time coordinates.

Where are we going? With no celestial guidance we feel like pilgrims traveling with no map and no compass.

Our glorious Quest for the true meaning of the Sacred Ten is reverting to a crude rudimentary investigation led by two detectives equipped only with the rough magnifier of sheer reason.

[105] Kavanah= in Hebrew means a goal, and more precisely a directional intent.

25. Interlude.

SUDDEN INSPIRATION! LET'S GO TO PARIS! "I suggest we take a few days rest in Lutece! We would stroll in the Tuileries garden, cross over the River Seine on the Pont-des-Arts, meditate in Notre Dame Cathedral, linger over a French café-croissant breakfast at an outdoor bistro, be Parisians again! Moreover, our friend Marie Tania will surely be there, as she always spends her summer vacation in Paris. She is high-spirited, and always ready to share in a lively conversation."

"And, concurs Albert, currently Marie Tania is the only person to whom we can reliably confide anything about our recent historical and metaphysical discoveries."

Thus, perceiving our agreement on direction and purpose, Angel YELIYAEL slowly extended a sky-blue ray of light, in the form of an access ramp, inviting us aboard, guiding our steps towards two dimly illuminated cradles. Relishing in the warmth of the familiar seraphic embrace I heard YELIYAEL whispering: "*Earth, France, Paris, July 1st 2000 AD*".

Instantaneously we find we are gently hovering high above the illustrious immense architectural island, ringed by successive boulevards retracing the paths of old times defensive walls, traversed by the calm albeit potent flow of the meandering Seine River.

YELIYAEL: "*We are presently flying above the city of Lutetia[106], which Julian[107] the Roman general and philosopher valued as a sanctuary for resting, thinking, writing, to devise social reforms, and bask in the glory of his military exploits; that small city later mysteriously renamed Paris.*"

---

[106] Lutece, Lutetia: name of Paris before and during the Gallo-Roman era.

[107] Julian, born in 331 AD was a man of unusually complex character: he was "military commander, theosophist, social reformer, man of letters". Furthermore he became Emperor of Rome (355-363 AD).

We have landed at the heart of the Quartier Latin, right at the corner of Boulevard Saint Michel and Rue des Ecoles, a few steps from the Sorbonne University, our alma mater.

What a wonderful gift, O Angel YELIYAEL! So tender a thought, mixed with energizing angelic humor. As this is the exact location, the exact street corner where Albert and I met and loved each other at first sight, commenced our uninterrupted philosophic, poetic, spiritual dialog, decades ago. A predestined encounter? Two pilgrims suddenly recognizing their eternal soul mate?

Since then we are traveling companions, united by our passion and common purpose: to discover more of the Truth hidden beyond appearances.

July 2000! YELIYAEL, aware of our uncertainty regarding the continuation of our quest, was offering us a celestial gift, a pilgrimage at the source of our ardent continuous love.

As we stepped out of the Angel's white translucent aura, for a short moment there, on the large gray concrete sidewalk, the shiny golden sphere opened in its center, each side elongating slowly into diaphanous iridescent wings. But neither too-rational students, nor too-busy street merchants, or too-hectic tourists, no one in the famed Quartier Latin[108] seemed to perceive the amazing magnificent spectacle unfolding before their eyes in the light of day.

We had come down to Earth, literally and figuratively, but the presence of Rabbi Yohanan BEN ZAKAI was still lingering in our psyche, the words of MOSES yet echoing in our hearts, and indeed on our cheeks, tears of farewell had not yet dried.

A fine July day in Paris; rare long white clouds swirling on a deep blue sky, a refreshing soft breeze stimulate a desire to stroll.

Our familiar traveler's light backpack materializes on Albert's shoulder, and I pick up the mobile phone. I am calling Marie Tania:

"Allo!"

"Bonjour Marie Tania!"

---

[108] Quartier Latin = Latin Quarter, location of Universities and Colleges since the 12th century, when scholars were speaking mainly Latin.

"Simha! Where are you?"
"In Paris, the three of us!"
"Come over, vite, quickly!"

Marie Tania was home, and immediately available for a long conversation with friends; very excited, waiting, eager to be updated on the progress of our time-space journey "on the wings of the Angel", as we have not contacted her since our departure from Manhattan to Mount Nebo.

We walked leisurely along the Seine River, passed near Notre Dame, made a detour by Rue des Blancs Manteaux[109] as a salute to the medieval Knights Templar who once maintained headquarters here, reached the old Marais district, where our friend lives whenever she stays in Paris.

We converse as we walk:

ALBERT: "The Order of the Knights Templar[110] is named after the Temple of Jerusalem, where nine French knights are known to have established their general headquarters at the time European crusaders conquered the old city…"

SIMHA: "About 1,000 years after the destruction of Jerusalem's Temple by the Romans and Yohanan BEN ZAKAI's daring escape..."

ALBERT: "Their first headquarters situated in Jerusalem, then general headquarters in Paris! A sure sign these two famous cities are linked, in spite of geographical and cultural remoteness."

YELIYAEL: "*The first nine French knights did more than reside in the monument's ruins. They conducted extensive researches and secret explorations below the Temple, discovering hidden tunnels, chambers…artifacts, appliances, maps and written documents…To accomplish their mission's true secret goal, as defined by abbot Bernard de Clairvaux, they spent most of their time underground, below the Temple's ruins…Nine years they stayed...* "

---

[109] Blancs Manteaux: the Knights Templar wore a White Cape. The street name reminds that Knights Templar Order was headquartered in this area of Paris, until the destruction of their order by the French King Philip le Bel, in year 1307 AD.

[110] In French designated as "Ordre du Temple", order of "The Temple" (of Jerusalem).

SIMHA: "Upon the knights' return to their abbey at Claivaux, their numerous carts loaded with ancient manuscripts and scrolls, the elite Cistercian monks went eagerly to work. Maps and drawings were assiduously studied, various mysterious appliances diligently reverse engineered, ancient obscure texts deciphered."

ALBERT: "Soon thereafter, and under the impulse of Bernard de Clairvaux, majestic cathedrals surged and mushroomed from the ground. All over Europe, France, Germany, England, Spain, Italy; audacious belfries conquered the skies, high pillars supporting elegant spectacular ogival ceilings relieved the lateral walls from excess weight, allowing opening of large windows for daylight to flow inside, glasses stained with eternal primary colors glorifying the sun rays as they reached immense frontal roses…"

SIMHA: "On construction sites, all architects, master builders, artisans, masons, sculptors, artist glaziers, of diverse origins and races were communicating in a single mysterious language, the "argot"."

ALBERT: "That lingo was mostly oral and a well guarded secret shared only by those involved in the "Renaissance Mission". Only rare writings in that language by medieval free spirit "escholiers" have been found. But, miracle, it remained alive until today thanks to its absorption in the Parisian "slang" used by the "bad boys" to avoid detection of their plans and misfits!"

SIMHA: "And, many words in that language sound like ancient Hebrew!"

ALBERT: "Therefore "argot" is ineluctably linked to ARCHAE LINGUA!"

SIMHA: "Hence the amazing mental and spiritual progress realized almost instantly by those who spoke "argot".

Consider, by example, the startling results of this "argotic" performance: dozens immense cathedrals, of a size until then unknown, even unimaginable, have been initiated and almost completed in less than fifty years!"

ALBERT: "O YELIYAEL, did the Knights Templar discover the famed lost Ark of Alliance?"

The Angel effaces his eyes. No answer…Have we reached the

frontier of another forbidden territory?

We have arrived at Marie Tania's home. To celebrate our reunion she opens a bottle of Burgundy, and we share the heady, "fleshy" wine, along with goat cheese and fresh baguette. As we just emerge from a timeless cosmic travel, those earthly, pungent flavors and scents make us feel like starting a new voyage, a rediscovery and reliving of past sensations and sentiments. Yes, life is good, all life is good!

Albert is an excellent truthful storyteller, patient, determined to develop each and every idea, main course and all tributaries, forgetting no detail, extracting from words and facts all relevant significant meanings. And, apparently drawing encouragement from Rabbi YOHANAN's recent request to tell all "in details", Albert, today, updating Marie Tania, has chosen the longest way, which as always annoys me a little, I confess.

While listening to the story of our story, my mind at times escapes from the main path, navigating from word to word, on the living flow of ARCHAE LINGUA:

The sound-word DETails, resonates like DATo in Hebrew, which means divine knowledge-revelation delivered to man in answer to faith…and the Hebrew DATo fraternizes with Arabic haDITa, the legend, the Arab Sufi culture so recognizing the crucial import of the content of tales and the irreplaceable value of good story tellers...and thus presents itself to my mind the Latin word DATA, used by the English speaking people to mean "full information".

So, Albert recounts for Marie Tania our complete saga, thoughts, joys, frights, unexpected twists and astonishing turns, celestial humor, laughter and tears, Mount Nebo, the mysterious multilayered map in the Tent of Assignments headquarters of the twelve tribes commanders, planned departures towards all horizons, Mount Horeb, first 9 then 10 Commandments, the friendly shade of the Galilean olive tree, Rabbi BEN ZAKAI's tender smile, Angel YELIYAEL's loving caresses…

And constantly surge, from the elevated sources of Universal ARCHAE LINGUA, radiant letters and resounding words singing the grandeur of the human adventure nourished by the divine promise of Eternal Life.

I observe Marie Tania, she is tense, passionate, happy, her soul ready to effuse and soar like a giant eagle heading to its nest on the highest summit of the Himalayas. Beloved daughter of a famed talented entrepreneur, herself Executive Vice President in one of these major supranational Corporations which so much vex and irk the anxious minds of our times, Marie Tania knows to disentangle the most intricate knots, find her way in the confusion of roads, quickly identify, explain and apply simple, effective procedures. In her presence insights blossom, thoughts radiate, Life broadens as her intents are pure, guided by her love for clarity.

Albert, happily noticing Marie Tania doesn't tire listening, adds on the spherical virtual canvas he just painted for us a few more fine impressions, color nuances, subtle personal feelings and philosophical concepts. Then, bowing slowly, deeply, he stops speaking.

We all remain silent, contentedly ensconced in antique armchairs, hardly aware of our position in time and space.

MARIE TANIA: "Yohanan BEN ZAKAI did not give YELIYAEL directions, but YELIYAEL brought you here, in Paris. I have the intuition it is here we will find useful clues, the indicators pointing at your next destination."

Albert and Marie Tania are now standing by an open window, commenting sotto voce on the peacefulness of the square garden below and the charming ancient arched vaulted galleries typical of Place des Vosges. I am sitting near the large coffee table, white Carrara marble still displaying the half-emptied wine bottle, glasses and platters, reminiscent symbols of our happy reunion.

Unnoticed until now, in the far corner of the table, lays a thin beige covered book. Curious, I stand up to look at the title. Marie Tania, surely intuiting the intensity of my interest, turns towards me and says:

"I meant to lend you this book in New York, but could not find it on my bookshelves there. In fact the book was here in Paris; I found it in my bedroom yesterday. After we talked on the phone this morning I put it on this table, with the intent to give it to you."

Marie Tania takes the thin unassuming beige book in hand, starts reading the title. She stops suddenly, stomps on the wooden floor, and almost screaming she announces triumphantly: "Voilà, c'est çà, that's it!" "Oui, oui! Yes, yes, yes!"

Albert and I, accustomed to her outbursts of sheer vitality, just wait for her to calm down.

"Look!" she exclaims. "The French translation of the poems written by Lao Tzu, the founder of Taoism. When you told me about your quest, I promised myself to give you this book! Only I could not find it in my New York bookshelves. Maybe it was meant I give it to you now! Here is the synchronic sign I was expecting! Lao Tzu! You are to encounter the great Chinese sage! It is marvelous; certainly you are destined to meet Lao Tzu!"

Warmth radiating from my solar plexus gently caresses my heart, a sure signal of closeness to "inspiration" and "truth revelation". My cheeks heated, I feel my eyes shining as lit by one thousand candles.

"Yes, this is the way! Lao Tzu we shall visit!"

So, that's it! MarieTania firmly put the pilgrim's staff back in our hands. Where is YELIYAEL?

A swirling gust of floral scented air flows into the room, as our Angel navigator projects in my mind vivid images of scores of colorful butterflies circling above the artistically designed flowerbeds of a Parisian garden.

YELIYAEL: *"Rendez-vous in front of cathedral Notre Dame. Tonight we shall offer the ultra rational Parisians the spectacle of a Grand Cosmic Departure!"*

26. Manhattan, July 6, 2000 AD.

FROM PARIS, ANGEL YELIYAEL instantly transferred us to New York. We are quite familiarized now with the pure and dreamless slumber typical of ele-guided transport. As described to us by the Angel our enseraphed bodies do not display any of our usual natural colors. And, some time ago, he informed us, like a Concorde's pilot would explain to his passengers the basics of supersonic propulsion:

"*Your corporeal shape and organic systems dissolve gradually while I am memorizing their imprint. The HA, mental principle imprint defining your Human Persona, intertwines with the EL circuits of my Angelic Persona. That EL circuit coils around spiritual energy columns as a liana on a tropical tree.*"

We thus understood that, embraced by the EL of Angel YELIYAEL our terrestrial form is safely dematerialized, its structure safeguarded in the universal GANA, center and reservoir of all archetypal GENES.

As our human forms are "degravitated", corpuscular matter transmuted into luminous waves, our material BODA survives as immaterial GANA. So our liberated human HA[111], the celestial divine presence in us, becomes free to travel through time and space without material obstruction.

YELIYAEL added: "*Transmuted into spiritual HA, and its dematerialized mind embracing the angelic spiritual circuits EL, the human persona becomes HA-EL, practically of angelic nature. And that is how, virtualized, you are able to travel with me, unhindered.*"

[111] Rouach Ha Kadosh= in Hebrew means Breath of the Divine Presence.

Chapter Five

Sensei Lao Tzu

27. Manhattan, July 16, 2000 AD.

BACK FROM PARIS, WE ARE NOW RESTING in Manhattan, our home base. A pleasant interlude spent in our familiar surroundings: books, CD's, living room fountain, and the quiet flowery garden below our windows.

During the day we take care of our tapestry business, checking quality, evaluating sales, creating new designs and products in view of the upcoming international trade shows season. In the evening we listen to music, mostly songs chanted "a capella" gathered under the flying arches of Santiago de Compostella cathedral. Avoiding the too-often bastardly cooked ethnic foods presented by most New York restaurants, we eat at home, simple savory light dishes prepared with nutritious natural ingredients.

Tomorrow morning, on the 10th day of our halt in New York, Angel YELIYAEL will appear. And kindly wrapped in the luminous multicolored angelic veil, safely ele-guided through time and space, we shall continue our Quest, carry on our sacred mission: to unlock the hidden meanings of MOSES' 10 Commandments.

Our next assignment is to decode the 9th Commandment, with the assistance of the Chinese ancient sage Lao Tzu.

In the common English translation from the Hellenic-Latin version that Commandment reads as follows: "Thou shalt not bear false witness against thy neighbors".

28. The House of the Sage. Cathay. Lo Yang, 6th century BC.

SMOOTH ELE-LANDING, AT DAWN. Angel YELIYAEL's melodic voice softly announces we have reached early 6th century BC, and continues:

"*You are now standing on the ground of the largest potential Federation on Earth. At the present time this immense territory is not a unified "China", but a heterogeneous composition of countless small duchies, united only in spirit, under the jurisdiction of a Grand Duke. That Grand Duke is an iconic descendant of the first Prince who received investiture from the Heavens, a long time ago, a very long time ago. The Grand Duke presently in office holds only a fictional and symbolic power. In fact each small duchy is ruled by a dictator, military leader of the most powerful clan.*

We have landed in Lo-yang, capital of the duchy of Chou[112]. *Here, Sensei Lao Tzu has spent most of his life, received inspiration from the heavens, and penned his immortal poems.*"

Invisible to the local inhabitants, guided by YELIYAEL's cloudy white aura, we start walking in the direction of the home of the sage. The houses are built along parallel streets, and as we go across, we see the foot of steep mountains covered with deep for-

[112] Duchy of Chou shall become, 250 years later the mighty Kingdom of Qin, soon to become the unified Empire of China, regrouping seven large kingdoms, under the first effective federating Emperor "Qing".

ests, their dark gray summits toped with sun reflecting snow. The facades are painted in bright colors, doors decorated with impressive flame throwing dragons.

Artistic talents appear to be widely developed in this part of the world; drawing from imagination, or from ancestral memory, artists have populated the town with fascinating architectural forms, fantastic birds and fishes, oversized plants and flowers.

We quietly amble across the main square facing the proud ducal palace, and enter a narrow street lined with small shops, fronts featuring simpler decors of the most universal beauty. This area of town is obviously unpretentious, more humble than the Central Square, and pulses true and living harmonies.

Following YELIYAEL's guiding beacon we turn left under a triangular arched portal, entering a paved corridor, clean fresh air caressing our face, a tinge of lavender scent greeting us as we enter the inner courtyard.

Noiselessly, on the right, a large massive wooden door opens.

The old man before us, face and demeanor characteristically oriental, slightly bends inviting us inside, and we follow him through the anteroom. Eyes wide open we step in a bright medium size space, high ceiling, no furniture in sight.

The walls are entirely covered with wood panels, carved bas-reliefs depicting forested mountains, hieratic animals, lush plants and small bridges traversing lively gushing brooks.

Delicately painted silky fabric banners are displayed at regular intervals, populating the room with long necked white herons, flamboyant celestial flying dragons, ponds covered with quiet lotus flowers. The brightness of contrasting colors balanced by the white silence of empty spaces, the overall decorative effect is quietude, serenity, harmony.

Facing the entrance, his back to the garden, sitting in the classic lotus position on a large cushion, dressed in a cobalt blue silk long robe embroidered with orange and white floral motives, a man is staring at us, intently, through half closed slanted eyes. His long hands resting on crossed legs reveal special ability for delicate writing and painting.

Albert, YELIYAEL and I move forward, side by side, reverently approaching our host, LAO TZU, the divine sage.

In truth, I avow, I now feel even more impressed and more apprehensive than when I met Prophet MOSES and Rabbi Yohanan BEN ZAKAI. Glancing askance I see Albert's serene composure, calm and poised like a granite rock. YELIYAEL has adopted the silhouette of an ancient Greek sculpture, Pythagoras[113] maybe, his luminous flowing toga bordered with tiny glimmering golden sparks.

The sage, still and silent, wide opens his slanted eyes, pointing at two cushions facing him. Albert and I sit on the soft silk, in the lotus position.

I am overwhelmed with utter joy muddled by non-describable fears. This is happening now! We are facing Chinese Lao Tzu, far from Israel, far from the 12 tribes, far from learned Rabbis, far from the Christian monks relentlessly preserving science in their scriptorium, far from the expert archeologists decoding the ancient messages from Sumer and Akad. How dare we even start asking LAO TZU to help us unveil the secret meanings enclosed in the 9th Commandment, an obscure phrase written in Hebrew, extracted from a list of 10 laws he surely never knew existed.

I cannot contain the flow of my anxiety:

Our savant Archaeo-Linguistic method he shall disdainfully disregard; the evocation of ARCHAE LINGUA will make him laugh; the very notion of universal language he will mock! Albert and I, ashamed, humiliated, shall lose face in front of LAO TZU, and in front of the world!

Almost reflexively I begin an urgent silent invocation to Angel YELIYAEL, hoping for immediate succor: "O YELIYAEL…"

"*Indeed*, whispers YELIYAEL, *you are on the verge of panic. Your emotions resemble the feelings of a Jewish girl entering a church during mass for the first time, or those of a Christian invit-*

[113] Pythagoras, 570-495 BC: famous Greek mathematician and philosopher.

ed in a synagogue on Yom Kippur!"[114]

Fortunately Albert, drawing confidence in his philosophical training at the Sorbonne, opens the meeting.

With a clear voice, and a tone somewhat formal, he says:

"On behalf of my two friends time-space travelers, I salute you, divine master LAO TZU!"

Voice light as mist, almost immaterial, the master answers:

"Heartfelt greetings! Welcome to you, Angel YI LIU YI LO!"[115]

YELIYAEL does not seem in the least surprised by the odd sonority of his name, but he is certainly pleased and charmed, showing his contentment by launching toward the high ceiling a vigorous volley of tender pink and sky blue crackling sparkles.

"Salutations to you ILI BI LI TAI"[116] says the sage, extending his joined hands towards Albert.

Albert containing a nascent laughter frowns and almost closes his eyes, his face now distinctly looking Chinese…

"As for you, my dear Shimeha, I am deeply pleased to welcome you under the name TCHI MEI HIAI."[117]

What a relief! The master kindly called me first by my Hebrew name! LAO TZU has even elected to vocalize the warm sounds TCHI, and not the hissing and cold sound SI.

Our names are ambassadors of our soul, they tell others who we are and who we want to be. LAO TZU chose to emphasize a warm facet of my persona, the way of the heart, the radiant expression of life. Rabbi YOHANAN said that in heavens the celestial beings think the warm SHI is more accurate to represent my soul identity, and they name me Shimeha.

However, and despite the converging judgment of the celestial Rabbi, the Angels and Sensei LAO TZU, I keep thinking that SI at the beginning of my name explains better my terrestrial purpose: mainly my eagerness to uncover truth by giving prevalence to

---

[114] Yom Kippur: the most important Jewish religious celebration.

[115] Yi-liu-yi-lo= Chinese resonance of the name Ye-li-ya-el.

[116] Ili-bi-li-tai=Chinese resonance of the name Al-be-re-te (Albert). The sound R, missing in Chinese, is replaced by the sound L.

[117] Tchi-mei-hiai= Chinese resonance of the name Shi-me-ha (Simha)

mathematics and scientific analytic approach rather than gaining and transmitting knowledge mostly by empathy and sympathy, often misinterpreted as too emotional, akin to a chimera.

Now, bracing for courage, I address LAO TZU:

"Salute to you, divine sage LA-OV-TZSE!"

His face lights up, his eyes open wide and large, unveiling shining irises; suddenly LAO TZU doesn't look typically Chinese at all! For a long moment he stays completely immobile, his mind seemingly traveling towards hidden dimensions. Then he says:

"During my sojourn on Earth I was never named the way you just called me. Most often I answered to the sounds LAO-TSEU, and sometimes LI-TZU."

ALBERT: "And which is your correct name?"

LAO TZU: "No name is true, and no name is false. No word is true, no word is wrong. As you call a being or a thing, so it presents itself."

SIMHA: "Do you mean, Master, that nothing exists objectively, and that our entire world is a complete illusive unreality?"

LAO TZU: "No, it's the opposite. Everything exists, absolutely everything! And every reality exists wrapped in a specific form, but also contains all non-specific forms. Everything exists in each reality; and not only each specific reality is a part of the whole but the whole itself exists in all specific reality.

And, as you call a being or a thing, so it presents itself.[118]

ALBERT: "By example, if I call you by the name LAO-TSEU, it is the reality LAO-TSEU that shall connect with me; and if I call LI-TZU, the reality LI-TZU shall present itself. And, as Simha just called you LA-OV-TZSE, truly LA-OV-TZSE is facing us now..."

The sage has now shut his eyes. His body remains motionless, however, although no movement can be perceived, I feel his position has changed; LAOV-TZSE appears to have retreated within a

---

[118] Genesis 2 19= "*and whatsoever Adam called every living creature, that was the name thereof*". In Hebrew: ve-col asher yikerah-lo ha-adam nefesh chayah hou shemo. Archaeo-Linguistic translation: "and according to the sound-resonance (ve-col asher) the terrestrial human (ha adam) uttered (yikerah lo), the essence of that life (nefesh chaya) manifests its celestial essence (hou) through its name (shemo)".

caring protective shell, now curved like a baby in a maternal womb. The sage has entered into a profound meditative trance.

Deep stillness and ineffable peace stimulate our desire to follow his trail within the intellectual circuits of invisible dimensions, our mind in spiritual pursuit, eager to soar as high as the master will lead us.

Then, after an indefinable silent time, a split second or an hour, we start perceiving again the background musical spurts of the garden cascades; we are all back in the sage's house…

Now returned invigorated from his cosmic escapade LAOV-TZSE, facing us, answers Albert's question:

"Though each individualized unit is unified within a larger whole, each being simultaneously manifests its specific identity. This specific identity is eventuated by natural causes or driven by aspirations and ideals, and almost always its motility, emotions and intelligence it draws from both sources: Cause and Intent, Necessity and Will, Matter and Spirit, Destiny and Providence."

Silence

"Except when, vigorously breaking the time-space eggshell, thus finding an exit door out of the constraining material world, the freed soul immediately enters the universes of eternity; there the being is directed by one unique force, namely the force of Finality, the force of pure Intent."[119]

Silence

"Within the central universes, near the gravitation center of the master Universe, the forces of causality have no power, but the principle law of Totality-Unity prevails; it is the dominant Law.

However, within all the universes encapsulated by the time-space double shield, though every unique entity contains all potential existences, each entity exists principally as a preferential specific form.[120]

Thus, a single liver cell holds the powers to eventuate the

---

[119] Pure Intent=Kavanah, the science of pure Intent -akin to Zen-, revealed as the highest aspiration through Kabalah.

[120] As perceived by Goethe's natural science, and Burbank's applications in modern agriculture.

whole body. That cell may, not only reproduce itself, but, under favorable conditions it generates the entire organic body in which it is hosted. However that cell is specifically a liver cell and normally functions as such.

Now, when that cell enters a vital expansion mode, it creates a door (DA) to exit its limiting eggshell (OVa) and develop all the potentials its wholeness contains.

In normal resting mode however, enclosed in its functional egg form (Ova), each cell in the liver acts according to the specific status imparted to it within the whole body. Each cell deferentially accomplishes the wishes of its host, the unifying superior principle of the whole body, its "Guide-God".

In normal mode each cell abandons its will to be the whole, renounces out of Goodness and Compassion its powers to be the whole, by simultaneously recognizing and obeying the Law of the Whole." [121]

New long silence. All is quiet in the room. Then I ask:

"Do you mean, divine Sensei[122], your personal existence contains all qualities and virtues defining a metaphysician master-poet, and one can give you any name designating any of those qualities? However there is certainly one particular name which best reveals more wholly your special personality. There is a name disclosing your personal mission, a name precisely indicating in what way you are participating to the grand universal design, the name that designates the best part of "you" in the whole."

LAOV-TZSE: "Yes, exactly; the analogy works in that case."

ALBERT: "Then, which name, which word-composition, evokes best your presence and existence within the Universal Wholeness?"

LAOV-TZSE: "The name Tchi Mei Hiai so kindly offered me this morning! LA-OV-TZSE it is! I shall clarify:

---

[121] If obedience of the part to the whole is disrupted then "mortal" disease happens.

[122] Sensei: master teacher in Chinese and Japanese. Notice within the name SenSei the 2 letter-sounds S which core meaning in Universal Language, or Archae Lingua is: "Superior Science". Those same adjoined letters appear in the English words SenSe, SenSitive, SenSible, all designating great abilities to perceive and master different levels of reality.

"Composed of celestial meaningful elements-sound-letters, a name not only illustrates the qualities of an individual being, it also *empowers* the being it is associated with.

The name LI-TZU has been often used to call me, but it was not adequate to best accomplish the mission I had undertaken on Earth. The linguistic formula LI-TZU lacks a major force indispensable to find the sublime celestial path I wished to open.

The melody LAO-TZEU was almost perfect, it contained most of the necessary resonances, but missing elements have limited the scope of my own inner awareness, and consequently reduced the understanding and influence of my message in the world.

In contrast, the name LA-OV-TZSE contains all the essential resonances and provides all the emotional, mental and spiritual tools needed to perfectly and completely accomplish my mission."

Turning my head towards the garden I see YELIYAEL has fractioned his shape into a multitude of colorful little dragon-butterflies. They vividly hop from leaves to flowers, rest on bridge parapets, and hover above the multiple rivulets, gushing fresh cascades and placid mirror ponds.

An intense gaze in my direction pulls my attention back to the room. For the first time since we started our cosmic journey, Albert seems to be perplexed by something he just heard. Though, to me, what the master just said is clear, as limpid as the water flowing in the garden nearby.

"LA-OV-TZSE, LAOV-TZSE, what is the core meaning of that name?" inquires Albert.

The Master slightly nods at me, signaling I must clarify.

SIMHA: "In every modern language maintaining closeness to ARCHAE LINGUA, the primeval source of all idioms, whenever the letter O is present, at the beginning or inside words, behind that vowel O secretly resides the consonant letter V.

Therefore the Archaeo-Linguistic exact formula of the O sound is in reality O+V, OV. Consequently, to fully deliver the cosmic value enclosed in the name LA-O, one should vocalize the complete LA-OV. However, not all vowels are hiding a consonant; some vowels are neutral, basically added to the consonants to facilitate the word pronunciation."

ALBERT: "Then, the peoples speaking only western languages, like myself, how may they differentiate neutral vowels from vowels hiding consonants?"

SIMHA: "For once, I shall answer with another question: How can a mail carrier deliver a letter in Tokyo in areas of the city where streets have no name and buildings are designated by the year of their construction?"

ALBERT: "Certainly, I assume the letter carrier has been properly informed, carefully instructed, well initiated."

"Ah! Master LAOV-TZSE exclaims, expressed so candidly, the idea of Initiation! Clear and simple! An "initiate" has acquired knowledge. True Initiation requires no ritualistic ceremonies, only a genuine will to acquire the knowledge necessary to attain a goal.

So a letter carrier in Tokyo has to be initiated, to know the principles underlying the structure of the city, thus finding his way in the maze and effectively deliver the mail.

And so must be duly initiated him who wishes to uncover intelligibility and universality in the apparent chaotic diversity of multitudinous languages and dialects on Earth.

There is nothing strange, or irrational in the actuality of a unique original founding language. Applying scientific methods to elucidate what now appears like a cacophony you shall contribute to the advancement of linguistic knowledge in regard to its cosmic universality."

The sage offers more details:

"The divine YEHOSHUA-JESUS during his mission on Earth shared on this subject a precise and limpid message, and so concluded: I shall come back on Earth when all humans of all nations shall understand and speak the same language.

Meaning that whichever national tongue one speaks, each individual shall become conscious that all languages are built and developed on the same foundations: the celestial principles of the Universal Language, namely ARCHAE LINGUA, the Stars' language."

The Chinese sage's discourse on the fundamental unity of multiple terrestrial languages and the confirmation of that fact by the teachings of the Galilean Messiah pulses like a deep drumming in my mind.

Westerner citizens, even at the edge of the third millennium, are bound, by legacy and education, to perceive Africa, and Asian China, as huge islands with no permanent cultural bridges to interconnect continents, the tongues spoken being so different, in direct contrast to the primary motive of our Quest which implies a fundamental language unity.

We do not see, presently, how to approach, this paradox, and in the secret of our heart we hope that LAOV-TZSE shall help us bring clarity into this pervasive and persistent contradiction. As we are actually facing LAOV-TZSE in person I decide to tackle this difficult question:

"Divine Master, please explain. Here is the situation. Modern historians, laboring in their universities, convinced themselves of the existence of a complete cultural incompatibility, an immense chasm allegedly separating West from Far East.

To sustain their view they even present those as two opposite zones of influence, China being identified as Celestial Empire, sometimes Empire of the Middle, and the other is designated as Western civilization.

For those inaccurate historians, and their followers, mistaken scientists of all categories, the chasm separating East and West is proven by an obvious, abyssal difference in spoken and written languages.

Divine Master, you know why Albert, Angel YELIYAEL and myself have traversed the fences of time and space to meet with you. The success of our present quest for Truth is largely based on the certainty that a Universal Language, the Stars' language, fundamentally founds all languages spoken on Earth[123]. Earlier you

---

[123] Genesis 11-1 states: "the whole earth had one language and one speech". The English word "One" is a translation of the Hebrew word Akhad, meaning "Unified". The same root designates Akad, the language of the Akadian-Mesopotamian civilization, foundation of the Hebrew language.

evoked yourself ARCHAE LINGUA presenting it as the primeval Universal Language."

The sage, immobile, seems hesitant to address the topic I just laid on his lap. Understandably cautious he is, like so many other savant and wise humans who know more than they are willing to disclose on this subject potentially scandalous.

Deep breathe in. Now LAOV-TZSE has resolved to navigate the dangerous waters. With a firm voice, he endeavors to explain; and, following the wave sounds of his discourse, we all depart with him on this challenging journey towards forbidden territories.

LAOV-TZSE: "Humanity's origin and historical development as transmitted by western "official history tellers" is pure folly! Those peoples who may justly be proud of their quasi-infallible scientific methods as applied to mathematics, physics, chemistry, astronomy, are only showing mind weakness, and awareness limitation, when addressing the domain of historical human progression.

In the name of science they boldly proffer and collectively endorse numerous illogical assertions, oblivious to the malefic consequences of their flawed vapid conclusions.

Particularly they effectively prevent genuine new accurate observations and theories not fitting into their conventional systems, albeit so necessary and crucial for the future disclosure of the Truth.

By example, according to these self-labeled scientists the first civilization emerged about 6,000 years before your 21st century era, complete, integral, with numerous schools, monuments, cities, and languages featuring sophisticated syntax. Recent archeological discoveries, and particularly the findings obtained by deciphering multitude engraved clay tablets, demonstrate that the city dwellers of Akad, Mari, Uruk, Lagash, Ur, Nippur, Larsa, were recording the quality and volume of their commercial transactions with many parts of the world, as far as the actual Isles of Brittany. The so-called scientists, blind to the fact that such transactions must be mutual, continue to present Sumer city-states as the only source of civilization, existing by itself for itself: nothing would have existed before, and nothing existed further its geographical expanse.

But the fact is that, according to numbers found on their clay tablets, Ur and Akad were growing and harvesting enormous quantities of wheat grains, greatly superior to their local needs. Large workshops manufactured pottery, jugs, plates, clay tablets, at a quasi-industrial level. And, on the qualitative aspect, the Sumerian skilful bakers could, and probably were baking 300 kinds of bread. Obviously, such production was matched by an equally enormous demand beyond the Sumerian territories.

How can your official history tellers proclaim Sumer was the only civilized area at that time?"

With a light move of the hand LAOV-TZSE brushes away those shallow and inconsistent assertions. The master continues:

"Listen carefully. I will now tell you what happened on Earth, from the beginning. All human beings intellectually capable and intuitively well endowed, attuned to the frequencies of the cosmic mind, know of humankind's *dual* origin.

The first, the natural origin, is rather well described by the 19th Century meticulous observer of animal life TCHAO-LI DALI-WEN Charles Darwin[124].

But his followers and disciples, less cautious than their master, made unjustifiable inferences from the observed facts, installed as proofs mere heuristic hypotheses, and finally persuaded most of the schoolteachers of the western world that human beings somehow are descended from monkeys[125].

They could as well have chosen the bear as their ancestor. In fact, enlightened biologists of your time prefer to affirm that, from the natural point of view, human, bear, lion, eagle, dolphin, and all other animals have a common primeval undefined forebear; each

---

[124] Original title publication 24 November 1859 *On the Origin of Species by Means of Natural Selection, or the Preservation of Favoured Races in the Struggle for Life.*

[125] Quote from 2nd edition January 7th, 1860: "But as my conclusions have lately been much misrepresented, and it has been stated that I attribute the modification of species exclusively to natural selection, I may be permitted to remark that in the first edition of this work and subsequently, I placed in the most conspicuous position-namely at the close of the introduction-the following words: *"I am convinced that natural selection has been the main but not the exclusive means of modification"*. This has been to no avail. Great is the power of misrepresentation". *Charles Darwin.*

particular species having branched out from the main life strand millions years ago. However, amongst all animal species the human ancestor has been the winner of the race to attain cosmic consciousness. How?

Due to greatest physical strength? No.
Due to superior instinctual power? No.
By developing the largest brains in the largest skull? No.

But Yes, the true supremacy was achieved by way of a *moral act!* By making a moral choice, that is a choice in utter opposition to the general instinctual combat rule for individual survival, a single individual instantaneously produced on Earth the most improbable status alteration: A Transmutation from ANIMAL to AMINAL (OMINAL). And, as any other valuable traits, that acquired ability to conceive and perform moral behaviors, organically embedded itself in the AMinal genotype, and became transmissible and potentially inheritable.

Furthermore, that lone sparkle of moral action, albeit weak and indiscernible on Earth, yet cast up an unambiguous resonant and luminous message of colossal import immediately recorded by the universal cosmic receptors: (((A-M A N))) (((AM E N))). Celestial beings, diligent expectant observers of Earthly human evolution, perceived the significance of that sound letter inversion: an ANimal creature had made a voluntary connection with the Universe Spirit! And that ANimal creature had acted according to the rule of universal Spirit! AMEN! AMEN!

Consequently, enthusiastically responding to the AMIN-AL call, majestic celestial envoys imbued Earth with their presence, so strengthening the eternal linkage between Earth and the Heavens. As a welcome gift from Heavens the AMINAL species received the supreme connective powers of the essential sound "He", and thereafter was forever named, portrayed and known as HOMINAL[126] in

[126] The sound Hey provides the ability to connect with the spiritual dimension. As Holy in English. As stated in the Hebrew Torah, Old Testament, Genesis 17:5 Abram was named AbraH-am following his connection with celestial Melkitzedek. Furthermore AbraHam's spouse Sarai has been consequently renamed SaraH. Genesis 17-15.

accordance with the universal resonance of the Stars' Language."

ALBERT: "So, this is the origin of the word HuMaN in English, and HuMaNité, HuMaiN in French, Ha-MiN in Hebrew?" [127]

LAOV-TZSE: "Yes. And as you call a being, so it presents itself."

The sage continues: "After receiving the H, Holy powers, the aMinal, formerly aNimal, became Human, humankind, truly standing up at last. Thus started the prophesized era of beneficent reciprocal relationship between Human and Celestial races..

Theretofore humankind had been a passive receptor of the divine celestial manna, it was now empowered with the capacity to become efficient "receptor-emitter", able to process and act upon the divine MANNA.[128], a potential perfect Human.

In that way, human beings are sanctified, as they do not entirely submit to entropy. Humans are not like spoon-fed babies anymore. They are rather like an adult able to find nourishment by himself for himself and, subsequently, also nurture various other types of living beings increasingly differing from his own species.

Thus Humans have become potentially able to step in and take their rightful position in the universal SANCTITY assembly, the SA-NAT-A cosmic SeNaTorial congregation, where celestial knowledge and science (SA) connect all sentients through the cosmic NETwork.

From mere "receptor", sanctified Human is now able to emit and give;, his personal melodic messages, albeit infrequent, can resonate, vibrate and be identified, acknowledged, accepted by all living consciences in the cosmos."

Pause. Silence.

The sage is pondering the next striking information he is going to deliver.

LAOV-TZSE: "Note that, in the entire alphabetical set, the sound

---

[127] Ha-MiN= in Hebrew means 1/Ha=connection with the Spirit, 2/MiN=species. Therefore, in Archae Lingua, a Hu-Man is identified as "a species conscious of its connection with the Spirit".

[128] Manna in Hebrew means that which is given, by the Heavens, according to the specific original entitlement of each individual. By a willed moral act, an individual may augment his Manna, so enriching his species and enabling it to evolve as a whole.

HE is the human sound produced by the deepest breath out. That special voluntary exhalation of air which produces HE, signals the capacity to consciously send away and give.

Earthly Humans have yet to learn how to primarily give more than they receive. Whenever individuals shall attain that phase of evolution, thus connecting with immensely potent spiritual energies, they will effortlessly renounce all non-essential desires. Humans will thus completely shed covetousness, as advised by MOSES in the 10th Commandment and subsequently promised to the Heavens, on behalf of all humankind, by Yohanan BEN ZAKAI BAR YOELLA."

LAOV-TZSE pauses again. I look at his long pointed white beard, slanted eyes, little round silk cap, ample robe and large sleeves, marveling at how the Chinese sage resembles a Jerusalemite Rabbi…

LAOV-TZSE continues: "From the moment a few human beings made themselves known as potential actors on the moral stage, and so joined in the universal chorus, planet Earth has been continually visited by celestial visitors, numerous and of many kinds! Some episodes of that history may be construed as beneficent, others as catastrophic, bringers of disaster and confusion. Walked on Earth gods and goddesses, semi-gods, heroes, and malevolent demons.

In spite of hindrances, numerous extraordinary celestial teachers, educators crisscrossed all parts of the planet. Schools diffusing astonishing knowledge were established, attracting many progressive humans of all genders and races.

And students from all peoples living on Earth came, and came, walking, riding horse-like animals, flying on eagles and giant birds, or on "chariots of fire", to hear, gain skills and learn how to disseminate knowledge. And those students became teachers, and went back to their tribes to transfer their newly acquired celestial information and expertise.

ARCHAE LINGUA keeps accurate records of those student-educators, whose intellects were elevated by celestial instructors.

Look for them under the name ELLEH[129], meaning elevated-by-elevated beings (EL), learning to use their intellectual powers (LE), with the intent to give and distribute the heavenly knowledge (H).

Later they have been called the Elamites, the Elect people[130]: EL (elect) AM (people).

During that long pre-historic era, as recorded in geological layers, occurred many natural disasters, glaciations and planetary warmings, floods and droughts, earthquakes, volcanic eruptions, gigantic land fires and natural reforestation on nourishing ashes.

Humans alternatively had to find refuge in the mountains, hide in caves, even climb on arks and fly away far from their familiar terrestrial horizons.

In vast areas on the stricken planet everyone and everything was destroyed, but in other planetary sectors unyielding survivors vigilantly preserved their genetic and linguistic treasures. Surely, at times, some physical and mindal qualities were on the brink of extinction. But as a whole Earth entity survived the million years of tribulations."

Almost in the same breath the sage continues:

"The celestial visitors were of opposite polarities. In larger numbers came and constantly intervened the positive Yin entities, recognized as utterly compassionate, kindest benefactors.

The visitors of negative Yang polarity were often perceived by most humans as haughty supervisors, arrogant and lacking compassion. However, in spite of their apparent severity, those celestials also contributed positively to the civilizing process on Earth.

The presence and actions of both types of visitors are partially recorded in numerous legends, more than often the positive mixed and confused with those of the other less positive divinities, as found in many narrations of ancient African myths, Greek tales, Brahmin traditions and numerous native American legends.

Then a sudden leap occurred: pre-historic earthly humanity reached its evolutionary peak with the appearance of outstanding

---

129 Elleh is the root of the word Aloha, greeting expression used to this day by Hawaians to welcome visitors.

130 El-am= the Elamites mentioned in the Old Testament.

Neanderthal Man, "Homo Faber", so apt at fabricating objects, the man with "golden hands".

Silence

"Afterward, celestial EVA-ADAM[131], the sacred couple, landed on Earth. Until then, for half a million years, celestial visitors had stimulated individual progress through education only, for they were to avoid any direct genetic interference on the human phylum. Conversely, EVE-ADAM, as planned in highest celestial circles, provided the powerful divo-genetic influx that was to benefit all humanity and all life on the planet, without exception.

EVE-ADAM's divine involvement took place about 40,000 years ago, terrestrial time. A relatively recent period, yielding traces accessible to modern archeologists, who discern the manifestation of a new, superior human type, "Homo-Sapiens-Sapiens", a man immeasurably cleverer than clever adroit "Homo-Faber-Sapiens" Neanderthal.

The enormous gap in skills and intellectual abilities between Neanderthal and vastly superior post EVADAM men and women cannot be explained by slow intrinsic genetic evolution."

ALBERT: "Modern researchers of proto human history coined the term "Creative Era" to describe the evolutionary leap that started sometime between 50 to 35,000 years ago."

Angel YELIYAEL, interrupting his leisurely conversation with flowers, rocks, water drops, dragonflies and frogs in the garden, suddenly appears in the center of our meditative triad, in the compact form of three cloudy golden spheres, superposed, slightly decreasing in size, capped with a sparkling purple star.

I exclaim: "AM SEGULAH[132]! The six-pointed purple star at the

---

[131] Simplistic doctrine presents Adam and Eve as the first God-created human beings. A study of the original text of Genesis and Talmud, reveals 3 kinds of Adam and Eve. 1/Adam be tzelem elohim: Gen 1:27, the Adam "built according to celestial patterns, referred at in Oral Tradition as Adam ha kadmon. 2/Adam asher chai Genesis 5:5 designating "the animal originated Adam (chai) evolving under our sun. 3/ Al Adam before the induced deep sleep, named El Adam when awaken, and from whom the woman is extracted. Genesis 2:22-25 designates the highly evolved human (el) elevated to compatibility with the Celestial Adam (ha kadmon).

[132] Segulah: in Hebrew means 1/Violet color 2/Liberation by elevation. In the Hebrew Bible as well as in prayer books, am segulah is mentioned in reference to hu-

top evokes the Violet Race!"

At the sight of this poetic evocation I burst out laughing, a sonorous, joyful, heartfelt expression of freedom and liberation. Simultaneously I hear Albert's hand clapping in delight. The sage LAOV-TZSE prolonged chuckling rapid breathing is accompanied by rhythmic up and down movements of his arms, mimicking the wings of a bird in flight.

YELIYAEL is now addressing us, enthralled audience, in a soft melodious fraternal voice, chanted words pulsating in all directions simultaneously from each of the six points of the violet star.

"EXTRACTS FROM ARCHANGELIC ARCHIVES the voice announces*: EVA-ADAM's violet progeny, when out of Eden, orderly scattered on the entire planet. One particular notorious son, named SETH, is recorded in collective memory of Ancient Egypt, Israel and China*

Those missionaries brought to every area on Earth new types of animals able to assist humans in their labors, new seeds to produce grains, nuts, fruits, plants and vegetables. And, for the indispensable essential nourishment of minds, they generously brought the ultimate gift, the core of all future tongues on Earth, the roots of the Celestial Universal Language, ARCHAE LINGUA.

EVA-ADAM's mission was the first planned attempt at genetic, linguistic and spiritual unification in the human inhabited world. In spite of great difficulties, obstacles, resistance and hostility, the results of their remarkable achievement are unmistakable.

Then, at the time Abraham was walking on Earth, his celestial mentor known as MELKITSEDEK[133] *launched on the roads of Earth an immense number of dedicated educators-missionaries. They went round the planet, teaching and revealing the existence of numerous celestial kingdoms, renovating the art of agriculture and techniques of husbandry, disclosing new sciences, new laws and*

---

mans as being issued from the Violet Race, liberated from animal darkness and elevated to sapience by the Celestial teachers. tokh emoune am segulah bohi be shalom.

133 Melkitsedek: celestial envoy, Abraham's celestial initiator temporarily incarnated as human, also mentioned in the Gospels in *Hebrews 5:5, 6; 7: 20, 21 "You are a priest forever according to the order of Melkitsedek".*

instruments for arithmetic, architecture, astronomy. That feat, accomplished 2,000 years BC, resulted into extraordinary cultural renaissance and human unity awareness, everywhere, from East to West, from North to South. [134]

Evidently, at that time also, as always, communications between teachers and students, as well as between individuals, tribes and nations, were greatly enhanced by the revitalized use of the magical vocalized sounds and core meanings of Universal ARCHAE LINGUA, the Stars' Language. Then MOSES, 500 years later, starting from Egypt[135]*, which, with Abraham's assistance, had become the main and safe depository of MELKITSEDEK's sciences and revelations, created and trained an elite people with the purpose to disseminate the ARCHAE sciences all over the world. The new missionaries traveled in all directions, toward Asia, Africa, America, also landing on the shores of Oceania, in the Pacific Ocean."*

LAOV-TZSE, smiling broadly: "That suitably explains the traditional Hawaiian greetings "ALOHA", similar to the Hebrew word ELOHA, meaning ELEVATED DIVINITY."

SIMHA: "The plural form of ELOHA is ELOHIM, "the Gods", as mentioned in the Torah."

YELIYAEL's voice continues: "*Most recently, a new knowledge of cosmic import has been spread, at the time of Jesus' mission on Earth. The "good tidings" regarding re-acquired human access to the celestial kingdoms have been announced by Jesus himself, then by the apostles, disciples and their disciples, in many directions, even penetrating into Kashmir, China, Japan. And, they also often*[136]*crossed the Atlantic Ocean, from the Spanish Galician penin-*

---

[134] The Brahmin religious movement, same word as Abraham, started in Northern India circa 1900 BC, soon after Melkitsedek instructed Abraham.

[135] Egypt: Genesis 12,1-5. Abram soon to become AbraHam is sent to Egypt by Melkitsedek, Genesis 12-10. His mission: inform, initiate Pharaoh and the priesthood about the revival of antique celestial sciences; establish a new covenant. Thus the valley of Goshen became the center of immigrations for all peoples from all races adhering to the covenant. That motley people became Am Ram, people elevated by Celestial science. 400 years later, Moses said to be the son of Am Ram, led that people out of Egypt.

[136] Often crossed: This Atlantic westernmost edge of coastal Spain offers a perfect port of departure, as well as the shortest distance at sea to reach the American continent. This point of departure has been used frequently at all times. It is at the

sula, called "Finisterra", reaching the land inhabited by the Mayas and Toltecs in Central America."

Master LAOV-TZSE comments: "SETH's missionaries and those who followed, MELKITZEDEK's envoys, MOSES' voyagers, JESUS' disciples, all went all around Earth.

Thus, you may see, China has never been an isolated sector of humankind, never been separated from human union. Rather has China always viewed itself as The Middle Empire, Europe to its far West, Amerika to the East, to the North the Mongolian Manchurian immensities, to the South the African mystery. And, unlike other human groups did over time, we never, ever forgot the dual common origin of humankind: we Chinese call ourselves Children of Heavens, as a reminder of the true celestial source of human unity."

Deep silence again. YELIYAEL's voice is at rest. Albert has now closed his eyes. I remember reading a legend mentioning tombstones in Kashmir attributed to MOUSSA and ISSA[137]. Probably are interred there Moses' and Jesus' disciples…

The verity of the historical outline traced by the sage and the Angel is supported by positive evidence on earth, but proofs are scattered like pieces of a broken mirror, facts partially described in countless different books and manuscripts, encased in results of thousands scientific works, not one decidedly seeking for enlightening inter-correlations.

Reading my mind, feeling my growing despair, YELIYAEL softly comments: "*Have no fear, Simha! Ever since the first moral action eventuated on planet locally named Earth-Eretz-Urthu, all essential human facts and thoughts are known to the planetary Guardian Angels and safely recorded in the indestructible, always accessible, archangelic archives.*"

ALBERT, calm and respectful, now addresses the sage:

"Master, you are asserting the existence of a genetic common source unifying all humans on Earth, but this affirmation goes con-

---

origin of the famous pilgrimage to Santiago de Compostella, whose symbol is a seashell, reminder of the ocean crossings of old.

[137] Moussa and Issa= Moses and Jesus in Arabic.

trary to the plain appearances: by example men's and women's skin colors are blackish, yellowish, reddish brown, pink-whitish!

Furthermore, Sensei, you, us, and Angel YELIYAEL vigorously aver the existence of ARCHAE LINGUA, unique source and universal foundation of all languages, tongues and dialects used on Earth. But looking at pages written in English, Slavic, Japanese, Chinese, Sanskrit, Greek, Arabic, Hebrew, how can we open the contemporary minds so they perceive and accept the premise of Unity?"

LAOV-TZSE smiles gently, his face expressing paternal love and understanding, and he responds:

"I know that you, Ili Bi Li Tai, and Tchi Mei Hiai, came here in ancient China to confer with me in regard with MOSES' 9th Commandment. I love you both for choosing me to elucidate the manifold meanings of that wondrous verse, not because I am flattered, but because it is exactly here, on this territory, the Middle Empire, that this seed-Commandment developed the deepest roots and unfolded as a fruitful tree necessary to insure humankind's spiritual expansion.

Therefore you had to come here to better understand the meanings of that particular divine law.

However, in the Heavens, we were in suspense, awaiting your decision. Yohanan BEN ZAKAI BAR YOELLA had opted not to direct YELIYAEL. You were on your own, celestial guidance temporarily denied. To solve the dilemma you chose to rely neither on reason alone nor on intuition alone, but to harmoniously combine both intuition and reason.

There were only two solutions to the riddle: LAO TZU or KUNG FU TZU. We both lived in China at the same epoch, and, though we never met here, both knew well the thoughts and teachings of the other.

You have accomplished two acts of bravery, which delighted many Angels and retained the attention of several Archangels!

The first act of bravery is to have selected China, a territory ostensibly contradicting the ideas of unity and universality which, justly, motivate the extraordinary exploration you have undertaken, and which fuel your daring Quest for Truth.

For, cultural manifestations and linguistic peculiarities seem to ineluctably separate China from the rest of the world.

The second act of bravery is to have chosen me, LAO TZU, who apparently only gave to the world a series of Chinese characters engraved on bamboo sticks, now read as metaphysical poems!

On the other hand, KUNG FU-TZU, known in the West by his Latinized name CONFUCIUS, deeply transformed Chinese social life, providing students, men and women with an efficient system of education and moral edification that endured the passing of time. Based on ancient knowledge received from the antique missionary-educators, KUNG-FU-TZU's teachings perpetuated the enhancement of morality at all levels of the vast Chinese society."

Silence

LAOV-TZSE, distraught, exclaims:

"Until the 20th century AD Red Plague brutally wiped out in a few years the ethical principles which had been benignly guiding the Chinese minds for the past 25 centuries."

Obviously the sage barely refrains from crying. From his present elevated station in Heaven he has been a reliable witness to many pitfalls afflicting humanity. But the brutal and destructive invasion of the Chinese mind and spirit affects him more deeply.

LAOV-TZSE continues: "The major instigators and perpetrators of this vast scale murder may have been since annihilated themselves, souls dissolved, having lost all spiritual coherence, thus now unable to fathom distorted malevolent intents. Our ancient Egyptian masters would enounce the celestial "Death sentence" verdict following their trial as the annihilation of the KA-BA, in which KA represents the mindal coherence and BA the life substance foundation.[138]

Or, as written by the cosmic poet Albert Haldane, sitting nearby me today: they died of a deadly death."[139]

---

[138] See the ancient Egyptian Book of the Dead or Book of the coming forth to the Light, explaining the function of Ka and Ba, both components of the potentially surviving soul of the individual after "Death". Consult also the Tibetan Book of the Dead, the Bardo Thodol.

[139] Albert Haldane, in Mémoires du Futur : *"ils mourrons de mortelle mort*".

Albert suddenly blushes, both surprised and grateful to being quoted by the sage. YELIYAEL casts a dense cluster of crackling violet sparks towards Albert's chest. And I hear my companion sotto voce chanting an evocation "O YERATHAEL, revive my memory, assist me in thinking the sage by reciting a poem he wrote:

Whoever Wants	The	Whoever
To	World Is	Abuses it
Seize	A	Destroys
The	Sacred Vessel	It,
World	Which	Whoever
And	Cannot	Steals
Enslave it	Be Stolen	It
Shall	And	Loses
Fail.	Abused.	It

Then LAOV-TZSE, with a high and sharp voice, like a 20 years young man, continues reciting the poem he created more than 2,500 years ago:

Some	Some	Some	Some
march	breathe	are	stand,
ahead,	softly,	vigorous	others
others	others	others	fall
follow	deeply	feeble	

And from the little purple six-pointed star spinning on top of the golden cloudy sphere forming YELIYAEL's head, radiate the last words of the last verse:

The sage avoids
all extremes
and
all extravagances

○

LAOV-TZSE is intensely moved by that collective recollection of his poetic creation. His prolonged gaze on each of us feels like a warm enfolding embrace, his large smile expresses thankfulness and joie de vivre!

LAOV-TZSE: "I shall now address Albert's dilemma. How are we humans so different in appearance whilst we are so profoundly unified? Are those the terms of your predicament?"

ALBERT: "As you surely know, Sensei, I have partially solved that quandary, walking on the paths illuminated by many ancient philosophers, who showed me how to leap from details to whole, and reversely from the whole to details, intuiting the whole in each detail, understanding the unique value of each detail through its relation to the whole. But, how can we inform those individuals in the Western world who rely only on manifestations observable by their five senses to draw their so called scientific conclusions?"

LAOV-TZSE: "Lets then explore that alleyway of the human logic and let's speak the language of those who commonly tread this path."

I am still under the charm of LAOV-TZSE's rhythmic verses, and the words he just uttered gracefully blend with those of the poem. But his last sentence piqued my curiosity. What kind of language is he speaking about?

29. Ten Adams, Eighteen Eves.

THE SAGE STRAIGHTENS HIS BACK, rearranges his long sleeves on his knees, then, pensively, says:

"Some months ago, you have traveled the way modern humans do, from New York to Paris, in a jetliner. And Tchi Mei Hiai, who notoriously reads newspapers only in planes, and even more rarely magazines at the dentist's waiting room, mentally clipped in the New York Times an article dated Tuesday May 02, 2000, titled "The human family tree: 10 Adams and 18 Eves", subtitled "Tracing history through genetic mutations". The writer Nicholas Wade, a renowned scientific journalist, reporting in that article the results of the most recent biogenetic research on Earth."

"TCHI MEI HIAI, asks the sage, please summarize for us the contents of that article…"

Stimulated by the Sensei's request, I am projected years back on a bench at the Sorbonne, answering the challenge presented by a professor, in front of a hundred brilliant college students.

"*I shall provide you with exact quotes, if neces*sary" adds Angel YELIYAEL, with a sympathetic wink.

I gather my reminiscences of that flight New York–Paris, the details flashing in my mind, in rapid succession, as they occurred: scanning New York Times title, smell of newspaper freshly printed, swiftly skipping bold front-page propaganda, leafing through slowly, dreamily, my expectations low, readying to abandon the paper and open a real book. Ah! Stop! Curiosity raised! Adam, Eve, ten Adams and eighteen Eves! I start reading the article.

I summarize: "In brief, several bio genetic researchers together with a team of archeologists analyzed the DNA of ancient skeletons unearthed in different parts of the world and discovered that a basic particular element composing the DNA of EVE, deemed first source of all women, is found in the DNA of all women on Earth, with only 18 variations of slight importance."

Says YELIYAEL, completing my outline:

"All mitochondrial DNA[140] *are all branches that stem from a single one, archeologists call Eve DNA*."

SIMHA: "And according to scientists, ADAM would have spread his male identity through the Y chromosome, and researchers at Stanford University, recently found "the tree is rooted in a single Y chromosomal Adam and lies in 10 principal branches."

And in that same New York Times article, striking conclusions are offered regarding time markers, providing a historical perspective."

Dutifully YELIYAEL further quotes the article:

"*The split between the two branches in the European tree suggests that modern humans reached Europe 39,000 to 51,000 years*

[140] Mitochondrial DNA: tiny rings of genetic material.

ago, Dr. Wallace calculates, a time that corresponds with the archeological dates of at least 35,000 years ago."

LAOV-TZSE: "You see Albert, even some rational academics are already recognizing that apparent multiple differences, like skin colors, races, sizes, are united in a common genetic stock. In their own way albeit slowly, they are discovering the Truth and, given more time, they will cease to combat its revelation.

That is, if they follow the advice of their peer, Dr Sykes from Oxford University in Great Britain, so quoted at the end of the same article:

"I don't think this stuff should be confined to academics."

LAOV-TZSE continues: "Now for the strong and brave seekers of Truth, I confirm that, actually, the celestial envoys EVA and ADAM landed on Earth about 40,000 years ago, and their genetic contribution showed perceptible effects, through Eve's and Adam's children born on Earth, only 5,000 years after their arrival. Those dates are well recorded in the archives of antique Sumer-Akad, ancient Egypt and Greece, and other more recent annals.

Yes, all modern women and men, including you and me, descendants of EVE and ADAM, pertain to the type "Sapiens-Sapiens", humans who think and speak, using in their speech a wide range of consonant-sonorities, exploring the widest array of wave frequencies human voice can produce on planet Earth. And, furthermore, "Sapiens-Sapiens" individuals not only "think and speak", but are fully *conscious* of speaking and thinking."

"Master LAOV-TZSE, exclaims Albert, thank you for linking ancient knowledge with the discoveries of our times. You are demonstrating that the gap of knowledge is deep in appearance only. Surely, somewhere, sometimes, maybe soon, modern science and antique wisdom will celebrate their grand Unity!"

LAOV-TZSE: "I have been always portrayed as an old sage removed from the world, an austere man sitting on top of a bare mountain, detached from everything and everyone, following the path of passive meditation, exclusively in search of a state of "do nothing, desire nothing".

That is a baseless fabrication. In truth, as attentive reading of my concise verses will clearly prove, I have been fully, vigorously engaged in the experience of progressive evolution of humankind, untiringly separating light from darkness, so allowing powerful joy of living to triumph over the enchaining sadness born of ignorance; pointing at essential knowledge regarding the divine origins of All Life and all beings, so providing all women and men with the prospect of an imperishable future life, in an eternal and limitless cosmic expanse."

Silence

Calmness and serenity prevail in the presence of our host. Again we take advantage of his tacit permission to remain still, let our thoughts roam and explore new territories, spiraling up to the confines of the mindal fields, daringly approaching the fires of spiritual frontiers…

Silence

Silence

Silence

Then Albert resumes the dialog:

"Sensei, what of the Chinese language? So visibly alien to most terrestrial languages, so remote from the root language, the Universal ARCHAE LINGUA?"

LAOV-TZSE, with great kindness, answers:

"You must understand that linguistic and genetic historic developments are absolutely correlated.

Before celestial EVE and ADAM landed and started the genetic enhancement of humankind, Earth was mostly populated by Homo Faber, genius artisan, then the dominant type among all humans.

At that time racial and territorial differences overpower the underlying similitude, humanity being still dominated by the forces of ANIMALITY. During the 500,000 years period preceding the EvAdamic divine merging, the human species had mostly manifested their vitality by differentiation and separateness, by race, skin color, gender, tribe, territory.

EVE and ADAM did not "invent" humanity; but they devotedly contributed to humans' increase in awareness of the ascending paths leading them toward celestial kingdoms.

By adding their divine genus to the genetic AMINAL-ANIMAL genome, they reversed the old values of instinctual survival, they increased the human aspirations towards the spiritual oceans, enabling women and men to become more sensitive to the pull of the universal gravitational spiritual centers. In fact they provided each individual with the capability to steadily develop a personal eternal SOUL."[141]

ALBERT: "And the human language on Earth, Master, how did it develop? How did it differentiate, how does it unify?"

LAOV-TZSE: "As earlier stated, linguistics and genetics evolved together, following the same path. On planet Earth existed pre-EvAdamic languages, which had been periodically enhanced by earlier numerous celestial visitors-educators, whose mission was to successively improve the different communication performances gradually developed over time by those individuals and groups having different life experience.

The genetic mission of EVA-ADAM was complemented with a specific linguistic mission. Thus pure ARCHAE LINGUA has been taught just as celestial genetic enhancement spread.

In fact, ARCHAE LINGUA and EvAdamic genes share in the same celestial origin, and are consequently inexorably twined.

Divine genetic enhancement does improve linguistic abilities, which in turn stimulates the manifestation of superior genetic traits, which in turn aggrandizes linguistic capacities, ad infinitum."

Albert summarizes: "Genetically divinized humankind ac-

---

[141] Soul: Genesis 2, 7. "And the Lord God formed man of the dust of the ground and breathed into his nostril the *breath of life*, and man became a *living being*". In Hebrew: va yitzer yahveh elohim et ha adam afar min ha adamah va yipach be apiv *neshamat chayim* va yehi ha adam le *nephesh chaya*. Literal correct translation of *neshamat chayim*=the breath of multiple lives=door to Immortality and potential Eternity=the soul. The common translation: the breath of life is incorrect for chayim is a plural form, thus meaning multiple lives. Literal translation of *nephesh chaya*: a living animal being (Chaya) inhabited by a soul (Nephesh).

quired the linguistic ability to converse with divinities using the same language, the Universal Language, ARCHAE LINGUA!"

LAOV-TZSE: "First each basic primeval sound has been clarified, vocalization sharpened, and, then, almost concurrently, to each basic voice-sound was made perceptible its specific "sense", its corresponding emotional resonance, intellectual meaning, and spiritual value.

The voice carries the sound, the sound carries the sense and the meaning. And to each different vocal-sound corresponds a specific meaning.[142] That aspect of ARCHAE LINGUA is well revealed by your Archaeo-Linguistic Analysis Method, as briefly presented in your "Angels Signs" book."

Angel YELIYAEL, who until now seemed remotely interested by this part of our conversation, unexpectedly projects in the direction of the room's darkest wall, precisely on a cream-colored narrow hanging banner, a brief extract of our work on "Universal Resonance" of the alphabet letters.

(((B as in Ba or Bi or Bo)))
The Basic universal paternal force,
which contains the code of all codes.
The formative energy generating all data and shapes.
The energy that Begins each and every life,
all manifestations,
all experiences.
The Basic Foundation of Life and Matter.[143]
The primeval house (Bayt in Hebrew) the Body

(((C as in Ca Co or Ka Ko)))
The practical, physical and material manifestation
of ideas and thoughts. A solidifying, Coalescing force

---

[142] Modern neurophysiology shows the triadic structure of the human hearing apparatus: 1-Sound receptor (noise). 2- Sound coordination (pre-meaning, "make sense" out of the sounds). 3- Perception transmuting sounds and basic "sense" into an "understanding" (symbolic function of the brains).

[143] B= The Hebrew BiBle Begins by Bereshit Bara, ordinarily translated as "In the Beginning (God) Brought into existence (created)"

within the fluidic substances of the universe.
Energies of Cohesion and Collusion,
Collaboration, Cooperation.
A force of impact and power, I Can.[144]
more…

The sage nodding appreciation gently smiles and continues his fascinating lecture:

"ARCHAE LINGUA-VOCALIS, namely the science of universal sonorities, has been henceforth spread among all human groups on the planet. Those archetypal sounds, sonorous effects of universal vibrations at various frequencies and amplitudes, are the basic foundations of all communications on Earth and throughout the Grand Universe.

Every type of creatures existing in the immense Cosmos, be they divine, celestial, vegetal, mineral, animal or human, ideally can perceive and make sense of those archetypal resonances.

ARCHAE LINGUA, eternally has always been, is and will be the absolute unifying source of all cosmic lives."

SIMHA: "Those basic universal resonances in the form of letters-consonants are preserved in various alphabets, the 22 Hebrew alphabet letter-sounds being the most exact, because through them are kept alive all the archetypal resonances, including those rarely used in modern cultures. And it is the purest, because only the consonants are recorded, not the vowels."

LAOV-TZSE: "Yes. The consonants and their corresponding meanings have been taught first, as it was easy to graft the most refined sounds on the previous rough animalistic grunts and groans. Those grunts being the natural primitive vowel sounds: aaaaaaaaaaa-ooooooooo-iiiiiiiiiiiii-uuuuuuuuuuuu.

With the ensuing clarification of the primitive fundamental vowels-sounds, the entire ARCHAE LINGUA communication system was made potentially accessible to humankind.

---

[144] Can: in Old English and Scottish "I ken" was often used to mean I can and I know how to do this, and I agree; in Old as well as Modern Hebrew ken= yes, and kana= know.

By example, the consonant "S", alone, un-vowelled, connotes the sense of Structured Science, Sapience. Wondrous nuances are made available when a complementing sound-vowel is added to the basic consonant."

YELIYAEL instantly enlightens our minds by projecting a new set of dark violet words on the yellow-ocher banner:

S+a=SA	S+o=SO	S+e=SE	S+i=SI
Infinite knowledge without specific directions. Expansive science without definite form or structure.	Polarized, oriented science, potentially radiating like a sun, "solar" ray or "soleil".	Enveloping, imbuing science. Embracing, loving, nourishing, caring science.	Science activated by an agent, a "persona", an "I am". A conscious science, active, dynamic, and transformative.

LAOV-TZSE: "That stage of language evolution is very well recorded on the Sumerian tablets found by the 19th and 20th century archeologists. The Sumerian language is typical of the syllabic system, where complex phrases are expressed by a sequential syllabic assemblage, like the word-phrase SU+MA+RI, which means:

SU = Science-knowledge,
MA = raised as a child by a Mother,
RI = shared as a sun shares its nourishing Rays.

Other examples of that stage of syllabic language development can be found in African tongues, as with the word-notion BO-KO-NO.[145] Also in Chinese, in the name-phrase KUNG FU TZU the last two sounds FU and TZU are syllabic; while KUNG is a word com-

[145] Bokono means, in an African dialect: Priest-Sage: the one who houses (bo) knowledge (kono)

pacting three syllables: Ku-Na-Go."[146]

The sage continues: "For a very long time the descendants of ADAM and EVE did not concern themselves with the establishment and propagation of a specific graphic writing system. Rather, they focused their attention on perfecting reception and reproduction of universal "sounds", the elements of "verbal expression", to instruct their human pupils to better convey emotions, share thoughts and goals, transfer complex skills.

In fact, when SETH's [147] descendants and missionaries brought civilization to the Middle Empire territory, their teaching contained no instructions regarding any script or graphic expression, while it conveyed exact and clear instruction concerning vocal expression and resulting powers of in-vocation and e-vocation.[148]

I shall expound on this subject later. As for now, I wish to continue the story of the spoken language on Earth, as it unfolded under the guidance of the celestial educators...

The first phase centered on the instruction-revelation of 22 pure, distinct consonant sounds, each conveying a core meaning, perceived by all beings in the entire Universe. Humans' hearing abilities were progressively refined, their acquired capacities to exactly reproduce sonorities by speech gradually increased.

The second level focused on the creation of syllabic sounds, by pairing consonants with significant vowels, potentially adding an infinite number of nuances to the human language. Thanks to the ancient scribes' devotion, Sumerian and Chinese languages preserve those teachings almost intact.

The third step in communication improvement concerns more specifically the expansion of mental development by introducing

---

[146] Kung = Ku-Na-Go, meaning Cohesion (Ku), Central, Nucleus (Na), Gravitation, attractive motion (Go). Resulting global meaning: *extreme charismatic personality*.

[147] Seth: the third son of Eve and Adam, as recorded in the Old Testament. See Genesis, 4:25-26.

[148] Genesis 4:26: "and as for Seth to him also a son was born and they named him Enoch. Then men began to "*call* on the name of the Lord". The Hebrew Oral Tradition designates humanity as Enoshout, thus indicating that True Humanity actually began when vocalizing Universal Sounds and therefore communicating with the Celestial Forces.

the "Word", built with several basic "letter-sound" elements. As a whole the Word expresses a global synthetic meaning.

And enclosed within the global meaning each separate verbal component keeps its specific connotation.

By nature, the whole word contains all the meanings offered by its components, and delivers an additional synergetic sense engendered by synthetic mental operation.

And, as a beneficial consequence of being inserted in the whole, the significance of each particular component is enriched by the global meaning delivered by the whole word.

By example, imagine one is presented with the whole word KaNaGa for the first time, therefore having no knowledge of its global meaning, one may separate each syllabic component, Ka, and Na and Ga and extract a global signification by adding the core meaning of the three components.

Ka= Cohesive power.
Na= Center of attraction, the Nucleus.
Ga= Physical Action and Motion, movement on Ground.

Thus Ka Na Ga = Cohesive Power becomes Center of Attraction which stimulates Physical Action.

The whole word KaNaGa, if applied to social organization, describes the chief, the charismatic heroic leader, insuring strong group coherence by attracting other individuals toward his central persona, himself acting and accomplishing deeds."

Surprise! Three crystalline musical notes dropping from the high ceiling, gaining in intensity as they slowly spiral downwards, gradually attract our attention towards the geometric center of the triangle formed by the sage, Albert and me.

And now, at eye level, floats and revolves a large golden shining circlet set with ruby red, amethyst blue, topaz yellow, the mysterious brilliance of the living gems reflecting the light of moving flames spiking from the upper edge.

"A crown! exclaims Albert. YELIYAEL has transformed himself into a gemmed golden crown!"

"The crown of a KaNaGa" murmurs LAOV-TZSE, lowering the tone of his voice to focus our attention.

SIMHA: "The crown of a KiNG!"

LAOV-TZSE: "Thank you Sensei YELIYAEL! Please interrupt my discourse as you please. I was weary, doubting my ability to appropriately reveal the wondrous grandeur of ARCHAE LINGUA!"

"Yes, says the sage. The word KING, similar to KaNaGa, expresses the nature of "kingness"[149]:

K= By cohesive power
N= be a center of attraction.
G= in order to conquer and maintain a kingdom by
physical action and motion.

You see, modern English language, like all others in the world, is permeated by antique ARCHAE LINGUA. In Chinese, the word KUNG FU, also rooted in ARCHAE LINGUA, designates the KINGLY FIGHT, FU pointing at the Fire, Vital Fiery Power to Fight. And indeed, in the Celestial Empire, KuNG Fu originated as a Royal Art!"

"Thank you, thank you Angel YELIYAEL!" "Thank you master LAOV TZSE!" Albert and I exclaim in concert.

We all take a deep deep breath, inspire-expire, rekindle our courage, and LAOV-TZSE resumes speaking:

"The greatest achievement of the third and final language teaching phase by the celestial educators is the full revelation of the principles underlying the lively, vibrant, dynamic, immortal ARCHAE LINGUA. Wide diffusion of that revelation among all peoples occurred just recently in the history of humankind, but ARCHAE LINGUA was long before known and used as a communication tool by the elite, mostly the direct descendants of celestial pre-EvAdamic visitors; the feats of those "supra-humans" are recorded in ancient traditions and mythologies as powerful Gods and heroic Semi-Gods. In fact ARCHAE LINGUA became widely

[149] Kingness/ kingship: Third century BC, the first unifier of China, renamed the Chou territory Qin and titled himself Qing Thus, in spite of violent resistance, the first Empire of China came into existence. Perfect "naming" made perfect result.

shared[150] on the planet only 6,000 years ago."

SIMHA: "Like yesterday on the time scale of evolution..."

ALBERT: "So recently, and humans have already forgotten! Obviously, humankind is afflicted by chronic amnesia..."

LAOV-TZSE: "The intensification and amplified transmission of that linguistic knowledge has been effected at the care of the descendants of the celestial EVE and ADAM. That knowledge is well preserved on the engraved tablets still hidden underground in the former territories of Sumer and Akad[151].

ARCHAE LINGUA's principles are embodied in the Sumerian analytic alphabet, which comprises 22 to 27 letter-sounds. Those principles are applied to convey basic emotions and notions as well as advanced scientific and technical knowledge."

Fiery visions swirl in my mind, Hebrew words resonate in my spirit, flamed letters illuminate my thoughts...Is that you YELIYAEL, shortening under your angelic light the shadows of my ignorance? I feel compelled to share my insight:

"ARCHAE LINGUA, ARCHAE LIN-Kua, the ARK of LINK, Art of Linking. Celestial ARCHAE LINGUA is safely preserved in the ARK of ALLIANCE! And the ARK of ALLIANCE is linking Heavens with Earth!"

Did I scream? Did I hush? Did anyone even hear me? Albert is smiling, LAOV-TZSE's eyes cast intense intelligent reflections. Neither of them comments on my verbal outburst.

And again YELIYAEL is nowhere to be seen or heard.

Unperturbed, serene, the sage pursues his historical linguistic revelation: "ARCHAE LINGUA manifested itself in full light about 2,000 years before Abraham's epoch. From Abraham to Jesus 2,000 years elapsed and from Jesus to your epoch another 2,000 years

---

150 Genesis 11-1: *Now the whole earth had one language and one speech*". In Hebrew Torah: "va yehi kol ha aretz safah achad ve devarim achadim" Through Archaeo-Linguistic analysis Safah-vocal language points at "the primary syllable roots and their sounds"; Devarim-speech points at "the designating function of the language, the root combinations producing the words".

151 Sumer-Akad territories: south Mesopotamia, between Tigris and Euphrates Rivers, recently invaded at the end of 600 century AD during Mohammedan hegira, now occupied by Arabs in Irak.

have passed. Therefore the Stars' Language has been fully revealed and relatively widely spread all over the planet since about 6,000 years.

This timing is well recorded by the Hebrew calendar, which indicates that something crucial has been initiated in year 3,760 BC, meaning 5,760 years ago, as of present year 2,000 AD."

More thoughts blooming in my head, more joyful emotions warm my heart. In few words sensei LAOV-TZSE has quietly enlightened for us the mysterious Year One of the Hebrew calendar!

I cannot refrain from commenting aloud:

"Master, I understand now. The traditional Hebrew calendar does not record the elapsed time since the creation of our world, as religionists stubbornly affirm. But it factually recalls the beginning of a crucial era: the foundation of potential and widely spread science of direct, frequent, recurrent, reciprocal communications between humans and celestial beings! At that time an unbreakable link has been re-established between earthly inhabitants and the entire Universe Sentience! A date worth recording, indeed!

Just imagine! Divine ARCHAE LINGUA was then fully alive, walking on Earth, nourishing human minds by the millions, with only 22 celestial sound-letters!"

"And, adds ALBERT, with 22 ferments UNIVERSAL LANGUAGE provided enough "spirit" to rejoice millions celebrating their union with all creatures on Earth and the Heavens!"

"And only with 22 beacons, illuminated the High Way to the Celestial kingdoms!" concludes LAOV-TZSE.

Enthralled we are! Human history as gallantly recounted by Master LAOV-TZSE dissolves much obfuscation that has persistently blocked our understanding of the true nature, origin and expansion of the human language.

ALBERT: "Marvelous, Sensei, amazing! You are handing us a potent microscope and a powerful telescope, all in one! Universal ARCHAE LINGUA illumes the near and the far, enlivens the small and the immense, embraces the temporal and the eternal, unifies human and divine…

But! But…(silence) after almost 6,000 years, separateness prevails on Earth, not union. That divisive reality is clearly illustrated by the different writing systems in use, the script differences overwhelming the potential unity of language. Have the celestial educators failed in their noble attempt? Or rather, has humankind regressed, not progressed, being now unwilling to maintain a firm contact with divinity?"

"Oui, answers LAOV-TZSE, I understand your French Cartesian mind[152] requests an elucidation of that apparent conundrum.

Let's travel back in time, to the long period before the human tribes received the Archaeo-Linguistic celestial teachings, namely the science of basic original sonorities, to be completed later by the full revelation of the ARCHAE LINGUA, the science of syllables assembly allowing the composition of complex sounds-words in order to communicate ideas and abstract knowledge.

At that remote time, when separateness prevailed, humans developed within each isolated tribal group, specific communication systems NOT BASED ON VOICE; since their groans and grunts utterly lacked conceptual nuances[153], carrying mostly emotional messages, through rhythmic breathing and throat racketing."

"However, emphasizes the sage, they all mastered another type of expression, of extraordinary sophistication: *GRAPHIC* expression, as expected from the adroit humans with "golden hands", Homo Faber! In fact, earthly humans SCRIPTED and WROTE long before they SPOKE…

They first "wrote" by drawing simple figures, representations of things and animals, and occasionally depicted "strange celestial aliens"; then their skills evolved into tracing symbols, points, lines and curves assembled to replace the former figurative messages, later on sophisticating the graphs, as the members of the tribes were sophisticating their abilities to seize their meanings.

---

[152] Cartesian: system of thought referring to French Scientist-Philosopher René Descartes (1596-1650 AD) who emphasizes the value of logical reasoning as a major tool for experimental science.

[153] Vocal expression similar to "click" consonants in Zulu and Xhosa language in Southern and Eastern Africa. Similar sounds may be found in the Australian Aborigine "Damin" ceremonial language.

The ultimate development step of that graphic expression has evolved into the Egyptian hieroglyphs, the Aztec glyphs and the elaborate Chinese characters. Of course, before the revelation and diffusion of the Archaeo-Linguistic sound system, the ancestors of those three languages I just mentioned did not demonstrate the same beauty, subtlety and exactness they have acquired in later times."

SIMHA: "O Master, you are implying that the diversity and differentiation of the original graphic systems are primarily rooted in terrestrial ground, while the source of the spoken languages is to be found in the celestial expanses, abode of the Angels and Divine Beings!

As an illustration one may evoke the word PAROLE[154], which means "spoken language" in modern French. It can be analyzed as PAR-OL, easily transferred into Hebrew PAR-EL, and decoded as PAR= the fruit-gift from EL= elevated, celestial…The celestial origin of speech is here clearly shown."

LAOV-TZSE nods approval and resumes his teaching:

"Contrary to VOCAL SPEECH, which nature is fully vibratory, silent graphs and scripts have little vibratory power, emit feeble architectonic and arithmetic resonance, retain only weak genetic, biochemical, or astral symbolism.

In blatant contrast with locally confined graphic script, Vocal expression unwaveringly links humankind to the Living Circuits of Cosmic Intelligence, the universal force fields of communication eternally crisscrossing all parts of all worlds; the spoken language connects all humans to those immense, albeit uncharted, networks concentrating and pulsating infinite mindal energies and supra-coherent spiritual lights.

Following the revelation and diffusion of ARCHAE LINGUA by the celestial teachers, *scripts* have been developed merely as practical recording tools. And, over time, different scripts have been used to record the same sound-languages.

---

[154] Parole: beware: modern English has drastically restricted the meaning of the word Parole to a legal term. However to the definition of "parole" is still attached the notion of promise under oath, indicative of a linkage with a superior divine authority.

SIMHA: "In recent history, during the early 7th century BC, the Hebrew language, sonorities unchanged, adopted a new lettering system, of Chaldaic origin. In modern times 20th century, the Turks, keeping their resonant language intact, changed the graphs only, overnight smoothly abandoning the Arabic script in favor of the Latin letters. Examples abound."

LAOV-TZSE: "Over time, many different cultural groups have attempted, with relative success, to adjust the newly acquired ARCHAE LINGUA principles, entirely based on analytical sonorities and melodic meaningful compositions, to their anterior system of graphic expression, which was pictographic and global.

In the Celestial Empire, today's China, the ancient college of savant "Name-Heads" "Name-Makers", an assembly of the wisest and learned linguistic leaders, chose not to adopt a new scripting system, dreading undesirable conceptual simplification. Therefore they voluntarily kept the previous quasi-pictographic script, global and synthetic, while attempting to combine it with the undoubtedly powerful analytic system.

During the third step of planetary linguistic development, the crucial phase of words creation by assembling and combining simple elements, the Chinese scribes endeavored to design ever more complex pictographic signs, each artistically compacted into an unbreakable whole, each aiming at representing an even more specific idea, sentiment, or perceived reality."

ALBERT: "And this is the cause of the enormous quantity of Chinese characters, more than 8,000 different signs!"[155]

Allowing LAOV-TZSE a well-deserved respite, YELIYAEL's soft voice continues the history lesson:

"*In their part of the world the AZTECAS pursued the same goal. Most samples of their linguistic effort, engraved on gold plates, are now lost, melted at the hands of the Spanish conquistadors; but myriads plates have been timely uplifted by celestial envoys and their contents are safely safeguarded in archangelic archives.*

[155] Chinese dictionaries record from around 10,000 to 105,000 characters. In recent times, around 1950 AD, the number of "official" characters in use has been reduced, and a well-educated Chinese person uses around 4,500 characters.

The ancient Egyptian sages kept their hieroglyphic system intact; while avoiding complication they astutely proceeded to make the necessary adjustments required by ARCHAE LINGUA's two levels system: first, basic sounds, then syllabic combination.

Before that, the Sumero Akadian writings, produced at the time of Guilgamesh and the epoch of the Tiger and Euphrates great civilizations, used classic global pictographic glyphs. And in other instances, they employed an alphabetical system which allows to compose any word by addition of simple signs-elements, and to employ the same signs, in different order, to obtain a different word, a different meaning.

Those languages were relatively easy to understand by many, their script being adapted to the two levels "sounds and syllables" linguistic system, as propagated by the celestial teachers.

ARCHAE LINGUA Lesson number 13478- Examples:

Whenever the sound "S" is being included in a word, it is represented by the same invariant graphic sign.

Whenever the syllabic sound "MA" is included in a word, it is represented by the same identical signs MA, whether the composed sign MA is employed in the words MARIA, MATTER, ADAMA or RAMA.

Such is not the case in languages constructed on pictographic structures, which, in spite of adjustments commanded by the two levels "sounds and syllables" linguistic system, are holding onto their global glyph systems, remnants of the pre-EvAdamic, non vocal systems, when tribal humans were only "speaking" by silently drawing pictures."

LAOV-TZSE, mischievously announces: "And this is the end of the lesson! You now understand the multitudinous visual scripts, graphs, glyphs and letter-character designs are the cause of the illusory, deceptive heterogeneity of the human languages. In truth, all languages, composed with the same sounds, are inexorably fundamentally identical.

ARCHAE LINGUA, unbeknown to multitudes, is in fact spoken by everyone on Earth, and understood by all celestial beings in the Heavens! And because they contemptuously ignore the presence of

ARCHAE LINGUA, most babbling humans don't know what they are really speaking about!"

LAOV-TZSE bursts into an enormous, joyful full-throated laughter, then, wiping his tears with his long silky sleeve, gently turns his head toward Albert, verifying that his question has been completely answered.

"Thank you, Sensei, merci!" confirms Albert, with a respectful saikeirei bow, expressing his profound gratitude.

I stand to add my own sincere expression of gratefulness:

"Thank you, Rabbi, TODAH RABAH!"

"AL LO DAVAR! You are welcome!" replies the sage.

Book 2

Quantum Leaps to Paradise

Chapter One

The Path and the Gate

30. The Sage's Garden.

TACITLY WE AGREED TO TAKE A BREAK. I chose to walk alone in the sage's garden. The sun is now high in the sky, early morning mist has completely dissolved, and a bright light reveals all the contrasts of the peaceful landscape.

Walking slowly, meditatively, I am immersing myself in the harmonious beauty emerging from the thoughtful arrangement of the various natural elements surrounding me: flowers, bushes, trees, brooks, cascades, stone bridges, ponds. Multiple pebble-covered narrow paths open in every possible direction, never impeding the wanderer's liberty.

Albert has climbed on the largest rock at the further end of the garden and is now sitting at the top. From that position he may enjoy a broad view of the entire interior garden, and turning his head, of the vast countryside beyond the fence.

My strolling between plants and rocks revives the earlier feelings raised this morning as I was contemplating the courtyard through the large bay window: from any angle this garden offers no obstacle, no barrier, and no limit, seemingly including the far away mountains and ocean, expanding even beyond the horizon.

Pause, observe, meditate, act without doing, travel without moving, swirl but follow the simplest path…

In my memory reverberates the echo of LAOV -TZSE's poem:

The Sky reached the Whole and became clear.
The Earth reached the Whole and became calm.
The Spirits reached the Whole, hence their power.
The Rivers reached the Whole and became filled.
The Beings reached the Whole and multiplied…

YELIYAEL is casting his angelic light on the multiple fresh cascading brooks projecting little droplets on the bordering rocks and leaves.

I hear the Angel's distinct voice calmly enouncing:

"The exploration of this Chinese garden is bringing back your fond memories of another magical garden near Tokyo, Japan. And you are comparing Japan's and China's destinies..."

Far from being shocked by the angelic intrusion, I feel honored YELIYAEL is again reading my inner thoughts.

The Angel continues:

"Japan started with a migration mostly motivated by spiritual evolution, first founded in, then departing from China: a migration preserving the Chinese foundations but stimulated by new desires, a soft form of rebellion.

Every component of the Japanese reality originates from mandarin China: philosophy, poetry, art, way of life...however the "whole" results in a completely different life experience. For, while the components are the same, desires and intents are differently oriented. In Japan LAOV-TZSE and BUDDHA are given a prevalent guiding role, over KUNG FU TZU...

You are wondering: What is contemporary Japan heading for? What specific voice is Japan contributing to the celestial chorus? Which permanent values is Japan carefully preserving? And which transformative revelation shall Japan disclose to the world?

You are trying to foresee the history of the future...You shall succeed. Ask Princess ARCHAE LINGUA to chant the ancient legends recounting the origins and future of the nations..."

YELIYAEL suddenly explodes into thousands brilliant sparks, reaching high in the sky, beyond the whitish little clouds leisurely traveling above. Then, each tiny star slowly falling transmutes into colorful fragrant flowers, luscious green leaves, sparkling droplets, vibrating noble dragonflies, all welcomed by a carefree chorale of twittering, chirping, peeping birds orderly perched on top of the graceful bamboo fence.

31. The Way.

WE ARE NOW BACK INSIDE OUR FAMILIAR informal ritual-free temple. Reforming on the floor our magic triangle, we now sit again on silky cushions, cobalt blue with embroidered hot amber dragons, ready to resume our dialog.

LAOV-TZSE: "This morning I have lectured at length and you both have demonstrated a great capacity for attentive listening and deep understanding. Allow me now to be a perfect listener and receiver…"

Peace and silence. Eyes closed, the sage keeps utterly still. My heartbeat gradually accelerates, increasingly warming up my entire body. LAOV-TZSE "doing nothing" radiates even more energy than LAOV-TZSE doing something…

ALBERT addresses the sage:

"As you see us we are children of the 20th century AD, born in the Western part of the world, far from China, 25 centuries after your sojourn on Earth. I can assure you that you and the results of your endeavors are famous, eminent and legendary amongst the most sincere seekers of Truth.

The excellence of your intelligence is as famed as are unknown the details of your daily life.

And paradoxically, while you are so celebrated for promoting inaction you have conquered the hearts and minds of millions across vast expanses of times and lands, by what you did and only by what you did: namely penning, on frail bamboo sticks, 5,000 elaborate pictographic Chinese characters.

The spiritual energy enclosed in each of your eighty-one short rhythmic poems is so powerful it has transpierced the language barriers and instigated multiple translations of those verses into all the tongues of all intellectually developed individuals and nations."

SIMHA: "And, you have universally implanted two lively vibrant philosophical seeds, two lively metaphysical core notions in the minds and hearts of humans: TAO TE KING and WU WEI."

ALBERT: "Certainly, Master LAOV-TZSE, from your present celestial station, you can measure the immensity and munificence of the philosophical orchard you have planted 25 centuries ago."

The sage opens his eyes, gently nods assent, and says: XIE-XIE[1].

Then, tilting slightly his head, staring at me, the sage asks: "Tchi Mei Hiai, would you interpret those Chinese words, TAO-TE-KING and WU WEI, with the help of Princess ARCHAE LINGUA? "

I answer:

"In truth TAO TE KING should resound as DAO DEH YING…"

The sage once more burst into a booming youthful laughter, vitalizing all beings, objects, plants, and atoms in the room and vicinity. Tiny luminous waves gently ripple from his face, coloring the transparent atmosphere as their circles expand in the limitless skies.

LAOV-TZSE: "Telluric energies have always that strange effect on me! But Tchi Mei Hiai, it is you who ignited the fire. Yes, yes, DAO DEH YING is a more accurate formula. The usual sonorities TAO TE KING are but a mundane pronouncement merely suitable for encouraging the worldly transient ambitions of princes, governors, kings, modern presidents. The sonorities DAO DEH YING better express the exact cosmic harmonies I attempted to reveal.

Please, Tchi Mei Hiai, let the melody DAO-DEH-YING resound in the Universe."

Swiftly I silently request again YELIYAEL's assistance. Feeling

1 Xie Xie = thank you in Mandarin Chinese.

so lonely, so shy, afraid to disappoint the sage, I timidly enounce:

DAO
Open the divine portal
DEH
Discover the short way
YI
Leading to the Verb
ING
of Eternal Presence

ALBERT: "Thus, the linguistic formula DAO DEH YING instantly connects the individual spirit with the Ultimate Source of all Spirits, Supreme Creator of all Life."

SIMHA: "How to discern and follow the DAO, the direct Way? At the time of our Birth we emerge in a state of panic out of the nourishing protective eggshell, the womb; at the time of our Death-Transition, stony ignorance often entombs our soul! How to find the short way to the Absolute Creator?"

LAOV-TZSE: "Sharpen your Intent at the time of explosion, and let your Intent float on the spirit ocean. Do not devise any mean, do not summon any force, do not invoke any cause that would push or pull, and interfere.

Fuse with your pure, good, true, beautiful Intent. That is all."

I am filled with the desire to emulate the Master, follow the track he so brilliantly illumed. And at the same time, I am not sure to find within myself the resources necessary to connect with the living spirit.

LAOV-TZSE's poetic words excite my sixth sense, expand the scope of my insight, incite my psyche to encompass the spirit essences which imbue and vitalize all existences, but cold Reason keeps raising obstacles and uncertainties.

I hear the sage's compassionate voice consoling me:

"I lived on Earth at a time when ARCHAE LINGUA was fully alive and constantly enlivening human minds. Everyone could easily perceive the rich melody emanating from each syllable, appreciate the spherical meaningful pulsation of every word.

Numerous mighty celestial initiators were still visibly roaming nearby, their beneficial influence vibrating concentrically from their schools built on mountaintops, like those you can see from my garden. Those schools nowadays you name Monasteries; in ARCHAE LINGUA monastery sounds as MIN-ASTER[2], which translates into "the species MIN from the Stars ASTER".

At the time I lived on Earth, one could perceive and easily assimilate spherical multifaceted knowledge. But at your epoch, the prevalent linear causal analyses obfuscate the comprehension of the living whole, forcing the mental spotlight on lifeless fragments." Silence

"Consequently a large increasing number of your contemporary researchers, and thinkers as well, lost all conscious connection with the Celestial Realms…"

Silence

Then the sage addresses me:

"Now, Tchi Mei Hiai let WU WEI cast its meaningful sound waves in the Universe."

Without interrupting my prior flow of thought I promptly comply with the wish of the sage:

"WU WEI expresses the essence of the original divine Verb. As DAO DEH YING is accomplished, the gate to the Cosmos wide open, the newborn soul is immerged in the essence of the divine Verb "WUWEI" "YAHVEH," which is ultimate "agent", ultimate "operator", ultimate "act". The Infinitely potent Divine WU WEI involvement absolutely nullifies any type of human action. Hence the "do nothing" notion generally presented to render the Chinese characters: WU WEI. "

Now YELIYAEL with a poised clear voice, like a Cistercian[3]

---

2 Min-Aster: Hebrew Min=Species. Latin Aster=star. Hence the word Monastery designates "the housing of the Celestial Beings".
A monastery in Hebrew, Aramaic and Arabic is a Min-Zar, the word meaning "the Species Min, alien to Earth zar". Note that Zar also means "enlightening power", as in Zohar. The word Zohar designating the famous kabalah book of the lights present in every synagogue literally means:" the beam of light (zo) which "descends from On High (har)".

3 Cistercian monks, of the religious order created in 1098, and fully developed under the guidance of the new abbot Bernard de Clairvaux in 1110 ad. That order is at

monk addressing his brothers assembled for the evening dinner, intones:

"Do not confuse the words, says the disciple, because when LAO TZE pronounces WU WEI, "doing nothing", he is not promoting ordinary inaction, contentment born of laziness. He is pointing at inaction of the terrestrial motion, desires, aspirations to things devoid of reality. Such "inaction" would then permit the real most energetic activity of the soul, which must be freed from its prison, like one opens the cage of a captive bird[4]."

I ask the sage:

"Master, aren't you a little annoyed by the dire distortions men have inflicted to the sublime message you have offered them before leaving Earth?"

LAOV-TZSE: "This type of emotion-thought has no place in my registry. It has no significance in the TAO-DAO. All I have been actively seeking is to restore the link between the Divine Creator and my own soul. I am a free traveler aiming at reaching ever-wider horizons. Although I did not egoistically conceal anything, I described my goal and discoveries with no intent to direct the steps of anybody else.

At times, surely, individual humans perceived the echo and rhymes and rhythms of the answers I was receiving from the DAO. And those individuals played the celestial melodies on the best instrument they could muster, chanted them with their own voice, at the best of their personal abilities.

If some disciples, by the grace of WU WEI's fiery cosmic vibrations, exploded out of their jailing eggshell, freed their soul, energized their being in the living cosmic ocean, I am unreservedly pleased by their success at embracing and being embraced by DAO."

The sage closes his eyes. His last word, DAO, reverberates in my mind, echoing as DAYO, DIOS, DEVA, DIEU, DEUS, all verbal

---

the origin of the Knights Templar Order and the source of the Gothic cathedrals all over Europe.

4 The Angel is delivering a free English translation of a short excerpt from the French literary book titled wu wei by Henry Borel, original edition 1931.

sounds expressing different facets of the Divine Totality, the Ultimate and One Source of Life.

LAOV-TZSE: "All around Earth, during the era of my sojourn on your planet, many great Masters contributed to the revitalization of humankind eternal alliance with the Creator of all that IS. Each master choosing to emphasize different aspects of the Whole, according to the abilities of the peoples they were addressing: Kung Fu Tzu in China, Kwezal Koatl in Central America."

ALBERT: "And in Greece Pericles, Pythagoras, Socrates, Plato, Aristoteles."

SIMHA: "Tarquinius, the Etruscan founder of Rome, Cyrus reviving the powerful Babylonian culture in Persia-Mesopotamia. Esdras transliterates the Mosaic oral tradition into written Hebraic Chaldaic scriptures as it has come down to us unadulterated."

LAOV-TZSE: "Gautama Buddha, in India."

SIMHA "The awakening of the Dogon people, and the birth of the Ghana Empire, in Afrika"

LAOV-TZSE: "All are disciples of Musaeus-Hermes, the great incomparable cosmic musician, guardian of the Ark of Alliance, HER-MAISTER supreme poet and propagator of Universal ARCHAE LINGUA, my Divine Initiator MOSHEH… MOSES …"

I cannot gauge the time of our complete stillness. We do not move, we do not speak, all action being suspended for a long, long time…or a few minutes? In the presence of LAOV-TZSE time is an elusive reality. All eons, eras, years, days, hours, minutes are only artificial fractions of the immeasurable, incalculable, eternal Oneness.

I feel the wondrous flowing powers of DAO DEH YING rippling in my mind, gushing in my heart, filling my lungs with renewed energies; I am making no effort to control the rhythmic gentle tremor shaking my whole body; all my bones and organs seem to willingly play a part in this wonderful celestial chorus.

(((DAO DEH YING)))
(((DAO DEH YING))) (((DAO DEH YING)))

I am aware of my increasing awareness, and my awareness expands into Albert's awareness, our combined enlightenments augmenting exponentially.

And suddenly I SEE, brighter than sunlight, and I HEAR, clearer than clear crystal, YELIYAEL's, LAOV-TZSE's and Yohanan BEN ZAKAI's SOULS, three revolving immense radiating white suns, calling, rhythming, chanting our names:

(((SIM-HA
((((AL-BER-T
(((TCHI MEI HIAI
(((ALBERTOV
(((SHI ME HA
(((ILI-BI-LI-TAI...
(((DAO,
((((DAO *come over,*
(((DAO-R *is open,*
(((DOO-R *is open.....Join us!...*

Answering the call, instantly Albert and I lock hands, and, together, side by side, body-mind-spirit united, facing Infinity, without hesitation, we jump up into Eternity...

32. The 9th Commandment.

LAOV-TZSE: "YOU CAME HERE TO CONFER with me in regard with MOSES' 9th Commandment..."

"Yes, I answer, and I must confess, when, after our encounter with Yohanan BEN ZAKAI, in the ancient land of Israel, we finally found we would be meeting you, in China, to decipher an alien text written in Hebrew, promulgated from the top of Mount Nebo facing the land of Canaan, I was personally very unsure whether we had made the correct choice. Those strange sonorities LAO TZE, LAO TZU, TAO, TAO TE KING, TAO CHING, WU WEI, dragonlike symbols of a Celestial Empire, mysterious China protected by gigantic walls, immense expanses of land, innumerable peoples speaking multiple diverse dialects, their elite only commanding a singular federative language as well, writing with graphically complex characters, all these oddities seemed to indicate we could find in China no real help for the accomplishment of our mission."

LAOV-TZSE: "Then what happened?"

ALBERT: "You know Sensei that, at the end of our encounter with MOSES, in the plain of Moab, in front of the famous Tent of Assignments, Master MOSES has given YELIYAEL clear precise directions regarding our next interlocutor, Yohanan BEN ZAKAI, and the space- time coordinates to find him."

SIMHA: "We clearly saw MOSES moving his hands and fingers to instruct Angel YELIYAEL and we effectively landed in Galilee. But, after our encounter, the Rabbi blatantly refused to provide YELIYAEL, with any indication concerning the personality we were to meet next. No name, no space, no time!"

LAOV-TZSE: "So YOHANAN did nothing?"

SIMHA: "Nothing! He did nothing! Nothing visible! Nothing audible! Nothing tangible!"

LAOV-TZSE: "And what did you do?"

ALBERT: "At first we worried, feeling lost in the void, unable to continue our mission."

LAOV-TZSE: "Then?"

SIMHA: "We decided to let all worries go, and YELIYAEL flew us to Paris, just for fun! There we found your book of poems waiting for us, on a coffee table, at a friend's home."

LAOV-TZSE: "Thank you! YOHANAN, Albertov, Shimeha, you are my first true disciples! You did nothing, you WuWei-ed, and you found me! Now, together, let's uncover and illume the multiple facets of the 9th Commandment."

SIMHA: "With your like-minded Yohanan BEN ZAKAI, we have uncovered the mysteries of the 10th Commandment, titled YoAa, and entered the covenant "not to desire anything inessential, not to covet anyone's mundane properties or intellectual and spiritual qualities."

"TOBA is the melodic title of the 9th Commandment" chimes in YELIYAEL.

Reaching with his long-fingered hand the low square black lacquered table on his right, the sage picks up an object wrapped in blue fabric, slowly uncovers a little paper cylinder. LAOV-TZSE opens the scroll, and briefly shows us the inside, covered with stylish Chinese characters, then, reading, enounces, with a clear barely accented voice:

(((((((((LOA))))))))))
((((((((((TA ÂNEH))))))))))
(((((((((((BE RE ÊKHA))))))))
((((((((((((ÂD SHE KER)))))))))))

Thrilled we hear MOSES' 9th Commandment, now scripted in elegant Chinese characters, directly vocalized in ARCHAE LINGUA, the Hebrew Version!

Without a pause, the sage asks:

"How do the non-erudite people of your time translate this rhythmic verse?"

ALBERT: "They say it means: DO NOT LIE."

LAOV-TZSE, smiling gently: "Naïve, off handed rendition!"

ALBERT: "However, in spite of the simplicity of the command, men and women keep lying, everywhere, often, and for countless worthless motives!"

LAOV-TZSE: "Natural predictable consequence! As you call a being or a thing, so it presents itself. The Commandment is incorrectly transmitted; that translation from the original text itself is a lie. Is there a more sophisticated rendering generally available?"

ALBERT: "Here is the Latin translation that has been used for almost a millennium: "Non loqueris contra proximum tuum falsum testimonium". Today the popular King James Bible proclaims:

Thou shalt not bear false witness against thy neighbor."

The sage thinks a moment, meditatively, slowly brushes his long white beard with two fingers, and says:

"Much improved version, nearer to the first level of truth. The short formulation "Do not lie" stands at the end of the paraphrase chain and ends being akin to a lie.

Obviously, men and women of your time can find remedy to error and ignorance by voluntarily accessing the original text, not contenting themselves with inexact commentaries and rumors."

SIMHA: "As you know, Master, each Commandment has been revealed to MOSES as a divine song, each with a specific title, each title being an indispensable key to unlock the powerful spiritual powers enclosed in each Commandment.

Angel YELIYAEL helped us decipher HOVA-LOVE. Then Rabbi YOHANAN illumed for us the structural correspondence linking all those titles, and told us how MOSES himself composed the 10th law, YoAa, I AM THE CELESTIALIZED MAN. Sensei, please help us free the genie enclosed in the 9th title, TOBA!"

LAOV-TZSE intervenes:

"Let's apply our Archaeo-Linguistic skills. First we separate the two syllables To and Ba composing the word ToBa. The sound "To" results from the vocalization symbolized by the Hebrew letter named "Tet"[5], which sound carries the energies and attribute of

5 Tet Hebrew letter Tet, connoting short Time and Short Cycle to be distinguished from the other Hebrew letter Tav connoting Great Cyclical manifestation of Time. In

Divine Instant-aneity, transmuted on Earth into Instinct-aneity.

At times of severe extreme crisis threatening "survival", the innate Instinctual response may prove greatly insufficient, and the situation requests Instant Divine intervention.

"TeT", the letter which mirrors itself, indicates that Instinctual energies and Divine Instantaneity can instantly act in concert.

Every terrestrial creature confronted with sudden and brutal danger which threatens its very existence, asking help from the Heavens with pure Intent and intense Will to survive, may be immediately embraced by the celestial hyper-energized circuits. The effects on the living being are multidimensional: electro-biologic, psycho-mental, chemico-hormonal, spiritual.

Thus wondrous Miracle occurs, Providence manifests, Grace saves instantaneously (TO).

Learn that the living pattern of this sudden miraculous potent response may engrave itself on the genetic physical body level (BA) thus serving as acquired transmissible potential model for future instantaneous and fully adequate reactions, at the bio-electric-chemical level, or psycho-mindal-moral-spiritual level.

That perfectly immediate-adequate response to present danger, the Sumerian and Hebrew scribes name TOBA, meaning what is Good, streaming from the cosmic reservoir of Goodness."

SIMHA: "At the beginning of the GENESIS book, the celestial supervisors, the ELOHIM, appraise the completion of each stage of planetary transformations with those words: VA YARE KI TOBA. Which means: "this is Good, valid for reproduction", for it is integrated within the superior circuits of cosmic GOODNESS."

ALBERT: "Oh là là! TOBA ! What a giant leap in understanding! TOBA transmutes the curt moral injunction "DO NOT LIE" into a promise of divine grace and compassion!

SIMHA: "The heading TOBA, announces that the principles conveyed by the 9th Commandment are offspring of the Divine Universal Organicity, and therefore Good to be imprinted and re-

---

the past those two Ts were pronounced differently. Tet sounding like T, and Tav sounding like English TH.

produced indefinitely, either through intellectual instillation, or emotional impression, or infusion of moral reflexes, ultimately by all these means."

LAOV-TZSE: "TOV! I approve the wording of your explanation. Abstract in the form but to me verily, intensely real."

SIMHA: "Thank you Master!"

ALBERT: "The short version "Do not lie" we can easily discard. Now, about the longer version "Thou shalt not bear false witness against thy neighbor". Is it a satisfactory translation of the original verse in Hebrew

LOA TA ÂNEH BE RE ÊKHA ÂD SHE KER?"

SIMHA: "The official translation hints at promoting the notion of "verity" against "falseness". Certainly that expression of the 9th Commandment is more in accord with the message delivered by TOBA, which emphasizes the natural "verity" characterizing the immediate unassailable alliance uniting humankind's reality and the Universal Creator. Thus this law asserts a spiritual unbreakable pact between true perfect Divinity and true perfectible Humanity.

But the now popularized formulation "Thou shalt not bear false witness against thy neighbor" has reached the status of certainty, at the exoteric level, only because no challenging popular translation has ever been proposed in the past 2,000 years.

However, that sketchy formulation under the guise of a firm social rule colored with tinges of individual morality, compared to the original statement in ARCHAE LINGUA, is a patent falsification."

Shocked, LAOV-TZSE and Albert, at the same time, open wide their eyes, straighten their backs, curiosity and attention raised up to maximum. YELIYAEL, my compassionate angelic friend, encourages me with a volley of undulating mauve and yellow light rays, aiming at my heart and forehead.

LAOV-TZSE: "And, Shimeha, are you now about to demonstrate the falsification!?"

I open my own biblical scroll, take a deep inspiration, and resolutely let ARCHAE LINGUA resound in the room, my translation from Hebrew:

LOA	do not
TA ÂNEH	respond
BE RE ÊKHA [6]	when *confronted*
	with neighbor's wickedness
ÂD [7]	by testifying as truth
SHEKER	that what is falsity.

"As you see, the original Torah text comprises essential details, blatantly overlooked by the common translation:

"Thou shalt not bear false witness against thy neighbor"

This common translation, in contrast with ARCHAE LINGUA'S version, does not mention potentially crucial circumstances under which we should not bear false witness.

Whoever hears this common version is implicitly induced to believe the neighbor against whom one is bearing false witness is innocent and has done no wrong. Therefore the temptation to bear false witness is almost nil.

The vapid vagueness of the official translation, under the guise of generality, opens the door to all exceptions and extenuating circumstances, which could be invoked; it hypocritically nullifies the practical value of the 9th Commandment during our life on Earth.

Conversely, the original text, when correctly translated, points clearly to the most crucial circumstances, as it noticeably states:

"Do not bear false witness in response to *your neighbor's wickedness*". Therefore this command is specifically pointing at situations in which urgent temptation to bear false witness effectively surges!

Consider this: I am under attack, surrounded, threatened by someone in my proximity, bearing false witness against me, wickedly endangering my freedom or my life! I see no escape! I must react, it is urgent, blow for blow, even oppose falsity to falsity lest I fall, suffocate in the clutches of wickedness…

To address that highly emotional and practical predicament,

---

6 Re ekha: this Hebrew word delivers simultaneously and unambiguously two specific meanings.:1/ Your Neighbor. 2/ Wickedness aimed at you.

7 Ad: this Hebrew word contracts two meanings: 1/ Witnessing .2/Truthfulness. It is the root of the verbs "to aid" and "to add".

the 9th Commandment anticipates the worse circumstances and draws all its value thereof, for it clearly specifies:

Do not respond to hostile falsity with your made up falsity, even for the good cause."

ALBERT: "I see now. The common formulation does not even allude to a "response", a "reaction". Conversely the original ARCHAE LINGUA text clearly does so, by specifying it with the second word TA ÂNEH, meaning: re-action, a reactive response.

The common formulation doesn't mention that I may be under attack, the victim of an aggression, and could find legitimate to reciprocate, by use of equal wickedness. In contrast, the common translation boldly asserts, not only implies, that the neighbor against whom I bear false witness is innocent of any wrongdoing!"

SIMHA: "And, enlarging the scope of application, the real 9th Commandment may be construed as justly proclaiming: "The end does not justify the means"."

Albert frowns his eyebrows, moves slowly his fingers, closing and opening his hands. I know those signs; his philosophical mind has perceived a contradiction. His request for clarification comes even sooner, and more calmly, than I expected:

ALBERT: "At the start of and throughout our cosmic journey, we have always firmly asserted, and experienced, that right Intent is the supreme energy and guiding principle for any successful enterprise. The very reality of Intention always encloses an actual aim, goal, purpose…an end.

The End-Intent being supreme, the Means employed to reach that End must necessarily defer to the End.

Is there a way to harmonize the law of right Intent with the ethical commandment "The end does not justify the means"?"

LAOV-TZSE's visage emanates perfect tranquility. The sage is attentive to the debate but apparently unconcerned by the ethical philosophical turbulences raised by Albert's question.

I close my eyes, remain still for a moment to reinforce my connection with my inner guide, my divine companion, my eternal beacon, and I say:

"Obviously there is nothing to harmonize, because there is no contradiction. True final Intents are always pure, limpid, aiming at Universal Goodness.

Every pure intention is necessarily aiming at "some-thing"; it cannot be intention aiming at "not-something".

NO-something is only illusory, has no real existence in the Universe. In the Universe all existence is inescapably ontologically positive, and consequently every illusory and unsubstantial NO is immediately converted into a YES."

ALBERT: "Just like in a music part a pause, a "silence" IS, equal in status to every note…"

SIMHA: "Yes. That is why we must incessantly scrutinize and refine our Intents, finely accord their frequency with the principles of Divine Universal "Organicity". So attuned, our Good Intents, aiming at Universal Goodness, will be naturally attracted by the Divine TOBA, divine GOODNESS."

ALBERT: "In that case, when the pure Intent is truly in accord with Universal Goodness, the End completely justifies the means, for the means are de facto part of the End, like the part enclosed in the whole; there is no separation between the means and the aimed at End."

SIMHA: "That is, if and when the Cosmic Mind recognizes the End as TOBA, GOOD. But in all other cases, when the Intent is qualitatively less than universally good, then the means cannot be justified by the End."

LAOV-TZSE: "Innumerable individuals attempt to hide behind a pretense of Goodness a purpose solely aiming at immoral self-serving selfish empowerment. They are willfully, slyly "scheming" in lieu of "aiming". However the Cosmic Mind in fact rejects the cover up and the apparent success is only transitory, or the obtained result is a complete reversal of the avowed desired effect."

ALBERT: "In practice, it is not easy for an individual to reach the level of Pure Intent. Therefore every individual willing to improve his situation on the scale of moral evolution must develop a perfect consciousness of the message contained in the 9th Law."

SIMHA: "Yes, consciousness of the message contained in the

9th law, including the title TOBA, the ultimate model of all Goodness, the seal "Good to Reproduce". "

ALBERT: "Whoever ignores the model TOBA is left without a guide, and chances for the 9th Commandment to be implemented at the moral level are low…as low as when one has only a partial, feeble awareness of the content of the Commandment itself."

SIMHA: "Without full conscious harmony with TOBA, the ultimate universal model of all goodness, our intentions are finally inoperative, ignored, dissolved, dropped into the universe "waste bin". Their flimsy pseudo-reality dissolves, enters and merges into the gigantic circuits of anonymous unidentified energies."

ALBERT: "Then TOBA is really akin to the keystone of an arch: two sides of an arch leaning on each other need a keystone to gain strength. TOBA provides the "spiritual keystone" necessary to transform those two weaknesses into great strength[8]."

Nurturing our meditative stasis LAOV-TZSE softly recites:

Long and Short	High and Low	Before and After
send for	lean	each
each	on	other
other	each other	follow.

Then the sage exclaims: "I really enjoy your company! I am so glad you did nothing foolish when my good friend Yohanan BEN ZAKAI apparently disappointed you by "doing nothing" and "said nothing" to Angel YELIYAEL. Had he interfered in any way, the attractive power of my poem book in Paris might have been weakened…and you would have ended visiting KUNG FU TZU, not me LAO TZU!"

Chuckle. Chuckle. Broad smile.

"Surely KUNG FU TZU would have been delighted to hear you both tackle moral dilemmas! His extensive repertoire offers a definite number of answers for every possible situation, a cure for eve-

8 Definition of the arch form by Leonardo da Vinci: "An arch consists of two weaknesses, which leaning on each other, become a great strength". "L'arco è una costruzione nata da due debolezze dalla cui unione risulta una grande forza".

ry possible sin! However nobody and nothing interfered with the Universal law of pure Intent, and by the Grace of TOBA, you are here with me, and I am here with you!

And now, let's celebrate our reunion by unveiling the marvels enclosed in the 9th Commandment!"

ALBERT: "Our Angel companion made us aware, at the very beginning of our quest, that every Commandment, enshrined in living ARCHAE LINGUA, is a sphere radiating rays of knowledge perceivable at different levels of consciousness.

Level 1: principles of human morality.
Level 2: divine recommendation.
Level 3: human pledge to divinity.
Level 4: scientific description of divine Law
operative in the Universe.

And, as do the radiuses of a sphere, all those rays converge toward the same unique center."

SIMHA: "And the circumference of the sphere being limitless, each ray expands into Infinity…"

"TOV, GOOD, says the sage. Ili Bi Li Tai, Tchi Mei Hiai, let's begin at level One."

Reading aloud, I let the cherished divine sonorities of ARCHAE LINGUA resound in the room, and, amplified by the surrounding magnetic spirit field, they concentrically ripple in the Universe:

LOA TA ÂNEH BE RE ÊKHA ÂD SHE KER

"The first sound, LOA, deserves special attention. That word, which comes first in seven out of ten Commandments, is repeated several times in three Commandments. And in spite of its banal common meaning, DO NOT, some clarifications are very much needed."

I can feel Albert is tense, made uneasy by my prelude to a probable long digression. But, encouraged by the impeccable serenity displayed by the sage, he swiftly calms his anxiety, opens wide his mind, readying for one more revealing deep incursion into Princess' ARCHAE LINGUA castle.

So I commence:

"In functional Hebrew, as spoken today in the land of Israel, the word LOA, pronounced LO, is quite equivalent to the English NO, DO NOT. As I just reminded you, seven out of ten of MOSES' Commandments begin by LOA, and systematically, during the past 3,500 years, in all published translations, LOA serves as official announcer of negative injunctions: "do not kill", "do not lie" "do not steal" do not covet" "do not commit adultery"...

But, in truth, NO and its reverse YES, retain no real substance in the Universe. YES and NO are merely signs, akin to algebraic symbols, for expressing polarities which operate in the real world: active-passive, male-female, past-future, yin-yang.

However each side of the polarity equally IS, neither could exist without the other.

Therefore banal use of NO and YES is akin to looking at a couple, a handsome man and a beautiful woman, and tersely name one NO and the other YES!

When, on Mount Horeb, the celestial envoy hurled his blazing light beams on the stone slabs, seven of his messages began with LOA, which, as revealed by Archaeo-Linguistic analysis, means:

The bright and flowing energies,
forces of elevation and living mental expansion,(LO)
soar and link directly (LO)
with the First and Ultimate Source of all Beings (A).

Therefore, the heading LOA indicates that the Commandment is altogether telling us what "not to do" to not impede our life progress, and at the same time, what we must "be" and "become" to reach our true goal, the ultimate source of existence.

Of course, when starting from the lowest human station, the experience of such an elevating motion and direct connection with the divine necessitates prior exact knowledge acquisition by each individual of the fundamental Universal Laws active in the cosmos he or she aspires to bond with.

Those laws apply at all levels of existence, in all dimensions of Life: material, mental and spiritual. They apply as well in human relations to all other forms of Life and, of course to social and inter-individual relationships.

The word LOA, at the opening of each apparently prohibitive Commandment, "do not", simultaneously says:

When you have found the way leading (LO) you to your source (A) then you shall be able to:

"*acquire without stealing*" thus completing "do not steal",
"*win over wickedness without falsification*" thus completing
"you shall not bear false witness even against the wicked"
"*enjoy without possession*" thus completing "do not covet"
"*prevail without killing*" thus completing "do not kill".

And that is how ARCHAE LINGUA may help perceive the different facets of a single word-diamond."

I pause. The sage smiles broadly, apparently appreciating the detour. Albert who also seems to enjoy the digression, appears stimulated by the new outlook I just offered...Both having so kind minds and generous hearts!

As for myself, I secretly feel dissatisfied by my own discourse, too didactic, resembling too much the academic psychology and high school philosophy classes of old.

But how would one possibly render the rich and versatile, flowing, dynamic and spherical reality of ARCHAE LINGUA? How to lead other minds to the understanding of the same expression of Life at so many levels, in so many dimensions?

I feel deeply depressed. Only 4 levels of interpretation, and even this extremely reduced number seems too much to cope with; it appears to be an unattainable goal. The task is almost akin to sum up centuries of extensive Talmudic commentaries into 4 short sentences…

ALBERT breaks the silence and, enthusiastic, enounces:

"An attentive listener with a clear mind can notice LOA sounds like the word LAW, as vocalized by English speaking peoples, and LOI as vocalized by the French speaking peoples. LOA at the start of a Commandment tells us: What follows is a LAW!"

LAOV-TZSE: "Unambiguous conclusion obtained by perceiving

and interpreting the sound similarity of the words alone! I would call that spontaneous Archaeo-Linguistic analysis! A proof that truth can be attained also by simple, uncomplicated ways!"

"TOV!" the sage exclaims. "Now Albertov, Shimeha, let's begin the interpretation of the 9th Commandment at level 1: principles of human morality."

ALBERT starts reading, his index successively pointing at each antique word, clearly vocalizing every syllable:

"When you find yourself inhabited or enshrouded (BA) by the obvious wickedness or malfeasance of someone (RE ÊKHA), you shall nevertheless treat that someone like a respectable alter ego, alter idem, (RE ÊKHA).

And despite the powerful pressure (RE) imposed on you by his aggression, despite his wanton will to persuade others to harm you (RE ÊKHA), do not react to that kind of aggression (TA ÂNEH) by developing "schemes" or scenarios (ÂD), by which you involve witnesses (ÂD) into promoting falsification (SHEKER).

Know that if you disregard this command and opt for forgery, you shall be utterly destroyed (RE Ê) by your own actions (KHA)."

SIMHA: "I am so proud of my student! Albert's translation at the human moral level is good; the humanistic contents of that Commandment are clearly shown, the underlying moral principle well illumed. Such striking progress in so little time at studying ARCHAE LINGUA!"

And now, the voice of Angel YELIYAEL resonates from the four corners of the room: "*This command is titled TOBA, universal resonance meaning "Good to reproduce". It proclaims that, by providential Grace, the pattern of an heroic human reaction may be permanently impressed in the genetic code and instilled in the mindal circuits, so becoming an automatic reflex, namely capable to adequately guide future actions and shorten the response time in dangerous circumstances.*

In light of Albert's excellent prior interpretation, what is the value added by TOBA, the title-code of the 9th Commandment? That Commandment evokes the manifold aggressions besetting humans in the course of their life. Those aggressions may be minor; they may also be major.

Reacting to aggressions specifically threatening physical life, the animal instinctual response, namely self-defense, is still, at the present stage of human evolution, generally adequate.

Yet, we the Angels know this 9th Commandment aims beyond those dangers threatening physical life in the material world.

The major innovation this Commandment brings to humanity as a whole, and to each individual human being, is a moral induction. Humans are hereby induced to assess aggressive incidents, distinguish the attack on life itself, authorizing immediate self-defense reaction, from an aggression which must be brought to justice, human and or divine.

*For those judicable cases, self-defense reaction is prohibited. And so is prohibited the falsification of facts, false witnessing, as substitute for self-defense. The aggressor, provoker, antagonist, must thus be justly regarded as an "other self", an "alter ego" (*RE ĚKHA*) lovable and redeemable, as frequently as possible.*

Whenever and wherever an aggressed individual, obeying the 9th Commandment's injunction, refrains to respond to wickedness-by-wickedness, he/she is justly behaving in harmony with the highest behavioral model of all, the heavenly law of divine Justice.
Thus is sealed the bond between the human individual and the miraculous TOBA, the Heavenly GOODNESS.

Recall that in ARCHAE LINGUA, the word TOBA signals: this is Good, valid for reproduction, perfectly integrated within the superior circuits of cosmic GOODNESS.

Conscious compliance with this Commandment shall cause the divine ethical principles to infuse spirit, mind and body, endowing the individual with an inner moral pattern, a spiritual reflex akin to the animal self-defense reflex, a "built-in" organic moral-ethical response system.

Thus the Universe thanks and rewards moral man and woman by facilitating their Just decision in all difficult situations of their life. Wide open before them is the majestic path leading to Universal Grace and Goodness.

TOBA, ultimate model of divine GOODNESS, is the keystone of the 9th Commandment. Those men and women who conjoin and unite with that 9th law, are endowed by divine decree with the powers to stimulate the moral ascending transformation of their "neighbors" and social "alter egos", and thus become the new rock-solid foundation of the ethical progress of all humanity."

And the Angel concludes: "*Imagine! Envision the beauty of a land, a planet, a world where humanity, in all thoughts, actions and cosmic connections, spontaneously, reflexively, abides by the Divine Law of Universal Goodness!!!"*

"TOBA-TOBA!" exclaims LAOV TZSE, looking at the high ceiling where YELIYAEL at the moment is floating in the guise of a ring of purple smoke.

"Now, who is going to voice and decipher Level 2, divine recommendation to humanity?"

As the sage is intensely gazing in my direction I slowly open my scroll, and start vocalizing, syllable by syllable, the message addressed by the Divine Envoy, through MOSES' mediation, to each man and woman on Earth:

LOA TA ÂNEH BE RE ÊKHA ÂD SHE KER

And I earnestly attempt to interpret these words, reaching beyond the veils interposed by exoteric ordinary translations:

"When you know and recognize the luminous mental circuits (LO) by which you shall be able to establish a link with your Supreme Creator, your original Source (A), it will be easy for you to transfigure your temporal destiny (TA) into un-temporal destination. For a long period you shall remain "temporalized" (TA), and controlled by sensibility (Â). However permanent connection with the divine generates crucial essential changes (NeH), your senses shall drink from a new source (Â), the immense original source of eternal substance (N), inseparable from the substance of the Mother Spirit pervading the entire Universe (Ne-H).

It is then that you will face a destructive danger (BE RE ÊKHA). Hence, be wary and recognize your own form of being (BE), the specific nature of sensations-emotions and mental achievements, which have been your own all along your life's path and your quest.

While experiencing the turmoil of transformations, respect your own nature, carefully observe and know thyself as much as you shall respect the specific forms of other beings by observing them impeccably.

For I tell you, no falsification, no false testimony can be justified, nor can enduringly succeed.

For you can transit toward the worlds leading to the Ultimate and Sacred Presence only by passing through the door perfectly, precisely, harmonized with "what and who is you".

And consequently, now, without delay, inquire, study, search, ascertain the nature and dimensions of your true self, so as to prepare yourself to produce the exact YES-I AM, and immediately recognize that which is not "you".

Understand that if you cannot perceive and pass through the unique door that is "for you" because it is "your truth", then, inexorably, the fragmented elements of your inessential personality shall dissolve, melt into the universe "impersonal nothingness", thus meeting absolute Death!

Neither Purgatory, nor Hell, nor Paradise. Simply nothing, for there would be "nothing" of universal value in that experiential, existential I AM.

That is why, I am asking you: now without delay, during your present terrestrial existence, constantly exercise a true moral attitude, do create moral reflexes and ethical instincts, so as to permanently impress on your behavioral circuits, the patterns of Justness and Verity. This is TOBA, this is GOOD."

After a long pause, ALBERT shares his thoughts with us:

"The import of that Commandment is enormous, for it informs us that a proper constant ethical training performed during our terrestrial existence creates mental and spiritual patterns, and these patterns will guide and facilitate the passage of mortal pilgrims on their way to immortality.

But simultaneously it asserts no act can attain moral or ethical status if it is not effected in accordance with those eternal laws that originate from the Celestial Source, which is the Ultimate End every human pilgrim is craving to attain.

By divine Justness, true moral patterns can be permanently encrypted in the individual genetic code, which forever will spurn any potential ethical dilemma. And as an effect of the same divine endowment a real path and passage leading to the worlds of eternal life is widely open to the human traveler in quest of eternity."

Silence.

"MOSES' 9th Commandment clearly points at the Means and Ends which enable to enter DAO DEH YING, the direct short path to Eternal Wholeness.

Truly, the knowledge conveyed by ARCHAE LINGUA is....so encompassing, altogether practical and transcendental! Magnificent!"

Maybe to prove Albert right in regard to the universality of ARCHAE LINGUA, Angel YELIYAEL is now sitting side by side with LAOV-TZSE, his new manifestation perfectly impersonating a typical Hellenic Aede[9], long brown curly hair, pearly white long toga, a cithara on his knees...Orpheus maybe? Or Protagoras?

The Angel and LAOV-TZSE seem to be engaged in a friendly private and inaudible conversation. Then YELIYAEL, plucking three harmonic notes on the strings of his cithara, announces:

"By elitist demand I shall now reveal level three, the human promise to the Supreme Creator, the pledge enounced by MUSAEUS on behalf of all human beings for all times:

"Because I do want to learn the path of light leading me to my true source and veritable origin on high (LOA), I pledge, during my life on this material Earth, to sharpen my senses and widen my consciousness (TA ÂNEH) to already perceive the eternal light, to observe precisely the variety of forms of being here on Earth and generate the vision of the ideal form of my future existence on high (BE RE ÊKHA).

I pledge to trust, and also pledge to question, investigate,

9 Aede= Greek word for Bard, itinerant storyteller. In Hebrew the word aed means witness and witnessing, one essential function of a bard.

study, understand and acquire firm knowledge, so as to be the truthful witness of my sensorial experience, my own personal mental and spiritual radiation, my inner diversity as well as the coherence of my unique personality resulting from my genuine mental and moral achievements (ÂD). I shall testify truthfully as myself only, but, on my way to You, I shall give evidence of all that I am and all I have experienced by myself (ÂD*). With this golden key, I shall cross the ultimate threshold which you have arched for me, so I can elatedly enter the sacred celestial kingdom (BE RE ÊKHA). And this will be both Your secret prize and my sacred reward (SHEKER)*[10]*."*

A drizzle of crystalline musical notes escapes from the angelic cithara, then YELIYAEL concludes:

"It is the sacred mission of all Guardian Angels, personal guardians, destiny guardians, to duly assist every and all human beings in faithfully keeping their pledge of indissoluble Alliance and eternal Union with their Supreme Creator."

SIMHA: "Now, to complete our inquiry, we must lift the veil off level 4, the scientific law present in the 9th Commandment."

LAOV-TZSE raises his right hand signaling his readiness, and although he probably knows all the words by rote, he conspicuously holds at eye level a scroll covered with Chinese characters, starts reading and, surprise, a Hebrew chant is now resonating in the room:

LOA
TA ÂNEH BE RE ÊKHA
ÂD
SHEKER

That tone, that rhythm…Albert and I attentively sitting in front of the master…I am immediately transported in the "Cheder" of my early childhood, the quaint ancient little room in Fez, where young children not yet of school-going age, were receiving their first alphabet instruction, sitting on small floor cushions, repeating

10 Sheker: Hebrew word conveying the essential meaning of: a reward (sukar-sugar), sacred (sakar). In Aramaic shoukran is an expression of deep gratitude.

in chorus, letters, syllables, words and short phrases proffered by the black robed teacher.

Thus LAOV-TZSE is chanting the 9th Commandment of MOSES, a simple melody, each syllable vibrating clearly, independently, letting each sound transport to our heart its unique sonority: LOA TA ÂNEH BE RE ÊKHA ÂD SHE KER And now, the master reveals for us the cosmogonic import of the 9th Law:

"Scientific Intelligence of the Universe (LOA) first requires awareness of Temporal Cycles, and intimate comprehension of the nature of Time itself (TA). Know that the primal source of all Space-Time worlds (Â) is the "Core-Nucleus" of the original fluidic essential Energy (NEH) from which the Universe of Universes has emerged. Thus, Time is an offspring of Eternity (TA ÂNEH).

Moreover, upon emerging from Eternity, Time was surrounded by a matrix-code described as spirit-principle bio-engenderer of the Universe (BE). That matrix's aim was to code-feed and code-inform the newborn Time for it to develop its own experience and its own identity (ET). That matrix itself is utterly immaterial and constitutes a virtual envelop, a womb, a "shelter", a "space" which contains, encoded, all bioorganic forms and structures, albeit immaterial and un-manifested (BE).

All structuring force-substances of free expansion-diffusion-radiation (BE RE), and all structuring force-substances of free compression-cohesion (BE ÊKHA), are enwombed by the cosmic mother-spirit who embraces the whole Universe encompassing all universes and all inhabitants of all the time-space worlds, without limiting them, without repressing them, without oppressing them.[11]

So spiritually encoded and cosmically energized, all terrestrial and all celestial beings can, by the means of quest, inquest, and knowledge of their true selves (RE ÊKHA), each testify and measure their own progress and advancement (ÂD), and pass the door (DA), which eventually brings them back in front of the Ultimate Divinity who is the sacred Verity forever residing inside them.

---

11 To our knowledge several religions call this ineffable non constricting womb mother spirit: "the Holy Ghost" or the "Shekhinah"

No false appearance can pass that door, and the science of passage must be exact and just."

The sage is now completely silent. And I sense our visit is coming to an end. In the presence of the Chinese master the 9th Commandment has indeed delivered wondrous teachings, a valuable knowledge until then encased and preserved like precious jewels in a sealed treasure chest.

I ask, my throat constricted like if it was my last question ever to Sensei LAOV-TZSE: "Why was it necessary to meet you, personally, to explain that Commandment? What kind of affinity correlates the Chinese sage LAO TZU to the 9th Commandment?"

LAOV-TZSE: "The answer to this question is very simple. First, as you can now see, that command relates, as much as myself, to the pursuit of the Ultimate End, the DAO DEH YING, the Universal Divine embrace. That path must faithfully be sought by men and women despite terrestrial tribulations, regardless of the numerous, powerful material aggressions which they inevitably face on Earth. To every man and woman it is imperatively demanded *not to* react to aggression-by-aggression, not to respond to terrestrial materiality by narrow-minded materialistic reaction. Such as negating the reality of Divine Presence in reaction to catastrophic events like earthquakes, tsunamis or man made genocidal mass murders!

Thus the 9th Commandment personally concerns me, LAOV-TZSE, its essence having been at the core of my preordained earthly endeavors, and later, the substance of my present celestial sphere of residence.

Moreover, for the best advancement of your quest and struggle in pursuit of Verity and Truth, China was the perfect destination. Because in China, since ages, the greatest difficulty one encounters is to adjust personal and collective thoughts-behaviors to the principles of true testimony. "Losing face", "saving face", are keys to the Chinese behavior and culture, since eons and eons. A perpetual game of "pretend", "make believe". The rule of that game is that you must say what is "expected of you to say", in defiance of truth; and acts are covered up with words to which twists and turns are applied to the effect of falsifying the witnessed facts.

Thus the constant safeguarding of personal dignity adjusted solely to the social status of the individuals always prevails over the universal ethical duty of preserving fundamental verity.

Also, Chinese peoples, on this immense land, in the course of collective history, have most often endorsed the social philosophy doctrine “the end justifies all means”.

The pursuit of Truth, true identity, has been supported, mostly in vain, by Sensei FO HI, Sensei LAO TZU, Sensei KUNG FU TZU.

The most social oriented among those masters, KUNG FU TZU CONFUCIUS, instructed thousands disciples, all taught, trained to develop a “moral pattern” and encourage its instillation in the constitutive fabric of the Chinese society at large.

But, even today, in your time, if a Chinese, to “save face” pretends a flower is blue, albeit its color is pink, he will declare the flower to be “blue”; and if to say this flower is blue saves the face of his interlocutors then the flower will remain “blue”.

Until by common agreement the whole group decides that when a flower is pink, everyone will say it is “blue”, all en bloc agreeing to understand the color of the flower is, in fact, pink.

Did you perceive the “torsion, the “distortion”?

That mental and spiritual stress is the cause of the confusion observed at different degrees in the language, thoughts and acts in China. False testimony here becomes so blatant that the sense of all discourses is essentially distorted, hampering all access to verity, true identity of things, beings and souls. China’s cosmic destiny, at personal as well as collective level, depends upon the eventual resolution of that radical predicament.

Consequently, in the past, a prominent Chinese Master, a genuine Taoist Sensei, deeply distressed by that enduring cultural falsification, emigrated to the northeast with all his disciples. Over the seas they permanently settled on a large archipelago, inhabited by few humans, but occupied by wild beasts and giant lizards.

They then founded “YA-PON”, creating schools of martial arts, the art of survival and arts of the “true act”, the NI-PON essence of verity, the NI-HON essence of grace and authentic honor.

Leaving China behind, the Sensei and his followers were actually fleeing the utter confusion of acts, things and words which their soul experienced as absolute "ugliness".

From then on, their hearts and that of their descendants filled with a deep and dominant passion: the pursuit of Beauty attained by total Simplicity. They later developed, based in part on my metaphysical poems, the ZEN philosophy and practice, which name ZEN reveals in ARCHAE LINGUA the "Beauty instantaneously nourished at the source of eternal substances of Verity"."

The sage is now silent. Soon we shall part.

Presciently informed of the imminent second departure of the great savant LAOV-TZSE, who knowingly was living in perfect harmony with all beings during his mission-pilgrimage on this Earth, all elements, minerals, liquids, gases, plants, animals present in the duchy of Chou, have sent an ambassador representing their kind to offer a heartfelt farewell to the departing Sensei.

Magnetic currents flowing and traversing our virtual bodies include us, Albert, me and YELIYAEL in their affectionate twirling. Crackling electric sparkles circulate at speed faster than light inside the sky's cupola, uniting all spirits and souls in a munificently living warm loving embrace.

The dreaded moment to part has come.

LAOV TZSE, Angel YELIYAEL, Albert and I join hands; our minds merge, recalling instantly the sensual essence of our magical encounter. By mutual agreement we each inwardly compose a "molecule of coherent light" to enfold and preserve the essential emotions, thoughts, ideals now inhabiting our hearts and spirits.

Four signed hologram creations join and unite in a single tiny submicroscopic infinitely small root of quartz which, riding the breath and light of the cosmic circuits, shall travel and sing our story to the four corners of the Universe.

Chapter Two

The Enchanted Forest

33. Manhattan, after July 10, 2000 AD.

WE HAVE LANDED IN MANHATTAN, at the edge of the third millennium, still stunned by the resounding echoes of our formidable escapade within sixth century BC China. Nobody, friend or foe, in our private and professional environment knows of or even suspects the nature and the scope of our enterprise. Our dear friend Marie Tania is the only person showing interest in the details of our cosmic jumps and discoveries. The great city is relatively calm as it is always in the days following the Fourth of July. The clanks and clings of the national celebrations now bygone, one may leisurely reflect on the profound significance of the American Declaration of Independence.

> "When, in the course of human events, it becomes necessary for one people to dissolve the political bands which have connected them with another/...../a decent respect to the opinions of mankind requires that they should declare the causes which impel them to the separation. We hold these truths to be self-evident, that all men are created equal, that they are endowed by their Creator with certain unalienable rights that among these are life, liberty and the pursuit of happiness."

A Declaration of Liberty to the world, announcing the future union of all human races, on this continent "rediscovered" [12] by European adventurers after 1,500 years of official amnesia. An illustrious Declaration which was also announcing the foundation of the First harmonious modern time democratic society founded on the principle of self-governance.

Manhattan wrapped in a thick blanket of heat enters into summer languor. However this seasonal slowdown is only perceptible in the traditional establishment area, Upper East Side, between Park and First Avenue, from 90th street North to 60th South. The buzz, the typical excitement, continues everywhere else in the densely populated island city. Residents, visitors, tourists, young and older, strolling or running or skating in all kinds of garb, experience the unique sensation of a freedom to be found only on the Manhattan Island. Hordes of hasty yellow cabs reluctantly stop at red lights giving way to motley crowds, daring explorers of deep urban canyons and dense city jungles, sporadically enjoying a respite in well-cooled restaurants, boutiques and museums.

Albert and I earnestly resume the regular course of our daily professional activities, reviewing our catalogs, preparing for trade shows which will soon open in New York, Atlanta, Dallas, Los Angeles, San Francisco, Frankfurt, Paris and Birmingham.

We are busy during daytime, and, in the evening, meditative, reflective, studious. Occasionally, rarely in fact, friends come and visit, and that special evening we happily share a festive gourmet meal, home cooked, spiced with French red wine, a fragrant Saint-Emilion, or sometimes a raspy Burgundy.

We enjoy conversing about the state of the world, recent historical developments, undercurrent metaphysical evolution. In the background Gregorian chants keep us aware of the everlasting

---

12 Re-discovered: During his long assiduous research in preparation for his cross-Atlantic voyage, Christopher Columbus perusing the wealth of monastery archives, learned of the saga of the 12 tribes "Coalition" expanding the post celestial Egyptian civilization all around the world including the American continent; he also learned of the existence of a Universal Language, akin to biblical Hebrew. Therefore, for his first voyage in August 1492 he embarked on his caravel several "interpreters" all fluent in Hebrew language. Later, Thomas Jefferson dutifully collected thousands of Native Indian words, among multiple tribal dialects, all bearing strong resemblance in sounds, roots and meanings, with Hebrew words..

connection linking Earth and the Firmament.

Time flows by. We look forward to resuming soon our cosmic adventure in search of the thinkers, philosophers, poets who shall discuss and explain with us the wondrous messages sealed in MOSES' Ten Commandments. As days and nights elapse we become even more eager, alert, attentive to any sign indicating who might be waiting for us at some yet unknown space-time coordinates, to unlock phrases and words and let surge the brilliant light of the 8th Commandment. Who shall speak to us? Who shall guide our steps on this path? The 5th Commandment HOVA, *Honor with love and loyalty your debts to all your sources and all your origins by faithfully knowing them and purposefully learning from them*, was set free out of its multi-millenarian tightly closed mysterious vault, here in Manhattan, under YELIYAEL's guidance, our angelic space-time ship and navigator.

The recollections of our wondrous encounter with MOSES are embroidered with shining gold threads in the recesses of my memory. MOSES himself led us to Rabbi Yohanan BEN ZAKAI at the beginning of the 1st century AD and with him we deciphered the 10th Commandment YoAa: *You shall not covet anything that is not meant to be yours, not covet that which is not your true unique identity nor that which is not defining your specific life purpose.*

Finally we ele-landed in Paris for a sentimental visit, where we learned that LAO TZU in China was to elucidate the mysteries of the 9th Commandment TOBA: *You shall not react with a falsified testimony to aggressions perpetrated against you.*

For several weeks we have been unsuccessfully tracking signs and hints to find the "mentor" and "master" who shall share our purpose to unveil the universal meanings of the 8th Commandment, popularly enounced DO NOT STEAL. To date no name has presented itself; we are yet to perceive the expected intuitive spark that will orient our next discovery journey.

34. Manhattan, July 19, 2000 AD.

TODAY, LATE IN THE EVENING WHEN WE RETURNED to our home, a bit tired from standing the whole day in a booth during the New York International Gift Fair, I suggested we review our manuscript and read at random excerpts from our memorable dialog with Rabbi Yohanan BEN ZAKAI. And with delight we started to relive various phases of our recent encounter, a spontaneous multifaceted discussion, so stimulating, at time grave, mostly filled with joy, happiness and elation!

Reminiscing the final moments of our meeting in Galilee, specific words and phrases pronounced by the Rabbi swirled in my mind, flashing messages I could not clearly fathom. Softly, albeit unrelentingly, words were moving like a circle dance, enliven by the rhythmic rhymes of happy children's ritornelle.

Light dawned on me! One statement, I just now remembered, which was not yet recorded in the manuscript, seemed to flash out an encoded message! Indeed YOHANAN has given us a clue, a course, a path…for the continuance of our discovery journey!

I recited the phrase aloud, and asked Albert if he "saw" what I had just perceived myself. "Judaism, Christianity, and Islam, a Trinitarian revelation is in the process of unification; Taoism and Buddhism, American and African Shamanism, scientific spiritualism, all are going to open up to everyone's understanding."

ALBERT confirmed and said: "In his farewell message the Rabbi made it clear, that after our encounter with LAO-TZU founder of Taoism, the next step of our journey will be India, to meet with the Buddha."

"And that is exactly what I understand. This conclusion seems accurate, and enticing!"

Moments later Angel YELIYAEL appeared in our living room, a scented mist gradually taking shape, virginal and pure, cloaked in pearlescent whiteness, large jade eyes smiling tenderly.

YELIYAEL: *"You have just discovered the path enabling us to continue our cosmic, linguistic and metaphysical journey!"*

SIMHA: "Yes. Presently though, I wish to study and learn more about Gautama's [13] historical context, before meeting with him."

YELIYAEL: *"Well, very well! Study, Simha, learn! When you and Albert are ready, call me!"*

On impulse I had taken the decision to immerse myself in the detailed study of texts relating the enlightenment experience of Gautama Buddha, and find books expounding on the emergence of the famed 6th century BC philosophy and epistemology.

Thus I began a large circular tour of the events known for the enlivenment and enlightenment occurring during that amazing era.

Exactly at the time Pericles in Greece enacts the first democratic laws, Cyrus descending from the Caucasus mountains revives the ancient Babylonian Chaldean civilization; Esdras, in Jerusalem brings together all the texts inherited from the archaeo historic Mesopotamia and Egypt, then transcribes in Chaldean lettering the Old Hebrew Testament as we know it.

Lao Tzu and Kung Fu Tzu recreate in China the collective consciousness of their celestial founding ancestors and illuminate humanity's divine origin. The Persian Zoroaster dictates the first chapters of the sacred Zend-Avesta; and the empire of Ghana extends its influence from west to east across Africa.

6th Century BC! Humanity's spirit is sparkling on all continents at the same time. And specifically in India, BUDDHA endeavors to stamp indelible moral and spiritual patterns in the minds of millions humans. For several days and nights drawing on the resources of both, Marie Tania's and my abundant libraries, I endeavored to immerse myself in the cultural atmosphere of the country where the enlightened BUDDHA taught; I revisited the intellectual and spiritual path followed, in the unfolding centuries, by countless brave disciples, whose ideas and words have shaken for over 25 centuries, religious and social structures in India and much

13 Gautama : original name of the man who will become the enlightened Buddha.

beyond. I then learned, nowadays modern Buddhism is a spiritual movement, as well as Islam religion, growing at fast pace in the world. These two philosophies seem also on the brink of confrontation and violent conflagration everywhere, in Asia, Europe and here in America. In my heart, I hope our investigation, and the ensuing book, will contribute to inspire a comprehensive understanding between two visions which are about to split the world.

Thus, I spent hot summer days studying old and new texts on Buddhism, the life of BUDDHA and his disciples, in various academic books, novels and essays.

And one bright morning, I asked:

"Albert, are you ready for another big leap?"

"Yes! I am!"

Our words: "ready", "big leap", "yes", made the call YELIYAEL was expecting.

The Angel instantly appeared and initiated the enseraphment process, enveloping us in his translucent veil, our physical bodies weightless and ethereal. The holographic image of our personal codes, genes and mind patterns are projected on the GANA spiritual fabric, safeguarded by Archangels as YELIYAEL swiftly adjusts to the cosmic ele-guidance circuits attuned to his melodic identity.

Immediately Albert and I confidently plunge into the state of alert unconsciousness created by the warm caress of coherent lights, the spherical form and ethereal substance of the Angel.

Maybe some observant New Yorkers, looking at the violet sky, perceived the flash of our departing opalescent sphere.

As for us, we are now zigzagging through profound darkness and absolute silence. Our angelic adept navigator purposefully shrinking space, deftly twisting time, is accurately leading us where and when marvelous knowledge flourishes, in the gardens planted by celestial visitors, the gods of yesteryear.

35. Rajagriba, India, 6th century BC. Friends among Trees.

NIGHT DISSOLVES UNDER THE PRESSURE of my consciousness. I wake up at the same time as Albert raises his head, and I see him smiling nearby me. The protective sphere of seraphic light opens like a providential egg as we are gently spiraling down towards terra firma.

Judging by the air temperature at low altitude, the location of our landing will be warm and humid. From above I see, on many straight paths people treading in well-defined directions, seemingly guided by clear goals. Among those numerous local trekkers not one gives the slightest sign our angelic sphere, now looking like a faded sun, has been noticed. Thus, unseen, we are hovering over a vast forested expanse, a sea of intensely green perpetual foliage.

However, over there, that old lady slowly walking, dressed in a dark blue cotton sari, perplexed, is fixedly staring at our exact location above ground. And the little boy, dark haired, sparkling eyes, who strolls by her side, is now gazing at the luminous sphere his grand mother is pointing at. Is he going to see something, or shall he ever remain "paranormal-blind", unable to penetrate the mysteries of virtual presences within material reality?

He is still gazing at us…closes both eyes…his pupils reflex adjusting…gazing again…Now, he sees something, jumps up and down, unrestrained, excited, points his hand towards us, laughing uproariously. The boy saw what his grandmother saw!

Tonight, at storytelling time before sleep, she, the ancestor, actual witness of a new wonder, shall recall and recount more astonishing events from the magical past, reliving extraordinary feelings and stirring emotions; and the boy shall better identify with those heroes "descending from the skies" vividly portrayed in ancient Hindu tales and legends.

Our spherical spaceship-Angel gradually flattens as it descends along giant trees, finally landing at the center of a large clearing, now becoming a smooth, springy shimmering triangular wing, on which Albert and I stand.

As if decompressed by enchantment, our cosmic presences comfortably adjust to the time-space terrestrial dimensions. We undergo a new re-birth, submerged with lively feelings, a mind-dizzying mélange of total familiarity and extreme novelty.

YELIYAEL kindly explains:

"Every angelic journey begins when your encoded personal substance leaves the corporeal form BOKANA to transmute into a state of fluidic and luminous vitality we celestials name VOLANA. The distinction between the BOKANA condition and the VOLANA state is micro differential, but the resulting effects of the transformation are strikingly dissimilar.

BOKANA is the corporeal principle by which manifests the state of mineral strength, whose archetype is calcium[14]. In the state of BOKANA life manifests in a solidified and fixed form, like bones in a body. Humans in the ordinary waking state, live mostly in the (((BO))) ((((KA))) (((NA))) dimension.

But when sleeping, dreaming, meditating and Angel-traveling, human beings enter a form of existence described in ARCHAEA LINGUA by three syllables:

(((VO))) (((LA))) (((NA)))

The VOLANA state has no solid form, yet it maintains in the human being an intention to be a form. The usual variations of the (((VO))) (((LA))) (((NA)) phase are Wish, Will, Vitality, Virtuality.

The angelic journey in virtual spaces beyond time is immediate when humans, like the Angels themselves, trans-code the BO, bio-form, into VO, VOW, the intent of form, while maintaining whole the Vigor of Life.

In this same movement the KA of the time–space traveler's body, the binding fixative force of cohesion is replaced by the lu-

14The Calcium atom is one of few "heavy" elements in the Sun, carried through the terrestrial atmosphere by Sun rays.

minous fluidic presence of LA. *Thus the human being attains the ethereal condition necessary for this transport mode."*

Our mentor Angel YELIYAEL continues his generous teaching, silently, directly impressing our psyche, as he often does during our journeys and our encounters, whenever he senses that we are ready to absorb practical and theoretical knowledge useful to the attainment of our goals.

Thus YELIYAEL informs us: "*Whenever you enter into the vital angelic structure to pass beyond the portals of Time, you are reborn as a VOLANA form, which is a form of primitive pre-human state of being, a racial heritage shared by all bio organic beings.*

Even the apparently most inert inanimate matter has the ability to be so virtualized. Matter is not "full", it is mainly made up of "empty" intervals. But in these "matterless" intervals live invisible microelements, called "spiriton". These microelements sustain the "life" of matter, and animate it, guiding its dynamics as would an intention. This intention is VOLANA."

The Angel continues: "*For most of the present day materialistic minded observers, matter is deemed "non living", its motions being allegedly determined only by external causal forces applied on its natural state of inertia; and any deviations they observe are so minimal in their space-time framework they are perceived and categorized as "chances and probabilities".*

However, these minute deviations are, in your time, the subject of new advanced scientific investigations and are now explained by many researchers as the effect of "living intentions" applied to matter by matter. The new sciences emerging in your world will soon study those sub electronic unpredicted effects as "intentional synchronicities" and incorporate in their logical reasoning the presence of invisible living entities, personality endowed creatures."

"Angels?" asks ALBERT

"Angels, yes, one kind among myriads other beings" answers YELIYAEL. *"The state of VOLANA is the natural state of existence for deities and celestial creatures.*

In a luminous, free, fluid form they actually live within the energy of pure Intent, by which they activate their ever-virtual existence, and manifest every potential aspect of their life within the whole, in unity with all.

That energy they do not spend ever, thus their living span and space are timeless and infinite. However these deities, despite their eternality are maximally ever changing, ever metamorphosing.

Their program confers them eternity, but without fixity.

By contrast, during their transient corporeal life in a state of BOKANA, mortal humans are minimally changing, therefore minimally adjusting, hence their noticeable predispositions to disharmonies and illnesses.

Human beings experience perpetual transformation only after their physical death-transition, when they attain the spheres of immortal survival and enter the perpetual state of VOLANA."

ALBERT: "Since humans can easily transcend the state of BOKANA to unfold their existence in the universe as a celestial VOLANA being, and as you stated earlier the VOLANA condition has been bestowed as an inheritance to all bio-organic beings of the universe, how is it that human beings, akin to the animals, feel forever fastened to the BOKANA structure?"

YELIYAEL then transfers to our minds, directly by a single albeit multifaceted clear thought, that "*humans have great capacity to achieve this state of fluidity; many individuals reached the state of VOLANA during their earthly life, some known as saints, others as fools, many others branded impostors.*

But the great majority of men and women who attained the state of VOLANA wisely remained silent and are, therefore, unknown."

"*However*, YELIYAEL continues, *the human species throughout its entire evolutionary history is moving boldly to reclaim this fabulous heritage, which has always belonged to it since the apparition of the first "amoeba ancestor of humanity", which amoeba, equally endowed with BOKANA structure and VOLANA substance, has chosen an existence of transformation, fluidity, illumination, and risk taking, akin to all genuine freedom seekers."*

SIMHA: "What then stops the human species, or slows its efforts at recovering its own "supra-natural" powers?"

YELIYAEL: "*Everything occurs through accurate adjustment and precise harmonization with the musical vibrancy invoked by the word "LIBERTY".*

What is LIBERTY? It is the highest and most spiritual form of TRUTH.[15]"

Inwardly pondering the amazing significance of the Angel's revealing definition of LIBERTY, Albert and I are now walking on a humid grassy ground, in the middle of a clearing surrounded by huge trees, virile trunks boldly soaring towards the skies.

YELIYAEL has changed his "VOLANA" spaceship form to adopt the vegetal appearance of an archetypal plant, its luminous shapes and sinuous serpentine contours constantly moving. The Angel's large oval eyes are now deep green, reflecting the color hues of the forest.

In this place and at this moment I intensely empathize with the ancient Keltic priests, the Gallic "Druidas"[16], who conducted passionate rituals in adoration of the Grandeur of Nature at the center of sacred forest clearings as majestic as the columned nave of a gothic cathedral. I share my thoughts with Albert:

SIMHA: "I wonder at the mysterious linguistic path by which the word DRUIDAS, pronounced DRAWIDAS, is found intact in India to designate the DAWIDAS, wandering holy men, priests and *music* players of the Hindu religion?"

ALBERT: "As much puzzling is the concurrence of names linking the European DRUIDS-DRUIDAS *harp players*, with the Hindu DAWIDAS priest-*musicians*, and DAVID, whose name was, in his time, pronounced DAWIDA, king of Israel and Judea, poet and *harpist*."

Thus, quietly discussing and learning from each other like

---

15 Lliberty: in ancient languages like Hebrew, letters B and V are interchangeable. So, liBerty can be decoded as liVerty. Therefore, Archae Lingua demonstrates that li-verty= verity, the Elevated state (Li) of verity-truth, hence confirming the saying "Truth sets Free".

16 Druidas: English-French word = druids, the Keltic Gallic priests.

Greek philosophers ambling under shaded arcades in Athens, all three side by side we continue our purposeful march forward. This forest is neither too dense nor too scary. One can feel wild and violent animals do not habitually roam here, and the presence of human civilization clearly permeates this majestic woodland.

The soil is soft and spongy and at times gives up under our feet. Kindled by daily rain showers, ferns are wet and fragrant, heathers shine an electric bright purple.

The trees and bushes surrounding us are of a kind unfamiliar to me; yet, the smell of a small piece of bark I just plucked reminds me of sandalwood, illustrious ingredient of subtle woodsy perfumes enjoyed for ages on all continents. All the aromas of the forest blend and contrast into a vigorous olfactory syntonic concerto.

We now keep perfectly silent, perfectly integrated within this pleasant warm obstacle-free nature. Trunks, branches, leaves, and grass, all exude an intense passionate living presence.

And suddenly I hear voices speaking directly to my heart:

"*BEHOLD, we the trees are born, like you, to evolve and join the Creator. Once upon a time, our parents, our ancestors, multitude of plants then crawling on the ground at our feet have sacrificed everything to share with us the tiniest particle of spirit they had in them. Thus defying the terrors of earthly gravity we could soar skyward and attain the celestial spaces.*

The firsts among us to rise up to the skies, I was told, were the fig tree and palm tree, did you know?"

"No, I answer softly, I did not know!"

I heard very clearly! Trees have spoken to me! I feel elated, my heart, my entire body infused with joy! I have long suspected these green giants were agents of human telepathy, filtering human thoughts and relaying the most beautiful and soothing sentiments to all creatures who are listening. And now, several trees reading my thoughts vigorously launch a full choir, chanting in unison:

"We soared into space
Upwards, as high as possible

We are the ancestors of birds
Who, flying to our crests,
From their fatigues could rest
Or release their fears and anxieties.
And when the moment came
Early humans did the same.
Fleeing stronger predators
They were clumsily climbing our trunks.
Did they know we helped them ascend?
Did they know we were "Angels",
Messengers of Providence and Divine Compassion?
And when at last they could touch our heights,
They experienced a passion for the skies!
So they learned to observe the horizons,
Liberated from their base condition,
No more creeping or crawling creatures!
We are your higher ideals,
And your divine parental archetypes!"

At that moment the 5th Commandment moral injunction flashes back in my memory: You shall honor your debt toward *all* your mothers and *all* your fathers, *all your ancestors.*

And, continues the forest choir:

"We have embodied for you the pattern of physical ascension to the skies. And you have honored us, perpetuating this gift by your marvelous spiritual elevation.

We were then your Guardian Angels whilst you were hopping on earth like frogs, or crawling like snakes. Now, you, humans, are our "Angels", your minds and hearts the temples and vessels elevating us to the Eternal Father."

A blue ray of consciousness suddenly breaks into my mind, revealing a new stream of pristine thoughts. I finally understand that whenever human souls transit beyond the material world, they pull and carry all the manes of all their terrestrial ancestors, as an offering to their celestial brothers and Divine Father in the Heavens, so presenting them with the great latest outcome issued from their good generous seeds, the seeds of Original Life.

In the distance, a baritone voice launches an enthralling solo:

The Tree is the major High Way!

The Tree is the Voice of Heavens!

"What a magnificent melody" says ALBERT.

SIMHA: "A melody resounding in the midst of an opera! Since we entered that part of the forest, all the trees here seem to be in the mood of singing wondrous lyrics!"

ALBERT: "What did you hear? What did they say?"

YELIYAEL intervenes in our dialog:

"*Albert, not so long ago, a few centuries past, your ancestors Keltic Druids conversed with trees and raised their prayers at the center of clearings, natural sanctuaries born of light and shade, in the dense forests of Gaul, where great cathedrals now elevate their columns and belfries, Notre Dame de Paris, Reims, Chartres, Lisieux and many elsewheres.*

You shall honor your ancestors by listening to trees and confidently talking to them."

ALBERT then asks the BARITONE TREE:

"Pardon my insolence, O venerable Tree, but, in my time, all academic historians affirm that the Hindu DAWIDAS, and the DRUIDS of Western Europe, were superstitious idolaters who have installed you, the trees, in a reverential pantheon, as equals to the Ultimate Divinity. True?"

A magnificent, long, slim, ELEGANT TREE answers with a soprano voice, exquisitely feminine:

"*ALABERT, ALABERT*[17]*, this is not VAHARAYATA*[18]*, this is not the "Light of Verity". These noble DRUIDS were well aware of our ability to mediate between Heavens and Earth, and they mastered the vital science of VOLANA. They were inspired by our audacity, our courage to defy mighty terrestrial gravity, our power to firmly*

17 Alabert: one of the several celestial names given to Albert in the Heavens, as revealed by Rabbi Yohanan Ben Zakai.

18 Va ha rata= Sanskrit version of the Archae Lingua source of the word ve ri ty. Va=v, e=ha, r=ra, i=ya, t=ta. Note that Sanskrit eases the pronunciations of the Consonants-Roots most frequently with the vowel A. Example: MaHaRaBaTa, RaMaYaNa, MaHaRaJa etc.

root in the soil and better soar towards the celestial expanse.

They endeavored to share in our absolute conquest of the ARIA *element, the transparent aerial substance, which widely opens the field of our vision and enables us to find the light beyond the opaque world of slithering creatures.*

These white robed druids and priestesses loved us as youngsters would love parents and older brothers willing to show them the better ways; and we were constantly conversing together, with open hearts. We taught them, instructed, helped and guided them, up to the far edges of our science."

A high STOCKY TREE, donning a thick coarse reddish bark adorned with dainty patches of green lichen, triumphantly announces with a deep and strong voice echoing in the infinite:

"I will now recount THE SAGA OF YOUR ORIGINS."

We are listening intently, impassioned by this extraordinary, super promising announcement.

"*When humans, in their primal frog forms, attempted to climb our trunks, they hopped awkwardly, repeatedly falling back to the ground without ever being able to hold on to our too smooth slippery bark. We could do nothing for them.*

Though we sympathetically watched them try to ascend our trunks, again and again. What a remarkable show of courage and tenacity! From failure to failure they persisted. Until the day the most intelligent among human-frogs, in a sudden flash of genius understood that, hopping and "leapfrogging" to skip stages, was not the solution. Thus that Special Frog outlined the intention, still obscurely, to crawl, in order to climb and explore the Tree of Life that each of us perfectly embodied.

As for the Tree of Knowledge, these humans in the form of frogs never ever suspected it existed.

And the frog, so sophisticated, so beautiful, who jumped so easily in water and in air, humbly consented to regress and slither on the ground. It vowed to crawl and "Zip Zap", it became a sinuous serpent!

Thus human dressed in serpent skin was able to glide over us, silently, absorbing our delicious juices, and we became for him a Tree of Life in Paradise.

Did human-serpents see us then as the ultimate Deity who created them? Maybe, but we never knew, because those serpent-humans who scripted their presence on our bark with their saliva and poisons, who coiled lazily around our branches, skillfully using our strength to rise, never knew of the Heavens.

Neither basic speech, nor the Divine Verb, to them was ever revealed!

We let these strange children of nature graphically inscribe their silent obscure messages…"

A new chant reverberates in the forest, a feminine voice smooth and melodious:

"*And, later, when birds with grace and elegance rested lightly on our slender limbs, we resisted the urge to shake and wobble impatiently. Instead, we gently swung our branches, and the birds played like children in a park. We taught them how to sing, whistle, shrill and trill, using airstreams, winds, storms, caressing breezes.*

Like the serpents before them the birds inscribed their story on the bark of our branches supporting their cozy little nests.

And came the time they could fly by thousands, reaching much higher than the boldest most audacious treetops.

Did they vaguely perceive us as their ultimate Divine Creator? Certainly not, for they soon flew above us and far beyond, as pioneers and conquerors, exploring all areas of the planet.

Then they returned to our crests, their original home, and bedazzled we listened as they were narrating for us all the wonders of their travels. They were filled with gratitude for the angelic help we had given them, for the food, for the resting and nesting places and, above all, for the elevated platforms we have provided for them to soar higher beyond our own highest heights!

Truly to them we have been "The Tree of Life", but it is they, our grandchildren who brought from their explorations the new and surprising idea of gifting us with a wondrous destiny, transforming us into trees of science and knowledge.

We, the trees, thus endeavored to archive tales and legends, in all scripted and sonorous languages, all the songs of striking thunderbolts and rumbling storms, fresh breezes, scorching rays of sun, pouring rains and fine mists and those stories of thousands birds crisscrossing the skies.

And Behold! Persistent heavenly breaths had announced the imminent arrival of new special emissaries. How would we indubitably recognize them? All trees together vowed to remain ever alert and vigilant! Then finally came the "envoys" we had expected patiently for millions of years."

Now, from our left rises the powerful chant of a large TENOR TREE: "*When these eccentric beings, these furry mammals began to awkwardly escalate us to avoid the terrifying claws of wild beasts, their emotions were confused, their bodies weak, their minds feeble and their voices dull. For a long time we remained oblivious they were the prodigal sons and daughters of the Divine we had been assigned to take care of, attentively, lovingly.*

They died by the millions caught up in the clutches of tigers, dismembered by mammoths. At first we were indifferent to their fate and did not hear the harmonies they were, in vain, casting at us. We kept tight guard at the entrance of the Garden of Eden. They could not enter."

The TENOR TREE continues:

"Then, suddenly, it occurred! The GAP! Two of those beings began to engrave signs on our bark, and by that "SCRIPT" we knew THEY had finally arrived."

"How did you recognize those scripts were the work of the "envoys" you were expecting?" asks ALBERT.

A LITTLE TREE, with a juvenile boyish voice chimes in promptly: "*By the special manner their bodies embraced our trunks, touching us affectionately. Earlier, we had rejected all the others when they were attempting to clamber on to us, because they wanted to use us without passion and without love; while these two "envoys" were different, noticeably. They touched us like lovers, caressed us, prayed to us. They were directly communicating with our spirit."*

ALBERT, inquiring: Two envoys?

The YOUNG TREE intones: "*Yes two! And they were both well recognizable although their message was not similar. One touched us in a firm motion, kindly imperative, claiming his due inheritance. HE seemed to know he was an "envoy", that we were the guardians of the Promised Land the Divine had given him; he seemed to know we would open if he was knocking at our door, using the rhythms and rhymes of the original code, the code of ARCHAE LINGUA.*

The other being, "ELLE-SHE", had a sublime touch, caressing, seductive, quivering like an early spring leaf. Ah! It is all here etched in our memory! I remember her! We all remember her! She was so beautiful, serpentine, feline. I stood there, helpless as a log of wood. I wanted to romance her, to make declarations of passionate love."

ALBERT: "Then what happened after you recognized them?"

Another sweet and melodious chant dashes from behind us, announcing more revelations, more delightful knowledge, more instructive marvels:

"You are well aware the human baby, in its fetal state before birth, reproduces in the maternal womb the main sequences of his animal corporeal development, from tadpole to superior mammal. Yes, all women and men of the third millennium know that..."

The HISTORIAN TREE continues: *"Well, these two new creatures, to conquer our heart, reproduced the same course. First they leaped like frogs, and we laughed heartily. They crawled like serpents sliding miserably on our smooth and friable barks. Then they fancied they had wings like nimble birds and, there, also failed. At last, drawing from the resources of their imagination they began to love us of pure love. They knelt at our feet, hugged our trunks, caressed our branches, kissed our leaves.*

And they fervently prayed to us in the silence of their heart, because they had no link with universal soul and knew not how to speak. But those prayers we could yet not perceive, for we ourselves were oblivious to their plea, as there had never existed on Earth a being who had a soul and who could speak.

Then, later on, with the help of the "Almighty", we did what forever remained for those two beings an incomprehensible miracle: for as soon as they were touching us we lifted them up on the extremities of our branches!

Furthermore, responding to their wishes, our protective barks made themselves less slippery, more supportive, and on our trunks we grew protruding bumps, to support their ascending efforts. So they learned how to stand upright, a noble posture they adopted and reproduced at will.

Our crests became for them the perfect refuge, for whenever these two pioneers were resting there we were blocking access to all dangerous wild animals.

We temporarily became their Guardian Angels, teaching them everything we experienced, everything we had learned from frogs, serpents and birds. From the frogs we transferred to them the art of high jumping and the virtue of perseverance; from the serpents we passed on instruction on how to select and draw nourishment from the trees of life.

Then we passed on to them all the marvels the birds had brought from their far-flung travels, adding nothing, retrenching nothing."

I am fascinated by this story which covers millions terrestrial years, and, in a quivering excited voice, I ask:

"What exactly did the birds teach you?"

An ELDERLY TREE looking like a millenary inhabitant of this forest, jumps at the opportunity to recount part of his accumulated knowledge, and, in rhythmic prose, akin to a Hellenic aede, intones his narration: *"Above all, birds taught us bravery, heroism, how to answer challenges and rise beyond obstacles.*

Later they taught us how to explore and observe the world.

They faithfully shared with us all their adventurous feats above plains, mountains and seas. And now they continue their teaching by recounting the tales, legends and histories of the various peoples all around the planet.

And, expounds the savant PHILOSOPHER TREE-, *birds have been great spiritual masters, as they also taught us the moral law, keystone of MOSES' Fifth Commandment, the initial HOVA, Love, the bright path leading to supreme advancement and absolute valorization.*

And here is how they instructed us! The birds went away to free themselves from our parental control; they winged away from us to grow, develop, transform, fecundate, multiply.

However they gave themselves the means to return regularly, share their hopes, expectations, aspirations and of course narrate the experiences gathered during their faraway journeys.

Thus, despite our roots and sedentarity, our fields of knowledge widened considerably. They respected, honored our basic needs, for our own earthly mission was far from complete.

Our own spiritual quest had elevated us from the underground to the skies, allowing us to be a very useful launching pad for the flying species. But we still had to become the Tree of Knowledge and Science for the benefit of humankind.

Indefatigable migratory voyagers, all the bird species went off everywhere, learning everything and with perfect regularity returned to instruct us. So when the time came, we were ready!"

"*And there is more,* adds a delicate and ELEGANT SHE-TREE, with the thrilling voice of an heroic virgin, *the crown of their lessons was less visible and it was this one:*

Since they had become valiant explorers with unmatched skills in the art of flying, supreme discoverers of lands, masters on water and in the air, as albatrosses, eagles, storks, they returned to teach their parents, "backward" and "outdated" as we were. They chose to share their knowledge with beings they could have ignored or despised as inferior.

The birds also developed the Maternal-Paternal founding patterns, by building home nests, developing the virtue of self-

sacrifice and giving, the ability to provide nourishment for their offspring.

And furthermore, they showed admirable love and magnificent courage in the education of their youngsters. Generation after generation, when time came for the "fledgling" yet to become independent, the father or mother threw him firmly off a high limb so that it takes to the air, flaps its wings and flies. As for us, compassionately, we often helped these frightened beginners for a moment cling to the safety net of our supple foliage."

"Thus, adds the MILLENARY TREE, *learning from the birds experience we have been able to educate human beings, in all respects, including the basics of universal morality."*

That thoughtful conclusion presented by this most ancient tree casts a glimmer of light in my mind. I finally understand why the bird shaped Egyptian hieroglyph is pronounced AV[19] and means "Universal Father", the primal source (A) of life energies (V).

I address all the trees around us:

"Since humans knelt at your feet, prayed in front of you, embraced you with love as the traditional Jews in my time hug the scrolls of the Sepher Torah, their sacred book of knowledge, have they finally worshiped you as their ultimate gods and creators?"

The PHILOSOPHER TREE replies:

"No! Humans never made such an error, let alone, further in time, the Keltic priests, the greatest initiates in human history. Humans never deceived themselves. They came only asking us to fulfill our mission as educators and instructors.

Intuiting the presence of their Creator through His continuous universal whisper, human beings were the first creatures demanding from us to fulfill the Divine Prophecy that we become the very center of their Paradise.

Without hesitation we taught them we were for them as we had been for serpents and birds, "the Tree of Life" and therefore they

---

19 Av=in Latin root for Bird avis. In Hebrew root for Father (av). In ancient Egypt the hieroglyph read as Av is the silhouette of a bird.

could eat from our nourishing saps, use our therapeutic foliages and absorb our vitalizing fruits, absolutely freely.

But, when they demanded we personify also the tree carrying the fruits of Ultimate Science and Knowledge we were bewildered, knowing not what to do. We beseeched them to wait before picking this kind of fruit, for we did not know if this fruit would kill them or awaken them.

We did not really know, because we had not as yet deciphered the mysteries of ARCHAE LINGUA.

Thus we sought guidance from the birds then living higher in the skies. The birds wisely advised to await the arrival of the celestial beings who dwell above and beyond, nearby our Universal Father. Meanwhile, below, the snake rushed everything, engendering chaos, a dreadful disruption which terrorized us all.

The serpent told men and women: Behold, I myself used the trees, I have eaten their fruit and I am not dead!

The snake resembled all these ignorant advisers now swarming by the millions in every corner of our lands.

The serpent malignantly confused the Fruit-physical food with the essential Fruit-vitalizing science and conscience.

The fruit humans required that the trees give them was not physical, tangible and visible. Clearly, as was later recorded in your Bible, it was not the nutritious fruit of the Tree of Life, but the intangible fruit of the Tree of Knowledge and Consciousness.

They begged us to release the deep and mysterious unrevealed science which would allow them to acquire the powers to ascend towards the cosmic heights.

Their guiding Volana-Will-Wish was envisioning, albeit dimly, the awesome emergence within themselves, during their earthly life, of an elevating Soul that will one day enable them, free of terrestrial gravity, to master water air and fire, soar into the interstellar spaces and join their celestial brothers and sisters, offspring of the universal Mother Spirit and the Supreme Father, whose existence we had so often evoked with them.

We, the trees, having attempted to reach those elevated shores through a strong vertical thrust, the birds themselves having auda-

ciously explored high airy apparently inaccessible continent, human beings thought we necessarily possessed the ultimate secret.

But we both soon realized the depth of that secret science of elevation far exceeded the modest scope of our current knowledge. Therefore, together as one, we composed and chanted in chorus the most harmonic symphony, a melodious plea and supplication from humans, trees and birds, aiming at the very center of the Grand Universe. While waiting for a clear answer to our prayers, humans decided to better acquaint their senses to perceive harmonies from above, and willed us to further their initiation and enlightenment, starting with touch and taste then colors and sounds."

Silence

"Time passed, cyclical seasons revolved, human senses sharpened. And one blessed day, providentially replying to our collective chant, a voice from Heaven echoed in the world:

"BEHOLD! Humans are setting a path to become equal to the celestial powers, and be like us and this is Good."

That is when the first celestial visitors arrived on Earth. They came with the mission to regenerate humankind, to enhance their "food and clothing", for they saw they were almost "naked" and "malnourished".

And, concurrently, they taught them the necessary basics of the transformative language that opens mind and enlightens spirit, ARCHEO LINGUA, the celestial language."

"Ah! exclaims ALBERT, dearest trees, it is now my turn to seek sound advice from you. Should we dare narrate this wonderful saga to our fellow contemporaries living at the beginning of the third millennium AD? Surely, some will smugly call it "fairy tale", good only for little children; others will label it "parable" at best, a fable akin to Adam and Eve biblical story, and many will even make a big fuss because that story flagrantly differs from the official scriptures! How should we recount it?"

A POET TREE interposes and says: *"Of course it is a typical children's story, but fairy tales are not worthless! Of course it is a parable but no well-inspired parable betrays the truth. The history known to the trees does not replace any other versions, biblical or scientific. It just adds to all the others, and everyone is free to accept it or reject it.*

And if your underlying question is: How to tell this story so it will be understood? Well, tell it exactly as you heard it narrated in this forest clearing, "without adding and without retrenching".

As well deserved, the POET TREE had the last word.

Enchanted, enthralled, we have resumed our march, and are now entering an area of the forest which resembles a park designed for the enjoyment of contemplative strollers. The soil on the spongy path is well-flattened, defined edges marked with rounded stones, the mossy undergrowth completely cleared.

Albert and I, pensive, suddenly halt in front of a tree, trunk colossal as a temple column designed by an architect of ancient Egypt. Its smooth shiny bark exudes a subtle refreshing floral fragrance, unexpected in this hot and spicy forest atmosphere. That tree seems to be holding the precious memories of a unique destiny, a personal history out of the ordinary…

YELIYAEL confirms my insight:

"This one tree is often visited by disciples as a sacred monument. Exactly here young Prince GAUTAMA SHAKYAMUNI sat meditating deeply for thirty days without interruption, nourished only by the potent floral aroma produced by this tree. And here he received full enlightenment on the ultimate finality of True Life. And that is why GAUTAMA was later called the BUDDHA, name which in Sanskrit, the Hindu's sacred language, designates a tree, a BODHA."

We respectfully bow in reverence to the ancient tree "who" received the celestial dazzling flash of universal consciousness and faithfully transmitted that intelligent light to the man who changed forever the social and spiritual destiny of India and the world.

36. On the Riverbank. Rajagriba, 6th century BC.

THE PATH WE ARE FOLLOWING NOW is leading us to the bank of a wide river lined with green and yellow dense foliage, bamboos and reeds. In front of us expands a riotous vegetal chaos, every plant, every leaf, every stem appear to be engaged in a final struggle to approach the shore and touch the surging living waters.

"*In a few weeks,* YELIYAEL informs, *the entire valley will be flooded, forming large seasonal lakes. Women and men will then travel happily on thousands small boats skillfully steered to avoid tree trunks and muddy little islands. The inhabitants enjoy this aquatic season, a cyclical event bringing into their lives new activity, refreshment, and a welcome diversion from their back breaking daily soil toiling routines.*"

Lulled by YELIYAEL's voice my imagination carries me above the luxuriant Nile delta, for ages a powerful vivacious life center born of the providential encounter of land, river and sea.

YELIYAEL: "*This vibrant and majestic river flowing before us is one of the many tributaries of the Ganges, the River of Rivers, the sublime, which after having briskly descended the steep slopes of the western Himalayas and rushed across countless rocky gorges, spreads wide and powerful in the open plains to run and hurl itself in the Indian Ocean, at the northeast tip, forming an immense fertile delta, nearby Cathay, the China of your time.*"

A narrow opening in the dense vegetation on the edge of the river offers the opportunity for a resting halt, and we are now, the three of us sitting by the rushing splashing waters.

The sky is cloudy, but of light gray almost transparent hue. On my skin I still feel a fresh tinge of early morning. YELIYAEL now wears a bright opal turquoise all over coat, edged with striped rays of indigo blue; the Angel's eyes reflect the exact shades of brown-green-yellow emanating from the surrounding luxuriant vegetal landscape.

I am fully enjoying this calm moment of contact with my inner mentor, an occasion to link to the true, ultimate Source of Life.

Undulating colorful arrows of light are lively spurting out of YELIYAEL's sparkling spherical shape, clearly signaling his desire to raise our attention.

"Here, says he, *exactly in this part of the world, natural evolution of man began, before spreading all around Earth."*

India at the origin of human evolution? I am deeply intrigued and alarmed by this remark, which again contradicts so evidently the consensual common credo of numerous anthropologists. However I keep silent. Albert stares at me, his grey green eyes expressing puzzlement, fervent curiosity and expectation.

YELIYAEL, perceiving our surprise, gently probes our minds to make sure we are both fully attentive, and begins:

"You have just heard, told by trees in this forest, an account of humankind's natural evolution. The memory of trees is one of the richest and most ancient planetary archives. There are many other repositories. And during your adventure in this world and the surrounding universe, you will have the opportunity to learn about origins and creations in many different ways. Each is unique, all are marvelously linked, combined, unified.

Ordinary human language apparently flows along a chronological timeline, while the universe is not linear but composed of circles and spheres. Before proceeding further on your path to the living BUDDHA you must stay here for a time, think, reflect and visualize, until the moment of your enlightenment."

Another alarm rings in my mind! I stare at Albert who seems to absorb and understand easily that message, his face brightened, his eyes illuminated. Focusing my thoughts, I refrain frowning; I am listening passionately, but I do not yet penetrate the sense of this angelic indefinable demand.

Patience, I tell myself, have patience…

Swirling a breath of iridescence on top of his body of light, YELIYAEL, eyes smiling, continues: "*I shall tell you the history of humankind without tapping into the terrestrial archives, but in those held by the Archangels of our universe.*

From the original origin, first, unique, ultimate and supreme, from that infinite and eternal pregnant instant, creation exists as a triadic tapestry interweaving three essential virtues: the Verity of the Father, the Beauty of the Spirit-Mother and the Goodness of the Son.

Of course I know this apparently archaic formulation shocks third millennium modern peoples, who contend those words and notions are religious nonsense, or, at best, ancient memorabilia just good to carefully fold and forget like a decorative pile of old linens in a grandmother's closet.

But when I say Father, or Son or Mother Spirit, I do not speak in terms of duality, Father-Mother, Male-Female, Son-Daughter. This duality does not exist at the origin, and the terms Father, Son and Spirit are only analogies simulating and stimulating terrestrial emotions, the nearest formulation to expressing the ineffable reality of the original archetypal concepts.

The life evolution of every species and genus, be they mineral, vegetal or animal, necessarily manifests its progress through three major archetypal stages:

Truth-Beauty-Goodness.

Thus Humanity's evolution on Earth also manifests through these three distinctive phases:

VERITY, bioorganic and mindal phase, completed.

BEAUTY, internal and external phase, nearing completion.

GOODNESS, ethical and spiritual phase, currently unfolding.

Goodness initiated about 35,000 years ago, was strongly reactivated by Master MOSES 3,500 years ago, brought to the brink of perfect completion as to its shape, light and direction by Messiah YEHOSHUA-JESUS 2,000 years ago, and continues to walk the world, with ups and downs, returns to darkness, and sudden renewals of clarity.

Goodness influential presence is now inscribed on Earth, it will not be effaced. And humanity will continue, painfully limping, or sublimely soaring, on its constantly lit ascending path toward spiritual and celestial enlightenment.

How did humankind advance toward TRUTH*? As the trees chanted for us, there has been a strenuous very very long natural evolution.*

SIMHA: "Natural? What does that mean?"

YELIYAEL: "*Natural evolution means that, at the time Earth was ready to engender*[20] *life, providentially appeared a mysterious seed. Your academic scientists name it "migratory interstellar dust", while shamans call it "the original egg", and modern religions revere it as the "Universal Verb of the Father".*

In universal ARCHAE LINGUA *dust is named* AVA-K, *the egg is* OVA *and the Father is* AVA *or* ABA.

Obviously, the scientist atheist, the animist shaman and the doctrinal religionist, all say exactly the same thing, by the grace of the celestial spherical language which has been transmitted to humankind. None of these three characters is either incorrect, or blasphemous. For human evolution phase through VERITY *being completed, no one can in effect actually disconnect from or betray* VERITY.

That original seed developed on Earth for millions and millions of years. But this natural evolution is not foolish or hazardous, or unintelligent. Because Nature is oriented, inwardly e-motioned by the ever-renewed vow to return to its primary source, directed by VOLANA, *the Universal cosmic Vow.*

Nature unfolds the laws of Life in the manner of a moving playing child, a youngster who spontaneously explores everything and anything, apparently haphazardly.

However Nature's harmonic flow, as well as the child, is directioned, intentioned by, inhabited with, and immersed within the all-encompassing Universal Spirit HU: *the complete unifying cos-*

---

20 Engender. See Genesis First verse ve ha aretz hayta tohu va bohu: meaning: "and the Earth was ready to engender". Tohu means time pregnant and Bohu means space pregnant. Archaeo-linguistic analysis: tohu, is composed of to=Time and hu=Spiritual life trigger. bohu: is composed of bo=foundation of home (Bayt-space) hu= spiritual life trigger.

mic breath, sustaining the entire perpetuated creation.

SIMHA: "Can every creature existing on or within the Earth, return to the Creator?"

YELIYAEL: *"In principle, yes; in actuality, no. For humankind, having won the race for mind consciousness attainment has become the focal spirit temple and spirit conveying medium for all creatures on Earth, and those creatures surrendered to humankind, to preserve and care for, all the spiritual vows and intents they had built up since the origin*[21].

That is why it is ever crucially important that humans respect and honor Nature, so they indefatigably continue and progress on the path towards fulfillment of Goodness.

After several million years of recurrent evolutionary cycles, the pre-human AMINals emerged through natural evolution. They appeared on the planet hardly distinguishable from the ANImals, their brothers. The gap between them was internal, bio-chemically caused, barely visible from the outside, the differentiation at first untraceable in the corporeal manifestation.

Then suddenly, here, in the region we are now visiting, the first major gap appeared amidst a regular group of new AMINals. The change which occurred in the brains and minds had profound and rapid effect on the characteristics of these primal humans. This new breed adapted itself to camouflage in the forests and their skin colors harmonically adjusted to those of woodlands and marshes; therefore dark pigments dominated much of their ocher-browns and dark-greens.

---

21 Genesis 1-26 Then God said, "Let Us make man in our image according to our likeness; let them have dominion over the fish of the sea, over the birds of the air, and over the cattle, over all the earth and over every creeping thing that creeps on the earth." Let them have dominion is translated from the Hebrew word va-yir-dou. Common translation: let them dominate, rule over. Archae Lingua shows that this word means exactly the opposite:
1-Va-yirdu is a conjugation of the root verb yored= to descend.
2- Descending from all living beings on earth, having ascended with their help to higher consciousness, man is awarded with the responsability of caring for them.
3- From the Hebrew word va-yored derive the English words "Ward" "Warden" and "Award". Therefore Genesis states: Man was awarded the warden-ship of all that lives on earth, to help them not to constrain or dominate them.

The evolutionary impulses of that human "Faber Originalis" were entirely directed toward brain development, correlated with use of hands and upright walk, so as to compete against the ANIM*al species, savage predators largely superior on the physical plane, who fiercely fought for their own right of primogeniture, the archetypal pattern of most combats.*

Thus "Homo Originalis" long remained a unique race, totally oriented towards chemical, physical and cerebral Verity, as yet far from envisioning the exploration of the realm of Beauty.

That human species, without discernible racial diversification, spread everywhere it could find terrain and climatic conditions favorable to its organic adaptation. These specific acquired traits spread mainly through Global Morphogenesis, very little by migration. And they started migrating only after their racial validity and mind Verity had been put to severe and continuous test, here, in the region of their origin, near the Himalayas."

SIMHA: "I am curious. How did that human species spread "very little by migrations" and yet manifested everywhere identical to its original appearances?"

YELIYAEL: "*As I mentioned earlier, by Global Morphogenesis. In your time that universal law of morphogenic field development is seriously studied, explored, analyzed by talented researchers and advanced thinkers.*

When somewhere, sometime on your planet Earth appears an idea, a form, a being, which is recognized as exact and true, meaning in accord with Universal Principles, they spontaneously manifest everywhere else and almost at the same time, without need for long distance physical transport.

Your scientists have recently identified and studied that phenomenon which they sometimes call "zeitgeist", "l'esprit du temps", "the spirit of the times".

Your planet exists as a whole bioorganic living spherical unit. Morphogenesis is a fundamental law of Life that allows all living creatures including humans to progress almost homogeneously on the "corporeal" and "mental" level as well.

Morphogenesis effect is a phenomenon, in some of its aspects, still construed in your time as chancy, miraculous or delusional.

One may easily interpret Global Morphogenesis as the most current expression which designates the same phenomenon the Bible is pointing at in Genesis: "the divine spirit that floats around the Earth": VE ROUACH ELOHIM MERA CHEPHET ÂL PENE HA MAYIM. And the breath of the Elohim-celestials was hovering over the face of the mother-waters-earth."

YELIYAEL continues his astonishing account of humanity's evolution: "*Homo Faber Originalis appeared everywhere on Earth around one million years ago, developed to the optimum of their potential as skillful utensils fabricators-user intelligent humans.*

They also reached an honorable level on the path to Beauty, and developed an embryo of Goodness.

500,000 years ago, amid that species, already long evolved and well defined, manifested the first racial diversification, again in the vast Caucasian expanse, west of the Caspian Sea, the current land of Afghanistan.

Homo Originalis species was then widespread and powerful everywhere it could adapt. Pre-human ANIMals had completely disappeared from the face of Earth, annihilation caused by genetic inferiority and daily mortal combats lost against the superior adroit AMINal individuals and their better skilled offspring.

So, Homo Faber Originalis was alone and no other comparable species was close enough to stimulate its progress. Solitary human then cast his vision-project of diversity!

Having explored the truth of its identity, humankind aspired to enter the field of Beauty, by diversifying its physical appearances.

Thus were born the natural races. They appeared on a solid foundation of equality, to play, as do basic colors, the harmonic game of contrasts, complementarities, and stimulating blends. The planet peopled with men and women of most varied physical appearances, emulating all colors, sizes, shapes and textures the earth was offering, to beautify the color tones of their bodies, skin, eyes, hair.

Humans so manifested the aspiration they had nurtured and cast to the effect of becoming unique, of acquiring distinctive characters and expressing specific personality.

In accord with the fundamental cosmic law of Verity[22]*, the various races were, through Variety and Beauty, originally aiming at generating attraction, not rejection."*

SIMHA: "So, racial creations 500,000 years ago are the ancestors of our third millennium fashion shows!"

YELIYAEL adds, almost casually, this startling information:

"Among the 6 races which emerged originally neither appeared the so called white race or black race, for both are the result of subsequent race mixing and influence of regional climate environment during multiple and repeated migrations."

Behind us trees are gently rustling their farewell to the refreshing morning breeze. Thirsty reeds accentuate their arches to reach the cool waters of the river. YELIYAEL has fallen silent, and the iridescence of its shape softens as a sign of quietude. Albert, sitting still has entered a state of deep meditation. I keep my eyes open and resting my gaze on the distant opposite bank of the river, I see through the fading mist, dense clusters of little houses standing at the edge of the town of Rajagriba.

At the heart of our silence echoes the Angel's melodious voice:

"Then, 500,000 years ago, descended on Earth, in this part of your world, the first divine beings called DEVAS[23]*, as recorded in the ancient Vedas texts, safeguarded until today by the Brahmin priests in India.*

These visitors enabled willing human clans to progress intellectually, transmitting them the refined significant sounds of the Universal Language, the vocal Archaeo sonorities. They also provided precise instructions on basic dietary principles which efficaciously contributed to the amplification of brain potentials already

---

22 The words Verity and Variety both originate from the biblical word Berith, meaning Original Creation and Covenant. In Hebrew B=V and vice versa.

23 Devas: in the Old Testament, Hebrew version, those "divine devas" are designated by the word Ne-fillim, translated vernacularly as "Falling from the skies". In Archaeo Lingua ne=immortal substance and fillim=beings falling. Note that the sound-root fill and falling are identical.

acquired, and to the manifestation of a more vigorous and greater physical beauty. Those competent divine beings helped Homo Faber Originalis in the same measure they assisted the newest colored races who had recently begun their wanderings on Earth.

Silence. Long silence.

Then, a long time after the DEVAS had earth-landed, stirs and strife occurred among the divine visitors, rippling conflicts erupted amidst humans, pandemonium punctuated by geological chaos of immense magnitude.

Silence.

Finally, 40,000 years ago, took place a great celestially planned event of which the Archangels do not allow me to presently reveal the details.

Since that time, humanity, having received additional forces to strengthen its Vow of Truth, to reinforce its Will of Beauty, has heartily commenced its long journey towards the high shores of universal Goodness.

Since that time humans are engaged in broadening their cosmic awareness concomitantly with the development of individuality as well as the manifestation of moral commitment towards all beings, aiming at achieving universal spiritual consciousness, thus completing the third evolutionary stage: GOODNESS, GODNESS.

This is the ongoing human saga since Adam's and Eve's sojourn, including the wondrous actions, teachings and revelations by the Masters MELKITSEDEK, MOSES, ORPHEUS, YEHOSHUA-JESUS. Every step and every revelation has added to the previous, enriching and complementing it."

YELIYAEL gradually discolors and disappears before our eyes, thus signaling he has completed one of the thousand and one stories that can be narrated on the origin and evolution of humankind on Earth.

We stand up and resume our walk along the river, hoping soon to reach the garden-monastery where BUDDHA and some of his many disciples reside at this time. YELIYAEL visible again, floats at my side. He informs us we have ele-landed in the country of MAGADA, at the eastern end of the life-thriving Ganges delta.

An authoritarian and buoyant monarch, Bimbasara, reigns on this small sized albeit advanced kingdom, enriched by resourceful artisans and dynamic traders.

To increase his power and wealth, king Bimbasara seeks hegemony over all the monarchies and republics which by the hundreds are scattered on each side of the Ganges River. We are here a few miles from the capital city Rajagriba, new intellectual and spiritual center. Bimbasara facilitates and finances the construction of dozens Buddhist monasteries in his kingdom, hoping to use their remarkable spiritual vitality to achieve political hegemony, in competition with the strong monarchy Varanasi, another important region of Buddhist expansion.

At the turn of the road we see emerging on the horizon, simple lines and modest size, the silhouette of a monastery, resembling the ashrams our contemporaries may visit on their touristy journeys: unadorned architecture, trapezoidal roof gable resting on plain slender columns.

We are now about to step on a warm ocher wooden bridge, one of the entrances to the vast park surrounding the monastery. The river is generously sharing its bounty with this welcoming garden, as lively waters flow through scores of irrigating canals pleasingly bordered with reeds.

Scattered amid stately trees I discern several bamboo roofed shacks, humble dwellings for disciples and visitors. On a small hill to the left, three men sit in perfect meditative stillness under the restful shade of a roof elegantly supported by four carved wood pillars. Their shelter is largely open to the four horizons. An aura of scintillating blue light surrounds the entire body of one of the three monks.

From afar I can see them clearly, but they seem not to have yet detected our approach.

YELIYAEL announces:

"There is BUDDHA and two disciples, SARIPUTRA and ANANDA."

Brusquely, I am stunned, shocked. I feel my body shivering

violently, uncontrollably. I am traversed and shaken by electric surges. Air vibrates, landscape and sky undulate, as if stricken by an intense heat wave.

Then, on a gleaming backdrop filled with pure white whiteness, I see **HER.**

At first fuzzy, her silhouette now more precise stands immobile in petrified time. Silence is absolute.

The Dame, majestic, luminous, is wearing a pale blue cape dotted with golden stars.

SHE speaks to me, I understand her words, but I hear no sound.

"You must go away! Immediately! Immediately!"

Did I scream or simply whispered, I do not remember. Before me Albert's face effaces itself, pale lines and fugitive curves. He seems to smile at me, but I am not sure of anything. The forest, river, bridge, are now evanescent mists.

And behold, YELIYAEL is enveloping us with his ethereal milky substance, which takes the form of a slightly ovoid luminous sphere. My last thought dissolves in the enseraphment unconsciousness that precedes the angelic travel.

Chapter Three

...and there was Light!

37. Galilee, 2nd century AD.

BERURIAH WAKES UP ABRUPTLY. Alarmed, concerned. Loose fringes of a recurrent nightmare? From her restless sleep she has brought back no image, no clear or fuzzy thought, no familiar or odd landscape; remains only a distressing latent sense of gripping anxiety. It is dawn. BERURIAH silently extracts herself from the warm and cozy alcove, her resting area.

Her husband is still sleeping soundly, breathing peacefully. She stares at him, heart imbued with love and tenderness. Meir is a stocky man, vigorous, freckles peppered face, green topaz eyes and red hair curls evoke the Jewish Moabite lineage of David, the poet-king. Meir nicknamed Baal-Hanes[24] is very famous in Galilee and well beyond, as a brilliant scholar who has studied history and the Sepher Torah with all Babylon's, Jerusalem's and Alexandria's great masters. A proselyte also, a convert like thousands Judeans, Samaritans, Greeks from Antioch and Athens, who since the beginning of this century, have come, enthused, to participate in the transmission of the Galilean carpenter's new message. They all came to receive Yeshuist[25] and Johannit messianic teachings, or

24 Baal ha-Nes; in Hebrew means: Master of the Miracle.
25 Johannites: disciples of John the Baptist, Yeshuistes: followers of Yehoshuah-Jesus

study and practice the ancient Essenes' spiritual discipline.

BERURIAH lets her morning thoughts wander: the situation in the land of Israel is perplexing. The new sects preach with passion the imminent second coming of the Messiah, who shall guide humanity to Heavens' kingdom. The Tzadokit establishment opposes them violently, as befits priests of an official institution which controls both the economic, religious-political life in the countries of Israel and Judea. Those Tzadokim operate in perfect collusion with the Roman rulers, and the king imposed by the Roman imperial power.

The occupying Romans themselves are tormented, fearing social chaos, harassed by the zealots, a rebellious group whose influence is strongly growing throughout this part of the Empire. And presently the ruling authorities are primarily focusing on a repression they want quick, massive and definitive.

Whenever a Tzadokit-Sadducee priest member of the Great Sanhedrin[26], or a king's police agent, points finger at a religious dissident, the Roman executors seize, crucify, flay alive or burn him at the stake along with his entire family and associates.

A vast majority among Israelites and Judeans, from Nazareth, Tiberias, Jerusalem, Caesarea, Bethlehem, Hebron, support firmly the new message; they live by its conveyed hope, either openly, so risking their lives, or clandestinely, to survive this social and political dreadful turmoil they hope will be only transitory.

BERURIAH prolongs her inner monolog:

The situation is confusing and perilous. A very large number of Jews and proselytes adhere to the new spiritual creed, whose principles take roots in the Messianic Essene tradition several thousand years old.[27]

---

26 Sanhedrin: the official judicial institution of Judea and Israel, established in Jerusalem. Composed of 70 judges, issued from different "schools of thoughts" (Tzadokim-Sadducees/ Pharashim-Pharisees, undercover political Zelots and mystic Essenes).

27 The Essene Tradition is a legacy of cosmic revelations carried by Adam and Eve, Abraham and Melkitzedek, Joseph and Moses, and revived by Yehoshua. These revelations are the core of the Hebraic and Christian Kabalah.

But unfortunately some members of the noisiest and most violent kind ostensibly stick to the new gospel only to use it as an effective weapon of subversion against the alleged materialistic Roman domination, and as a powerful lever to resist the political oppression of Judea and Israel imposed by foreign kings established by Roman decrees. And the Roman soldiers, themselves terrified, strike blindly, arbitrarily, violently.

The spiritual guidance and social tenets of the new creed are both conveyed by Galileans, Judeans and proselytes newly evangelized, all over the Mediterranean world traveled in every direction by passionate preachers.

Some of these preachers, direct witnesses, boldly spread the message of Messiah YEHOSHUA of Nazareth, the incarnate son of God, resurrected. Often those preachers have latinized their names to facilitate rapports with non-Jew proselytes: Shimon-Petrus, Yaacov-Jacobus, Shaul-Paulus.

Other missionaries still purposely bearing their Hebrew names trek the roads of Anatolia, Byzantium, Persia, Babylonia, Egypt, Ethiopia, Cyrenaica, and find an attentive audience wherever reside members of the powerful Israelite diaspora, recent and ancient. Those disciples do not refer explicitly to the Messiah as son of God, but talk about new times, convey the new gospel, the new promise, the advent of the heavenly kingdom on Earth.

Already the rituals of the Israelite official religion have changed, many reforms have been adopted, the practice of animal sacrifices progressively abandoned, and the institutional priesthood nowadays almost powerless and obsolete.

Now the time of leadership by scholars and learned rabbis has come. These Hebrew missionaries are also permeated by the new message, but keep secret their adhesion to the messianic verb. The contents of their teachings, the routes they follow, and the tragic end they often meet at the hands of the Roman legates easily reveal the true character of their adhesion to the new faith. But the chroniclers' honesty completely dissolves in the burning acid of sectarian antagonism. "I shall always keep those scholars' names untold and respect their desire for secrecy."

Parallel to BERURIAH's train of thoughts conveyed to my mind, Angel YELIYAEL has started streaming images and information issued from archangelic archives:

"BERURIAH herself is a secret leader of the sect called MINIM, which means "both sexes", a name of derision and irony, attributed to the members of that Jesuist group by its detractors. For the teaching of Rabbi YEHOSHUA-Jesus has changed the nature of relationships between men and women.

Now, since decades, groups of both sexes assemble to study the Torah, as well as to attend liturgical services for Shabbat and traditional holidays. Boys and girls, teenagers and maidens, women and men, pray and study in natural proximity the same way they live, love, marry and weave together the fabric of family and society. Like many women today, BERURIAH has benefited from the deep laceration the arrogant male monopoly, until then uninterrupted for centuries, has recently suffered. Among scholars and rabbis she is recognized and admired as an exceptional woman, a brilliant intellectual sun illuminating the entire land of Judea and Galilee.

Her teachings on Talmud law and wisdom are sought even by some ultra-traditional rabbis of the country. Although, to them, she is only a voice they hear from behind a thick curtain. But what voice, what clarity brought to the intellect!

All those who have heard her commentaries marvel at the imperative, competent tone by which she calls the sonorities of each word and letter, in order to reveal their true essence, their deep meaning, their life force. Women and children who can see her face to face perceive the radiant waves of knowledge which illuminate her handsome beaming visage."

Shabat day! BERURIAH dedicates this holy day to a very special project. She will teach a class of young boys and girls in a village, near Tiberias. She is smiling inwardly. Ironic coincidence! The great house where she will speak in a few hours, after sunset, is a history lesson by itself, for it is the beautiful home of Mattathias ben Yehuda, grand-son of Mattathias–Matthew the tax collector, one of the twelve YEHOSHUA-JESUS' apostles, who stayed with his teacher throughout the three years of his public life. During that period, this house was often used as a place of meeting, study, and truth-seeking discussions, for this amazing group of fishermen, preachers and fated martyrs.

YELIYAEL resumes his parallel streaming:

"BERURIAH is an expert interpreter of MOSES' Scriptures. Of all the texts she has ever read and explained, nothing delights her more than the 10 Commandments, the 10 laws which contain buried like the roots of a tree, all the wisdom of the Universe.

BERURIAH is not merely reading the Torah and its commentaries. She has studied and contemplated the Egyptian legends, reflected on the Greek philosophy of Socrates, Plato and Aristotle; she has analyzed antique manuscripts of the masters geometers and mathematicians Pythagoras and Archimedes; she has wondered reading, in papyruses from Babylon and Persia, historical tales of famed Sumer and Akad.

She even managed, O miracle of these times of adventurous travels and long distance trade, to meet with a silk and precious stones merchant, who sold her texts of Hindu Vedas, translated into Aramaic by a poet from Isphahan[28], who had long lived near the Ganges delta. And currently she is soon to acquire a rare Greek scroll originally written by Sariputra, who is said to have been the greatest disciple of BUDDHA. She knows little yet of this divine philosophy, only hearsays, but her inquisitive mind is already glowing with anticipation for the new lights and revelations it shall receive from that great teacher as yet unknown to her.

BERURIAH is definitely a learned woman gifted with a wide encompassing intelligence. She insightfully interconnects notions and ideas apparently unrelated, breaks the fragile vessels housing the echoes of ignorant refrains sung for generations by "religionist" men who have long forgotten the wondrous power of creativity, imagination and personal reflection. And many an itinerant seeker

28 Ispahan: ancient capital city of Persia.

of knowledge has come knocking at her door, beseeching enlightening answers from this most brilliant mind of the century.

Her beloved husband Meir Baal-Hanes, surnamed "miracle illuminator" is also a bright mind of his times. But he shines often in places she has not yet visited. However, above all, BERURIAH prefers to teach children. And today she is to meet a great challenge: Teach a class of youngsters aged from seven to twelve, lead them to perceive and experience inwardly the world's creation wondrous advent. She will resolutely avoid intellectual acrobatics typical of the Greek Sophists. Equally she will endeavor to keep away from the inextricable confusion presented on this topic by supercilious pseudo kabalists, though true Kabalah knowledge she excels in clarifying more than most."

After much thought, she finally opted for telling the story of the world creation in the form of a fable…

BERURIAH, the great woman scholar, senses she has very little time left to live. Her husband Meir will depart tomorrow for a destination unknown to her, for one of those long secret missions which he is accustomed to accomplish. Is he going to Rome, that hornet's nest filled with prickly men of dogmatic faith, that seductive deadly trap? An inner voice, insisting whisper, tells her this time he will not return to the land of Canaan.

She feels he has taken an important, irrevocable decision, since their sons, lovely seventeen years old twins, her light on this earth, were executed by the dagger of stealthy assassins. Victims of this common form of execution called "sica"[29], performed by the zealots Sicari, but also by Roman secret agents who are using the same lethal daggers thus pretending the murderers are Judean zealots.

Horror! Their two sons were executed, furtively, ignominiously, without public trial. Their bloodied bodies were returned home, a day of Shabat, in the afternoon. An act of black vengeance by which the institutions of Rome and Jerusalem had warned the parents they too, were judged subversive and dissident.

---

29 Sica: in Hebrew designates a very sharp pointed deadly dagger, used by the Zelots. Hence their surname: Sicari.

BERURIAH and Meir are both holding faith in their upcoming re-birth in the celestial realms. Their consolation and joy they draw from this hope and dream: next year in the *Other* Jerusalem! Shana Ha Baa Be Yeroushalaim! All members of the new faith know this venerated phrase conceals a secret meaning, the revelation of the celestial Jerusalem[30] in the heavenly kingdom.

Soon, very soon, she will exit this Earth to expand her life in the Heavens; that ascending journey, she calls for, she hopes for, she is longing for.

YELIYAEL casts a new string of information, this time not parallel, but intertwined with BERURIAH's flow of thoughts:

"M*any on Earth, faithful to their materialistic opinions, affirm humans live many successive lives through perpetual reincarnation in the midst of terrestrial tribulations. That is a belief they share with the magi of ancient Persia and Brahmin sects in India. BERURIAH, like many disciples in her era, has finally learned this common belief is not the exact truth. She knows these new lives and re-births occur mostly as post death-transition, experienced by ascended soul-pilgrims, in the seven worlds of Heaven, in quest of the ultimate gate that leads to the field of eternal essences, into the promised land of the infinite spirit.*

On this luminous path of the true Life BERURIAH will meet without barriers, and without obstacles, the peoples she has cherished during her earthly life, a life full of challenges and sacrifices but also replete with the immense joy springing from the exhilarating experience of birthing a distinctive eternal soul.

Did BERURIAH also hear YELIYAEL's silent words I thought were only for our own private instruction? I empathize with her transfigured inner vision; her heart overflows with happiness and her body is on the verge of levitation. BERURIAH clings to a heavy wooden table to block her nascent flight. Now she runs to the gar-

30 Jerusalem: transliteration of the Hebrew name Yeroushalayim.
The final yim is a dual form. The grammar thus confirms the statement found in the Talmud commentaries and Kabalah revelations: there are two "sacred" cities bearing the same name, and therefore ineluctably linked: one on earth in Israel, and one in the Heavens. Tradition says they are "mystically connected".

den well to extinguish with fresh water the flames of the fire surging in her mind. To complete her thorough morning toilet she perfumes her hair, hands and neck with discreet orange blossom fragrance.

Standing still in the garden adjacent to the humble stone house she inherited from her father, inhabited by her family for several generations, BERURIAH glances at the familiar snowy peak of solitary Mount Hermon silhouetting on the misty lavender horizon of the farther Golan Mountains.

In the valley, beyond the forested low slopes, shines the large Kinneret Lake, the inland Sea of Galilee. The many surrounding villages are hidden by luxuriant trees and large rocks. It is Shabat day, no smoke can be seen rising above the roofs.

Looking at the sky, tiny airy white clouds floating in the pale azure, the day will be sunny and mild. Northern Israel accustomed to frost and chilly morning mists is blessed this year with an early and warm Spring. White daisies, buttercups and bright red poppies gaily dress all the hills around Nazareth, Safed and Hatzor. Scattered blooming fruit trees radiate white and rose beauty, equally attracting bees and butterflies. From the old large fig tree in the garden, countless birds rhythmically greet the new morning and offer salutation to their creator.

BERURIAH picks a pretty little green fig, soft cheeks reddened by her lover the sun, then snaps a second, still freshened by the dew of dawn, and a third quickly reaches her small hand. Tasty, exquisitely tender, delicately sweet, this will be her only meal until sunset, which will announce the end of Shabbat, the end of the day of peace and grace.

Tomorrow BERURIAH, and all Galileans, in tears, will again be assailed by the cruelty of Rome and Jerusalem. But tomorrow is tomorrow, today is today…

In a few hours she will walk down slowly along the road to Kfar Nahum, to her long planned appointment with the boys and girls assembled, waiting for her in the valley, eager to hear the story of the Creation of the World.

Albert, YELIYAEL and I, invisible inside a translucent virtual sphere are gently floating above BERURIAH since the moment she awoke.

Our human minds embedded like tiny bright droplets within the vital ethereal substance of the Angel perceive and read all BERURIAH's inner thoughts and emotions, main streams and nuances, shapes, sounds, colors and aromas emanating from her magnetic mind field. These waves of energy are angelically transcoded-transposed into words, phrases and sensations within our personal consciousness.

Now our angelic ship is flying away from BERURIAH's house, like a tiny cloud, rising high, very high in the pristine atmosphere.

ALBERT asks: "Aren't we to attend the lesson BERURIAH will present to the children in Kfar Nahum?"

YELIYAEL, with a reassuring kind voice:

"*We have ample time to move towards the village by the lake, in the late afternoon.*"

Amid a field of wild flowers, we smoothly land, near an old abandoned stone fountain in a deserted patch, away from human dwellings. A little dazed, we regain full usage of our visible bodies, progressively feeling the pull of terrestrial gravity. YELIYAEL recreates for himself a luminous white iridescent silhouette, toped by those large jade green eyes I love so much to stare at whenever they appear.

I enjoy the respite. We three sit side by side on large square cut stones, remnants of an ancient farmhouse, like the fountain, long ago abandoned.

ALBERT addresses me abruptly, sounding extremely concerned, and even somewhat accusatory:

"What happened in India, near BUDDHA's monastery? Why that sudden scream:

"We must go away! Immediately! Immediately!" Your face went pale; you were on the verge of syncope. You even said: "We are on the wrong way!"

SIMHA: "I am not aware of having said "We are on the wrong

way!" though the whole frenzied scene, the precipitous sudden dramatic departure, remains deeply etched in my mind. I remember every nuance, every detail."

YELIYAEL is serene, neutral. I gaze at his eyes and, instantly, perceive his thought: "*That wrong way*, says he silently, *was perfectly on the course you had to travel.*"

I turn to Albert, and explain:

"We were not wrong to think we should go and meet BUDDHA in that monastery at Rajagriba. It was a meaningful move; an essential step for you and me, so our initiation continues in the right direction and our cosmic saga blossoms as a galactic rose. We were meant to enter that enchanted forest, listen to the trees chanting, and walk along that great river, near the ancestral lands, repository of our most ancient origins. But, converse with BUDDHA and his disciples on the subject of the 8th Commandment was not the way…"

ALBERT: "How did you learn that? Why just at that moment?"

I answer calmly: "As we were walking in the park of the monastery and at the very moment I saw the silhouette of BUDDHA and his two disciples, my whole body started to shudder uncontrollably, like a tree assailed by a hurricane. And I found myself locked in a trance of deep-white silence. A Lady, a Dame, appeared a few steps in front of me, spoke to me mind to mind, soul to soul, revealed her identity and her message. I am now to tell you what she authorized me to disclose.

She said the 8th Commandment THOU SHALT NOT STEAL-LOA TA GANOV, was destined to be explored with her, the ARCHAE MATRIA, Mother of Humans.

She illumed the letters of that law and I became excitedly aware the popular regular translations stand ten thousand miles away from the cosmic message it truly contains.

This Commandment, she added, may be revealed only by reaching spiritual dimensions far beyond the opaque physical and material spheres.

She confided to me many other marvels, which at that moment clear like crystal, became afterwards vague, blurred and utterly incomprehensible to my logical mind.

Then she declared commandingly: "Now go away from here! Leave this place immediately!"

I asked her, ecstasy mixing with panic: To go where, Mother? She gently wrapped me in a cloak of love, and simply said:

"Go and Trust!!"

Angel YELIYAEL has now adopted the outline of a compact, concentrated light shining at the exact center of a spherical cloud. Dense and glistening spirals whirl at high speed around his fuzzy form. All shades of green, the colors of serenity and peace, scintillate on the irises of his wide-open eyes. My evocation of the Dame seems to have produced dramatic effects in the spirit of our cherished angelic guide.

Albert, quiet, hands joined touching his chest, is standing, staring at the snowy peak of faraway Hermon Mountain. He seems to converse with invisible beings, I see his lips move slowly, like a child learning to read. Is he conversing privately with YELIYAEL? Or with his personal Guardian Angels? Maybe with the Lady herself?

After a long moment of silent prayer, Albert looks at me, smiles broadly, and says: "If you agree, Simha, let's go now and join BERURIAH. I look forward to enter this 2nd century school. I would not want to miss the beginning of the lesson. What a challenge! Explain the Creation of the World to young children!"

"Ready!" I said.

And so was YELIYAEL! The landscape unfurls at high speed under my eyes. From above I search for BERURIAH on the yellow dusty road heading to Kfar Nahum. Nobody. Not a lonely traveler, not even a donkey or a wayward goat!

Suddenly we find ourselves floating invisibly above a flat roofed house surrounded by a large blooming orchard. Jumping out of the fresh and airy protective angelic crystal dome, I enter a large room, windows fully open to the evening breeze. I see Albert and YELIYAEL are already fluttering here and there, exploring the scene, apparently in search of the finest angle and most favorable perspective to best enjoy BERURIAH's lesson.

"Look, look, exclaims Albert, we are not the only visitors! Do you see these wavy forms in the back row, behind the children?"

I see. And YELIYAEL seems now to be animatedly conversing with these iridescent pastel cloudy shapes. Albert is now floating by my side, and the ubiquitous Angel reports:

"The celestial guests welcome you! MOSES, LAOV TZSE, Yohanan BEN ZAKAI are here to attend the lesson of the luminous BARURIAH[31], Master of Light."

"But I discern four distinct forms, I say. Is there another visitor you have not named?"

"*GAUTAMA BUDDHA is the name*" says YELIYAEL.

38. The Creation of the World.

BERURIAH IS SITTING CROSS-LEGGED ON a broad floor cushion. Rounded face, petite, well built and good-looking. Shiny black wavy hair discreetly attached down her neck with a pastel blue ribbon. Her light-olive complexion radiates health and energy acquired from sunshine and natural harmonious diet.

At the center of the atrium, thirty boys and girls, the older twelve years old, sit side by side, forming a wide semi-circle facing BERURIAH. In the background, the orchard of this stately mansion flows in successive terraces down to the lakeshore.

Behind BERURIAH, almost touching her back, a floor to ceiling thick heavy curtain, lapis-blue velvet finely embroidered with golden threads, is masking the entrance of a large cavernous room. There, in the dark, are seated adult male listeners, rabbis, scholars,

31 Bar-uriah=another way to read the name Beruriah, delivering the true meaning enclosed in the name: Master of Divine Light. bar=Master, ur=Light, iah=Divine power, an attribute of the Divine Creator.

disciples who came from afar to hear this special lesson. Amidst this silent assembly, in a corner to the right, inconspicuous, a few women, heads covered with silk scarves. BERURIAH only accepts a male audience on the stipulation the room be open to feminine assistance. Most of those present today are the wives, daughters or sisters of Talmudic judges and eminent Torah scholars.

Now everyone is silent; children in the atrium, adults concealed behind the curtain, are expectantly waiting.

BERURIAH slowly extends her right arm, hand open facing the skies, and begins:

"YALDE YAMENOU, Children of our Time, how can we describe what we cannot know by direct evidence? The Creation of the World! BERITH HA ÔLAM! The sounds of those words are running along my body, make it shiver with awe, love and joy. How can we represent the Creation of the World?

I ask you, you Mikhail of Caesarea, and you Angelos of Corinth, and you, Hannah of Babylon, you Ramona of Toledo, you Rachel from Nazareth…

Well! I already see part of the answer on your bright faces illuminated with enthusiasm. Yes, what cannot be seen with eyes, touched with hands, heard with ears, you may feel it in your chest, following the strong beat of your heart.

Within the depth of our minds, holding that feeling of warmth and happiness, we can ride the beams of our imagination and sail on the wings of Angels in the luminous wide space of the Spirit. In this space we can hear the joyous gush of invisible fountains telling us what they have always known.

Together, let us embark on this fabulous angelic ship and listen to the story whispered by the infinite:

"ONCE UPON A TIME, far in time, beyond everything, there was a world where there was nothing, NOTHING!

That NOTHING was a being which existed alone, without voice, without vow, without law.

As there was NOBODY else who was there, we never found out

who was that NOTHING who claimed to be there!

No witness has ever been able to report on that NOTHING who knew nobody and whom nobody knew.

NOTHING not even knew himself, because he was engulfed in absolute silence, enclosed in total eternity, without voice, without vow, without law.

How do I know? Who has ever been able to testify? Nothing and nobody!

And yet something has come up to us, later, much later, when EVERYTHING was already there, suddenly present with voice, vow and law!

That's when we knew of this extraordinary birth, and here's how the story was told:

Once there was a world without men and women,
Without homes and without countries,
Without lakes and without mountains,
A world without voice."

Little Shoshanna muffles a squeal in her hand, her innocent face mimicking intense fear, but her eyes, color of freshly harvested hazelnuts, glimmer with happiness and anticipation.

BERURIAH charmed, smiles gently and continues:

"And yet that world without vow,
Without law, without voice
Was full of thrills of joy…
And nobody knew how and why!
Those thrills of joy were hanging
Like black filaments
In the midst of a black ocean."

"But, but, then, exclaims Rapha, the slender Ethiopian Kousha, jet black eyes, curly hair, lanky boy who loves to laugh and talk, then how could we see the black threads hanging in the black night?"

BERURIAH, unruffled, replies: "There is no clear answer to your question, Rapha! As there was nobody there, nobody to look at anything, every thing remained hidden in the dark.

In that surprising world there was
No white to pierce the black because everything was black,
No outside to go inside because everything was inside,
No sorrow to spoil the joy because everything was joy,
No door to close the mind because everything was mind,
No head to love thinking because everything was thought.
And because ALL was there, there was Nothing, nothing there!
ALL was giving gifts to no one, because there was no One there!"

Lydia, daughter of a recent proselyte from Athens, bursts in a cascading laughter, launching waves of happiness in the atmosphere already electrified by the imagination of all those children whose minds are exploring that strange and frightening world, blacker than a starless night…

Calming her youthful laughter, Lydia exclaims in a passionate tone:

"We must help that world!"

"Ah, answers the teacher: How do we help a WHOLE which has NOTHING to hold on it?"

David, usually a rebellious little boy, timidly proposes:

"Maybe I could shoot from here with my sling a small white pebble into this black world!"

A little girl, mischievous looking, announces theatrically:

"We could send my little sister Rachel who cries and whines all the time. It will change everything down there in that world where everything is joy!"

BERURIAH smiles and encourages:

"But it is so far away, how to get there? That world is engulfed in a deep space and nobody knows where to find it, because it is everywhere!"

Solomon of Nazareth, young descendant of a long line of scholars, intervenes, calm, controlled, his boyish voice already grave and serious:

"I have an idea! That world is made of thoughts, we cannot

send a stone and we cannot send a whining little girl, he will take neither. We are all going to think, think hard. And we are not going to think with the head only, but we will think with our spirit. That world will love these special thoughts, he will accept them, and that will change everything!"

Some children look at Solomon curiously, twisting their brow, they do not understand. Others are really excited by this solution which seems clever and amusing.

BERURIAH, nodding approvingly offers assistance:

"Solomon is right, that black world is all made of thought and spirit, and it is with thoughts and spirit we can touch it. But then, which thoughts are we going to send to that world where all is black, all is silence and all is joy?"

"Me, me! exclaims Neferta of Alexandria. I am going to enter in my mind, inside my head, doing like this!"

Neferta joining action to words covers her face with her hands, pressing very hard on her closed eyes, so that no particle of light reaches in. And, in front of all attentive, amazed children, Neferta completely immobilizes herself, silent. Under the admiring gaze of the youngsters a tiny golden halo materializes around her head.

All are quiet, expectant…

Behind the blue velvet curtain, among the hidden audience, some faces mark surprise, frowning and squinting. Some hand movements question silently: What's going on? What's happening? But nobody utters the minutest sound.

Neferta finally lowers her hands, freeing her intensely radiating face. Her large jet-black eyes slightly slanted evoke the vast Asian steppes; her slender gracious neck reminds the black princesses celebrated by King Solomon, her delicate freckled and milky skin conjures up the great plains of the Caucasus. Her birthplace, Alexandria in Egypt, is once again a cosmopolitan city. Her tone serious, Neferta excitedly announces:

"Morati! Morati! My teacher! my teacher! Ni Tza Chati! Ni Tza Chati! I did it! I succeeded, I won!!!"

BERURIAH whispers softly to herself. In her heart and spirit resonate and amplify the sacred sounds of savant ARCHAE LINGUA:

((((Ni)))) ((((Tza)))) ((((Cha Ti))))
"I have ridden the waves of eternity,
I entered the ocean of essential substances (Ni)
and swiftly exiting out of my own physical shell, I succeeded,
with sudden force, to break into the other world (Tza).
There I have placed the seed of life and suffering (Cha),
and the musical melody of perpetual cycles (Ti)"

"Tell us more, asks BERURIAH, what did you do, Neferta?"

"I went into my head, in the most inside place in my head, where all was black and all was silence, I raised a tiny white dot in the blackness, a little white idea, a drop of light, I transformed it into a transparent teardrop, a tiny drop of water that wept from being alone in the world, then I prayed:

BARUCH - ATA - ADONAI - ELOHENOU - MELEKH - HA ÔLAM - CHE - LAKACH - ET - HA - BETZA - BE-ROSHY - VE - SHAMAH - BA - ÔLAM - HA - CHOSHEKH - LI - PTACHO - VE - MITHOKH - HA - SHACHOR - YATZA - SHAM - OR - VE – OROT. "

BERURIAH asks: "Who will translate the prayer Neferta has composed, and whispered in her mind, inside the black silence of her head?"

Little brunette Olivia, the only daughter of Roman Porteus and beautiful Ishtar from Damascus, volunteers for this challenging task. She hastily scribbles a few sentences on her papyrus, stands up and recites:

"*Blessed art thou, O Adonai-our Lord, King of the Universe, who now takes the egg out of my head to place it in the black world, who opens it, and in the middle of blackness, there far away, surges the light of luminous stars."*

BERURIAH: "Did you go there Neferta, with your thoughts, riding the Divine Spirit with your prayer?"

"Yes, simply says Neferta, it just happened that way."

"And what have you seen?"

All children, fascinated, are listening intently.

Neferta recounts calmly:

"As soon as the egg has been deposited, there happened an extraordinary powerful explosion, the egg opened and everything was shattered. But nothing was destroyed. Everything was beautiful! Colored ribbons were dancing in the air, sweet music was coming from everywhere, Angels flying between spheres of gold.

I saw strange blooming flowers, long winged birds bigger than in my grandmother's tales. Fruit trees spoke together and with the birds, and with the breeze! I saw filaments of joy weeping, kissing little globes of sadness, snakes escalating giant baobab trees; I saw clouds of darkness that ran like storms to escape the arrows of light thrown by smiling Cherubs. I saw...I saw…"

The girl stops recounting, laughs with all her heart. Neferta is renowned for her rich magnificent overflowing imagination. She has already written many poems, often read and admired in the women's circles of Galilee.

BERURIAH looks fondly at this beautiful bouquet of girls and boys as an immense wave of profound nostalgia suddenly engulfs her chest, almost blocking her breath. Soon she will go away, leave this Earth and journey to the Heavens. That is her wish; she is waiting for her Angel to lift her in his ethereal embrace.

She decides to conclude this lesson harmoniously, as she wishes to conclude her life on Earth:

"Behold now, with the Almighty's help, we sent a small drop of white light into the sea of dark night, in total silence, inhabited by living filaments of joy. Then, that ocean that was black because it was NOTHING has just received a white and yellow musical sound, the AV, the OV, the L-OVE, the egg of life, the seed of the Father AV, the visitor, the seed from elsewhere. Now that world is created and everything in that world is created, everything that exists shall flow from that unique Source, naturally.

YALDE HA ROUACH, Children of the Spirit, the lesson is completed!"

Boys and girls, shocked, resist leaving their seats. They want, they wish to know more, much more.

"Morati, teacher, a little more!"

"More, teacher, more!"

Wonderful chorus of all children everywhere in the world, asking for more, more, ever more!

BERURIAH offers consolation:

"This story is only the beginning of the Creation of the World. Children, ask Neferta to give you the Hebrew text of her prayer, study it again and again. Compare it with the first paragraph of the Torah. You will see that prayer uses every letter, every syllable and every word of the first seven verses of the Book of MOSES. The order is different, but everything is the same.

This is the miracle of liberty!

If you keep all your intentions very clear, you too can do what Neferta did. Respect the letters and the text, but change the order of syllables, change the words order, break and reconstruct new words. You will then discover thousands wonderful stories!"

Behind the blue curtain the audience is in total pandemonium, indescribable excitement.

"MISHIGANE!" some voices claim, "crazy, she is crazy, crazy!"

"Verbiage without head or tail, it is pure nonsense! She does not understand the scriptures!"

"She invents it all, she studies nothing!"

"NES, NES GADOL" whisper others, turning faces and arms to the sky.

"This woman is a MIRACLE, this woman is a marvel!"

"This is truth combining freedom with science!"

"This is truth reaching the peak of imagination and audacity. "

A third group has formed, around poisonous ideas, spit by dangerous serpents: "This is dissention, subversion, blasphemy of the most sacred texts!"

"She is tearing down everything, tradition, law, order!"

"This is the ferment of social dissent and chaos!"

"Hush! Hush! Chtok! murmur some women. You will alert the Roman soldiers and their throng of spies!"
"Enough tears and blood shed!"
"The pyre that burned her father and her whole family is not yet extinguished. Shame, shame on you!"

"May she burn at the stake in sacrilegious Rome, before roasting in the perpetual fires of hell!" mulls a man of quiet appearance, his foxy eyes never looking straight at others' faces. But his inner thoughts are so viciously noisy everyone can hear them as if he was shouting.

A frisson of anxiety traverses the assembly. All think of those martyrs being flayed alive, burned, crucified, surrendering their soul while proclaiming their love of the Lord in Heaven, for decades past.

As for us, venturous space-time travelers, invisible witnesses of this frenzied scene, we know that to this current series of violence will be added lions pits, bloody religious wars, recurrent merciless multiform inquisitions, genocides and holocausts.

But, surely, one day, from afar in the vast universe, a little child shall send to our world a golden luminous egg of harmony and peace.

BERURIAH knows in her heart what is going on there, behind the blue heavy curtain of shame, the hypocritical fence planted by those arrogant bearded faces who edict as rigid rule that no female may teach a male face to face.

Her thoughts soften, however:
"Among those men can also be found the jewels of humanity, loving, tolerant, ready to travel the path of Liberty.

Think Just, aiming at Truth, seek Beauty in accord with the harmony of the celestial spheres, find Goodness by the Grace of the Divine…

There is no point in arguing, conflicting and proving. True

thought is RISHIT, Reigning Principle, radiant fundamental law, Royal Princess of the Creation of the Worlds.

Think True, Just, Good, and patiently, wait. Thoughts and imagination are Fire and Light, offspring of the Verb of Life."

Chapter Four

Edenia

39. Manhattan, March 2001, AD.

OUR STOPOVER APPEARS INDEFINTELY PROLONGUED. Since our wondrous expedition into 2nd century AD to attend BERURIAH's lesson, months have passed, the seasons have provided their harvests of sunlight, rain and fog, storms and winds.

The city's cycles also have produced their fruits and flowers, traffic jams and noisy Sunday parades, New Year's Eve 2001 in Times Square, new buildings launching towards the sky, and the continuous flowering of yellow cabs on the broad avenues.

This evening unfurls like a pleasant dream. Albert and I sitting on the windowsill, lulled by the music of the waterfall in the garden; windows wide open we breathe in wave-particles of absolute energy darting through the cool night, embraced by the same simple joy of existence, aware of the immense beauty of the surrounding universe. Pensively looking askance, in the corner of my eye I notice the pink marble of our living room small fountain is now basking in a diaphanous mist, adorned with tiny sparkling pastel reflections. The rhythm of the water gush accelerates or slows like a song springing under the fingers of a harpist...a melodious and gentle voice approaches our escaped consciousness....Albert has turned his head towards the interior of the apartment and I see his eyes shining with contained excitement. He too has recognized the signs of the Angel's presence!

A simple clear image enters my inner vision, entwined with an electric whirr on my forehead.

"Is that you, YELIYAEL?"

The caress amplifies on my brow, feeling like the soft drone of two fluttering dragonflies flying sometimes in accord, sometimes in asymmetry.

Two forms, alabaster colored, gradually emerge three feet above the floor, distinct but connected by a fine net of purple strings. Without hesitation I recognize our cherished angelic companion, Seraph YELIYAEL. His ethereal aura now takes the shape of a downwards open fan, crisscrossed in all directions by a network of fine lines of light, his large green jade eyes throwing undulating arrows spangled with gold specks.

On the plissé veil figuring his angelic body I contemplate vast landscapes, mountains dotted with green-forested slopes and quiet mirror lakes. For the first time, YELIYAEL radiates a feminine aura: effect of the skirt shape of her current appearance, or suggested by the white crescent moon floating freely above the snow-capped peaks?

And YELIYAEL is not alone! At her side glides between floor and ceiling, a chubby baby face round as a rising sun, full lips, eyes wide open, silvery bright skin glowing like white gold. Luscious aromas are reaching us in waves, replete with jasmine and cypress notes, warm woodsy and lightly floral, forming a double helix of contrasting fragrances intertwined in a love trance.

"My name is YE-ZA-LA-EL" enunciates the chubby sun face with a solar bright smile.

And the round head zigzags in our living room, bouncing off the walls like a beach ball, conspicuously traverses YELIYAEL's fan shape, and finally abruptly lands on Marie Tania's favorite armchair, mischievously emulating the posture of a wise and serious child!

This new energetic presence sparked a cascade of laughter,

Angels and humans united! Intoxicated with joy we were rolling on the floor, our happiness so great, our surprise so intense. Two Angels with us, YELIYAEL and YEZALAEL! How wonderful! Bedlam and freshness of childhood now added to the profound wisdom of our friendly familiar travel companion.

"Where are we going O Angel YEZALAEL?"

"Who are we meeting next O Angel YELIYAEL?"

"The Saga of the Sacred Ten continues, exclaims ALBERT. I am ready for immediate departure!"

After a halt several months long, almost one year, our quest starts again, with a strong beat, vibrant like the gongs awakening the novices in the Tibetan temples.

Merry we are! Determined to unveil more truth embedded in the Ten Commandments, we shall take off again, penetrate the interstellar spaces, reach beyond the abyss of time, explore the enigmas etched on Earth by this extraordinary Egyptian sphinx, the Master of the Mysteries, the man with multiple names, MUSAEUS, MOISHE, MOUSSA, MOYSE, MAIS, MOSES. We shall resume the deciphering and understand even better the messages of HER-MAIS, the great HERMES, the initiator of the rites of Eleusis at the dawn of Greek history, who transmited the ancient Egyptian wisdom, the celestial laws of eternal science, the unbreakable hyperlink between Humans, Angels, Archangels and Deities.

40. Edenia. Universal Time.

"ALL ABOARD! OUR GEMINI SHIP IS WAITING FOR US!" Albert exclaimed humorously before safely diving into the sweet trance-dream of seraphic transport.

Our twin-captained ship is now composed of two very contrasting angelic textures: the familiar diaphanous evanescent refined veil of YELIYAEL propelled by the sensuous intense solar power of Seraph YEZALAEL.

"Our entwined angelic substances-energy deeply unified and harmonized release exponentially increasing overdrive powers necessary to perform our upcoming translation towards infra-atomic spaces" explained YELIYAEL before our complete enséraphment. *This journey will be different, because it now requires a double twist, and we will effect several ultra cosmic translations.*

Angel YEZALAEL and I shall spiral as a double helix, around a single axis, like a huge caduceus, added YELIYAEL. *You too will be split and re-formed several times before our arrival. Let us depart, we are expected... "*

41. The Encounter.

OUR SERAPHIC TIME-SPACE SHIP EMERGED and stabilized at the center of an immense perfectly polished crystal surface on which scintillate multi-colored interlacing geometric shapes, amazing pictorial masterpiece of an artist gifted with superlative abstract imaginative powers. Nothing here closely or remotely resembles terra firma, nothing is dense or opaque, all is translucent, fluid and gaseous.

"*Welcome to ZA-MARI-YAH*" murmurs a melodious voice rippling from everywhere around us.

Our celestial twin friends have not beforehand provided any information as to the destination or specific purpose of this new expedition. The two Angels surround us amicably a few moments with their transparent glimmering substance, then the double veil withdraws. Released from the protective immaterial shell, Albert and I slowly exit from the luminous Egg-Ship.

"Where are we?"

Minds extremely alert, thoughts agile and flexible, wide-ranging awareness, our emotions uplifted, thanks to the double enséraphment, we listen to our inner senses. No fright, not even the slightest anxiety, though nothing is ordinary or familiar in this place imbued with colored light and shimmering reflections.

"This is EDENIA sphere, capital of constellation ZA-MARI-YAH, YELIYAEL informs. *Let's go forward..."*

I wonder...Are we still enséraphed, did we arrive in a real place? Or is this a dream vision, virtual embodiment of a distant planet? However, we start moving forward, Albert and I side-by-side, flanked by our angelic navigators, deeply inserted in a soft sphere, somehow encapsulated in a kind of sub aerial sub substantial vessel. Above us the depths of profound volcanic furnaces, chimneys spewing scorching supercharged red-hot lava. Our virtual bodies effortlessly traverse multiple strata of geological aspect, irrigated by vast networks of sinuous roots emerging from an immense forest of innumerable trees, scattered with transparent sea-floors populated with a rich diverse marine life.

I feel like I am advancing in the bowels of a living earth, where all underground beings find protection and vital substances, living in a huge benevolent matrix, the womb of a loving mother. All necessary foods of life are here, around us, caring, nourishing, permeating all.

Exhilarated, we are now navigating an area where volcanic fires explode into luminescent cosmic conflagrations, burning nothing; scorching winds transmute into breezes, freshening our souls. Syrupy geological veins carry us on their colored fluids, vast network of "river-roads", directional and intelligent, transporting us towards our destination, naturally, telepathically, safely.

Godly Chronos[32] seems inactive in ZA-MARI-YAH, for my mind

32 Chronos: God of Time. Root for Chronology, Chronograph, Chronic, Chronicles.

doesn't perceive the presence of time, at least in the capital EDENIA, garden city built in an eggshell made of transparent particles of immaterial energy.

I see her! Near a spring spurting crystalline water, stands a sublime creature, a statuesque woman radiating a halo of white light traversed by a multitude of gleaming rays whose color evokes dense molten gold in an alchemist's athanor[33]. Each golden ray aims at her chest while it simultaneously emanates from her heart.

She comes to us wrapped in an egg-shaped brilliant aura, human woman of eternal essence. A pastel blue cape adorned with golden stars covers her body and head, color contrast revealing abundant dark hair glinting with purple reflections. Her satin skin hue matte copper-tone revealing shades of pastel indigo, her face finely sculpted, evoke all human races at once, a pure and perfect archetype of all women across the lands of Earth.

Slowly raising her right hand, she presents herself to us:

"I am AVA-MARI-YAH."

"On your planet I am known as Archae Matria, the Mother Goddess, Ishtar, Isis, Eva, the Virgin Mary. My archaic name AVA ZU-MARIAH, EVE from SU-MARIA transliterated into AVE MARIA, a beautiful prayer which rises up to me, since the 12th century AD of your time, from the humble churches and the majestic cathedrals of GAIA."[34]

"So, I ask, when we chant Ave Maria, it is you we address, the Archae Matria, our Source, our Goddess, our Mother?"

"*It is she who appears frequently on your land,* comments Angel YEZALAEL, *more often than chronicles relate. EVA may be seen only with the eyes of the heart. She is the Lady of the Lake, Our Lady of Fatima in Portugal, Our Lady of Lourdes in France and La Virgen de Guadalupe in Mexico, and more, more, always her, under various names...*"

Spark! That's **Her**! She appeared to me on the bank of the

33 Athanor: a furnace used to provide heat for alchemical process.

34 Gaia: ancient Greek name to designate planet Earth. Root of the Hebrew word goy, meaning people of Earth. Also root for Japanese Gai jin meaning foreigner. Both refer to people whose origins are only earthly and not from the Heavens.

Ganges River in India!

She is the Lady who asked me to leave immediately BUDDHA's monastery garden! I was then crushed by fear...Now I feel I know her as a friend, even know her very well…

Now mother AVA-MARI-YAH more commonly named EVA de MARI, the twin angels YELIYAEL and YEZALAEL, Albert and I, forming a circle, are sitting on low rocky platforms, transparent and supple, as comfortable as an English lawn. To our salute a vivacious brook responds, spraying our hands and faces with lively virginal waters, fresh like early morning dew. A majestic turquoise blue tree, similar to an immense umbrella pine offers us his fruits of kindness and inner peace.

YELIYAEL rises suddenly, and from his diaphanous veil slowly emerges a dense swirl of light tracing the perfect silhouette of a gloved hand holding three white roses, two pristine buds, one blooming as a love poem. Lowering his jade eyes respectfully, YELIYAEL tenders that swirling whiteness to EVE, who, with both her copper tone open hands, smiling, accepts the Angel's homage.

As she graciously elevates the angelic bouquet to her chest, near to her heart, rippling from below, above, all around us, the chirpy sounds of hundreds lyras, harps, phorminxes, citharas, konghous and kouxians, invisible cosmic string orchestra, unite and contrast their vibrations in an enthralling symphony.

Albertov has lowered his head as a sign of humility before the nobility and elevation of this exalting feminine presence, and I, Shimeha, as I am called within the celestial orbs, heart swelling with love and eyes misty with tears, I felt like paralyzed, my lips tightly closed, not knowing who I was or where I was, my memory and my identity completely dissolved.

Hail Shimeha!" she said.

EVA spoke as whispers a source of water emerging in the grass, pure, limpid and discreet:

"I heard your personal destiny's frequencies calling me, their colors harmonizing with my name and my mission; I energized my love-attraction HOVA field and thus waited for your psyche to rediscover the celestial roads leading to me, on Edenia.

I am here ready to help you succeed in your current quest and mission. I shall answer your questions. And this time, Shimeha, you shall open the dialogue!"

I am elated! Until then, whether with MOSES, Rabbi YOHANAN, or LAO TZU, albeit kindly, the male forces have dominated every situation...This time, eternal feminine has control of the game and I truly enjoy my advantage. Our Master, here, before us is a woman, and what a woman! The Heavenly Mother of all men and all women on Earth, EVE, the unique, the One…

I remember my first sentence was long, tangled, so much I wanted to make up for prior deferrals:

"I am standing before you with my traveling companions so that together we study the 8th Commandment MOSES received from our Father, the Father of all, EL ELYON, holding in his strong arms the twin stone slabs while the heavenly messenger engraved the laws, one by one, on Mount Horeb rocked by tremors, roars and flames."

"The present descendants of the peoples of the Exodus, how do they enounce this Commandment?" asks EVE.

"Since 3,500 years, I promptly reply, the official versions of the Beni-Israel[35], who have become Keltic, Hebrew, Hindu, Chinese, European, African, American, Japanese, more often enounce this Commandment as THOU SHALL NOT STEAL."

EVE now faces ALBERTOV, staring at him directly, a long moment, for the first time since we are with her. What do you think? she seems to be asking...However she remains silent.

"O EVE, inquires Albert, shall we also meet Adam?"

"ADAM and I, EVE, are a couple for eternity. Our identities are always complementary and in perfect harmony. When I appear, ADAM manifests simultaneously on my side. And vice versa."

"When EVE appears "in reality", ADAM also manifests "in po-

35 Beni israel: children of Israel, a name designating the 12 tribes.

tentiality", comments YELIYAEL

"When ADAM manifests his presence "in reality", simultaneously "in potentiality" EVE manifests, adds YEZALAEL.

"As the blue color calls orange in the dark chamber of the retina!"[36] exclaims Albert.

"As yellow calls purple, continues YEZALAEL, *and conversely, purple calls for yellow."*

"Our complementarity and harmony are indestructible" EVE concludes.

"Eva nostra Dama murmurs Albert, Nostre Adama, Notre Adam, Notre Dame. Thank you O EVE, Notre Dame! "[37]

Both Angels silently tender Albert a virtual clay tablet engraved with golden letters; he stands still for a moment, then reads aloud:

"Commandment 8th in rank, as engraved by the celestial messenger, official translation: THOU SHALL NOT STEAL."

And ALBERT continues:

"O EVE, the sentence here, at first, is conspicuously clear. It demands to show respect for other people's property, thus ensuring the stability of social groups, from the simplest couple or family to the larger nation or people."

EVE nods and says: "Shimeha, what do you make of this 8th law LOA TA GA NO-OV!"[38]

EVE's request awakens me. The banal enouncement of the Commandments has always a strong soporific effect on me. But EVE has just vocalized the original sounds of the law in ARCHAEA LINGUA. The letters-sonorities composing this 8th Commandment start dancing a magnificent ballet in the folds of my inner thoughts and I can admire them lighting up one after another, freeing at last their sparkling meanings:

---

36 As confirmed by Goethe's life time research on colors, the complementary colors, primary and secondary, are naturally generated within the human eye. See bibliography for details.

37 Notre dame: Our Lady in French. Hence the name of many cathedrals: Notre Dame de Paris, Notre Dame de Chartres, Notre Dame de Lisieux, and Notre Dame du Lac University, in Indiana usa.

38 Loa ta ganov: 8th Commandment in original Hebrew version.

LO "On the path of Light which ELEvates you and Links you
A to your origins and your ultimate source[39],
TA you Transmigrate and Traverse Times and cycles,
GA to connect with the Force of universal Gravitation-Attraction.
NO Only then the Nucleus-kernel of eternity, that everlastingly contains the essences of your existence,
OV becomes the egg-OVA in which, and through which,
NOV your new eternal life draws its forms, its new-novel beginnings."

EVE smiles tenderly as a mother proud of the progress and achievements of her child learning to walk and talk. Then she says:

"You have correctly applied the Archaeo-Linguistic method and each letter separately has sounded its own melody to deliver its exact message. We are now revealing the core meaning of the 8th Commandment, the seed it actually implants in the collective unconscious consciousness of men and women since millennia.

To transfer from the worlds of mortal existence to the globes of divine essences you will have to transmigrate beyond the worlds of Space-Times and Cycles..."

ALBERT: "Why and how this law has been construed and fixed in the official texts as prohibiting theft or larceny?"

EVE, quickly, without hesitation: "Because this law LOA TA GANOV precisely aims at the form of theft which is the source of all thefts…"

ALBERT: "How so?"

EVE: "It is Shimeha, highly learned woman and close friend of Princess ARCHAE LINGUA, who will first answer this question."

Startled again! My mind was leisurely drifting, with the distinct impression I had satisfactorily accomplished my task and extracted the meaning of the Commandment letter by letter. Thus I had allowed my psyche to wander in idle daydreaming. I understand Mother EVE is asking me to reveal the sense of the 8th law in

39 A= Hebrew letter Aleph, Greek Alpha, Arabic Alif. Archaeo-Linguistic analysis shows the sound A (with variations e, i, o, u) signals the reality of "Absolute Energy, Original and Ultimate before form, Universal, Infinite, Unifying.

ARCHAE LINGUA, no more letter by letter, but word by word.

"LOA TA GANOV", pronounces EVE, clearly separating the three words.

And I so translate:

During your earthly incarnation,
while you live in your transient mortal organic form,
any "genetic" (GAN) metamorphosis (NOV)
would entail a transformation of your magnetic
and gravitational identity,
such as the sensitive circuits of light
which direct you towards the Divine Presence,
might not recognize you
and not take act of your reality (LOA).
Take utmost care when you "innovate" (GA NOV),
to study the pattern-models of universal principles,
in order to "identify" them
and be recognized by them, be known to them.

EVE confidently completes the deciphering: "Know that aiming at "gaining time" by "skipping steps" (GA NOV), leads to outright "theft", ...and therefore ends in failure."

The Angels listen carefully. I silently nod approval. ALBERT frowns and asks:

"I would love to understand better how that genetic theft is the form of theft that encompasses all the types of thefts that may be perpetrated."

EVE simply replies:

"Any theft of any kind is based on the desire to seize and absorb the goods and riches of another, depriving him or her of rightful ownership. The thief is motivated by the unjustified desire to monopolize the riches that define the identity of another; the thief undertakes to quickly acquire a different identity by skipping steps and stealing time.

Does the thief succeed? Yes, almost always on the material and physical plane; on all the other planes, never! For stolen riches provide only an illusion, a mask placed on the real identity of the wearer.

The thief steals the fruit of the tree...but by this act he cannot steal the vigor of the tree that produces fruits through the cyclical return of seasons. And he will have to face the hard fact, that, being a thorn bush he can never become an apple tree by stealing apples...The bush stole the apple fruits, but he will make illusion only for a time...wanting to possess the identity of the apple tree he has only stolen the fruits, skipping the stages of flowering, fruiting, creating a fruit itself bearer of seeds."

"Thus, the thief is an identity thief, an usurper who necessarily fails" says ALBERT.

"Yes" murmurs EVE, with a deep sigh.

Mother Goddess EVE, observes us for a long moment, her face slowly opens like a rose in concentric circles. A shower of faded petals fleetingly darkens her brilliant aura, now tinged with hues of suffering and melancholy

ALBERT asks: "This Commandment "thou shall not commit identity theft or steal personal riches", why was it important and necessary to explore it and to enlighten it with you, our Archae Matria? How does it concern you? Is theft the source of that mysterious original sin you are accused to have committed? Is a theft the cause of your fall and your exile from Paradise?"

EVE: "I attempted to *skip steps*, I attempted to *steal time*."

Shock!

Distressed, Albert suddenly swivels on his seat to hide his tears, I see his shoulders tremble in a long uninterrupted shiver. I hide my face in my hands. My heart accelerates, races, gallops in my chest, desynchronized by the sudden furious emotional storm and immense pain overcoming me. Like Albert, I cannot bear this plain, humble admission of guilt by our Mother EVA. So much confidence, so much goodness radiate from her eyes, her open hands and her noble demeanor, toward us her distant children of space and time...

EVE, tenderly: "Do not cry, revive your "joie de vivre"! I will answer your questions. I will help you accomplish your mission.

Our meeting is a necessary step to the success of your Quest.

O YELIYAEL and YEZALAEL, please help dry their tears and light up their temporarily darkened spirits!"

42. Black and White. Confusion and Clarity.

ALBERT AND I, OVERCOME WITH GRATITUDE, release the flow of our questions, streams of accumulated nonsensical thoughts and troubled feelings all major religious traditions have obstinately assembled over the centuries as regards EVE, ADAM, "the shaming fall", "the harrowing exile from Paradise", "the childbirth punishing pain", "the woman's original sin", "the indelible fault" for which all females must forever pay the price, and the muddied tale of the "forbidden tree of knowledge".

Even more black spots jump out of the biblical records:

"First "God-made man ADAM", and "ADAM rib-extracted woman EVE", then here they come: "the sneaky sly serpent", "the harsh punishment", "natural nakedness" uncovered then covered again with fig leaves…And ever more muddy spots:

"The serpent prophesizes: God said you will die if you eat the forbidden fruit, but you will not!"

"EVE eats the forbidden fruit from the tree standing in the middle of Paradise, sharing it with ADAM and voilà! the snake was right! It is not Death that occurs but the "disease of being", because EVE did not obey to the letter a discipline the divine guide had allegedly imposed!"

"When the divine master of the garden realized that, in spite of His instructions, you EVE, then ADAM had bitten into the fruit of the "tree of knowledge", and consequently "knew you were naked", the "voice in the garden" said:

"You the man, and all men thereafter, "*shall eat your bread in the sweat of your brow*"; you EVE, and all women thereafter, shall give birth in pain and, you both, and all men and women thereafter, shall remain forever away from the Garden of Eden."

And the divine master ADONAI ELOHIM said:

"Behold, the man has become as one of us, to know good and evil: and now, lest he put out his hand, and take also of the tree of life, and eat, and live for ever."[40]

and the Lord God sent him forth from the garden of Eden."[41]

YELIYAEL and YEZALAEL again entwine their vibrant white veils, recreate a double helix caduceus, throw a volley of tender green light filaments towards the top of our pine tree canopy. Giant rainbows traverse the transparent sphere of our crystal dome, spin and dash towards the nearby stars, flooding the firmament with vibrant colors.

Leaves, needles and buds activate their conscience, ready to absorb in their sap cells, the words of EVE, the new revelation of Edenia, the chant, the tale, the legend they will transmit through the vegetal network, running down the cosmic slopes, to the edges of the worlds.

Albert and I, certain we will never find again an opportunity to litany without fear all the fantasies our memory has been fed with since we are born, we resume our cacophonic recitation of the history of the alleged wickedness of the alleged first human couple.

"And there is the endless string of phantasmagoric stories of world creation transmitted by ancient Egyptians, Babylonians, Aztecs, Amerindians, African Dogons; those are a thousand times more intricate, inextricably complicated, ineluctably inducing, beyond perplexity, bemusement, migraine, hebetude, and intellectual coma..."

"*And there is the Voice in the Garden, and the Cherubim hold-*

40 Genesis 3-22
41 Genesis 3-23

ing their fiery spades...The Angels also have a part in the play"[42] adds mischievous YEZALAEL.

EVE -CHAVAH[43] smiles, her eyes slanted, gold stars embedded on her blue cape fly away, crackling like a dry wood fire, spiral and dance around her velvety face. On her damask long robe, Byzantine embroideries are moving slowly, forming ever new decorative motifs, butterflies and multiple flowers, alternate, vibrate, shine, then golden threads stretch into languorous arabesques, artistically embroidering silky feelings and thoughts of fine gold.

After a long silence, EVA starts speaking and says:

"Confusion, darkness, confusion...The text of Genesis as known to you tells and jumbles several differing stories at once. The history of archaic times of primeval humanity emerging from the terrors and superstitions of the animal condition is fused with the story of more recent times when the destiny of humans has been imbedded in the heavenly divine and exo-terrestrial community. Are haphazardly mixed and confused eras, locations, the nature of the actors in the story. These superimposed patterns produce a pseudo historical tapestry on which the identity of every protagonist is indistinct, human-animals, celestial-humans, Deities, Angels and Demons, often undistinguishable."

ALBERT: "O EVE, the first sentence of Genesis says: *Bereshit bara elohim et ha shamayim ve-et ha aretz.*[44].: In the beginning God created Heaven and Earth.

Is it our world's creation that is thus described?"

EVA: "Listen to the first meaning your intellect can grasp, among the 12 versions we are taught here on EDENIA:

By the initiating principles, *(Bereshit)*
the Commencer engendered *(bara)*
all evolving creatures, the ELEH, *(elohim)*
namely the Totality, Integrality *(et)*

42 Genesis, 3-24 "So He drove out the man and He placed cherubim at the east of the garden of Eden and the flaming sword which turned every way, to guard the way to the tree of life."
43 Chavah: original Hebrew name of Eve.
44 Original Hebrew version Genesis 1-1.

of the fluidic spirits emanating from the Mother's fluids,
called celestials, *(ha shamaim)*
in living synchrony contrasting and complementary
with the Totality, Integrality *(ve-et)*
of the beings born from the explosion of the primordial
fire of the Father, called the earth-terrestrials *(ha aretz)*."

ALBERT: "Does this text refer to the first Genesis of the world, the first beginning, the beginning of beginnings?"

EVA: "No! There were other beginnings before this beginning, many others before the beginnings of these other beginnings. Ad infinitum, because the Supreme Creation is Eternal.

And the beginnings succeed the beginnings; the creation of the Ultimate Creator is continuous, uninterrupted, permanent: ÂYIN EN SOF[45] THE INEFFABLE SOURCE OF ESSENCES WITH NO END."

ALBERT: "This lucid deciphering of the first phrase of GENESIS unambiguously evokes the creation of celestial beings and earthly beings. It clearly states both types share a common attribute: the ability to evolve…"

EVA: "Permanent creation is permanent evolution. The force of the beginning is the force of Life, force indefinitely beginning again. All creatures created by the Ultimate Commencer inherently possess the power to change, evolve.

I, EVE can evolve, ADAM can, Albertov you can, Shimeha you can evolve!"

"We are evolving!" exclaim gleefully together YELIYAEL and YEZALAEL.

Albert's eyes are shining with amazement and happiness. We are both dazzled by EVA's interpretation of the first phrase of Genesis condensed by MOSES in 7 words composed with 28 Hebrew letters.

The sounds of ARCHAE LINGUA echo in my mind, and I utter

45`Ayin en sof: At the center of Hebrew Kabalah this notion of "Eternal unending Beginning" describes a creation with no commencement and no end, infinite and eternal. Bereshit, the first of the Hebrew Old Testament begins with the letter B, second in the Alphabet, for the first letter A-Aleph, connoting Infinity and Eternity cannot resonate as a Beginning.

them aloud, recommencing the reading of the Bible for the thousandth time maybe, as do every day millions of people on Earth and in the Heavens: "BERESHIT BARA ELOHIM ET HA SHAMAIM VE ET HAARETZ.

The celestial and terrestrial beings, the ELOHIM, were created, complementary and harmonic, and since, endowed with the powers of a constantly renewed life, they move, change, evolve on all the Earths and all the Heavens."

"I love you so much! exclaims suddenly EVA. It is good to hear my children from planet EARTH-ARTZA echoing the sounds of celestial ARCHAE LINGUA. My children, I want to teach you more, for you to transmit my message of life to your sisters and your brothers on your planet.

My children, she said in a whisper, my children, I wish, facing present humanity and future humanity on EARTH-ARTZA-ERETZ-TERRA-GAIA..."

She again lowered her voice now barely audible:

"I, EVA, your mother, I wish to CONFESS!"

As if stricken by a magnetic lightning, I fall on the ground. A sudden fear causes my heart to beat at a furious pace. I close my eyes, with my hands I cover my ears. In my head a dam is bursting, walls collapsing in a huge uninterrupted roar, green water mixed with blood is boiling in the valleys of my memory.

I am screaming. Albert is screaming, whirling like a crazy spinning top. I see him descend suddenly kneeling at the feet of EVA, burying his head and tears in the folds of her divine starry cape.

43. Archangel Gabriel.

"BEHOLD GABARIYEL, THE ARCHANGEL OF LIGHT, is speaking! announce YELIYAEL and YEZALAEL in perfect tandem. *He greets you, EVA, he greets you Albertov and Shimeha. We shall now transmit his archangelic message, without adding anything, without retrenching. Hear, Listen..."*

A deep peace has now settled in our minds and our hearts. The terrible storm, so sudden, strong and fugacious, moved away, leaving as a sign of terrors past a slight bitter taste in our dry mouths.

Angels YELIYAEL and YEZALAEL, with one voice, continue the announcement:

"Listen to GABARIYEL, the Luminous Archangel: Archangelic words, concepts, notions and emotions translated into human language:

"This is the true story of Adam and Eve as it happened 39,617 years ago solar time, recorded in the archives of EDENIA sphere, capital of constellation ZU-MARI-YAH.

1,000,000 years ago, GAIA-ARTZA-URTHU, your planet, by divine watchers from the central capital of your universe, was identified as holding primitive original human seeds and so registered in the terrestrial records, transcribed in the Old Testament MOSES bequeathed to the 12 Tribes of the Federation of the Exodus, and consequently to all peoples. As inscribed in your Scriptures[46]:

VE HA ARETZ HAYTA
TOHU VA BOHU
VE CHOSHEKH ÂL PENE TEHOM
VE ROUACH ELOHIM MERACHEPHET
ÂL PENE HA MAYIM

And here is how the celestials report their observations:

46 In Genesis - Hebrew Original Version 1:2

Behold! The Spirit-Life field (VE HA)
on Earth (ARETZ)
became stable and self reliant (HAYTA)
thus enabling the mortal humans of animal origin (TOHU)
into blossoming and reaching
the state of Bio-Minded humans (BOHU)
including the ability to connect (VE)
with the Spirit-Mind of the Celestials (ROUACH ELOHIM).
Albeit, the celestials observed,
darkness, opacity
and unconsciousness as yet prevailed (VE CHOSHEKH)
when scanning the Faces-Minds (ÂL PENE)
of most mortal humans (TEHOM).
Hence,
the breathing Living Mind-Spirit (VE ROUACH)
of the Celestials (ELOHIM)
manifested and incarnated (MERACHEPHET)
into Bodies and Faces (ÂL PENE)
incorporating all the essential Fluidic Forces of Earth:
Waters, Blood and Plasma. (HA MAYIM).

500,000 years[47] *of your ARETZ-EARTH-URTHU standard time then unfurled, and the history of those early days has been recounted to you by the trees of the antique forests whose direct descendants still stood at the foot of the Himalayas near the banks of the Ganges River, in India, when BUDDHA lived and developed his living doctrine.*

It was then, past 500,000 of your ARETZ-EARTH time, mandated by the one Deity humans were calling EL ELYON, the Creator of your local Universe, eternal Son of the only Son of the Ultimate Engenderer, I GABARIYEL, sent to GAIA-ARETZ the celestial prince SATANA along with his celestial aids, under the high authority of divine Lucifer, then divinity Governor of your cosmic local system.

---

47 Clay tablets found in Sumer and Akad record historic events, like royal dynasties, starting 450,000 solar years before the actual reporting (around 6 to 8 thousands before 2000 AD).

To begin his planned mission, prince SATANA established his headquarters in the highlands of the Caucasus Mountains near the sources of the Tigris and Euphrates Rivers, in the regions currently known as ARMANIA, near the actual shores and gentle pastures bordering the Black Sea.

Linguistic traces of this SATANA settlement persist until your days, the only areas in your world where countries are named with a final STAN: AfganiSTAN, PakiSTAN, BeloushiSTAN, KurdiSTAN, UzbekiSTAN...

For over 200,000 years those celestial envoys, Gods of the Earth, guided, helped, taught primitive human individuals, providing their knowledge only to those who expressed the demand to be educated.

In the span of those 200,000 years, the celestial envoys proposed pattern-models of evolution on Earth, without pressure applied on groups and clans, and strictly without genetic interference. For over 200 millenniums the rules of Utter Patience and Total Respect for human specificity were never broken by the celestial educators.

Then it happened that the divine Lucifer was more and more dazzled by the penetrating rays of his own divine light, and seduced by the unlimited powers of his own free will.

Realizing his freedom could find no other restriction than that imposed by his own will, noticing that his being was forever, at will, changing and growing, he projected that he had the power to become the radiant center of an immense universe, with borders ever pushed forward by his own desire for growth and expansion.

Lucifer in his brilliance, facing the depth of his universal person, aware of the extreme puissance of his will power, soon perceived only one guide valid for his evolution, and this guide was himself, and himself alone.

Evolutionary expansion had dissolved the memories of his origin in the time and space immensity; he repudiated the action of his original Creator and thus conceived he was the genuine Creator of Himself.

Thus divine Lucifer informed all beings who roamed his local sub-universe that his own light was to illuminate forever their times and their spaces, and that they would eternally benefit from his own sole authority, majestic, unsurpassable and benevolent. Some call this event "Lucifer Rebellion", others call it "Lucifer Revolution".

"*I am a witness,* comments YEZALAEL. *Almost all celestial beings in our local system perceiving Lucifer's declarations of expansive divinity were consistent with their own experience of freedom and will, did accept Lucifer's conclusions."*

A few, however, refused. I did refuse!"

"*I also declined giving my allegiance to Lucifer,* intervenes YELIYAEL. *Before that time, over eons and eons, I traveled the worlds, guided only by my Free Will and Intent, supported by the vital forces which have been given to me unconditionally, exploring on my own impulse the ways open to the evolution of my being. The Ultimate Creator and the Mother Spirit had stringed their creation with no demand for obedience. I was, and I am, a free creature, free to know the generosity of the One who gave me Life, free to ignore it. Lucifer's declaration, and collateral demand of allegiance, contained the seeds of subservience, violence and tyranny..."*

Archangel GABARIYEL resumes broadcasting: *"On your planet, the envoy SATANA rebelled not against Lucifer's declaration of power, and two thirds of the group of celestial instructors naturally followed Satana's leadership; two thirds of the Guardian Angels of Earth, and two thirds of cosmic messengers did the same.*

And almost all humans in contact with the celestial instructors never perceived a war was looming in the heavens. However ancient Hindu Sanskrit texts make an attempt at recording those events. [48] *Nevertheless, Lucifer's and Satana's followers pursued their educative mission on Earth, with force and success, in apparent continuity with the actions previously undertaken.*

As for the celestials "faithful to a Nameless God", they reject-

---

48 Maharabata, Ramayana.

ed the new Proclamation, dissented and separated from the Luciferians-Satanians and established new educational facilities to the south west of ARMANIA, near Lake Van.[49]

Some humans, gifted with insightful awareness, then perceived there were now two kinds of gods on Earth, but for a long time that dual reality had no discernible consequences for them."

"*Yet,* comments YELIYAEL, *after another period of 250,000 standard years, subtle signs, then more and more perceptible hints, indicated that Lucifer's followers were gradually losing their power. Markedly their spiritual energy waned, while that of the celestials "faithful to a Nameless God" was constantly increasing, albeit slowly.*

It became apparent the Luciferians had access to the vast energy sources in the sub-universe controlled by Lucifer, but ONLY IN THAT SUB-UNIVERSE, while the other celestial beings had access, by Archangelic relay, to the spiritual superabundance of the Infinite Grand Universe.

All celestials thus knew Lucifer's sub-universe continued its expansion as an island growing in the center of an ocean forever limited and relatively shrinking, destined to ultimately become an isolated lake.

The Luciferian island in the Luciferian ocean were inexorably cut off from all other created worlds, separated from all other creations, infinite in number and quality, in perpetual expansion, constantly renewed, issuing from the inexhaustible creativity of the Supreme Engenderer, the True Eternal Creator of Life."

Since Archangel GABARIYEL is casting his message, we hear, like a lasting resonant cosmic backdrop, a roaring rumbling sound resembling a faraway continuous thunderstorm, dotted with rippling crystalline cadenced musical notes, like punctuating signs separating paragraphs on a long text.

---

49 Lake Van: Nearer to the ancient center cradle of natural evolutionary civilization, south-east shores of the Black sea. Much later, Abraham aware of the existence of those educational facilities, when seeking a bride for his "son of promise" Isaac , sent his most trusted assistant to the city of Haran, situated near lake Van, far away from Ur Kashdim, origin of Abraham's clan. Genesis 24:1,2,3,4.

Suddenly the music and the rumble are replaced by a series of string shrills, of so high a frequency the Archangel's voice becomes blank, inaudible.

Angel YELIYAEL promptly informs us that "*the messages sent are now ultra-condensed*" and that many parts of the story are directly etched in his angelic memory. *"You may read them later"* he says...

Then again the voice of archangel GABARIYEL becomes clear, and attuned to human hearing frequencies, thus perfectly understandable to us.

"Soon on your planet began a fierce battle between the celestials loyal to Satana and the heavenly dissidents faithful to the invisible, unfathomable Supreme Creator. And many Satana's supporters understood the choice made 250,000 years earlier had a negative impact on their own personal evolution.

Consequently, two-thirds of these followers freely decided to continue on Lucifer's path, while a third opted for secession and later joined the resistance groups of the first hour.

The seed of confusion took root and grew. Many humans became aware gods were now fighting gods; as there were friendly or ferocious animals, there were now good gods and bad gods.[50]

The Satanian gods, basing the expansion of their power on the number of their allies, made grandiose promises. Instead of letting humans progressively exercise their free will, they offered full license, en block, to all clans who joined their ranks.

Thus, for a time Satanians were perceived as the generous good gods, grantors of unconditional clanic liberty.

In the opposing camp, the "faithful to the nameless unknown God", less numerous, cautious to the extreme, continued to encourage persistent individual efforts and improving individual performances, ignoring requests for general immediate alleged "liberation". Those were, paradoxically, often referred to as the "evil

50 See legends all over the world, amongst civilized nations or isolated tribes in forest and jungles: Dogons-Aztecs-Egypt-Greece-Hindu BagavadGita: the Gods' war.

gods."

Confusion reigned still for 50,000 years, but human evolution continued. The chaos grew.

Finally, 40,000 years ago, standard time, the non-luciferian celestial dissidents, "the faithful to the Supreme God" and their human allies, "the faithful to the Invisible One", received from the Heavens the answer to their fervent prayers:

Two new celestial beings, luminous, immortal, came down on Earth and landed in their garden camp."

"We have here a copy of cosmic Archives" exclaim together YEZALAEL and YELIYAEL.

"Specific mission of the heavenly ADAM-EVE:

Phase I Mission of heavenly ADAM and EVE: Based on Edenian Principles, teach nutritional rules, the art of selecting and preparing nutrients; teach body hygiene, basic principles of health maintenance, prophylaxis, and healing; assist in the selection, development and growth of useful plants; clarify and qualify the terrestrial species: animals, fruits, foliages, vegetables, cereals, and train in agricultural skills and animal husbandry; teach the craft techniques, the art of weaving, home building ...more...

Phase II Mission of heavenly EVE: Based on Edenian Principles, lead firmly and gradually the evolution of positive human relationships, interpersonal, clanic and social; guide humans towards inter-family and inter-tribal cross breeding favorable to positive evolution and genetically inherited talents. more..."

GABARIYEL's voice, angelically relayed, resounds and continues the cosmic chronicle:

"The mission of the celestial envoys, 460,000 years before the arrival of ADAM and EVE, had ruled out any interference on the genetics of human phylum for a very long period. However, some time after their "revolution", as a result of their isolation, the celestial Satanians modified the original program, bent the imperative divine instructions, and began an unplanned development of new lines of "celestialized" beings by mixing their non-terrestrial

genes with the genes of humans on Earth."

Comments YELIYAEL: *"Here is the literal most accurate available translation of the Hebrew text Genesis 6:1-2 : "When men began to multiply on Earth, the sons of the celestial-divine race, noticing that the daughters of earthly humans had become beautiful, took them as wives, whenever they so desired. Their descendants are known as the Giborim-the giant heroes", the Nephilim-the fallen from the sky and Rephaim-the healers, the half gods."*[51]

The Archangel's voice continues dispelling confusions and dissolving black spots in our minds:

"In contrast, ADAM and EVE, the immortal celestial couple, whose genomic characteristics had been, previously to their landing, rendered exactly compatible with those of the most highly evolved humans on Earth, were instructed to improve the human "genome". A change planned to occur not through direct interference of EVE and ADAM themselves, but through gradual infusion by relay of their own children, who were to cross-breed later with best evolved humans, to stimulate, enable, enrich their yet dormant vital potentials."

51 Genesis 6:1-2.The King James version translation is less accurate than the original Hebrew text, but nevertheless the message comes through very clearly: "Now it came to pass, when men began to multiply on the face of the earth, and daughters were born to them, that the sons of God saw the daughters of men, that they were beautiful and they took wives for themselves of all whom they chose". Genesis 6:4: "There were giants on the earth in those days and also afterwards, when the sons of God came in to the daughters of men and they bore children to them. Those were the mighty men who were of old, men of renown".

Note from the authors: In writing the previous and succeeding lines we are only transcribing the words of Archangel Gabriel, as they have been decoded for us, on EDENIA, by Angels YEZALAEL and YELIYAEL. EVE herself was present, and nothing in her attitude or in her words permits to conclude this report concerning her mission on our planet is incorrect. It may be incomplete, as the Archangel and our two angelic companions have clearly indicated they would not present us with knowledge our current mental level cannot grasp. Albert and I have often revisited the words of these revelations, during many discussions, face to face. We decided to keep the text intact, without adding or retrench. We realize that reading these texts is a roller coaster for the mind and spirit. The only difference with a full speed roller coaster ride is that, here, the reader can exercise her or his freedom, and, at any time, safely get off.

44. Terror and Salvation.

GABARIYEL'S VOICE REVERBERATES ANEW: *"To fulfill their mission, the heavenly ADAM and EVE had adopted a human appearance, a body of spiritualized flesh. They offered their protégés a model of beauty, intelligence and goodness, according to different ages and levels of development of their wards. Both always presented the aspects appropriate to the level of their students, at an ideal stage everyone could hope to achieve.*

And so, held in the arms of EVE and ADAM, protected by Angels, sheltered from the dangers of wild ferocious nature, human children in the Garden of Eden dreamed of reaching the skies.

The situation outside the walled Garden was very different. Over the years, and century after century, waves of human progress had spread on Earth chaotically. Evolutions and regressions crossed their forces, under the pressure of animal genes tamed by the lessons and discipline of good gods, unleashed by the license of evil gods.

A lasting devious genetic storm was overwhelming Earth. And ADAM and EVE, temporarily humanized celestials, sometimes despaired of ever achieving on the entire planet a result comparable to the success attained within the high walls of the Garden of Eden.

For, outside the Garden, none of prior knowledge acquired through education could resist the savagery of primitive humans. Almost all the messengers instructors educated in the Garden perished before they could pass on their precious legacy. The bits of knowledge that had been inculcated to the students in the Garden were almost erased with the death of those individuals, without benefiting next generations.

After several centuries on Earth, Adam and Eve, chagrined, saw their mission's progress was infinitesimal.

Those words from archangel GABARIYEL pierce my tympanum like flying arrows, reach the center of my deeply buried unconscious memory reservoir.

I am fainting…I faint. From the depth of my unconsciousness...I remember…I vividly relive…

I see, I see, I feel…I am sitting…the ground is cold…the strong smells…crushed grass…a pile of rotten fruits…urine and feces…I hear the voice of the messenger...he talks about the camp of the god and the goddess...from the skies they came together...he is a giant…she is a giant…there is a vast garden down there…the messenger says…flowers…fruits…brutal animals…cannot enter the garden…come over…come over…he says…the hairy man who imprisons my mother growls and grunts…hits and hits the tree trunk with his fist…I am hiding…I run to the thorny bushes…

I run...leaning…rushing towards the edge of the forest where the messenger came from...I shall wait for him…when he returns he will pass by here...Now I do not hear the groans of the hairy man who imprisons my mother…

Where am I? Laying on a soft tender grass. I am breathless after such a long furious chase. My bare feet are bleeding, my legs lacerated, deeply cut by thorns. I am cold, I am hot, I cry, I laugh.

EVE took off her starry cape and laid it on my shivering body. Albert, down on one knee, is holding my right hand. My two angelic companions form a square protective canopy with their diaphanous veils. I see thousands galaxies and nebulae twinkling in the distance, the blue night dew caresses my forehead.

EVE addresses me:

"At that time you have safely reached the Garden of Eden. The pursuit lasted five days and five nights. The messenger often did bear you in his arms, on his shoulders, for crossing streams and marshes. The brutal hairy man finally fell off a cliff and broke his skull. I remember Shimeha, I remember the day you came to us!

What a brilliant student we have gained that day! And what a magnificent schoolteacher you became, in the Garden of Eden!"

Lulled by these sweet words, I fell asleep well protected under the starry cape. When I awoke, I saw Albert in conversation with EVE, who was holding a blue book, from which she read, pointing to a passage Albert seemed to comment.

I stood up slowly, freshened my face and hands at the crystal fountain, prepared to hear more of GABARIYEL's revelations.

Sitting on our soft rocks, we are again forming a magical circle; EVE's comforting loving left arm is leaning on my shoulders; in her right palm she is holding Albert's hand.

GABARIYEL: *"Compassion won the heart of EVE. And it happened that SERPANATA, beautiful half-human offspring of gods descendant of a Satanian lineage, was very supportive of the program of the Garden. With this friendly young man gifted with a fine subtle mind, head of a large tribe living outside near the Garden, EVE was often sharing her impatience, disappointments and hopes...A parallel program was born of their agreement: by mixing EVE's celestial genes with the genes of finest and most advanced humans evolving out of the garden, now repentant descendants of Luciferian gods and semi-gods, humanity on Earth would rapidly attain a superior level of progress, and the added thrust would eliminate all accumulated hindrances.*

EVE never expected the original program would be negatively altered. On the contrary, she envisioned, when the children's children of ADAM and EVE having reached the requested quantum threshold, would finally step outside the walls to mix with the terrestrial humans, as projected in heaven's plan, her purely divine direct daughters and sons would find her other mixed offspring born beyond the Garden's boundaries, and merge their celestial genes with humans already advanced, genetically prepared for a grand evolutionary leap!"

EVA whispers softly: "Faster, faster! Skip stages! Everything seemed so slow...My celestial mind was diluting in my earthly flesh, often I lost consciousness of my immortality. I accepted the supreme sacrifice. To ADAM I masked the colors of my project and the rhythms of my actions. Hastily, I mixed my genes, I conceived a son *directly* with the descendant of a semi-god, a handsome, young and intelligent man, from the SERPANATA tribe. And I engendered KAIN! HINE ÂSSITI ISH LE ELOHIM."[52]

"Behold (HINE) I have been able to produce (ÂSSITI) a man (ISH) in the essence of the race of the Celestials (LE ELOHIM), a man equal to the Divines" translates YEZALAEL

"And it thus happened that the Angels who were watching over the Garden of Eden observed the harmony of the divine universal program had been shattered. And ADAM instantly perceived the disharmony caused by EVE."

Says YELIYAEL: *"The initial divine program of the Garden was based on universal laws, the laws of complementary and harmonic contrasts. EVE, tempted by a speedier implementation of the original plan, had committed an act "outside the law of Universal Harmony."*

Says YEZALAEL: "*The consequences of this disharmony were multiple. You will learn 10 by visiting the Edenia archives. There are many others. On Earth, you can find six enclosed in the sonorities of ARCHAE LINGUA."*

---

52 Genesis, Hebrew Original Version 4:1.

EVE intervenes: "To accelerate humankind's progress on Earth, we skipped stages, I myself voluntarily, then complementarily ADAM. Thus our direct earth born new offspring would engender "celestialized" children; the future evolution would be greatly accelerated, humans would escape more quickly the slippery ruts of animality."

I understand EVE's fault! Impatience! Jump over the principial necessary stages. But I also understand EVE's belief that acceleration of cosmic consciousness by direct divine genetic legacy would insure rapid desirable progress on the evolutionary ladder.

YELIYAEL adds: "*By merging her genes with those of a handsome descendant of half-gods, gifted with healthy body and bright intellect, EVE's intent was the immediate improvement of human physical performance and mental abilities.*

She intended to accelerate the EV-O-LUTION of humankind. But the original divine program was aiming much higher, beyond the boundaries of physical animality, beyond time.

In contrast and based on universal laws, the original mission of ADAM and EVE, was to make possible the spiritual EL-EVA-TION of primitive humans emanating entirely from the animal original terrestrial evolved phylum."

YEZALAEL confirms: "*What was the intent, the finality of the divine original design? From the bottom of earthly humanity, its unstable mind buried within mortal degradable bodies, emitting mental radiation so chaotic its wave energies dissolve into cosmic anonymity, the divine design was to stimulate the progressive emergence of coherent Spirit-Souls.*

Each soul designed to be a work of art, original and signed, to go and illuminate the universes, fill and enrich them with the specificities, the diversities, that eternally enchant the ONE, the UNIQUE, join HIM as a Soul in love with the intrinsic totality of the UNIQUE ULTIMATE DEITY, He who from afar is invisible, ineffable, inconceivable."

Archangel GABARIYEL's revelation, fascinating and captivating, has now become enlightening. We now comprehend that although Serpanata's and EVE's intentions were pure, the consequences of EVE's impatience have been grave; but her misjudgment has not resulted in the annihilation of humankind's potentials.

Then, I ask myself, keeping silent, this 8th Commandment which casually states "THOU SHALL NOT STEAL"[53] what is so crucial about it that mother EVE willed to explain it herself?

"The masters of spiritual science and divine wisdom understand that" intervenes YELIYAEL who has read my thoughts, as he always does.

"Here is one possible interpretation of the 8th Commandment:

LOA TA GANOV, THOU SHALL NOT GANOV, literally means:

You shall not innovate genetically only (GAN-NOV).[54]

You shall not attempt to extract a "Genie" from an "Ova" belonging to a defined species and insert it within another "Ova" belonging to another species. For every specific "Ova" is alive only because it contains a particular identifiable "Genie-spark" eternally linked to and recognized by the Divine Creator.

You shall not steal genes that belong to a species to merge it with another species of different essence and nature...for that "genetic theft" disregards the law of originality, specificity, differentiation, which is the foundation of the existence of the "whole"; the principial law which alone justifies the rule of Love and Union.

It is vain to "alter" and "steal" what makes the essential identity of another ova-being, and that is what the thief is doing, whatever the object of his theft, be it an egg or an ox."

"Here is another version of the 8th Commandment" immediately adds YEZALAEL:

"You shall not exceed your limits by appropriating new Genes

---

53 St-e-al: as an Archae Lingua formula ST stands for Satan / e for h=universal spirit / al stands for evolution towards the celestial kingdoms. Therefore in Universal Language the word Steal means: you shall not regard Satanism as the letter and spirit of the path leading you towards the celestial kingdoms. The verb stagnate also takes root in the name Satan.

54 Ganov: Hebrew word commonly means stealing. In Archae Lingua the elements of the words ganov convey the following meanings: gan for Gene pool, nov for Novation Innovation. N=New essence, New Nature of the ov, the Egg.

Genies not inscribed in your original Nature and Final Destiny."

ALBERT: "In clear, once the word GANOV is deciphered, this Commandment may be understood as such: "Radical innovation on the genotype ineluctably produces profound disharmony."

With an inward shudder of passion, I am realizing: EVE's intent and purpose were good and pure, then, how can it be that her action has been construed as a crucial sin?

Archangel GABARIYEL certainly heard my inner debate, as he answers my unspoken questions:

"Human evolution, even at the stage of very primitive cell, is oriented on finding the essential substance of which it was extracted at the origin, the Essence-Substance Creating Life. To achieve this promised final re-union the human being, at every step of his metamorphic life, must attempt to "prolong his days in a land that has been promised to him".

To that end he must constantly, cyclically, without respite, leave the usual form to which he has been bonded, his house of Egypt, to reach a new state of being freed from slavery, freed from stagnation in a fixed state of being.

Each of the 10 Commandments highlights one of the key stages indispensable to achieve such liberation, from the 10th Commandment: "Thou shalt not covet", to the 1st divine Commandment which leads to the ultimate stage of human liberation.

For as the 1st Commandment asserts:

ANOKHI YEHOVAH	*I am the Lord*
ELOHEKHA	*your God*
SHE HOTZETI OTEKHA	*who brought you*
ME ERETZ MITZRAIM	*out of the land of Egypt*
MI BEIT ÂVADIM	*out of the house of slavery.*

The personalized human soul, who has advanced on the path, who has experienced all the stages, from the 10th up, without skipping a step, may so announce:

ANOKHI YEHOVAH: *I am the eternalized being, the spirit lover.*

ELOHEKHA[55]: *the elevated being ascending towards you."*

At that moment Archangel GABARIYEL's voice roared like a gigantic thunder, accompanied by a light dazzling like hundreds colossal cosmic fires blowing myriads cinders, and above our heads, crackling sparks gathered in a multitude of bright luminous sheaves, gigantic burning comets rushing towards the cosmic abysses.

Then silence returned to EDENIA, and the voice of Archangel GABARIYEL enounced:

"Tell the people of ancient GAIA ERETZ that any spiritual evolution is directed towards Immortality...but also tell them that, contrary to what the notorious Guilgamesh[56] did, men and women should not seek immortality for their bodies but for their spirit-minds and their souls.

In the dimension of the mind and spirit, MEN AND WOMEN ARE ALIKE, both receive the celestial seed and both become pregnant, because in every man and every woman grows and develops, all throughout their lives, a soul, who shall migrate to and pilgrimage through the celestial kingdoms.

Tell the people of ancient EARTH that what they call Death is actually a Birth. Yet no gestation is guaranteed, neither is birth. The innumerable Deities created by the Universal Father are eternal, the Angels are created immortal, but humans are experimenting mortality thus specifically experiencing and spreading in the universe the vibrancies of hope, evolution and progression. The eternal Deities are not evolutive, they do not consume nor recycle, they exist eternally and perfectly...Angels and human beings are eternal in potential, they are evolutive and e-motional in essence.

On all the millions inhabited planets, the evolutionary beings of human nature live and die according to sequential cycles, both predictable and unpredictable, both exact and probabilistic. Those

55 Mirror translation of the first Hebrew sentence of the verse, as enounced from the elevated spiritual human point of view.

56 Gilgamesh: Sumerian hero of old times, who among other great feats has journeyed as far as he could in search of the formula granting physical immortality, and did not find it. Refer to Epic of Gilgamesh.

human beings have all been generated and raised physically and spiritually, issued by an "EVO" (OVA)[57]*comparable to your Archae Matria, EVA.*

It is fundamental for the equilibrium of laws which maintain the existence of the Divine Creation that the evolutionary beings evolve within the vital essential principle which brought them to Life. If humans, while physically alive in the terrestrial-material dimension, merged with the OVA of the Eternals, ignoring the law of Universal Harmonies, their worlds would "implode", their universe and their identities explode. Within the 8th Commandment are embedded the spiritual elements insuring the relationship of potentially infinite human soul with actual Divine Eternity.

Tell men and women on Earth that the figure 8,[58] *written as the symbol of the double zero of infinite, is the guarantor of eternity. Tell men and women that, as material creature, human is not "finished". Humankind is the ZERO OF THE NOT FINITE, the un-finite, while the immortal beings engendered by the Universal Mother are the ZERO OF IN-FINITY.*

The Elohim of Heavens, the Angels, harmonizing with the Elohim of Earth, the elevated humans, together form the sacred marriage, which linking the zero of infinite to the zero of not-finite create the **8**, *the perpetual cycles of life, that is to say, Life itself.*

EVE's attempt to metamorphose "humans-created-human" into "eternals-created-eternal" is first and foremost a scientific error.

Such a project emerges from temporary oversight of the law of Universal Harmony, the law of attraction-love of complementary opposites, the love inflamed and synchronized by the Life spark transmitted from the origin of origins, the spark of the Supreme Divine Father present in every living creature.

Tell men and women on your planet the fault of your Mother Eve, so called original sin, is not a sin or a malediction, but a simple misunderstanding of the founding principle of life, a lack of wisdom.

---

57 Ova=egg of evolution.
58 8= evokes 8th Commandment.

"EVE did not willfully default on her ethical obligation" adds Archangel GABARIYEL, his tone distinctly compassionate.

"There has been no fall, EVE has committed no moral fault that justifies the women of your world must pay a never ending debt, nothing legitimates the arrogant domination of male over women, nothing validates the terror and serfdom violent males impose on the life of their female companions. The women's tremors of suffering and pain even during your era still reach the Heavens today by continuous streams of shrieking waves originating from the Earth of men.

Tell All, Men and Women, the real fall was that of the misdirecting celestial princes and misdirected angels; the initial fault was never committed by celestial EVE and ADAM, but by Lucifer and Satan."

"And, intervenes YELIYAEL, *this fall caused by Satan began 150,000 years ago, Earth Standard Time, long before the arrival of EVE and ADAM. That was before the dawn of evolved human history, 120,000 years before Homo Sapiens, your Cro-Magnons, roamed the earth and dominated the primitive Neanderthals.*

After the Lucifer-Satan rebellion, the celestials incarnated on earth engendered a new human race by mixing their celestial DEVO-GENES with earthly human OVO-GENES, in contravention with the original divine program of NO GENETIC INTERFERENCE. The human being named SERPANATA was one of their descendants."

EVE is beaming with happiness. YELIYAEL and YEZALAEL, armed with transparent bows, like cherubs of love, start throwing at her short arrows of wavy light. At impact each arrowhead transforms into blooming flowers typical of Earth, pansies, jasmines, tulips, carnations, lilies, marigolds, white anemones, roses, which soon form a superb fragrant vertical garden embracing and silhouetting the curvaceous feminine forms of EVA's presence.

Enthused by that brilliant blooming spectacle Albert applauds, clapping his hands and shouting Bravo! Thank you! Wonderful! I smile and admire the humor of our heavenly angelic companions.

EVE is beautiful, shall always be beautiful, and she will always be an ideal of Beauty, for all humans on Earth and in the Heavens!

ALBERT now asks, addressing no one in particular:

"The 8th Commandment LOA TA GANOV, THOU SHALL NOT GANOV, literally means YOU SHALL NOT NOVATE-CREATE NEW GENES. This is a hot topic nowadays. Routinely agricultural technicians genetically modify various plants and fruits, livestock technicians genetically transform farm animals pursuing strict economic goals, such as extending the legs of sheep, degreasing the shoulders of oxen...And then, of course, I must mention the cloning experiments, on animals today, humans soon, maybe..."

Shocked, I remain silent, mute. The Angels have both shrunk their luminous veils, reducing themselves to the size of a tiny lace handkerchief so tenuous they are almost absent. Elusive Archangel GABARIYEL seems to have diverted his attention from our group, and I sense he is now busy elsewhere…

Albertov, I shall address your question, murmurs EVE:

"Your current information on animal and human cloning is too weak, too sparse for you to even start intelligently thinking on the subject, even less to envision the outcome of the current actions undertaken by some scientists, bio-technicians and others, on your planet.

My answer to you would necessarily have many features of a prophecy. I know that you and Shimeha practice, in private, the art of prediction and prophecy with great success, but, by celestial pact inherent to the essence of your souls, you never disclose the so obtained revelations to anyone.

Your present mission is to enlighten without prophesying. Every celestial being you are encountering is helping you interpret the past to illuminate the present, and so enrich your current experience of life, on multiple dimensions.

In your presence, none of those beings is prophesying, although they hold the powers to do so. The intensity of your questioning might induce in me the temptation to offer a revealing answer that includes details on future events...My own experience in "skipping steps" and ensuing disastrous consequences commands me not to repeat the same error in a different guise."

ALBERT: "But, there have been many prophets and prophetesses in the past, even the recent past. Certainly they obtained help from celestial beings…there cannot be a prophet or prophetess without celestial inspiration: Prophet Elie, the Pythia at Delphi, the Sybille of Cumes, Michel de Nostre Dame-Nostradamus, Mother Shipton…"

EVE: "All those prophecies were expressed in languages or utterances not immediately understandable. When transcribed in the common tongues of their era, they are presented in the form of riddles."

SIMHA: "I understand, O Mother EVE. If my intent, and Albert's intent, had been to record in riddles our discoveries about the 10 Commandments, surely Angels YELIYAEL and YEZALAEL would never have taken us on their wings through time-space, and we would not have met you…here, on Edenia,….learning from you how not to "skip stages", by prophesying or otherwise…."

EVE: "Continue to expand your cosmic consciousness, refine your concepts of Life, enhance your knowledge of the hyper-powers of the senses, including the sixth sense. Keep close relationship with Princess ARCHAE LINGUA and you shall think more, intuit more clearly, ever more clearly, and so contribute to the advancement of mind-spirit evolution, yours and others'."

The voice of Archangel GABARIYEL suddenly rumbles, like muffled by distance, from afar:

"EVE's fault was a lack of wisdom; she also made an error of biopsychic science."

I start, alerted, both happy and worried. I have often envisioned psyche science, anthropology and linguistics being studied in relation to advanced biogenetic sciences, and the Archangel now evokes biopsychic science as a reality obvious and familiar in the celestial spheres! I crane, tense, hoping to learn more, but the voice which had surged from the heights of the cosmos cannot be heard.

And it is EVE who volunteers to complete the confession of her famous error: "Each form of existing creature has its corollary in reverse mirror in the universe. In this pair of opposites, I am the archetype of my contrary, and my contrary is my archetype. Each exists in interaction with the other and one cannot exist without the other; when one appears the other appears.

When I mixed Serpanata's genes, a descendant of terraformed gods', himself issued from a tribe of repentant Luciferians, with my own physical-material-divine phylum, I engendered KAIN. And with KAIN appeared a biopsychic form until then non-existent in the universe, a form which had no mirror opposite, no existing archetype to harmonically respond to its presence.

With no rival to attract and love, no contrary to ignite his desire, KAIN embodies absolute separateness. Without harmonic complementary, without synchronic alter ego, KAIN nowhere could find his other self, contrary but harmonic, his tranquil antagonist.

Thus KAIN was a solitary ADON, a Puissance without counterpart in the entire universe. Nothing within him could experience attraction towards another being; from KAIN would emerge no aspiring soul, since there was no complementary alter-ego elsewhere and beyond waiting for him, no potential attractor to fuse with and make him complete.

Thus I had given birth to a destroying contraption, a killing machine, a superior power without an invisible companion to love, and therefore without balance and control. Intending to offer humankind a faster achieved immortality, intending humans to escape the anxieties and miseries of physical death, I created the most deadly human phylum, because it would remain indefinitely, exclusively, terrestrial.

I engendered the most murderous man, because being powerful and alone he would perceive himself as incomparable, therefore superior, racial dominator.

VE. KAIN HARAG[59] ET ABEL: *and KAIN murdered ABEL!*

Wanting to accelerate my descendants' accession to Immor-

59 Harag= in Archae Lingua: dominating (har) mutant (ga).

tality I obtained the exact opposite effect, as often happens in analogous situations whenever one undertakes to attain a goal by "skipping important and major stages", the stages of consciousness expansion and progressive maturation.

In my haste to accelerate progress I initiated a process of REVolution, thus rejecting the wise divine design of EVOlution.

For I, EVE, created the seed of a new race of extra long living absolute human mortals who at time of death would find no synchronized gate opening before them, no harmonized mansion in the heavens to host them…"

YEZALAEL, now taking the appearance of a medieval parchment held by YELIYAEL who donning the white robe of a monk, belted at the waist with a brown cotton cord, sometimes recites, sometimes chants in a deep, grave voice:

"Celestial ADAM, genetic engineering expert, perceived and understood the specific rationales behind mother EVE's unfortunate scientific slip-up.

He unambiguously expressed solidarity with EVE, his complementary partner, and undertook to correct her miscalculation by applying all principles of the cosmic knowledge he possessed. His science was deep, vast, incorporating exact celestial invocations, divine trust, wisdom, spirit power, mental energies as well as biophysical and bio-psychic skills.

Celestial ADAM and EVE together sought permission from the heavens to remedy the transgression and, by archangelic relay, authorization was granted.

To achieve their goal EVE and ADAM had to relinquish their access to immortalizing energies; ADAM working "at the sweat of his brow" and EVE giving birth to babies in pain, they themselves became comparable to all other super humans on Earth.

KAIN, as engendered by EVE, had been endowed with quasi-immortal status on Earth only, but had no access to cosmic immortality, and paradoxically, it made him, an absolute mortal on the broader universal stage.

Thanks to ADAM's extraordinary expertise in biogenetic and

biopsychic sciences, KAIN's absolute mortality was offset. ADAM succeeded in restoring the original Edenic ADN–DNA, including its inbuilt inherent program of deferred immortality.
In Eden's genetic program human beings are to conquer immortality status through the personal experience of recurring Life-Death cycles[60]*, energized by the love of the Other Self, the Oneself who is not Oneself.*

Then, bearing deeply etched on the forehead the sign of his restored humanity, the circle mark of his regained membership in the human race, KAIN was sent by ADAM and EVE as ambassador to the country of NOD, across wild and dangerous mountains. His mission was to spread among the people of Nod the EvAdam genes, as their own divine inheritance made him bio-psychically compatible with them, the repentant descendants of the heavenly celestials, the half gods.

As it is written in your Bible Genesis 4-15-16:

"And the Lord set a mark on KAIN, lest anyone finding him should kill him. Then KAIN went out from the presence of the Lord and dwelt in the land of NOD to the east of Eden[61]*."*

The angelic monk stopped his recitation. Long silence…No interrupting rumbling…just a faint rhythmic whisper, discrete music of the spheres to sustain our meditation.

Notre Dame de Mari, EVE the Sumerian, opens her golden hazel eyes, and speaks, smiling cheerfully:

"All's well that ends well" she says, with an unmistakable touch of humor. "I learned to my cost why and how to respect the 8th Commandment" she adds, this time with a tinge of melancholy:

LOA TA GANOV!
You shall not skip genetic stages
in your haste to cross the border of Time and Space,

60 The mentioned program does not imply the Life-Death cycles occur only in regard with planet earth.

61 East of Eden: This would position the country of Nod in the north of Persia, nearby the Caspian sea, from where later spread the sophisticated tribesmen riding domesticated horses, then called Medes or Parsis. They may be the ancestors of the Parisi tribesmen, founders of the city of Paris.

in your haste to spread the "GANO"
Ultimate Verb of Life,
which guides to the Island of Paradise,
in your haste to live the New Life
energized by the vitality of the Ova,
the Egg of the Original Creator.

YELIYAEL: *"As per Albertov's silent request, here is a primary term by term correspondence in English and ARCHAE LINGUA:*

LOA *Do not cross*
TA *the Time barrier*
GANO *to enter the Ultimate Garden center of Eternity-Infinity*
around which gravitate
all the force fields of all universes
OVA *by stealing the original Egg, Supreme Giver of Life."*

Mindful of my own moral and intellectual responsibilities in regard with the decoding of the 8th Commandment, and encouraged by EVE's warm smile, I comment:

"This Commandment commonly translated as "THOU SHALL NOT STEAL" in fact edicts "Do not commit genetic theft", do not transfer your DNA to create another species that has no harmonic counterpart in the universe.

It also says "Do not skip steps", so do not steal TIME.
But as in each of the Ten Commandments which proceed by negative injunction "Do not do this", pattern of the primary moral imperative, the 8th divine law also provides positive complementary corollary, and it enounces:

"When you shall start your quest for me, when you shall search for the path leading to me, the Ultimate Source of your existence (LOA), know you shall actually need to pass the test of Time (TA), experience many lifetime cycles, before finding the way and the gate (GA) which put you on the path to Eternity (NO) and the Ultimate Eternal Life (V)."

Thus, through MOSES, the divine messenger tells us that any innovation during our journey, on Earth and beyond, must conform to the laws of Time; we must not steal time."

I stop for a moment, sigh deeply, hesitate, then ask:

"But, by providing this translation at a metaphysical level, illuming a law that for many may seem to apply mostly after Death, aren't we "skipping steps" in our endeavor to explain and clarify the 8th Commandment? Aren't we at risk to disconnect our fellow humans from the simple, albeit effective, millenary moral and social command "Do not steal"?

How does LOA TA GANOV connect with a man, a woman or a child who steals a toy, a car, a cow, a house, an insincere seductive kiss, a playwright, a computer program? Does it concern the ordinary human actual or potential thief at all?"

AVA MARIAH rises gently from her seat, plucks a daisy from a whiteness patch in the firmament, a white and vibrant flower resembling that which Rabbi Yohanan BEN ZAKAI picked in the vineyard at Brur Hayl, Galilee, in the 1st century AD. She looks at us intently, saying:

"All the thieves, be their acts small larceny or theft of genes, common stealing a cow, or a car, make the same mistake: they skip steps, they steal time, they falsely anticipate their future needs, their proper destiny and the paths leading to it. For, the man who possesses no cow should first consider whether if to feed himself he needs a cow or a fruit tree; a cow will certainly give milk, but that may be a poison to him; and if he doesn't have a cow it is not by chance.

The fruit of a tree might do for him what the milk could not. Thus, the thief, before acting, should spare time to think, know, weigh, refine his knowledge and wisdom.

Taking the time to think and ponder, he/she will meet the adjusted responses to her/his real situation and state of being, and no longer need to steal.

So LOA TA GANOV also means: Do not haste to break in the egg-life of others, do not steal unless stealing is the only option to insure your very survival"

YEZALAEL promptly interjects:

"And only under the irrevocable oath you shall soonest give

back what you borrowed under the direst circumstances!"

YELIYAEL: *"For borrowing with the intent of not giving back is stealing."*

My heart is heavy, dreading the ineluctable parting. I feel Albert's sentiments, they agree with mine: we would love to stay here, with EVE on Edenia, eternally.

EVE consoles us, encourages us, with her gentle singing, perfumed voice:

"Shimeha, Albertov, you must now depart...You have still a few stages to go through."

EVE's desires are orders to Angels. Our cosmic angelic navigators instantly joined their domed diaphanous veils in a perfect sphere, completely enseraphing our hyper-virtualized human presence.

Chapter Five

My name is Zoda

45. In Transit.

LAST IMAGE OF EDENIA IMPRESSED ON MY RETINA: EVE, our Lady of Zamariyah, watching our departure, sweetly smiling. She was hovering above us, elongated slanted eyes, blue cloak studded with myriad stars of polished gold, dress elegantly embroidered with floral slightly bluish patterns.

EVE's body haloed from head to foot, clasped hands raised to her olive-tone visage, seemed to cast a prayer of protection for us and our two Angels dashing again, set to traverse the immense darkness of cosmic oceans, skirting swirling magnetic storms while riding the living rays of nascent suns.

Alertly unconscious, comfortably enseraphed at the care of YELIYAEL and YEZALAEL, Albert and I are channeled through the GANO[62]circuits[63], guided beyond space and time at seraphic high speed, to a destination yet unknown to us.

62 Gano: the cosmic field on which are imprinted and stocked the genetic codes of all living beings. In vernacular Hebrew means Garden; hence Gan-Eden, the Garden of Eden.

63 During our first travels, through time without traversing trans-cosmic borders, our space-time ship was ele-guided, meaning directed by celestial angelic principles. In the current journey, to traverse the borders between microcosm and macrocosm, our navigation is oriented by gravitation force of the central universe nucleus, the gano.

46. Back to Rajagriba, India 600 BC.

OUR GAZES INSTANTLY MEET. AS WE SPOT HIM he symmetrically notices our arrival. BUDDHA is sitting at the same place, having seemingly not moved since we briefly observed him from afar during our previous visit to this monastery garden.

We have just ele-landed at the precise location our Archae Matria AVA MARIA had appeared suddenly, commanding imperatively we depart from this place "immediately". Same mound covered with short grass, same surrounding landscape, the giant trees are here, reminders to the passing pilgrims of the everlasting power of Life. Dampness announces the upcoming rainy season.

"Apparently, we have returned to India, says Albert. I've seen this place before. Monastery, irrigated garden, BUDDHA sitting under a canopy…"

"Yet something has changed, the ambiance is not exactly the same" I say.

"Maybe we have changed, as we traveled much and far since our rushed extraction from this place."

"Perhaps we have returned here exactly to the same day and time, before our visit to Beruriah, before our meeting with EVE; as a pilot missing the runway in the fog gases up, flies in a loop and returns immediately to land the plane."

"It is very possible because YEZALAEL the Angel most adept at zigzags, zips and zooms is no longer with us!"

The veil of uncertainty suddenly lifts, clearing my vision. I now perceive what has really changed. At present BUDDHA is *alone,* meditative, sitting under the shelter wide open to the four winds. His two disciples SARIPUTRA and ANANDA are absent. Therefore we have ele-landed in a different time, may be a while before the disciples arrive in the ashram, and we shall see them later?

We now move forward decisively to meet the master, the great sage, the visionary who enlightened and illuminated our world, from his time to this day, 25 centuries after his last incarnation on Earth as the famous Prince Shakyamuni Gautama BUDDHA.

Angel YELIYAEL, in the guise of a little misty cloud adorned with elongated lavender filaments, aerial jellyfish, is floating behind the face of BUDDHA. Calmly he enounces in a long breath, one of his precious lessons:

"Terrestrial tradition says he meditated 30 days and 30 nights without water and without food under a giant tree which harvested the Truth from Heaven and transmitted it to him in a full, perfect, unifying, final vision. Pure wisdom free of all illusions, mistakes, and confusions Brahmin priests had infiltrated in the original spiritual teachings, which were still true and accurate when brought 15 centuries before BUDDHA's time, by devoted missionaries from Mesopotamia, sent by MELKITSEDEK, on behalf of his major disciple, ABRAHAM, thus at the origin of the BRAHMIN doctrines."

We have now reached the open ashram and offer our respectful greetings to BUDDHA; he welcomes us with the simplicity and grace of a great master. An enigmatic smile slightly disturbs the perfect order of his imperturbable face, nearing indifference, but showing no hint of arrogance or superiority. With a slow ample move of hand he invites us to sit, and we emulate his comfortable lotus position, emblematic of BUDDHA's wisdom all over the civilized world.

"I was hoping to meet you, he says, without waiting for you. I saw you approach this very spot during your previous visit just before the last rainy season. I saw you both near the little wooden bridge that crosses the creek...you were walking on that narrow tree-lined path that leads to this mound, where I like to sit at the foot of these mighty oaks...and then, poof, you totally disappeared, dispersed in the molecular intervals of matter, invisibilized, virtualized.

I was then in silent mind-to-mind conversation with my two most ardent followers...they remained unaware of your presence, too busy playing their mystic inner dramas, convoluted meditations…

Then, reading your minds I knew, at this stage of your Quest you intended to explicit with me the 8th Commandment of MOSES, THOU SHALL NOT STEAL, and I laughed in my sleeves..."

Suddenly the sage burst into thunderous laughter, frantically clapping hands on his thighs barely protected by his saffron brown cotton robe...

Another commonplace belief breaks into pieces! GAUTAMA BUDDHA we always imagined displaying imperturbable positive indifference has transformed into jolly passionate laughing BUDDHA, cheerful companion BUDDHA!

"Master, why are you laughing?" asks ALBERT, respectfully.

"Because as you would say in your 21st century American language, your actual quest was futile, irrelevant, a mirage without substance, a fire without flame, a love without passion."

I watch BUDDHA thoughtfully. The present situation conjures in my mind a strange sense of familiarity, even more, a certain feeling of "déjà vu". Then, laughing uproariously, I recall the vivid image of Rabbi Yohanan BEN ZAKKAI in Brur Hayl Israel, under his time withered olive tree, erupting into laughter when Albert informed him we had come to meet him for we were in QUEST of the truth concealed in MOSES' 10 Commandments!

I am amused and intrigued by the similar reaction of the Rabbi of Israel and the Hindu Sage to the evocation of our Quest for Truth. Would the word Quest always trigger a tender and affectionate mockery in men of wisdom?

Regaining a serious and reflective mental attitude, I address the Master:

"How were we wrong, when attempting to meet with you earlier, expecting you to reveal the hidden deeper meanings of the 8th Commandment?"

BUDDHA: "There is no mysterious reason for that. The 8th Commandment states, apparently, YOU SHALL NOT STEAL. And as it is well known that little larceny is the most notable weakness of the Hindu people, it seemed perfectly justified to come here in India to study the evident and hidden meanings of that Commandment.

Of course, since your first aborted visit, you have searched beyond appearances, and learned that the 8th law refers first and foremost to the misuse of biogenetic science and biopsychic knowledge, generating beings and concepts devoid of their corresponding universal archetypes, so engendering solitary hybrids creatures and disharmonious entities ipso facto becoming destructive monsters and monstrosities. The 8th Commandment is a prophylaxis for misdeeds of would be Doctors Frankenstein, and for the criminal errors of modern ill intentioned social theorists. Hopefully, human civilization, advancing on the path of spiritual science and scientific wisdom, shall gradually renounce these temptations, partly thanks to the Buddhist doctrine of which I am the initiator.

Therefore I repeat what I have clearly and unequivocally stated a few moments ago: Coming here to explicit with me the 8th Commandment was futile, irrelevant, a quest, a mirage without substance, a blaze without flame, a love without passion."

Indeed now I perceive the accuracy of BUDDHA's statement. We have been regrettably shallow, making a very common mistake, basing our judgment solely on appearances.

ALBERT intervenes, candidly, a little timidly:

"This time. O Master BUDDHA, we have come to receive your lights and your teachings on the 7th Commandment, so enounced in English, the language most commonly spoken at the time we are living on Earth, at the dawn of the 3rd millennium: YOU SHALL NOT COMMIT ADULTERY."

We see BUDDHA nodding approval, his demeanor now serious, eager to participate in our quest. This time we have come to him with a Commandment that suits him; he unmistakably signaled he is the adequate protagonist!

Euphoric, I begin the dialogue with the Hindu sage:

"This 7th law, LOA TIN AAF in Hebrew, commonly translated as

"You shall not commit adultery", is a real Chinese puzzle. For some it is a sacred vow and for others a pure nonsense, a pseudo law interfering and unreasonably condemning personal intimate choices that should affect only two privately consenting adults.

At certain epochs, the penalty for breaking that law was death, primarily and almost exclusively when the alleged offender was a woman. Today this extreme harsh punishment inflicted on females is still enforced in some particular countries."

"Can we trust, asks ALBERT, the divine messenger on Mount Horeb dictated a particular law, in a particular historical period, limited to certain types of societies, and invalid at other times in the history of certain peoples?

All the sacred Commandments we examined so far embody a universal principle and are therefore applicable to humanity across all ethnic and social peculiarities. Would the 7th law be an exception?"

The Master answers very slowly, softly, calmly, and a real mental storm explodes in our mind, shattering our misconceptions and shaky beliefs.

Here are the words of BUDDHA: "The mystery is easily solved, as we revisit the original resonances of ARCHAE LINGUA, transmitted by the Hebraic tradition: [64] LOA TIN AAF

The common version "thou shall not commit adultery" is completely and totally falsely translated...There is in the 7th Commandment no reference to any sexual behavior, near or far.

Common adultery, namely adults engaging in sexual relationship out of wedlock may be regarded as a serious infringement of a marriage contract. However, proscription of this kind of adultery is in no way inscribed neither in the 7th nor in any of the other nine Commandments."

Funny law, I thought, strange law that 7th Commandment! Since we began our quest it is the first time I hear that one of the 10 laws is characterized as a total falsity. And, flash! Now I re-

---

64 Archae Lingua is best preserved in those 3 ancient languages: Hebrew, Urdu and Sanskrit.

member MOSES' wrath commenting on the popularized version of this Commandment when we met him at the entrance of the Tent of Assignations.

YELIYAEL, swiftly projects MOSES's vigorous words:

"Thus said MOSES:

"No, it is not correct. Although I cannot provide you now with a "spherical" revelation, I can tell you the common translation is a hideous perversion of my message, one of the saddest and most oppressive errors impressed on human intelligence.

You shall find the truth yourselves, by going over the original text, word by word, sentence by sentence, with your magnificent "Archaeo-Linguistic" method. You shall uncover the secret!"

BUDDHA's statement, clearly in agreement with MOSES's lament, re-orients the direction of my thinking. I absorb the shock. I notice Albert is also recovering his customary serenity. In fact, deep inside, we had been forewarned of a looming scandal regarding that particular 7th principle "DO NOT COMMIT ADULTERY". Our modern mind is troubled that a personal intimate act of love should become the object of a universal negative judgment, at the same level as killing, stealing, particularly in view that societies, ancient and recent, have applied lethal penalties, mainly if not exclusively, in case of female "adultery".

ALBERT courageously restores the dialogue with BUDDHA:

"I am presenting myself to you as a student before his teacher. I am glad to be in the presence of a wise man who practices the art of happiness, and who does not believe himself so highly placed that he can't play and laugh...It is a fact that all the sages we encountered so far were not arrogant, never bringing their nose so up to the sky that they could not speak to us and instruct us, we little children in the kingdom of mind and spirit.

O BUDDHA, kindler of enlightening fires, can you burn our delusions, illuminate our path, help us clarify this archaic phrase LOA TINA-AF engraved in incandescent letters by a divine messenger?"

BUDDHA with an alert and swift movement turns towards me,

points his finger at me and asks:

"You, Shimeha, what do you think?"

His voice tone is imperious, impetuous, communicates a sense of passion, a feeling of urgency and immediacy. It appeals to me and breaks the routine of my mind, forces the gate of my psyche. And I who respond to urgency almost always swiftly and impulsively, I undertake instead to ponder his request for a very, very long time. I remain still, living the moment as a slow motion film, a lasting emotion fully internalized.

After an interval that seemed to me eternal I answered:

"An honest linguistic analysis of that law does not actually deliver the slightest hint it contains any prohibition of *sexual* infidelity. Yet it is under this guise this 7th Commandment has acquired its extraordinary reputation…

If it were true this law meant DO NOT COMMIT ADULTERY, namely "thou shalt have no sexual intercourse but with your spouse", then we could say without doubt none of the Ten Commandments has been so betrayed, ignored, transgressed, by both males and females in the whole world and throughout all ages.

It is also clear that males have seized and appropriated this version of the 7th Commandment, leading women, raised in ignorance of the original texts, to believe this sacred law sanctions and punishes only the sensual conduct of females. This famous Commandment has always been used for centuries to legitimate cruel punishment, beating, locking, stoning, lynching, multiple forms of violence inflicted by men unto women."

My heart imbued with sadness, I hold my thoughts for an indefinite time, attempting to escape from a sense of impending oppression.

Then, I hear a distressing prolonged scream, a piercing human complaint. A feminine voice distorted by acute pain, exclaims:

"Between the 10th Commandment by which we are equaled to donkeys, slaves and oxen, the 8th which refers to an original sin, alleged cause of a fall attributed to feminine nature only, and this

7th Commandment that justifies all kinds of abuses against women who committed or are only suspected of committing adultery, our troubles are deep, and our perpetual submission to males is absolute."

Was I the only one to hear this heartbreaking complaint? Was I hallucinating? I find reassurance by watching YELIYAEL. I distinguish, emerging on top of the Angel's opalescent luminous form, the sculptural head of a beautiful woman with red abundant hair, turquoise blue tears clear and transparent as pure aquamarines flowing from her hazel eyes, irises enlarged by emotion. Despite her pain, she is smiling at me…And, slowly, gradually, the apparition fades and disappears completely.

YELIYAEL concludes his visual animated message of compassion by throwing in the air a spherical cluster of crackling multicolored sparks.

I observe the faces of Albert, and BUDDHA and I realize they have not seen the Madonna face in tears nor heard the lament of the wives of men...Some experiences cannot be shared with others but Angels, I think…

During the whole event, my human companion Albert and the sage BUDDHA remained still, waiting patiently for me to continue the exposition of my thoughts on the 7th Commandment.

Hundreds of birds hidden in the deep foliage above are whistling contentedly, responding to each other, offering to all listeners a morning concert, musically reporting that nature is awakening, young and refreshed...

Our Master BUDDHA has adopted the classical detached serene poise for which he is universally famous. Albert is looking at me, tensed by curiosity.

I resume speaking:

"Neither in ARCHAE LINGUA, nor Aramaic nor ancient Hebrew, can be found in this expression LOA TIN AAF the slightest hint these three words prohibit or punish sexual infidelities, even less the ban should apply to women in particular. And yet, I must face the facts: over the centuries, the translators of the Ten Commandments never *totally annihilated* all the possible meanings enclosed in the Mosaic texts.

They never totally sever the link between the avowed exoteric sense and the more profound esoteric message encrypted in the original words.

Therefore, reason and honesty command to consider the 7th law is no exception.

This 7th Commandment however, is a dark cavern and that cavern smells of sulfur."

Then again I hold my tongue, my lips clamed under the pressure of an unknown force. Encouraged by my silence, everyone starts riding the golden waves of his spiritual inner world; time and space melt and expand in the infinite and four dreams dash, united into a powerful ample spiral, attracted by an immaterial shining sphere which speaks to us of Void and Absence.

And that shining sphere presents itself, a voice echoing in our inner sanctuary, revealing its secret name:

"*My activation code is ZODA.*"

That name suddenly opens a tiny recess in my ancestral memory and I remember: 5th law, title HOVA, 10th law YOAA, 9th law TOBA. And ZODA is title of the 7th law…

Now, from the perfect silence of the cosmic interstices flows the crystalline song titled ZODA, and this chant reveals the secrets of the cavernous 7th Commandment, illuming it with an intense white light powdered with pale golden specks.

And Angel YELIYAEL, transforming the celestial flashes into a brilliant chaplet of human words, unveils for us the mystery of ZODA:

"*The 7th Commandment primarily warns against the malefic sin of ARROGANCE TINA-AF*[65]*. It literally points at individuals ele-*

65 Tin-aaf: in vernacular Hebrew translates as to "nose up", to be "arrogant". Also to look at the world only at the level of one's nose, neither higher (negating any superior force) nor lower (where only inferior beings to oneself crawl and creep). Thus this law points at the "sins" of "Pride" and "Prejudice".

vated by Divine Providence and aided by Angels, who boldly deny any celestial intervention, even disclaim having benefited from the help of men and women who arduously contributed to their ascension. Those ungrateful arrogant individuals proclaim "not existing" either the Divine Force or the Angels.

Then they treat as mere slaves and worthless instruments the humans who brought them to the pinnacle.

This kind of individuals place their nose above terrestrial ground, well above, preparing themselves for self-deification. They persuade the fellow humans who suffered for them and gave them so much, to deify them, to idolater them!"

ZODA the sphere of Void and Absence, ZODA faithful support of the luminous compass arrow eternally pointing toward the Almighty, gently caresses our minds and souls, we feel loved, comforted.

A huge hot flash blazes in the sky and etches LOA TIN AAF in giant letters above us. YELIYAEL translates:

"*Beware your boundless ambitions do not induce you to ADULTERATE the reality and truth of your human condition!"*

The chant of the sphere continues:

"This 7th Commandment of MOSES, *reminds humans rising to the summit of the pyramid of social power or to the heights of divine grace, not to fall into the temptation of passionate self-pride and be tempted to ADULTERATE the truth as to how they came to ascend this high...*

All human beings perpetrating ADULTERATION are perpetrators of infidelity, infidelity to Higher Divine Forces and their Creator.

This law, cautioning against the cardinal sin of self pride and arrogance, does not address humans only but the Angels as well, all divine beings, planets, suns, all living energies operative in the universe. And if, by inner illumination, one finds the way of DAO and ZEN, the direct path toward the Ultimate and the Supreme, as it is the case for exceptional women and men, as it has been the case for BUDDHA, beware not to become idolater of oneself, and not to induce or constrain others to one's undue worship.

And when that exceptional being, like the flying arrowhead touching the exact center of the target, finds the luminous path, perfect line-hyphen of instantaneous union, leading toward the ultimate goal of all living creatures, the Center of the Universal Creation, BEWARE not to fall into the Luciferian arrogance, induced by incommensurable egotism, a limitless and fenceless narcissism!"

Our souls united as a flame issued from the same blaze, we listen intently to the words of ZODA, the white sphere of Void and Absence:

"Adulteration is idolatry, the love of idols that MOSES sought to root out from the people he prepared to roam the 4 corners of the world to love it and civilize it.

Idolatry is IDOLA-TERRA, golden calf in multiple forms; it is adulation of terrestrial energies and matter, equaled to adoration of the Creator."

"And behold adds ZODA the white sphere, relayed by YELIYAEL's angelic energies, *here is exactly the true intent and purpose of the law now known in the popularized version of the 7th Commandment YOU SHALL NOT COMMIT ADULTERY.*

Far, very far from invoking sexual infidelity stimulated by emotional instinctual passions, LOA TIN AAF is an admonition not to willfully ADULTERATE AND FORGE AND FALSIFY the deeper truths of Divine Creation. And that is why Jesus invites to distinguish which belongs to terrestrial Caesars from that which belongs to your Eternal Father, your Soul and Spirit."

Thus sang ZODA the bright sphere of Void and Immaterial Absence:

You shall not ADULTERATE terrestrial realities.
You shall not transfigure materialistic elements of the Earth,
were they gold and diamonds, into idols
as substitutes for the Lights of Celestial Divine kingdoms.
You shall not abuse the powers of Grace and Providence
the Divine Himself bestows on you
by crowning yourself as prince on Earth;

That would be an act of IDOLA-TERRA, IDOLATRY,
an absurdity without essence or value.
Human creative generative powers manifest fully
only in union with elevating Divine Universal Spirit.
And this is the Sacred Marriage
To which each and every man and woman
Owes ABSOLUTE FIDELITY.

The heavenly song stopped gradually, leaving behind a swirling melody fading away like echoes ricocheting in the gorges of a profound valley.

We all gradually came back to self-consciousness, feeling relieved, refreshed, invigorated, revived, fully energized by a simple joy of being, happy under the shade of friendly oak trees, in the Rajagriba garden monastery.

BUDDHA becomes animated, his eyes open widely. He raises his hands palms up, expressing gratitude to the Heavens and says in a low and calm voice:

"Everything you have heard from ZODA enlightens you Shimeha, Albert, YELIYAEL, on the fact that this morning at dawn I have been waiting here *alone* without my two disciples SARIPUTRA and ANANDA. I know they shall, after I am gone, diligently spread my doctrine, the doctrine of enlightenment, the path leading each living creature to its Ultimate Source.

But it was in their absence that we needed to unlock the secrets concealed in the 7th law. A few months ago, at the time of your first ele-landing in the Rajagriba forest, you thought we were destined to explore the 8th Commandment THOU SHALL NOT STEAL, because it is known to the world that Hindu peoples transgress that law today as they will in centuries to come. But you well know that theft is far from being the specialty of the people of India.

Verily, what India today does the most is A*dulteration of Truth*, a practice leading to spiritual chaos and idolatry.

Idolatry greatly encouraged among the credulous by the Brahmin caste and its myriads priests and gurus who infiltrate the lives of Hindu peoples, control and lock them in gilded cages, maintain them deeply attached to earthly realities.

Yes, the forte of the peoples of this vast continent is garish idolatry and will remain so for a long time.

My own disciples shall spread another facet, another version of blatant idolatry, the worship of BUDDHA.

My own disciples, Ananda and Sariputra, their disciples and followers, in their fervent endeavor to spreading the pure truths I have received from the Heavens, shall lack wisdom, shall generate and encourage gaudy idolatry toward my person.

They shall make the mistake of magnifying me as a god, whereas only the truths that I bequeathed them were divine."

"This is your lesson! Farewell!...We shall meet again…"

"Master, O Master! exclaims ALBERT If your disciples Ananda and Sariputra had been able to attend our meeting, they would have heard this wonderful lesson, they could have avoided making their mistake, they would not have divinized you excessively, thousands, millions of human beings on the planet would have approached more quickly the pure truth you entrusted to them..."

BUDDHA replies:

"And Ananda and Sariputra would have skipped some steps necessary for the conquest of Truth, they would have attempted to steal time..."

ALBERT rejoins: "Master, you know this newly revealed version of the 8th Commandment!?"

BUDDHA: "I know EVE-MARIA, our celestial Mother, we meet often, we have a common mission..."

YELIYAEL: "*Observe attentively the statues and paintings of inspired artists on your planet, BUDDHA and EVE de SUMARIA display the same enigmatic smile...*"

Feeling abandoned, we sadly wave to the vanishing form of the sage BUDDHA, master of the doctrine of enlightenment, while his earthly appearance and smiling face dissolves slowly, inexorably. Progressively enseraphed, inwardly caressed and gradually imbued by the luminous energies of our celestial navigator, we hover for a moment, circling above the three noble oak trees. As our intangible time-space ship leaps over the giant Himalayas, we hear our angelic companion softly chanting:

"O BUDDHA of the three Ages, PADMA SAMBA HAVA,
remove all obstacles, be they Inner, Outer or Secret.
May our Thoughts come True spontaneously."

Then YELIYAEL instantly flashes us, hyper-virtualized passengers, across the starry firmament.

47. Back Home, Manhattan, March 2001 AD.

WE ELE-LANDED IN MANHATTAN ON THE EDGE of twilight. Dozens of peoples going about their daily "down to earth" business in the city of New York saw a brilliant object float in the sky. A few of them tried to share this "sighting" experience with their acquaintances, and those who had not seen anything were amused by the story, staring up to the skies with skepticism and various degrees of arrogance. Yet a breaking news segment "UFO over Manhattan" was hurriedly programmed by a TV network and as hastily cancelled following a mysterious authoritative phone call which insisted the network delete this information, and so it was done.

YELIYAEL did not fly us directly to our apartment.

Our Angel friend loves drama! In Paris he opened his dome in the middle of the Latin Quarter, one of the busiest areas of the city. This time, in New York, after hovering over Central Park for a while, maybe to give us time to regain "normal" consciousness, he landed his golden egg right at the center of Columbus Circle, and noticing that, once again, no one seemed to acknowledge the extraordinary event, poofed away unceremoniously.

And so, here we are, facing the large stone fountain, palpating our face, chest, legs and feet, to be sure we are not offering the spectacle of disembodied ghosts to the six or seven tourists who are still lingering on benches behind us. From the top of his 70 feet column Christopher Columbus[66] is smiling at us, fellow voyagers, re-discoverers of ancient worlds and languages.

"All is well, says ALBERT. I love this place, a few blocks from our home anyway. But I wonder why YELIYAEL dropped us here."

"Our angelic navigator never misses a target, or a set landing pad. There must be a reason for this bold initiative…Look, here, at the bottom of the pedestal, that statue of an Angel, watching at a globe, apparently protecting it…"

"That's it! YELIYAEL wanted to make it clear Angels are present on Earth, everywhere…Very thoughtful, our angelic companion, as always…Let's go home now."

But Albert cannot leave a place without reading every single notice, warning, new or obsolete...His mind, like a magnet clasps to all that is written, etched, engraved, painted, scripted...

"Simha, look, look! There is an inscription on the pedestal. Up there it is written in Italian:

IRRISO PRIMA
MINACCIATO DURANTE IL VIAGGIO
INCATENATO DOPO
SAPENDO ESSER GENEROSO QUANTO OPPRESSO
DONAVA UN MONDO AL MONDO

And here they carved a translation in English:

SCOFFED AT BEFORE,
DURING THE VOYAGE, MENACED,
AFTER IT, CHAINED,
AS GENEROUS AS OPPRESSED,
TO THE WORLD HE GAVE A WORLD.

---

66 Coordinates: 40°46′05″N 73°58′55″W .at the intersection of Central Park South, Broadway, Central Park West and 8th Avenue

Albert and I gasp at the same time, as we both immediately perceive YELIYAEL's intent in landing us here, near this statue.

We got the message, O YELIYAEL! We shall be careful, careful…in sharing our wonderful discoveries…

Let's walk home. Let's enjoy Spring in the City.

Chapter Six

America

48. Philadelphia, Pennsylvania, America, 1782 AD.

SITTING BY A DARK WOOD TABLE in a vast high ceilinged room, windows protected by thick crimson velvet drapes, walls decorated with paintings and mirrors lavishly framed, we gaze at a large fireplace animated by hundreds crackling bright sparks, warming our souls. Albert and I are facing a mature man, heavy reddish-brown hair streaked with shimmering blond strands, aquiline nose reminiscent of the great Renaissance Europeans.

I am flooded with happiness, I reach the 7th heaven! Even in my childhood's wildest dreams I never imagined I would find myself one day in the same room with the man I admired and loved so much, who throughout my life was my model and my inspiration. I still remember: I am 8 years old playing hopscotch in the narrow and crowded streets of the old Jewish Medieval neighborhood, in Fez, singing and dancing to the refrain recently learned at the French school:

Ben-ja-min Fran-klin	*Ben- ja-min Fran-klin*
le cé-lèbre Amé-ri-cain	*the fa-mous Ame-ri-can*
qui a in-ven-té	*who has in-ven-ted*
le para-to-nerre!	*the light-ning rod!*

That same year, in my primary school's main courtyard planted with majestic mulberry trees and paved with ancient stone slabs, all young girls assembled in perfect rows, hair garnished with a large white tied bow, watched in amazement a unique spectacle.

A scene which would never be repeated in history: facing us, a tall lady, thin and lanky, wearing a sky blue typical American country dress printed with white and coral little flowers, Eleanor Roosevelt, wife of President Franklin Delano Roosevelt was listening attentively to our youthful well rehearsed chorus, our song surging directly from the source of ancient Israel, the Liberation chant of Hanukah, successively in Hebrew, French and English.

Our children's voices heartily sang for her, Eleanor Roosevelt, wife of the late President of the Americans we already knew to be our brave and courageous liberators, who slashed, just in time, the genocidal claws of the savage Nazis occupying our birthland.

I remember my joy was doubly increased, for, standing beside her, I also clearly "saw" BENJAMIN FRANKLIN, the famous American, who has "invented the lightning rod". I would have loved to sing again and again for Eleanor, wife of a Franklin and BENJAMIN FRANKLIN himself, two ambassadors from distant America, the wonderland of freedom.

That day, America was represented by a woman, and she was displaying signs of a status and power which no one of the feminine gender, here in our backward social environment, could ever dream to access. To me, to all the girls maybe, Eleanor Roosevelt was the equal of BENJAMIN FRANKLIN, a feat only possible in America, where energetic cowboys horse ride on vast green prairies, immense high buildings boldly rise above the clouds, without fear, without reproach...The free encounter of old and new, to me, this was the America of BENJAMIN FRANKLIN.

And here I am now firmly set in an 18th century armchair facing BENJAMIN FRANKLIN, undeniably albeit virtually.

We remained silent for some time. Albert was leafing through a thick volume he had picked up from the bookshelf wall, as he does in every house in which he feels welcomed; BENJAMIN

FRANKLIN warming his bones by the fireplace, hands in back; Angel YELIYAEL exploring the room, like a mobile theater spotlight, successively beaming on each gilded framed paintings hanging on the walls.

ALBERT, pointing at the inside of the hard covered volume he is holding: "Well, well! This is surely a very interesting book! And a startling angle to explain some specific aspects of today's America! Just consider this peculiar amazing title: *The New Atlanteans. Essay on Population Expansion on the North American Continent through Intentional Cyclical Reincarnations."*

SIMHA: "And the author is?"

ALBERT: "Anonymous!"

SIMHA: "Could the author be Ben Franklin himself?"

ALBERT: "Or Francis Beacon, as a sequel to his "New Atlantis" essay?"

SIMHA: "Maybe! Either or, I would not be surprised!"

Long reflective pause.

I was inwardly revisiting my recollections of the recent events that led us here. After BUDDHA's abrupt farewell, comforted with a promise of a future meeting, we have ele-landed in Manhattan. In the nurturing peace of our home we have been studying maps and books, situating the scenes and revisiting the words of wisdom we have encountered since the beginning of our saga on the wings of the Angel. But we were also looking for a personage in the past or present, terrestrial or extraterrestrial, who could be the best partner to assist us in investigating the mysteries of the 6th Commandment: THOU SHALT NOT KILL.

Is this Commandment a novel moral instruction resounding like a gong in 1500 BC for the first time? No! Is it a major innovation improving on the social contract of the time? Certainly not!

Even before it appeared in the legal code of Hammurabi[67], in cuneiform script, this law was known and enforced over many cen-

67 The Hammurabi code has been written and largely publicized around 1800 BC. It is based on previous jurisprudence, encompassing hundreds of legal judgments rendered for centuries in the long lasting civilization of Sumer-Akad.

turies. For public view it was scripted on dozens headstones in all cities of Sumer and Akad in the rich and prosperous valley stretching between the two major Mesopotamian Rivers, Tigris and Euphrates.

Certainly in MOSES' time the murder taboo proclamation was not a patent social innovation. A more appropriate example of significant social progress can be found in the rule of obligatory weekly day of rest and recreation, the Shabat, dedicated to spiritual quest and religious rituals.

That rule edicted and legitimized as Fourth Commandment by the pronouncement of the divine messenger on Mount Horeb, was soon to become the unalienable right of every man, every woman, every child, be they free or slaves.

However "You shall not commit murder" was a moral imperative already taught, and widely practiced 35,000 years before MOSES, when ADAM and EVE propelled the new Homo Sapiens-Sapiens race onto the evolutionary scene.

After having researched, analyzed and discussed the subject and taken advice of our Angel friends, the name of BENJAMIN FRANKLIN presented itself on the forefront.

BENJAMIN FRANKLIN is a key proponent and founder of a new nation on a land vast and diverse enough to attract a massive emigration. A land actually welcoming an ever-growing number of men and women, eager participants in the new historic Exodus. A reverse exodus indeed, since, this time, instead of spreading out to all horizons, peoples of all walks converge towards the center of a New Federation. Like the future members of the 12 tribes converged towards Egypt, 400 years before MOSES, the American nation was meant to become the crucible of a vast melting pot, the new "valley of Goshen" on the re-discovered American continent.

We diligently shared our thoughts and data with YELIYAEL our angelic ship-navigator, who thus determined the precise spatio-temporal current coordinates of our hero, and here we are, in Pennsylvania, in BEN FRANKLIN's home, ready to explore all the intricacies of MOSES' 6th Law: murder taboo…

I observe our celestial host comfortably installed in his familiar terrestrial surroundings, his past living space. As if he has followed the path of my private reverie BENJAMIN FRANKLIN let go of his immobility, bends dropping a large wood log on the fire, which merrily responds with bright lively crackles. He stirs the coals and reactivates the flames now thrusting their flares against the blackened stones.

I notice with pleasure that already in the early days of its recent foundation the American people had a yearning for vastness and immensity, for in this place, absolutely everything is grand: the volume of the room itself, wall hangings, reading table, very high backed chairs, large carpets, massive stone fireplace and wide gilded frames enlarging original oil paintings…

Our host has moved to the beautiful square cherry wood table where Albert and I are sitting, then, with his elegant musician's hand lifts an etched crystal decanter, fills three little glasses with a glimmering amber liquid, and offers one to each of us.

On a chair nearby the table he sat down opposite us. I was curious to taste the liquor. Is it close to bourbon or port wine?...Sweet or bitter?...Cautiously, slowly, I started sipping and was delightfully surprised by the savor, a fruity wine, sweet but flavorful, accentuated by a composition of fragrant spices among which I recognized the delicate tang of orange peel mixed with clove's warm fragrance, all exotic and rare ingredients, costing a fortune in that time, I thought.

I began to enjoy the "cordial" at the same time I savored the present moment, intensely, like a precious gift.

Yet for an unknown reason, my simple happiness is insidiously tinged with doubt and anxiety. I watched Albert at my side wondering if he was also worried. Were we on the right track? Had we correctly chosen our interlocutor for this particular mission?

BENJAMIN FRANKLIN, a Founding Father, very active in the conception of the U.S. Constitution, was he really the path and the voice to release the hidden meanings of the 6th Commandment

THOU SHALT NOT KILL? That question was burning my lips and I knew not how to express it without breaking the quietude and harmony of the moment.

Fortunately within the dimension of virtual existence a silent thought is often sufficient to communicate efficiently.

BENJAMIN looked at us, two humans and one Angel, with a dash of thinly veiled amusement, then said:

"You have come to the right door, the door to the right house at the time of growing America.

You are here at the historical confluence of well-ordained social progress and needs for individual liberty, both encouraging the full exercise of free will. Thus, here, you may find the key opening the vault in which the 6th Commandment is locked and deliver its concealed messages to share them generously as you would pour celestial nectar and ambrosia, the drink and sustenance of the gods and goddesses."

Relieved, all my fears effaced, I again feel relaxed, lighthearted. We exchange long friendly gazes, probing the undercurrent feelings and aiming at finding out who among us will initiate the discussion, maybe the debate, on the ultimate crime, the murder, the homicide.

Generously, BENJAMIN manifests with a hand sign he will be the initiator, and he begins:

"Since the time of Christopher Columbus memorable journey, and the famed Caravels landing on this continent, hundreds of thousands peoples of all races have reached the shores of the American land, and this movement will only increase and continue for many centuries.

Why are they coming? What do they seek?

What did they find first in this dreamland? Hard work, poverty, indenture, slavery, violence, brutal death! And yet they came, they come and shall continue to come even more numerous, for a long time, and from all parts of Earth...

Are they attempting to better their social condition? Yes. Are they looking for material wealth? Yes, of course! Wealth for itself as an end? Or are they in search of wealth for the power and unrestrained domination it allows? It may be true for some people…

But what we all seek out here, is hope. What kind of hope? The sort rarely found in the rest of the world: *Open Hope*!

At the bottom of their heart every man and every woman who these days land on the shores of this rediscovered continent, are in search not as much for wealth as for the exciting adventure of personal and shared liberation. The sails of hope which here brought and shall bring millions peoples from all Earth's horizons are the sails which swell under the winds of liberties and liberations of all kinds.

Breaking free from all pressures and oppressions, grips of political and tyrannical unbreakable forces, greed of financial powers unleashed without legal-moral fences to resist them, clutch of rogue justice imposed in societies paralyzed by secular indestructible status quo, racial and ethnic prisons each strangling its people with its national rope, and last but not least, the jails of divisive religions. Leave all prisons behind, in the new land organize progressive legal framework of all liberties, this was the major aspiration for this migration which aims at reviving MOSES' multi-millenary CO-ALTICA, COALITION, union of the liberated peoples.

America is the new Center of the Federation of free nations.

At the dawn of the 3rd millennium this federation of united free peoples, United States of America, is an evolutionary foundation, admittedly imperfect but unique and perfectible.

This is the new people that will design and erect the pyramids of the new age. It is the one which will finally open the main road to divine compassion that leads to unified global humanity, including all races, a new humanity once more respectful and loving of all its ancestors, plants, trees, animals and the entire planet...

When the 3rd millennium Americans shall fully realize this is the true celestially ordained purpose and universal destiny of America, then again the brotherhood of liberating Angels shall descend on Earth to help you."

We listen, tense, fascinated by the powerful rhythm of BENJAMIN FRANKLIN's words of truth. Albert and I, like voyagers aboard a frail bark floating on the Hudson River, are expectantly waiting to see where the great Mother Waters[68] are leading us.

BEN FRANKLIN continues the history lesson:

"In fact, peoples of all kinds, some wearing the clothes of tyrannical potentates, some the rags of the poor and the slave, have come here to live free or die free. And many have also come to kill with impunity.

From the beginning the game was open, extreme behaviors and extreme ideas had free rein, absolutely. Pell-mell, flourished rampant criminality, fearful settlers killers of Indians and enraged Indian killers of settlers; the murderous savagery of slave merchants and slave owners, side by side with legalistic idealism of builders of democracy; the Quakers established their ethical society and the Amish of Pennsylvania developed their rigorous moral code, while at the same time city bandits and road robbers obeyed no law but that of theft and murder."

"Here we are, softly interrupts ALBERT, we start here the debate on the 6th Commandment "THOU SHALL NOT KILL". How many murders have been committed on this territory by violent and cruel individuals, or collectively by armies at war? Even today violence leading to murder is a scourge of American society; violent death can strike anywhere, from top to bottom of the social pyramid. The newscasts, day and night, constantly recite the litany of these heinous crimes while evil perpetrators frequently not found remain unpunished!"

Evidently amused by the vigor of Albert's diatribe, BENJAMIN FRANKLIN smiles warmly, then, calmly, says:

"Our Declaration of Independence contains also a chapter denouncing to the world the killings perpetrated on our people by the British tyrant, unpunished killings committed by the mercenary troops of their king, murders perpetrated during the unjust war

---

68 Mother Waters: name given by Native Americans to the Great Lakes. The main River born of the Mother Waters has been named after the explorer Henri Hudson. In Archae Lingua Hud-Son sounds as "Head-Son", meaning the Major Son of the Great Mother Lakes.

waged against the colonists, murder of American prisoners forced to fight at sea against their sailor brothers..."

"Yes, rejoins ALBERT, and you responded in kind by killing your enemies to prevent more murders in your ranks. In such dire circumstances the moral imperative of the 6th Commandment seems impossible to implement..."

BEN FRANKLIN gently continues on his train of thought:

"Reality is denser and more diverse than it appears in history books, partially released documents, and vapid historical ritornellos incessantly repeated in modern television series.

Just as the very existence of a person can never be fully disclosed in a biography, much less in a magazine article, the true reality of America cannot be encompassed in a social and political vision only.

America represents a new manifestation of individuals and peoples; novel are their births, achievements, lives and deaths..."

ALBERT: "Death! O Master, in your time, when you were living in the 18th century, what did you know about death? Did you trust that after your life on Earth, after the decomposition of your physical body, your life would be prolonged and even revitalized?"

"Honestly, BENJAMIN FRANKLIN replies, we were, most of my contemporaries and I, facing exactly the same dilemma, which troubles men and women of the 21st century. Our intellects and emotions were torn between certainty of a thereafter, and constant doubt induced by the messages of our senses and the illusions they construct."

His eyes sparkle with contained mischief, and the vivacious flame emanating from his gaze alerts us; our attention is fully mobilized.

BENJAMIN, assured our minds are perfectly focused, commences: "All trips, long or short, occur in stages, show discontinuities that may surprise the curious investigator, friend or foe, or scientific observers claiming "objectivity". Consider the example of a traveler, a man in search of adventure, or a man seeking a better social position, boarding a boat in London and heading to Boston.

On his arrival in this city, leaving the boat, he hails a coachman and by horse-drawn carriage reaches the Boston railway station. There he boards a train and after several stops and connecting transfers, he reaches a remote small town in Kansas.

Then, walking, he follows a narrow grassy path, knocks at a door and enters an isolated house in which he expects to meet an individual to whom he is delivering an important message.

After a few days halt, he continues his journey hoping to reach a "beyond" eventful and fertile, rich in favorable encounters, fitting his initial project or any new other project he has devised en route…

At another time, a lady passenger boards in London, leaves the boat in New York and seeks the most suitable and fastest way to reach San Francisco on the Pacific coast. According to her financial and intellectual means, her family connections, her social class, the trip will be modulated as of duration, comfort and safety.

So what do our "objective" senses perceive of the reality of these trips? Nothing or almost nothing!

Some will say that this or that person left London, and is now "beyond"; and others who have learned that this person was seen leaving Boston will say he has disappeared from that city. Is that the entire truth? Where is that person now? "*Beyond*!"

Our host continues, in the tone of a questioning teacher who knows the right answer:

"What would say a sage who does not believe that all knowledge derives only from his sight and other physical senses?

First the sage will inquire, to find out what was the final destination intended by this or that person, and, if it is unknown, he shall investigate about the known intermediate destinations and stages; he shall inform himself as quickly and effectively as possible, according to his level of wisdom.

The sage researcher may assume the traveler he is inquiring about was lost at sea and when investigating discovers the vessel which that passenger has boarded did not sink, he shall have good reasons to believe the man disembarked at Boston, and has decided to begin the second leg of his multi stages voyage.

Given accidents and incidents that might occur en route, possible changes in the original project, positive potential unplanned outcomes which may deviate from the path originally envisaged, is it reasonable or wise to think and conclude with certainty that this person never reached his distant destination? Is it "objectively" justified to estimate at zero the probability for that person to reach the intended goal?"

BENJAMIN stopped to observe us. His face shines with a light similar to YELIYAEL's ethereal substance. His abundant hair, which at the beginning of the meeting was drawn and neatly attached to the rear in a ponytail typical of gentlemen of his era, has opened, several escaped strands forming an artistic halo around his fine rosy skin face. He is passionate, having a lot of fun, enjoying this discussion and happy to feel we sense the import of his allegory.

ALBERT exclaims enthusiastically: "No, Master of Liberties, such a conclusion is not justified! We can never cancel the possibility of reaching the set goal, and on the contrary a sage philosopher will favor the opposite conclusion.

Anyone who has set the goal of his travel and who also clearly envisioned his route has every chance of arriving at his final destination. The chances of reaching the goal are much stronger whenever the traveler has beforehand well planned his route and clearly identified the forces that will propel him all along his journey, up to the point of arrival."

YELIYAEL seems to wake up, suddenly compacting his golden atomized glimmering reflections into a perfect luminous sphere, and intervenes for the first time in the present debate:

"*What forces are you talking about?*" asks our space-time Angel-navigator.

ALBERT replies swiftly:

"When the traveler, planning his route, envisions the obtainable material resources, train, boat, plane, he would be wise to also study and anticipate the available psychological means, such as gathering accurate and relevant information about peoples he might encounter on his way, peoples who could either help or hinder him, or even stop him."

YELIYAEL, relentless interrogator, asks again.

"Is this good enough?"

ALBERT: "No, the psychological and material resources are not sufficient to achieve most surely the goal set for a journey. And here occurs the divorce between the deep cosmic awareness of the sage and the limited mental thinking process singled out as "objective" by shallow science, prevalent in our days.

We have reached the crossroads of Terrestrial Mindal Light, of which REASON is the best feature and Cosmically Enlightened knowledge, of which FAITH is only the first stage.

To sincere truth-seekers, spiritual mastery heightens and broadens awareness of "the luminous path". This path calls for the intervention of a science our ancestors well mastered, and our contemporaries are just preparing to explore. Explicitly this cosmic celestial science may be designated as "quantum metaphysics", revealing the "laws of supra nature", "aid of Angels", "laws of Providence", or "intervention of Divine Grace"...

If the genuine intention of the thoughtful traveler is to reach San Francisco and if she has also envisioned the services she may provide to the human community when arrived, then yes she is giving herself much more chances to finalize her project. If the Kansas traveler's ultimate trust is that his presence in Topeka serves a deep purpose in his own life and the life of other living beings, whomever these "others", here or elsewhere, he has every chance of fulfilling his set goals."

BENJAMIN: "Yes, since every travel is on a par with the journey of life, it would be sheer folly to undertake it anticipating *only* the material and mental means necessary on the way; and this madness is called "reason only" or "certainties" based on illusive data produced by the five physical senses only.

It is of course absurd and barbaric to claim one might understand the journey of life without studying the underlying "intentions", for they are the major variables orienting the performances of individuals, groups, societies, peoples and nations.

Often, obviously, the set goals are not met; sometimes we reach a lateral goal, sometimes we obtain the opposite of what we originally projected.

Why? If the goal apparently aimed at is not achieved, it is because all aspects have been studied, analyzed, understood, planned, *except the essential Intent and its collaterals…*"

Angel YELIYAEL manifests his elation by throwing arrows of pastel yellow light at all the mural paintings adorning the room. At the impact point each arrowhead explodes into a myriad colorful shining sparks. For the first time since I know and can "see" him, YELIYAEL projects burning hot tones of red-oranges, ocher yellows, indigos and purples, on his diaphanous veils.

I also notice the angelic arrows always converge exclusively on the flowers, large or tiny, plainly visible or partly hidden behind leaves, exactly touching the pistils, irrespective of the location of the artworks hanging in this large comfortable lounge which hosts our gathering in the memory of time and the folds of space.

Albert's eyes follow with interest those rapid successive volleys of light, impeccably precise. He smiles and exclaims:

"Our angelic companion is having fun, and casts a metaphoric message as well..."

At that moment, suddenly, my heart pounds against my chest, excitedly starts galloping, stunned by a brutal assault of mixed feelings of wonderment and dismay.

The peace of my present virtual existence explodes like a falling mirror breaking on the ground, since, before my astonished eyes, the head of celestial BENJAMIN FRANKLIN both pivots and spins like a sphere driven by a super powerful engine. The effect is startling, terrifying in its evocation of death on the scaffold or under the strike of a samurai's sword.

Panic receding, in the silence and quietness following my emotional tornado, I realized that myself at that moment I could easily accomplish this same feat, and that I could have manifested similar "magical" performance, since I began this journey in the virtual dimensions, inserting, with the Angels' help, my ethereal self in the intervals of cosmic matter particles, behind the white veil of time. I have never "thought", never "projected", never "intentioned" it, and therefore I have never "done" it.

Now the mesh of fear does not constrain my heart, I feel liberated from the nightmarish heavy net that fell over me, and, BENJAMIN's handsome head which sometimes rotates at great speed, sometimes slowly, sometimes straight, sometimes bent, sometimes facing the ground and then oriented towards the ceiling, appears to me as a wonderful work of art, a dance of the mind.

Sitting in the middle of this virtual space populated by the works of European and American 18th century artists, I have just received three beautiful lessons on the science of intention, a science still ignored in academic circles of early 21st century and yet the oldest and most practiced by the masters of ancient wisdom.

Where was I! My imagination wandering…for how long? Gradually my mind resurfaces in the present, a "paradoxical present" indeed, the "present" of the "past". A peaceful silence fills the crimson-red velvet curtained living room, each of us deciding to suspend our train of thoughts and extend the state of grace engendered by the miracle of our "out of time" co-presence. I see our host BENJAMIN is now sitting quietly by the fire, displaying a posture of patient waiting, head and neck slanted.

What is he waiting for, so impassively? I feel embarrassed, confused, as if confronted with a vital challenge without knowing what-how-why. I pause, silently calling for celestial inspiration, then looking resolutely at BEN FRANKLIN I address him specifically:

"What happened? How did we reach the point of discussing "intentions"? What mysterious link can be found between the 6th Commandment of MOSES, THOU SHALL NOT KILL, the narrative of the travel and the traveler, and the lessons on the Science of Intent?"

BENJAMIN chuckling humorously stabilizes his head with both hands, keeping it straight up, in perfect balance on his broad shoulders, then turns to Albert, encouraging him with a long gaze to express his thoughts on that Commandment which reasserts the multi-millenary murder taboo.

ALBERT: "Obviously, Death is the central theme of the 6th Commandment, more specifically violently inflicted Death. This law addresses mainly the discontinuance of the travel brutally imposed on the traveler..."

BENJAMIN: "But this is just the tip of the iceberg! Tell us about the invisible part, deeper, vaster…"

ALBERT: "There are in this law that prohibits homicide, there are troubling paradoxes…"

BENJAMIN: "Which paradoxes?"

ALBERT: "First there is the notion of murder. First examination shows the 6th Commandment lacks precision.

Thou Shall Not Kill! That's all…nothing more…no railing to hold onto, no shore to land on. Nothing, no instructions to guide us on the path regarding the nature of this taboo...

In the 6th Commandment the divine messenger has transmitted a law that leaves us to ourselves, with no safety net, no guiding rules to help us control our passions and instincts. And if one obeys this law, what reward can one expect? What will be the punishment for violating it? Herein resides the first mystery of the 6th Commandment DO NOT KILL.

And, furthermore, whom or what should one not kill?

In any detective novel or murder trial we are informed immediately about the victim and we avidly read the book or follow the proceedings revealing the identity of the murderer, one who has perpetrated the murder. But on the contrary, in this Commandment it appears the mystery lays in the identity of the murdered, the victim.

Thus, again, who or what should one not kill? The bothersome wasp buzzing in the room, disturbing one's rest? The lion running through the savannah, the donkey who refuses to obey, the slave or prisoner who wishes to free himself, the man who beats his wife, the cheating rich merchant, the neighbor's dog barking at night?...Who or what should one not kill? Herein lurks the second mystery of the 6th Commandment."

ALBERT, raising his hands, palms open in perplexity, declares: "Currently, I do not know how to clarify these two enigmas."

"Is that all?" asks BENJAMIN

ALBERT: "No it is not all; the invisible iceberg plunges even deeper. Since all divine revelations assert there is no real death, only an apparent discontinuity in a journey that continues perpetually, from stage to stage, thus my question to you is: What differentiates so profoundly *natural death* from murder?

In one case the "interval" called Death manifests as a result of natural causes, like old age; in the other, Death is the outcome of a violent act, like murder, or suicide regarded as murder perpetrated by oneself on oneself."

Angel YELIYAEL passive and quiet since his last burst of love arrows thrown at every flower on the murals now intensifies the density of his pearlescent alabaster shades, his forms enter into a state of rhythmic movement, signs of emotion and disarray. Even the subtle aura surrounding the head and body of BEN FRANKLIN is darker, more opaque.

"Finally, says BENJAMIN, looking at each of us in turn, you have at last pronounced that phrase. I was wondering if you would ever get your hands on this major key of the divine mysteries!

Why is it so important to stay alive on this land, experiencing fleeting moments of joy mixed with long dreadful bouts of misery, even as the "Beyond", the real destination aimed at by the traveler, Life after Death, is by all prophets, visionaries and sages, described as a wonderful, attractive magical kingdom?

This is the biggest mystery, the most essential enigma for the truth seeker to solve.

Over the ages, many tribes, sects, civilizations have affirmed that Death, the portal leading to the divine realms, contains all the true values of Life and therefore Death may be sought for itself. Hence recurring human sacrifice rituals, holy wars, individual and collective suicides. This is the theory of "beneficial death", which should appear to all as a just and logical conclusion."

"However, BEN continues passionately, we the living celestials know this line of reasoning is false, its premises false and their conclusions false. And through the most basic primal instinct human beings react with utter disgust to murder, be it motivated by patent criminality or masked with mystical ideals."

BEN FRANKLIN stares into my eyes, insistently, his piercing gaze making me anxious and tense as a bow. He seems to discern my obscure fears and uncertainties; perhaps he knows better than I do the feelings now emerging from the maze of my inner sanctum.

BENJAMIN: "Can you tell me Shimeha, what is the source of that veiled shadow swirling around you?"

Oh the beauty of ideas and thoughts! Hardly had he uttered the words "veiled shadow", that a laser like bright beam illumed the dark recesses of my mind, instantaneously revealing the impasse we were all facing right now. All concerns dissolved I turn to my friends and say:

"In the allegory of the travelers who journey from London to Boston and San Francisco, was ever mentioned the importance of death? Nowhere and never!

Surely it is the traveler's journey and destination one must primordially explore and enlighten, not the frequent intervals, such as the passages between boat and train, between train and coach."

49. Life and Death.

SIMHA: "THE MYSTERY BEFORE US RIGHT NOW is certainly not that of Death, but rather that of Life. In recalling and revealing the stages of Life we can lift the veil of this mystery, and finally understand.

Death is a necessary interval, an inescapable passage…but it is Life which is at the center of our essential reality, our unfolding Destiny. The perspective changes completely, the light that shall beam on the 6th Commandment will illuminate Life and not Death.

Thus, it is no more THOU SHALL NOT KILL we must enounce,
but DO NOT DELIBERATELY, INTENTIONALLY, THREATEN LIFE.

This law does not prohibit causing death, but forbids the interruption of the natural course of life so that the journey may continue and the goal eventually be reached."

"But then, exclaims ALBERT, if Life is a journey primarily led by the intention to continue until the end up to the sublime frontiers of celestial Paradise, to enter the transcendent divine bosom, why not voluntarily interrupt the trip in this lower world, thus accelerating the Soul's passage towards its ultimate goal?"

BENJAMIN: "That would be stealing time by skipping steps! The 7th Commandment warns about the catastrophic effects caused by "stealing" the time of the experiment, the time necessary for the evolving Soul to gain maturity through attainment of its purposed destinations encompassed within each individual Destiny."

Short pause.

"Now resume your reasoning, Shimeha."

During that verbal exchange I secretly called YELIYAEL for urgent help. A bittersweet liquid of unknown composition titillates the tip of my tongue, a pungent unfamiliar albeit pleasant fragrance invades my nostrils, and in my mind swirl, dance and rhythmically resonate multicolored sounds ELIXIR...ELIXIR...ELIXIR, choreographed in ascending spirals, unfolding luminous David's stars, patted crosses, double zeros icon of infinity, Greek letters from Alpha to Omega, Hebrew Alphabet from Aleph to Tav.

All symbols and letters swirling in a joyous vital ballet, entering and exiting every tiny cell of my body, illuming nerve synapses, cleansing all my emotions and thoughts, even in the darkest deepest forgotten recesses of my psyche…

Then, through indefinite time and space, I hear BENJAMIN's kind voice:

"Resume your reasoning, Shimeha."

My thoughts now clear and limpid, revitalized by the angelic biopsychic Elixir, I respond to BENJAMIN's prompting:

"The crime in question, be it murder or suicide, does not take root in giving Death. How could that be since we are well assured that Death does not exist, is an illusion of the physical and material world, an illusion of the five senses…

The crime in question is the attempt at severing the continuous thread of Life, aiming at interrupting the flow of the Soul's voyage, breaking the living unity the traveler has created between himself, his itinerary, and his intent to reach his very final destination.

Why is this so crucial?

Because, more than any plant or animal, a living human is bearer of the Divine Verb, is endowed with divine consciousness.

We need to face this fact: every human being is a vessel that holds and joins with a mysterious spark of the Creator's original blaze. In the intention of twisting and breaking this sacred union takes root the real crime, crime perpetrated on another being, in case of murder, or committed on self, in case of suicide.

Therefore one can understand why the 6th Commandment gives this brief, curt order:

YOU SHALL NOT BREAK THE UNION
OF THE LIVING WITH THE DIVINE,
THE ONE SUPREME GIVER OF LIFE. "

Our host, the man from Heaven, BEN FRANKLIN, interrupts imperatively:

"Everything you say is true. However, when the divine messenger dictated the 6th law, he could have chosen a more specific formulation, more complete, or at least he could have inscribed a clue, a sign, an indication that can help men and women better understand this law, and better implement it!"

I reply: "Revisiting your potent allegory of the traveler, O Master of the spheres, we first discern that "uncertainty" being the permanent companion of the Life traveler, to continue and complete his journey he needs to consistently appeal to the energies of Open Hope and Enlightened Faith.

Faith is essential to undertake the journey and continue up the road, as much as water under the boat and the steam in the locomotive, because Faith is a supra-powerful spiritual energy.

Intelligent Faith is the necessary harmonic complement to Uncertainty. We understand that Uncertainty maintains an indispensable state of alertness and wakefulness, but it needs the force of Faith, its essential vital complement, to withstand and overcome the incidents and aggressions that may interrupt the flow of Life."

"Then, intervenes ALBERT, one who perpetrates murder is less guilty of having given Death than accountable for having misused his free will in attempting to break and damage the link uniting the traveler and his final destination.

And as this final destination may be intended to be the Supreme Deity, the murderer is guilty of severing the link between the Creator and his Creature; it is as if one separates the river from the upspring source that feeds it and to which it is intimately linked."

YELIYAEL whirls wildly. Is he impatient? Or simply happy?

BEN FRANKLIN relentlessly hammers:

"Is that all there is? Has everything been uncovered and said about the 6th Commandment?"

I buoyantly rejoin: "Certainly not! since we have not yet invited Princess ARCHAE LINGUA to participate in our debate!

BENJAMIN: "Let's hear her voice chanting MOSES' words:

LOA TI RATSACH!"

SIMHA: "The Hebrew keyword of this 6th Commandment is RATSACH. It has been transmitted for centuries as meaning KILL, to commit murder. But this popular translation is far, still very far from the original sense of the root RATSACH. It does assume the meaning KILL, only as a shortcut, a voluntary limitation impressed by scholars in the course of Western spiritual and religious history.

Here are the meanings which unfold when applying the Archaeo-Linguistic method:

RA: Radiate, Reign, dominate.
TSA: Implode, Metamorphose, Exit.
H: Spirit of love that envelops and unifies.
or: CH[69]: Instinctual passions oriented by survival.

This root RATSACH is the origin of the word RACE, which designates human racial groups, as well as competition, race for domination.

Over the millenniums, the search for absolute domination has motivated the largest number of killings, perpetrated on individuals or groups such as clans, tribes, nations. It is Domination, Will of Power, Der Wille zur Macht, Volonté de Puissance, clearly recorded in the roots of the word RATSACH, which often leads to blood crimes, in order to satisfy instinctual passions."

ALBERT: "This explains why, in ancient Greece as well in modern times, the Olympic sports competitions are wisely used as a substitute to "race for racial domination", an alternative activity leading to victories without killings.

Likewise the modern political races for election or re-election to official positions are a welcome replacement for duels, violent riots, clanic or tribal exterminations, and perpetual ducal, royal or international warfare and their resulting mass slaughters…"

---

69 Ha, letter He in Hebrew, vocalized as a soft expiration, connoting "Spiritual Connection". Cha, letter Chet in Hebrew, vocalized as a raspy H sound, connoting instinctual primal forces, emotions and sensual primitive passions. Those letters are interchangeable, according to the intended meaning of the word, idea or emotion described. Ha will give to the word a spiritual nuance, while Cha will give it a terrestrial quasi animal tinge.

BEN FRANKLIN and the Angel YELIYAEL now seem more relaxed.

In the lull Albert takes the Olympic torch in hands, and undertakes to continue the clarification of the 6th law, by revealing the meaning of each letter-sound of ARCHAE LINGUA:

DO NOT INTERRUPT LIFE, EITHER YOURS OR ANOTHER'S,
YOU THE PLANET DOMINANT HUMAN-ROY (RA),
FOR, YOUR DOMINION, YOUR CHARISMA,
YOUR ROYAL LEADERSHIP (RA),
ARE BETTER EXTRACTED (TSA)
AT THE VERY SOURCE OF SPIRITUAL LIFE (H)
AND NOT FROM YOUR INSTINCTUAL PASSIONS (CH).

"And behold, exclaims BENJAMIN, also revealed by ARCHAE LINGUA, here is MOSES true ciphered message, when on Mount Nebo, he reiterated that 6th law in front of the pioneers who were to start their long peaceful civilizing march towards all horizons on Earth:

THE TIME IS RIPE
FOR YOUR JOURNEY ON THE PATH OF LIFE
NOT TO BE DRIVEN
BY THE EXPLODING FORCES OF VIOLENCE,
THOSE ENERGIES, INSTINCTS AND PASSIONS
YOU HAVE ACCUMULATED
ALL ALONG YOUR EXISTENCE AS KING
IN THE ANIMAL KINGDOM. (RA)

THE MAN WHO KILLS TO DOMINATE,
TO AUGMENT HIS PERSONAL PUISSANCE (TSACH),
HE WHO INTERRUPTS THE LIFE OF AN OTHER
TO AUGMENT HIS OWN LIFE,
IS AN "INSANE" WHO BELIEVES IN DEATH.
IF HE WAS A LION OR AN EAGLE
HIS ACT WOULD UPHOLD A BASIC NATURAL PRINCIPLE;
BUT HAVING ENTERED IN THE KINGDOM OF HUMANITY
AND CONSCIOUSNESS

HIS CRIME IS PURE FOLLY,
ILLUSION OF A "RETARDED"
WHO ADHERES TO THE BELIEF THAT DEATH
IS TOTAL ANNIHILATION,

FOR HIS ASCENSION AND ATTAINMENT
TO THE STAGE OF KINGSHIP OVER THE SPECIES
MAKES IT HIS SACRED DUTY
TO PROJECT HIS SPIRIT TOWARD LIFE
WHICH IS SUSTAINED BY THE PRESENCE
OF THE CREATOR WITHIN EVERY LIVING BEING."

And BENJAMIN resumes:

"Ordained by their instinctual natural program and urge for life continuity, mosquitoes sting and drink blood. Hungry leopards, crouch waiting for the right moment to pounce upon their prey, fated by their programmed combat for survival. By design, "sane" animals kill only when "necessary"; their aggressive forces are integrated in the flow of life itself. So when plants, minerals, animals "kill", they do it as part of the natural fabric, the continuous stream of life, the terrestrial global ecology.

And, furthermore, as planetary evolution progresses, there occur more and more coordination and inter-species associations within the animal-vegetal-mineral kingdoms, namely interconnections between diverse animal species, between different plants, and between plants and animals, cooperation between mineral elements and plants, even much more than can perceive your modern ethologists, chemists and naturalists.

By example, the fruit trees in my courtyard are in permanent contact with many trees in the country, and communicate with certain giant trees in a monastery near Rajagriba, in India. And so I was alerted of the time and location of your arrival here, by a cherry tree planted in George Washington's estate..."

ALBERT: "Is it through benevolent telepathic trees you gather your information, so enabling you to write and publish your famous and notoriously exact Farmer's Almanack?"

BENJAMIN, in a roaring laughter:

"I cannot tell you. Trade secret! I am a celestial now, but I am still an American businessman!"

We all share in the sudden hilarity set off by that humorous rejoinder, then BENJAMIN continues his elucidation of MOSES' 6th Commandment:

"Humankind having won the RATSAH, the race for global dominion on the planet, entered a new dimension, a new ecology that de facto makes it "co-sentient", meaning joining its science with the broader science of the Universe. Human beings are on the way to be integrated in the supra-natural cosmic fabric, thus to become potential extra-terrestrials, possible immortals.

Earth humans draw and shall draw more and more their knowledge, their strength and inspiration from the inexhaustible reservoir of the sacred universal trinity, source of all life. Their powers are and will be increased tenfold, hundredfold, and exponentially...

Therefore "Thou shall not kill" is a prophecy announcing that the spirit of man which enters in union with the "Ultimate Source of Life" shall no more be dominated by the devious intention to interrupt the flow of Life! For the intelligence and conscience that strengthen and enhance humankind's union with the "Universal Unity" are means of survival more powerful, more efficacious, much safer than exclusive use of physical force..."

BENJAMIN has more to say:

"Thus spoke MOSES to the assembled tribes. Thus spoke the prince, the leader, the King of the Human Kingdom, the human being you shall learn to emulate. Thus spoke the great leader of those peoples the Father Creator has elevated, "elected" to represent Him on Earth and endowed with Ten divine powers so they can win without killing.

And tomorrow you shall be this Prince and Princess, whatever your race, social status, free or slave, your intellectual level, grand or humble, your form of being , Human or Angel, you in your epoch, and those generations living in future times."

BENJAMIN concludes: "Thus spoke MOSES when he pronounced his final testament on Mount Nebo and repeated the 6th Commandment: LOA-TI-RATSAH."

We are mesmerized by this vivid evocation of that ancient event. For a moment MOSES, Musaeus the Egyptian Prince Musician, master of Tanakh and Kabalah, has been here with us, alive.

As always when I feel that a celestial encounter may come soon to an end, I attempt to prolong the debate by playing the role of an elephant entering a porcelain store:

"And Self-Defense?! What is its status and value when confronted with the murder taboo, the interruption of the journey of life? Facing blind aggression and sheer brutality of others, our energies and instinctual passions resurface, explode, and we might enter the forbidden territory, that of violent blood crime. Overwhelmed by fear, we become again animal amidst animals, surviving by force and by eliminating the enemy."

BENJAMIN FRANKLIN, his face beaming with intelligence returns to the helm of our explorer ship:

"Ah, mes chers amis, c'est la bouteille à l'encre[70], he says, it's as clear as mud…Self-defense, killing to prevent an attacker from interrupting our own life!?

ALBERT: "Is the answer encoded in the 6th Commandment?"

BENJAMIN: "When does one kill in "self defense", "en légitime défense ", or when does one kill criminally?

When does one kill to self-preserve the embers of divine Life bestowed on him at birth?

When does one kill to dominate, to monopolize wealth and power, leaving thousands corpses on the road?

When does one assault and kill to physically eliminate an adversary that could have been confronted with and pacified through intelligence?

When an animal kills it is clear its intention is to survive a present urgent situation; when a man kills, one is certain of nothing and certainly not about his hidden "true intention"!

---

70 Ben Franklin has been an American Ambassador to France, thus he speaks perfect French.

A Murder occurred presumably in "self-defense"!?

Was the intention of the defender not to interrupt the journey of life of his attacker? Or was the hidden intention of the defender to cut the thread of life of that attacker? Who is defending? Who is attacking? What are the intentions of one or the other?"

"And voilà! BENJAMIN pensively reflects, that is obviously why the 6th Commandment explicates nothing, neither the "who", or the "when" nor how, nor why.

The truth lies in "the intentions and finalities" of the acts of *both* the aggressor and defender. This is the truth that Justice must weigh on both sides of the scale. And the ruling can be made neither too rigidly nor too simplistically.

The 6th Commandment is vague, floating in a vacuum, so that human justice be sought and found in the eyes that observe, the ears that hear, the thoughts that explicit. In brief the 6th Commandment's directions to a "jury of peers" could be enounced as follows: FIND WHO ATTEMPTED TO DOMINATE BY THREATENING TO INTERRUPT THE FLOW OF LIFE.

The 6th law remains very conspicuously imprecise in regard with the designated victim, the circumstances involved...It is for human justice to adjust, adapt to all the circumstances, times, manners, and psychological realities, as humanity progresses on the ladder of evolution. This is how justice is rendered in the civilized nations deeply influenced by the descendants of the pioneer emigrants from ancient Egypt, the 12 tribes of Exodus."

And BENJAMIN stopped. His face suddenly turned around, offering to our view the back of his head. Tiny multicolored sparks crackled over his long curly hair now chaotic and unruly. His friendly eyes separated from his face sparkling with joy, hover freely in space. Then the whole scene gradually stabilizes, the particles of virtual substance progressively recreating the familiar face of BEN FRANKLIN.

"Is that the final conclusion?" asks Albert, with a resolute tone.

"No that is not all, responds our celestial Master, that is not all. I still have to teach you this: the divine messenger who engraved the 6th sacred law did not deem it necessary to designate the potential victims humankind could threaten on its rise to global planetary dominion. He decided that human beings would be free, totally free.

Again, we may ponder: Who should we not kill? The tree in the forest? The rooster in the barnyard? The fish in the pond? The deer in the mountain? Or the human newborn child? The victims will not be specifically designated so that the intention not to terminate life is the only proposition of this message, it and nothing else.

In the hope that human beings during their ascending evolution on the path that leads to the celestial kingdoms, freely expand the circle of life forms to which the murder taboo will be applied. In order that there shall be no more human instinct to terminate life, whatever form is encountered and whatever the place it is met..."

Angel YELIYAEL reinforces BEN FRANKLIN'S lesson: "*That is justly why the Ten Commandments of MOSES are not obsolete or perishable, for they are truly scalable and evolutive. Humankind evolves with them and makes them evolve at the same time it develops.*

Thanks to these Sacred Ten laws the human covenant is sealed with the Supreme Creator for eternity.

The Ten Laws are interactive; and they are themselves living laws interacting with living beings. Thus interrupting their flow would also interrupt the flow of Life.

The creation of the Ten Commandments is a perfect Sphere, a Sepher-Torah[71]*: each phrase, each word, each letter is a "Universal Key" that opens and releases the message of the TOTALITY."*

BENJAMIN, mixed tears of melancholy and happiness streaming on his face, continues:

"All utterances pronounced on our worlds vibrate in unison

71 Sepher Torah: Hebrew words which designate most often the Old Testament. Literally they mean: The Book (Sepher) of the Law and Wisdom (Torah). Also the word Sepher is the root for many words in many languages: Sphere-Cipher-Safari- and many others. The word Torah is root for Terra, Tour, Tower, Tarot, and many others.

with the music of the spheres. Our mind-spirit picks up these notes as fruit donated by the tree of universal knowledge. Each fruit conveys the sounds and rhythms of a new truth, a new beauty, unlike any other and yet so close to all its sisters and all its brothers.

All the living beings speak the same language, ARCHAE LINGUA, single language with multiple resonances known to all voyagers, explorers, pioneers, builders of new worlds.

The source Verb is given by the Heavens to all those who want to listen and hear it, in spite of the deceiving din and disturbing clamor interposed by the incessant prattle of ordinary human societies.

It is the duty of those who can Hear and Speak this Universal Language to raise their Voices and Songs and thank the Angels, their companions, their future celestial guides for exploring, beyond the ocean of Death, the new continent of Life and Liberty."

50. Interval.

WE SAID FAREWELL TO BENJAMIN FRANKLIN, certain we shall see him again, but uncertain about the "when" and "how" of our next meeting.

Upon entering the seraphic trance preceding departure, I glimpsed at BENJAMIN standing nearby his beautiful cherry wood desk, finely adorned with artistically designed geometric marquetry.

Surrounded by a golden aura lightly streaked with purple veins BENJAMIN was pointing at YELIYAEL, beaming from his forefinger a dense stream of microscopic electrical energy particles, thousands of photons reaching by successive bursts the dome still half-open of our time-space angelic ship.

I discerned, like wintry frost on a windowpane, inscribed on the diaphanous substance of YELIYAEL, series of ancient cuneiform characters, similar to those engraved on antique clay tablets in Mesopotamia 4,500 years ago.

Before comfortably settling in the alert unconsciousness of enseraphment, I remembered that MOSES, at the end of our meeting at Mount Nebo, also cast signals towards our angelic navigator...I thought: So BENJAMIN FRANKLIN well knows our future destination, but he chooses to let us free to discover the time and space of our next journey...

Vive l'aventure! Vive la vie! I fell asleep and dreamed of Angels.

Chapter Seven

Strangers in Paradise

51. Where are we...When?... Who are we?...

OUR AWAKENING THIS TIME is very slow, gradual, hesitant…

Where are we?

… …. … …   When?.. … …   Who are we?

Strangeness…None of the usual sensations while emerging from enseraphment…Everything here seems odd, and even more, utterly foreign…I can sense more than hear the multilayered echoes of an immense celestial song, surging from far away, a cosmic chorale of angelic voices maybe…

In my inner sanctum I hum a very ancient Andalus song whose melody alternatively clings to and falls off my lips.

Words stretch and contract, depending on the elastic state of my consciousness, oscillating between me Shimeha and no-me-at-all, caressing like a slow moving pendulum all the nuances of presence and absence, being and non being, separation and union with the world...

Where am I? Who am I? What are we? When are we?

My awakening is slow, gradual hesitant...I am alone, I am not alone...Albert's ironic humor traverses my misty memory, am I alone? I am entirely surrounded by a lite phosphorescent blue gaseous aura; powerful translucent lightning flashes crisscross a space without horizon, cobalt, turquoise, ultramarine, indigo shades spring from the black abyss, streaking across the firmament, ricocheting from star to star, and fall with a crash into an immense moiré lake, boundless liquid mirror of amber color…

Ideal lake, honey lake fluid like ambrosia...From the depths of my memory ancient reminiscences emerge; slowly decant into my flowing psyche an archaic hymn chanting the delights of a Promised Land:

From all horizons of life
On our way we rise
Towards the land streaming
With milk pure,
Honey suave,
And ambrosia divine.

52. The Corridors of Paradise. Off Standard Time. Eternity.

THIS TIME WE HATCHED OUT of our angelic time-space vessel without ele-landing, for nothing here resembles a land; nothing surrounding us offers the support of a dense solid matter, not even a substance slightly opaque.

Angel YELIYAEL also has adopted a different aspect, his hyper translucent veils stretching out of sight; he seems to have no more substance, no identifiable form. A crystalline voice is reaching us, although we cannot detect its source:

(((((((((((*I am YELIYAEL*)))))))))))

sending a message to SHIMEHA and ALBARDAN. When we left the sphere of blessed Benjamin Franklin's virtual residence, we connected the ele-guided circuits which led us to a miniature transitional station.

Up to then, your two VI-IMAGO-LIVING-IMAGE coordinates had always been embedded within my angelic substance. On that transcendental-transitional sphere, ultimate limitless frontier between sub-microcosm and ultra-macrocosm, our ship has been ARCHAE-ANGELIZED, fitted with ARCHANGELIC powers and hyper space-time coordinates, sole able to transfer us to this "NO PLACE", this here where we are and are not. Do not ask me why and how, the mystery is as total for me as it is for you..."

Away from our time-space ship, en route transformed into an archangelic vessel, we now literally float in the wide currents of an arachnean matrix replete with nourishing essential life waves.

A soothing melodious trill touches the pulsating circumference of my personal consciousness, sinuously emerging from myself and simultaneously from outside my self...

"Shimeha, Shimeha, I think we have entered PARADISE!"

YELIYAEL's joyful effulgence emanates from his moving wave particles of light, flowing like the fresh laughter of a happy child:

"PARADISE is MIKDASH ADONAI[72] *the Holy of Holies...Neither you, Shimeha nor you Albardan nor I YELIYAEL can transfer and reside there...Paradise is not a destination within our reach, since we do not possess the energy frequencies to harmonize with ADONAI, the D N A of the Absolute Universal Force.*

To acquire perfect attunement with Paradise frequencies, we, time-space creatures must trek the immeasurable pilgrim's paths, passing through thousands stages-lives, birth experiences, death intervals, mutations, transitions, metamorphoses, resurrections.

In our actual archangelized form of existence, we have ap-

---

72 Mikdash Adonai: Hebrew common translation = the sacred living place of the Adon, the Lord of Lords. As deciphered from Archae Lingua: the womb (Mi), in which Concentrates and Sums the gravitational force (K) of the divine (D) Sun-fires (SH) of all universes. See Hebrew version of the Song of Moses -Exodus 15-17 Ou mikdash adonai konenou yadekha.

proached the closest possible to BAYT HA MIKDASH.[73], the PARDES, PARADISE.[74] Behold! We have entered the ***Corridors of Paradise****!*

The Corridors of Paradise are attuned, harmonized, to achieve synchronization between the "elevated Divines", the "very perfect paradized" beings and the time-space pilgrims whose journey has not been completed, those as yet on the quest, the path, the way..."

"The Corridors of Paradise, how surprising this name, how beautiful, I thought..."

Successive waves of powerful rays of light, yellow and cobalt blue lightning streaks, storm my inner vision. And wherever I rest my gaze, panoramically, like a soft wide stamp it impresses, all around me, still reflections of flowers, trees with green foliage, colorful birds, hills, large rivers flowing into golden sea...then the reflections come alive, leaves rustle in the breeze, curvaceous fragrances emanate from pistils, exotic animals, slow or swift, move in all dimensions of a powerful nature, dazzling with life...

I turn my head, marveling at all the beauty emerging before me. Whenever my gaze moves, to the right, or deeper, or to the left, surge even more colors, more shapes, more dancing emotions...

"HERE, comments YELIYAEL, *each thread of existence "ME-SELF" is entwined with a NOT-SELF, weaving a kind of being whose external life is unified with inner life.*

Here everyone is at once "within oneself" and "out of oneself", both self-identity and alterity-otherness, the whole is one and one is much more than the whole."

And I understand, laughing and crying at the same time, I understand that I am present in the totality of all the universes, past and future. I am inserted in a holographic universe, where each point exists by itself within its particular coordinates, in its small

---

73 Bayt ha mikdash: in Hebrew = House of the Holy Ark of Covenant in the Temple. Also one of several names of Paradise.

74 Pardes: Hebrew root of Paradise, Paradis, Paradisio. In vernacular Hebrew it means wondrously fruitful orchard. In Archae Lingua, and Kabalah par= peri=fruit, result of, produce of; and des=divine essences. Therefore pardes=wondrous fruits directly issued from divine essences, hence Paradise.

and humble position as a single point in the midst of the whole universe, while it contains the totality of the information composing the cosmic whole.

YELIYAEL: "*As in an ideal hologram, each individual point of the virtual image may be extracted from the whole, and reproduce out of itself the totality of the hologram. In bio-mathematical language describing physical reality, each body cell holds its position and acts as a specialized cell, bone or liver or blood.*

However, if and when cells are extracted or isolated, each cell shall signal it potentially contains the "whole" body and can physically reproduce every detail of "all" the living body from which it has been extracted…"

Angel YELIYAEL's words carried on a Gregorian chant reverberate in my consciousness, their clear resonance, amplified by the rumbling echo of a colossal cathedral nave. To the perfect musicality of his words responds a simultaneous perfect "silenciality".

"HERE, intones Angel YELIYAEL, *in this place-no place, all our thoughts and emotions manifest instantly as an existential presence, a real presence, albeit not stable, not fixed, utterly fluidic and pleasantly metamorphic.*

Here, in the Corridors of Paradise, all creatures, presently including us, move and expand within the original fluids substance of perpetual creation.

The profound transfiguration which has been effected within us on the Archangel's sphere of Mutation enables us to live and experience the unity of the whole and the specificity of each part, simultaneously, at the conscious level."

"I understand, chimes in ALBARDAN, here, none of our thoughts will provoke a "clash", a "discord"; no thoughts, no sensations-emotions can be disharmonic, everything harmoniously exists in perfect synideation and synaesthesia."

As I contemplate in my imagination the various geometric shapes engendered in correspondence with YELIYAEL's and Albert's words, a slow and soft chant crosses the barrier of my lips:

"Have we been archangelized during transit on the transcendental sphere in order to achieve super control over our minds?"

"On the contrary, intones ALBARDAN with an ample voice intertwined with a syncopated melody in muted tones, here each of us is "one" perfectly tolerated by the "totality"...we have entered the realm of perfect tolerance. Each of us is 100% free and 100% tolerated."

"Yes, 100% Tolerance and Zero Intolerance" agrees YELIYAEL joining his chant to Albardan's melody, thus producing a musical harmonic duet that penetrates everything from inside and outside.

A gigantic bubble of clear sparkling crystal suddenly soars and metamorphoses gradually into a Gothic ogival arch. Now a huge cathedral stands over and around us, clear and bright, decorated with munificent rose windows of pure colors chiseled as finely as lace. I see the silhouette of Albardan, who is studying a bas-relief carved at the foot of a column, while attentively listening to the explanations of Angel YELIYAEL, now wearing a long white robe, long hair, in all ways resembling a genuine ancient Gallic druid.

YELIYAEL: "*Here, in the Corridors of Paradise, woman, man, Angel, uniting our thoughts, our reminiscences and our hopes, we are building a cathedral altogether ephemeral and permanent, bright and shaded, immanent and transcendent, sculpting its walls, composing stained glasses, carving portals, inserting the buds of our questions and the blossom of celestial answers.*"

In a deafening crash of thunder a giant lightning flashes across the immense nave, zigzags between columns, firing up in passing massive candles that suddenly illuminate the little side chapels which hitherto had remained in darkness. The whole cathedral is animated now, candle flames project dancing shadows on stonewalls, wondrous stained glass colors vibrate with life.

But, utterly terrified, I threw myself on the slab-stoned floor, arms extended like a supplicant, pressed by an invisible presence, an irrepressible force...Forehead against the cold floor of the cathedral, waiting for the imminent punishment that had just been heralded by violent thunder cracks. The overwhelming simple joy I sensed at the sight of the fabulous cathedral I had helped build has vanished, shattered by this brutal terror.

I cry, my tears watering the seeds buried in my Jewish child's memory. I entered a church! I built a Christian church! I crossed the boundaries that separate established religions! The flood of my fears is dissolving my hopes; I am afraid that thunder is MOSES' voice, the Great Prophet of the Hebrews urgently coming down to judge me and punish me...

"*Stand up Shimeha*! orders a stentorian voice muffled by the gentleness of a caress on my shoulders stiffened by suffering, I am MOSES, the man you met at Mount Nebo, the Egyptian Musaeus, the founder of the Keltic Co-Elet Mission, the messenger of the Sacred Ten Commandments, destined to facilitate the ascent of all men and all women to the Celestial Paradise...

Like you, like Albardan, like Angel YELIYAEL I have projected my thoughts, my hopes and my love for life, and I contributed with you to the reconstruction of this magnificent and magical cathedral of Chartres, here in the Corridors of Paradise. I love the proportions of its architecture, I love its engravings, its sculptures and symbols; I love the contrasting colors of its stained glasses; I love its master architects and its masons; I love its foundations and the rivers secretly flowing under its transept; I love the majestic resonance of its organ. I love every detail and I love its totality, I love its past, present and future; I love those who protect it and those who visit it, I love the route it traces, for all of you, women and men, towards the Heavens…"

"HALELUYAH![75] HALELUYAH!" exclaimed Albardan and YELIYAEL, in unison.

---

75 Halelu-yah: transliteration from original Hebrew found 24 times in the Old Testament, generally transcribed as Praise the Lord. Archaeo-Linguistic decoding: 1/ha= the universe pervading spirit 2/ lelu=reciprocal enlightening links, one coming from the Divine (le=lh) , the other lu= emanating from the "praiser" to the Divine/ 3/yah= Divine Force casting and receiving. Haleluyah in Archae Lingua thus means: Sense of Joy-Ecstasy the Human heart-spirit experiences from his immersion in the Divine Field Force. Origin of the word ho-ll-y, which contains all the consonants-vibrations of Ha-Le-Lu-Yah! A vibrating trigger for direct communication with the Divine, in churches and synagogues.

"HALELUYAH!" I responded in a timid, uncertain voice. Despite the assurances given by MOSES, now looking very much like a Knight Templar, long curly hair reaching his broad shoulders, gently standing in front of me, I was still afraid of being victim of an illusion I had myself created.

And MOSES, simply, as a man of Earth addressing a woman from Earth said:

"Shimeha, I would love to hear you decipher in details the First Commandment. Please do it in the manner of a learned Rabbi, a Master of Talmud who would liberate himself from his Pharisee prison, to walk free on the royal road of pure Kabalah."

Stage fright! I am like paralyzed by the request of this extraordinary interlocutor, Prophet MOSES himself. So I try to resist and argue:

"Master, O MOSES, if I speak freely I shall offend the Jewish conventional Rabbis for having revealed secrets they want to keep as privileges for themselves. I shall provoke their anger and ignite their furor for daring disclose the mystical core ideas of Kabalah, I who, to their eyes, is an ignorant woman, a nobody."

"This does not reflect all what you think" rejoins MOSES.

"Yes, I also understand the sagest among the sage Rabbis have had many good reasons for protecting, over the centuries, the precious knowledge encrypted in the Kabalah science. And I admire the courage and resilience of those who have preserved the integrity of the greatest and maybe the only authentic Kabalah book, the Sepher Torah[76]. In spite of all dangers, repudiations, burning at the stake, auto da fe, insults, humiliations, social discrimination, they made certain that every verse, every word, every syllable, every letter, every dot, every sound of the original ARCHAE LINGUA has been preserved intact, undamaged, each copy of the Torah exact, integral."

ALBARDAN: "This feat is comparable to the replication of

76 Besides the word Torah, the Old Testament is also designated as Tanakh, which translates into: «that which is "revealed to you". On the other hand the word Kabalah translates into: that which "I receive and accept". Therefore the major book of Kabalah is the Torah.

heaps of grains resting on a gigantic checkerboard. Each "copy" would necessitate the counting of the grains on each pile for each black and white square, the replication of the exact position of each grain, on surface and inside, each layer, each orientation…"

YELIYAEL: *"All Angels can do that easily; Archangels accomplish similar feats customarily….but humans, for such an achievement need, and must obtain, celestial help."*

I heartily continue answering MOSES' question:

"On the other side of the coin, most Rabbis, as well as other religionists end up jailing themselves behind the impenetrable intellectual fences they have devotedly erected to protect the divinely revealed knowledge… "

"And, intervenes ALBARDAN, if, coming Spring they discover a grain-letter has started germination, aiming at expressing the irrepressible will of life renovation it contains,…the defenders, now jailers, cut the surging sprout, so attempting to prevent a new expression of life…"

MOSES, in a firm and tender voice:

"But the master book of Kabalah-Torah still exists, has not been buried in an unknown abyss, not destroyed in fires, not flooded in deluges, and ARCHAE LINGUA, within the Hebrew language and all languages still echoes on planet Earth…"

My stage fright now dissolved, I continue arguing with MOSES:

"And the millions non-Israelites, all those who know nothing of Jewish tradition, a discussion on the model of the ZOHAR, the Book of Light, will appear obscure, abstract, boring!

You know, MOSES, the unruly children of the Twelve Tribes of the Exodus, with the passing of time became Christians, Hindus, Buddhists, Mohammedans, Taoists, they are not familiar with the traditional Jewish way of thinking, which even their savants regard as outdated, too dry, too rigorist, too complex. In short, the style of the Zohar seems tedious, it lacks pizzazz and modernity..."

"I know all that, says MOSES...But you did not cite the Americans...They are all at the same time, Anglo Saxon, Latino, African, Japanese, Chinese, Arab, Jew…a true alchemical potion in a large boiling container...a blend of all the cultural riches and languages of the world…

Moreover they are enthusiastic and daring. America is the Federation of the new pioneering tribes, ready to launch the ships that shall explore vast extraterrestrial expanses and new dimensions of the mind...It is these new men and women you shall address to explain the First Commandment, in the *most archaic* manner possible."

"Speak up, encourages MOSES, as if you were sitting on the ground, two thousand years ago, under the shade of a millenarian olive tree, firmly rooted on a hillside in Canaan.

Open your memory Shimeha and give generously, give to these children of America a piece of the spirit of ancient Galilee, Safed, Tiberias, Nazareth, open for them the recesses of your personal abyssal ageless ancestral archives…and tell them, in the manner of old masters, the manner of Jewish Kabalah, the Kabalah of Jesus himself, yes, Shimeha reveal the contains of the First Commandment, the message the celestial envoy engraved on the slab I held in my arms on Mount Horeb in the Sinai desert.

Tell the Americans the ultimate knowledge recorded on stone tablets, the AVEN TORAH[77], tell them the truth about their ADVENTURE, talk to them, they will understand!"

I started to cry again. Heavy tears, without control, covered my cheeks...An extraordinary heat wave invaded my body mind and soul...I felt myself disappearing, melting...a gigantic blowing wind swirled me away…all consciousness stopped…"me" was here no more….was nowhere else... "me" was no more…

77 Aven= stone, torah= revelation. aven torah: the stone receptacle of the revelation of the 10 Commandments. AvenTora is the root of many words in many languages. Italian aventura French aventure, English adventure. In Sanskrit avanatara means "Propitious Advent".

53. The Memory of Centuries.

SHIMEON BAR YOHAI [78], *the verb of life* says:

It is said by the sages, the witnesses of time: And from a fountain in the firmament a celestial fluid streamed through open gates and the celestial fluid traced in letters of shining gold the first word of the 1st Law:

ANOKHI
I AM.

HANINA HA KADMI, *the ancient* says:

When the fountain ceased to flow, the gates of the firmament closed, and behold, a giant granite rock split open, a stream of lava burst out of the rock and liquid ember engraved in letters of fire the second word:

ADONAI YEHOVAH[79]
THE ETERNAL

SHIMEON BAR YOHAI, *the verb of life* says:

When the fountain of the firmament stopped flowing, and the rock closed the opening of the volcano which had awakened, a powerful whistle sound was heard, and suddenly a cobra appeared and spat a long stream of purple venom which designed and engraved the letters of the Third word of the First Law:

ELOHEKHA
YOUR GOD

---

78 Shimeon Bar Yohai: famous Rabbi and Kabalist who lived in Israel in Roman times after the destruction of the Temple in 70 ad. Usual translation of the name Bar Yohai is: Master (bar) of the Verb of Life (yo-hai).

79 All Biblical exegetes pronounce Adonai whenever the written word is in fact Yehovah. The verbal formula Adonai Yehovah is commonly translated as "the Eternal".

HANINA HA KADMI*, the ancient:*

As it is said at the very beginning of the First Law:
"I am the Lord thy God."
Then humans began to inquire, questioning and searching:
Who says: "I am"? Who is He who Is "I am"? Mi Hou?
He is ANOKHI, the source of sources, the fluid of Infinity,
He is the founder of Attraction.

SHIMEON BAR YOHAI*, the verb of life* says*:*

ANOKHI says I AM ADONAI *YEHOVAH*
I am the source of Infinite,
Potential of the Eternal Principle
I am the Intelligence of the Assembler.
I am "First Person".
I AM ADONAI *YEHOVAH*,
I qualify My Self "ADONAI *YEHOVAH*"
and ADONAI *YEHOVAH* is my Identity.

SHIMEON says more: As it is said:

ANOKHI "*YEHOVAH*", I AM "ADONAI *YEHOVAH*".
Who is HE who claims "I AM a Person"?
He is *YEHOVAH* THE ETERNAL.
Who is THE ETERNAL? He is *YEHOVAH*.

YUDA THE YOUNG asks:

Who is "I AM THE ETERNAL"?
What is this living hidden emotion, which emanates from the person of ANOKHI, and radiates to reveal itself
as *YEHOVAH* THE ETERNAL?

SHIMEON *the verb of life* asks:

ANOKHI *YEHOVAH* ADONAI, what does this mean?
Clearly and simply I translate it by I AM THE ETERNAL.
Is that all? The message is ended? Who is THE ETERNAL
whose sacred name is ADONAI *YEHOVAH*?
HE IS the Free Breath of Eternity in a State of Life.

HANINA HA KADMI, *the ancient*:

As it has been said "ANOKHI-I AM" was revealed by the celestial fluid on Mount Horeb.
It is the universal fluid that flows everywhere, that pervades the whole.
ANOKHI I AM is the Absolute of the "Infinites", and through HIM what is nothing and nowhere, becomes everything and everywhere.
By HIM, that what is "Not-finite", the Infinite, penetrates all that which is Finite, thus metamorphosing all Finites into fluidic, ever changing beings and things.

HANINA HA KADMI, *the ancient* says:

Who is ANOKHI?
ANOKHI is "WHO I AM". Mi Ani? It is "MY PERSON IN *INFINITY*"
Who is ADONAI?
YEHOVAH is "WHAT I AM", Ma Ani? MY IDENTITY IN *ETERNITY*.

SHIMEON BAR YOHAI, *the listener of the Verb of Life* says:

Thus taught our master Rabbi Akiba [80]:
ANOKHI is the person of God, the Infinite Fluid.
YEHOVAH is the Identity of God, the Fire of Eternity.
That is why it is said by our forefathers,
ZIKNE HA YAMIM [81], the witnesses of old:
Thus the messenger of God, released the SHAMAYIM, the Firmament Waters, to manifest ANOKHI, and released the Fire Earth ERETZ, to manifest ADONAI *YEHOVAH*.

YUDA THE YOUNG says:

Now I understand the Verb of Life,
ANOKHI-I AM "HE WHO IS".
I AM is the Infinite Fluid of Attraction.

---

80 Rabbi Akiba: famous Rabbi and Kabalist in Israel (circa.50–135 AD). Master of the greatest academy of Talmud and Kabalah studies (more than 6,000 students).
81 Zikne ha yamim: in Hebrew means: our unknown forebears from very very old times, who have initiated the legacy of cosmic consciousness.

I AM is Expansion,
I AM is the Spreader, the Sower.
I AM is Attraction.
I AM is the Convener, the Unifier.
I AM is both the Spreader and the Unifier.
I AM is the Complete Encompassing Breath of Life.

HANINA HA KADMI, *the ancient* says:

Now I know the original manifestation of life: THE ETERNAL.
YEHOVAH is the quality by which "I AM" is qualified,
the Substance from which I AM is WHO HE IS.
Thus God finds Himself and recognizes Himself
by being Eternity, ADONAI *YEHOVAH* THE ETERNAL.

HANINA HA KADMI, *the ancient,* says:

I AM = ANOKHI = the INFINITE,
primordial Essence of the Matter (NO)[82].
I AM the Spirit of the Matter,
the Totality that spreads, penetrates and assembles,
the DIVINE PERSON, THE FLUID OF THE INFINITE.

I AM = ADONAI *YEHOVAH* = THE ETERNAL,
the UNIQUE manifestation of the Assembler,
Primordial Substance of the Spirit (HO)[83].
I AM the Substance of the Spirit.
I manifest as the Fruit, the Son,
the offspring of the Assembler,
the Central Fire which Centers Himself
and Concentrates Himself.[84]

---

82 No: the word a-No-khi is the first word of the first Commandment, and translates into "I" (am). In this formula A=Unknown Ancestral Force, akin to infinite. And No=Essence of Matter, akin to the Spirit of the Matter. The final Khi=Attract, Assemble, Unify, conveying the notion of friendliness and love.

83 Ho: the second word of the first Commandment, traditionally vocalized as Adonai in the stead of the written word Ye-Ho-vah. In this formula ye=The perfect ideal Acting Agent, ho=the Substance of the Spirit, and va=Life.

84 The ancient kabalistic tradition states that, simultaneously and perpetually, the Divine Force expands itself and Contracts Itself. In Hebrew Archae Lingua, Expansion= zim, and Contraction= tzoum. Thus the concept of tzim-tzoum designates the First and forever perpetuated motion of Creation.

I AM THE OFFSPRING, *YEHOVAH* ADONAI,
THE SON, THE FIRE OF ETERNITY.

SHIMEON *the verb of life* says:

ANOKHI the person of the Infinite Father
Identifies Himself in ADONAI *YEHOVAH*,
the Identity of the ETERNAL SON.

RABBI HANINA HA KADMI, *the ancient* asks:

Does Yuda the Young understand the third word
of the first sentence of the First Commandment of MOSES?

YUDA THE YOUNG responds:

Regarding the word ELOHEKHA,
it is taught that it means YOUR GOD,
as it is said : I AM THE ETERNAL THY GOD.

YUDA THE YOUNG chants:

ANOKHI ADONAI ELOHEKHA [85]
I AM *ANOKHI*:
This word was inscribed on the tablets of the law
by the celestial fluids. For I AM is the Verb of Waters,
the formless Infinite, a motion that penetrates all.

The ETERNAL *ADONAI YEHOVAH*:
This word was inscribed on the tablets of the Law
by the Fires of Earth.
For the Eternal is the concentrated energy of the nucleus,
the Center of all centers.
The Eternal is the principle of living Attraction.
YEHOVAH the ADON is the Lord,
the Son, the First Manifestation.
He is the kernel Primordial Substance of the Spirit, the Eternal.
Thus, the Son of the Infinite I AM
is the Father-Mother of the Eternals.

---

85 These are the three first words of the first Commandment of Moses. They commonly translate into: I am the Eternal thy God.

THY GOD *ELOHEKHA*:
This word frightens me,
I cannot understand a word that was inscribed on the tablets of the law by the venom of the cobra[86].
My mind is darkened. I am dying to my own consciousness.
My consciousness effaces itself…fades away…

RABBI SHIMEON, *master of the verb of life* says to Yuda the Young: Heighten your courage and open your mind to the Light of Life. For here resides the great mystery of Creation.

ANOKHI I Am *Who* I Am.
Infinity, the Fluid Initiator,
the Father of the Whole.

YEHOVAH I Am *Wha*t I Am.
Eternity, offspring of Infinity, the Son,
Lord of Revelations, Principle of All Manifestations,
Father-Mother of the Deities.

ELOHEKHA Thy God.
I Am your GOD
To WHOM are addressed those words
"ELOHEKHA", "Your GOD"? Who is "YOU"?
One knows who God is, but who is "You"?
Who is the "other" in the universe,
the "ME" to whom GOD says "You"?
The I AM is revealed to us
by *YEHOVAH* ADONAI the Eternal Fire.
But who will reveal the "You"?
Him who shall say: O YOU my GOD!

And it is then that God answers:
I AM THE ETERNAL YOUR GOD. The "ME" and the "YOU" recognized themselves at the same instant.
"ELOHEKHA" "YOUR GOD". Who hears the word scripted

86 Cobra = ko ba ra meaning co-herent (ko) creation (bara). Co-creation born of co-operation between "I' and "You".

by the venom of the cobra?
He who hears it, let him adhere!
As it is said: "If you hear me, adhere and follow me."

RABBI HANINA HA KADMI, *the ancient* says:

Now I remember. I knew Mattathias the tax collector, the apostle of Jesus, the ADON–the Lord, Son of the Eternal, who said this to anyone who would hear:
"He who listens well finds salvation."

RABBI SHIMEON says:

Whoever hears this, he who understands this, he is saved and starts on the road, the path of the pilgrim who returns from the confines of the infinite cosmic spaces to the nucleus eternal center, the Great Revealer.

And he who starts on the path adheres and says: "It is towards You that I am moving, for, you are "Magid', my GuiDe, my GoD.

Thus all the living beings who hear and understand, they start *speaking*. The living beings turn their face towards the Creator and chant:

"*YEHOVAH* ADONAI YOU ARE THE ETERNAL,
You awoke me, You revealed yourself to me,
and here is my response: O YOU MY GoD "

And it was at this very moment, says SHIMEON, that the creation set ablaze, resonated, was formed, manifested. Motion began. And the Universal Engenderer, the Ultimate Creator, spoke out loud:

ANOKHI *YEHOVAH* ELOHEKHA
I AM THE ETERNAL THY GOD.

YUDA THE YOUNG questions:

The mystery of ELOHEKHA, has it been unveiled?
Who is this "you"? Who is the one who has heard everything from the beginning? Who has heard the word of God even before it resounded in the Universe?

Who is the one who spoke before knowing how to speak?

Who heard before having ears to hear?

Who is the "who" among the infinite variety of creatures
who perceived the fluid of Infinity before a single droplet
reached him? He who saw the light that shone
while only obscurity reigned?
He who proclaimed "ATA ELOHAY" "YOU ARE MY GOD",
as he was still mute and wordless?

SHIMEON BAR YOHAI says:

With regard to the other worlds, O YUDA, I cannot answer you, but regarding our world, the "me" who says "You" to God, this one I know who he is.

For, the ME to whom God said "YOU", God has designated him. As it is said: "I AM THE ETERNAL YOUR GOD".

HANINA HA KADMI, *the ancient* asks:

Who is he? Will you tell me this before I leave this Earth, and start my journey toward my Lord, the ADON?

SHIMEON BAR YOHAI says: I will tell you now:

The one who has joined our world and has saved us from oblivion, the one who opened the door of the kingdoms of the spirit is *the cobra*, the mute, who has projected what was most precious to him, the essence-venom it had retained over millions of years in his innermost, and gave it to engrave, on the stone that MOSES held, the third word of the First Commandment: ELOHEKHA YOUR GOD.

YUDA THE YOUNG:

Thus all serpents responded to the call. But if it is so, why the ADON, the Lord, as it is said, cursed the serpent of Eden, and all the serpents on Earth?

SHIMEON BAR YOHAI replies:

Neither all serpents responded to the call, nor all the cobras. Only this one responded who was on Mount Horeb, this identity, this personality, this cobra, *the Ko-Ba-Ra.*

This cobra was born from a long chain of cells-of-knowledge and he alone held the memory. This cobra preserved the memories of all his ancestors who received the revelation.

As soon as he perceived the activation of his memory he went into hiding, to secretly brood new little cobras to whom he passed on the instruction to conceal their cells-of-divine-knowledge.
But all the other serpents of all species began to hunt for that special cobra and his offspring with the will to interrupt the thread of their life, for they were jealous, coveting their uniqueness.

The enlightened Nabi Prophet Kobara fled far away and hid under a large rock at the summit of Mount Horeb.

As he possessed a perfect spark of the living verb he remained hidden for millions of years without eating or drinking.

He waited and waited, living, totally asleep, totally alert.

He waited for the time when MOSES twice climbed the mountain, and twice this cobra heard the call of God ELOHEKHA.

In his millenary mind he transcoded the Divine sounds into words and engraved them on the tablets with its precious venom.

Thus was completed the union of the Trinity.

ANOKHI...	*I AM.........*	FATHER OF THE INFINITE
YEHOVAH	*THE ETERNAL*	SON OF INFINITY, AND FATHER-MOTHER OF ETERNITY
ELOHEKHA	*YOUR GOD*	THE HIGH GUIDE FOR THOSE WHO VIBRATE AND RESPOND WITHIN THE COMMUNITY OF THE SPIRIT, YOU WHO FOREVER ADHERE TO THE SPIRIT OF SANCTITY

YUDA THE YOUNG asks SHIMEON:

O my Master, who passed on to you that what you are teaching me now?

SHIMEON BAR YOHAI says:

I received it from Rabbi Akiba, who received it from Rabbi Hanania, who was told by Rabbi Dossa, who received it from the great Yohanan Ben Zakkai, the giant Light, who himself received it from a Master of Mystery whose name he never disclosed.

54. The Stellar Cathedral.

THE RABBI'S VOICES GRADUALLY FADED. Silence reigned in my mind. I abruptly regained clear consciousness standing immobile in the eye of a furious photonic hurricane. Motionless at the center of this maelstrom I was gazing at myriads stars, comets, suns, cosmic spirals moving amid vast empty lightless, nameless expanses...Then without walking, without flying, without moving, I headed towards the cathedral of Chartres embedded in the Corridors of Paradise.

From afar, I hear and feel the voice of YELIYAEL conversing with Albardan:

"*After this savant debate, Yuda the Young and Hanina the Ancient took leave of their host and Shimeon Bar Yohai was left alone in his secret dwelling.*

In this deep windowless room shaded like the grotto of his inner self, he has lived for nearly 10 years, never emerging outside. His son Rabbi Eliezer the famous detective, the chaser of criminals who swarmed in these troubled times, came to see him once a week, every Friday at dusk, for a solemn entry into Shabbat. Both were worshipping the Divine and studying the Torah until the moment when Shabat, the day of glory, was leaving to visit another country, another world, another solar system."

Back in the nave I saw my companions were not alone, and many aspects of the cathedral had changed. Looking more attentively I knew suddenly where I was!

Golden statues, metallic dry sounds of pilgrim's sticks slamming on the floor, motley crowd, whispers in all the languages of the world, pungent smell of incense floating in the aisles, no doubt, I had emerged in the Cathedral of Santiago de Compostella!

Albardan winked, beckoning me to join him in the center of the transept on a second row wooden bench facing the altar.

Still bedazzled by my extra temporal escapade in Galilee, I am now watching the funniest and most poignant spectacle created before my eyes in the Corridors of Paradise.

For, MOSES himself, has joined the eight young red-robed men at the center of the nave and, adding his enthusiasm to theirs, with his powerful arms pulls on thick ropes, rhythmically, propelling higher and higher, ever upwards, towards the top of the ogival ceiling, a huge silver censer spitting flames, dense clouds of blue smoke profusely spreading in the cathedral the mystical fragrance of burning incense[87].

And our playful friend Angel YELIYAEL in a majestic wide-open winged flight, sometimes follows sometimes precedes, the rapid censer-pendulum, broadly smiling to us at each passage, happy as a child on a swing.

"Ite missa est" murmured Albert as the spectacle and the Sunday pilgrims' mass ended. In awe, transparent and invisible to all, we exited the cathedral, and regrouped on the front plaza. MOSES, always paternal and empathetic, scanned my mind to make sure of

---

87 Censer: the famous Butafumeiro, weighing 80 kg , 180 lbs and measuring 1.60 m, 5 feet 4 inches in height. When in use in the cathedral, on special Sunday masses, it is filled with 40 kg, 85 lbs, charcoal and incense. Eight red-robed *tiraboleiros* pull the ropes and bring it into a swinging motion almost to the roof of the transept, reaching speeds of 60 km/h, 45 mph, and dispensing thick clouds of incense, spreading in the entire cathedral, over the crowd of local Spanish churchgoers, and pilgrims from all countries of the world.

my regained serenity.

MOSES: "The sage Rabbis of Galilee invoked by Shimeha helped us decipher and understand the profound meaning of the sonorities ANOKHI ADONAI ELOHEKHA, the first three essential words of the First Commandment:

I AM THE ETERNAL YOUR GOD.
I AM THE INFINITE UNITED TO THE ETERNAL ,
YOUR CENTER, YOUR FOCAL POINT.
I AM YOUR AWAKENER, YOUR ATTRACTOR "

"*But there is even more,* intervenes YELIYAEL. *The Commandment begins with "I am the Eternal your God ANOKHI* ADONAI ELOHEKHA", and the celestial messenger went on adding:

CHE HOTSETI OTEKHA	*Who extracted you*
MI ERETZ MITZRAIM	*from the land of Egypt,*
MI BAYT ÂVADIM	*from a house of slavery.*

ALBARDAN asks:

"What did the celestial messenger mean, when he cast those words? How does the affirmation "I AM THE ETERNAL THY GOD" connect with the confirmation of a historical transient event: WHO EXTRACTED YOU FROM THE LAND OF EGYPT A HOUSE OF SLAVERY? What is the meaning of those last words, when carefully deciphered?"

Angel YELIYAEL answers:

"The vibrations of the 1st Law orient the pilgrim souls advancing towards the Supreme Deity. These few words encode and contain the Secrets of the roads leading to the ultimate destination of the journey of the livings.

Those seven last words, apparently disconnected from the initial statement "I am the Eternal your God", enfold a detailed geo-cosmic map of the itineraries, peregrinations, stages and possible dead ends, dangers, that may be encountered.

They also evoke the exalting liberation from material slavery experienced by the living beings when they answer the call of ELOHKHA "My God the AWAKENER, the ATTRACTOR", the call hu-

mans hear and sense by the mind of their heart, in spite and beyond the signals of their five senses."

MOSES nods briefly and adds:

"The adventures that await the survivor souls, the more-than-living, are also described in the Egyptians and Tibetans Books of the Dead. The first divine law contains the secrets of these voyages, which must be retrieved from the text transmitted in ARCHAE LINGUA. It recounts the allegoric story of the "Exodus out of Egypt", loaded with obstacles, dramas, accidents, conflicts, adventures, projects, and unexpected happiness, consolation, rewards, and glories.

Thus it also conveys metaphorically the deed of "extraction out of the house of slavery", namely the state of stagnation, fixity, lack of fluidity, fear of change, fear of Truth and correlated fear of Death."

We are now sitting on the stairs leading down to the vast paved courtyard, attentive students readying to listen first, before questioning. Undetectable, we are traversed by walking pilgrims, who, backpacked, skin tanned by sun and rain, march up the stairway to complete their journey in the cathedral, at the end of the Camino de Compostella, the long pilgrims' road with many stages.

The divine master, the great MOSES, looks at me ironically, his eyes sparkling with fatherly goodness:

"Shimeha, long before you began your journey on the wings of the Angel you had clearly identified the message hidden under the veil of the 2nd Commandment: YOU SHALL NOT HAVE ANY OTHER GOD BEFORE MY FACE - Non habebis deos alienos coram me.

So tell us, with no detour, what you know of the secrets enclosed in the 2nd Commandment."

Albardan is startled, amused and surprised. I have kept this information private, never finding a favorable moment to share my thoughts on this topic. I always deferred, pondering, unsure whether I was or not on the right path. This time, at MOSES' personal request, I accept the challenge without dithering:

"The second sacred law is identified on Earth as the religious foundation of monotheism. On this law is based the dogma "There is only one God", assuming the text means: I am the only One God, any other deity is imaginary and false."

Albardan intervenes: "With per consequence the following tyrannical instructions: burn symbols and break artful statues, remove, even by violence, all beliefs in multiple local deities. Woe to superstitions and idolatry!"

I promptly rejoin: "And this attitude and odious outcome is wrong! Since the 2nd Commandment "YOU SHALL HAVE NO OTHER GOD BEFORE MY FACE" is not related to idolatry, does not prompt to punish polytheism, does not require tackling superstitions, nor burning magi nor prophetesses..."

"LOA YIHAYE LEKHA" intones YELIYAEL, on a slow rhythm, first like background music, then progressively more discernable. The 2nd Commandment, in ARCHAE LINGUA, accented like original Hebrew, unfolds its message of truth:

LOA YIHAYE LEKHA *You will not "make be"*
ELOHIM ACHERIM *other Deities*
ÂL PANAY *above My Face.*[88]

And MOSES himself continues: "Consider this: If there exist no "other gods" why would the divine messenger mention them, and command not to revere them above the I AM, the ONE?

Long before the emergence of monotheistic religions, Jewish, Christian and Mohammedan, the savants and sages of the great civilizations were aware of the unbreakable human union with the One Supreme Being. In truth the One Deity is revered since immemorial times. However, "as below, so above"! As many forms of terrestrial life are existing and evolving on Earth, as well there are in the heavenly kingdoms, many kinds of manifestations of celestial life[89]. Our ancestors were well informed of the existence and life of these celestial beings, and some were spiritually en-

---

88 New King James Version, Exodus 20-1 "You shall have no other gods before Me" The original Hebrew text says: "...no other gods higher than my face"
89 Celestial life: in private conversations with Angel Yeliyael, we learned these celestial beings exist as "non incarnated visitor spirits" as well as "bodied physical creatures" born on other advanced worlds and often identified as "extra-terrestrial visitors".

dowed enough to converse with them. Furthermore, all those Deities themselves, contrary to many humans, are perfectly cognizant of their ultimate origin, the One Eternal Supreme Creator of all existences." Silence

"Now SHIMEHA, continues MOSES extending his open right hand towards me, if this law does not only mean "You shall have no other gods before me", what does it really convey to men and women on Earth?"

SHIMEHA: "I have long studied these words. I reflected on their significance, analyzed their hermetic message, I dialogued with them and here is what they disclosed to me:

When you set out to join My Face,
heading to the Infinite and Eternal Space
of my Sacred Residence,
when you will seek the path
that leads to your ultimate source of existence,
you shall meet a multitude
celestial beings-gods-the ELOHIM[90]
puissant and powerful life forces
living creatures of the universe
who shall attract you to them.

You shall witness extraordinary feats,
you will be amazed-fascinated
by the beauties offered to you
on the path that leads you
towards union with the Infinite
who manifests as the Eternal.
Beware,
do not give in to the temptation
of stopping along the way,
saying: here I am, I reached the goal

---

90 Elohim: in Hebrew, is the plural form of Eloha, God. Hence Elohim means the Gods. Albeit, in more than 2500 occurrences in the Torah, the same plural form Elohim is always translated as One God. The only exception being the Second Commandment in which the same plural form Elohim is emphatically acknowledged as designating *multiple* Gods.

of my journey, because here I am enthused!
Am I not in the Divine kingdom?
For, behold, I am surrounded
by the puissant celestial ELOHIM! The Gods!
Pilgrim! Know, though, that you are not yet
at the end of your road,
because those are not God the Supreme.
These celestial Elohim-gods, are your brothers
and sisters, your alter ego, your ACHERIM,[91]
ultimately sons and daughters
of the same Unique Father-Son-Spirit.

And if you want to be united with them and to them
you will have to resist the fascination
exercised by their beauty upon you.
Mobilize the resources of your personality,
and your ability to communicate
with the Integral Invisible[92]
in order to continue on the path
leading to the Unique Law,
the Unique Truth,
the Presence of the Unique,
whereby thou shall be united
to your celestial brothers and sisters.

When finally you will enter
in my sacred Home,
the Infinite Center of all Eternals
it is your own living personality

91 Acherim: in Hebrew it means "the others". It also designates the "alter ego"; in that case, acherim means the others on an equal footing with me. A deeper reading of the word acherim delivers the root ach=brother, which by adding R becomes acher=the principle of being a brother; the plural form acherim means brotherhood. Therefore the words Elohim acherim, conventionally translated as "the other gods", also mean: "our brothers amongst the divine creatures". Thus the divine creatures and the humans, both have one only Father Creator, the One Supreme God.

92 Until the celestial pilgrim reaches the consciousness level of perceiving the "Face" of the Creator, until that last moment when the pilgrim comes before his face, he, the creator, remains invisible, veiled.

your integral identity,
which shall appear before My Face.

I stopped. Yet I feel an intense desire to continue listening to ARCHAE LINGUA revealing more words of Truth, messengers from beyond time and space, from elsewhere; the inspiring sounds of the Stars' Language are calling other meanings, other interpretations, multiple facets of a luminous sphere, transparent, intense and light as a free spirit. I did not want to stop this journey into the living invisible, I did not want to leave the broad way that leads to the Supreme Attractor ADONAI ELOHEKHA...

I remember, we all drifted quietly into the inner refuge of our freedom, wherein resides the infinite spark of the "I am the Divine", the truthful companion of our consciousness who keeps watch within each of us, for each of us, as the prophet said:

HINE LO YANOUM *And he shall neither slumber*
VE LO YISHAN *nor sleep*
SHOMER ISRAEL *the Guardian of Israel.*[93]

After a long silence, MOSES spoke to me:

"Shimeha, you know that ISRAEL is not a nation only defined by geographic place of birth or distinguished by institutional religionist peculiarities. First and foremost the people of Israel encompasses all men, women and celestial beings of *educated, intelligent and practiced Faith*, as revealed in the Sacred Ten Commands, wherever they live and roam, on Earth as well as in the Grand Universe.

He-She who wants to enter in the House of Israel, if He-She has searched and found the gate keys, let them enter! He-She who hears the cosmic universal call, responds!"

I observed attentively my two companions, Angel YELIYAEL and Albardan. Like me, they were radiant, transfigured by the heartbreaking beauty of MOSES, his truthfulness and profound goodness. I could feel they also were elevated by the pure joy of

93 Old Testament - Psalms 121- 4

being again in the presence of this great hero, after so many peregrinations and enlightening encounters.

MOSES, Musaeus the Master of the Mysteries of Egypt, the Sphinx, had finally agreed to open the door of the inner temple-academy, to let us hear his voice.

Timidly, I ask him to explain the arcane intricacies of the 3rd Commandment.

> YOU SHALL NOT INVOKE THE NAME OF THE ETERNAL THY GOD IN SUPPORT OF LIES BECAUSE THE ETERNAL DOES NOT LEAVE UNPUNISHED HE WHO INVOKES HIS NAME IN VAIN.

ALBARDAN, master of exact principles frowns and says:

"Is this not somewhat a repetition of the 9th Commandment DO NOT BEAR AGAINST YOUR NEIGHBOR A FALSE TESTIMONY?"

"No, replies MOSES, the 3rd Law is not a mere repetition of the 9th. The 9th Commandment concerns life on Earth, it is primarily addressed to terrestrial men and women. The 3rd Commandment must be understood from an entirely celestial perspective."

"That lifts a very small corner of the veil but does not add much light" I think silently.

MOSES, accomplished diplomat, says: "You shall have ample time to study the 3rd Commandment later...and I will not be the only instructor to help you raise it from the darkness in which it is buried since more than 3,500 years."

Oh! I know this tone...this "wrap up" rhythm suggests the very imminence of our separation. I am alerted, immediately panicked. I hastily interject: "And the Shabat! The 4th Commandment, the Law of the sacred Saturday rest. Can you reveal its mysteries, help us understand its true cosmic universal meaning?"

And Angel YELIYAEL, eager to provide assistance, promptly enounces, in a single breath:

> *REMEMBER THE SHABAT DAY TO SANCTIFY IT.*
> *FOR SIX DAYS YOU SHALL LABOR AND DO ALL YOUR WORK.*
> *BUT THE SEVENTH DAY IS A PAUSE FOR THE ETERNAL YOUR GOD;*
> *YOU SHALL NOT DO ANY WORK, YOU, YOUR SON*

OR YOUR DAUGHTER, YOUR MALE OR FEMALE SLAVE,
YOUR LIVESTOCK, OR THE ALIEN RESIDENT IN YOUR TOWNS.
FOR IN SIX DAYS THE ETERNAL MADE THE SKIES AND EARTH, THE SEA,,
AND ALL THAT IS IN THEM, BUT RESTED THE SEVENTH DAY
THEREFORE THE ETERNAL BLESSED THE SHABAT DAY
AND SANCTIFIED IT.

For a fleeting moment MOSES looked at the three of us with astonishment, as if he was suddenly facing a retarded trio competing for a prize in limited intelligence.

MOSES: "But this law is the simplest one, the most obvious, there is no mystery here! There is nothing to disclose, no message to decrypt, this law says everything it has to say, in an ordinary way, without extra finesse. It says what it says; it says only what it says…and it says everything there is to say on this subject."

MOSES continues:

"A welcome refreshing pause for the investigating mind, is it not? The Shabat is like a beautiful tree yielding nutritious and tasty fruits, everyone can reach out and pluck them. Everyone can sit under its shade or find shelter from stormy rain. The Shabat is the sacred day of rest, absolutely necessary for humans to liberate themselves from material slavery and work bondage, to regenerate, and build up the capacity to reach the shores of the spirit."

Shy and slightly quivering, I venture to intervene, at the risk of appearing stupid:

"O divine master of divine sciences, certainly this law appears to me not as simple as you state it is, and I confess I do not understand."

MOSES: "You do not understand the meaning of those words?"

SIMHA: "I understand all the words and their meaning, but..."

"So?" asks MOSES, wrinkling his forehead, his laughing eyes twinkling with irony.

Angel YELIYAEL promptly rushes to my rescue, giving me a few moments of respite to prepare my questions.

On the folds of his white veil now spectacularly extending widely over the entire front of the cathedral, huge banner floating in the wind, the Angel projects rotating swirling beams of light.

In front of us, unfurl colorful images of a majestic forest in the tones of the four seasons of nature. All is quiet and serene, when without the slightest hint, on the angelic panoramic screen, a thunderous storm breaks out, huge, strong brisk winds twist and crumple the banner now deeply soaked and darkened by a torrential rain. And before our anxious eyes tumbles and inexorably falls to the ground, the oldest and strongest oak tree in the forest...!!!

I turn to MOSES and question him silently: "A strong and venerable tree as Shabat can suddenly become a fragile and dangerous shelter? Nothing is ever simple..."

Then I, again, bravely confront the Master: "O MOSES, this Commandment is indeed a great mystery that I cannot elucidate unaided. Since, to enounce all the other important laws, so fundamental to the conscious enlightenment of evolving souls, individuals, societies and humanity, only a few chosen words have been sufficient:

Thou shall not steal genes, you shall not adulterate the truth, you shall not interrupt intentionally the flow of Life.

But, this 4th Law on the Shabat day of rest contains 41 Hebrew words. In contrast the 9th, 8th, 7th, 6th, 5th, even the 1st voluntarily strip details to allow humans to progress, let them be free to interpret, free to think, free to act.

However, visibly, the 4th Law about the weekly day of rest is detailed, explaining the what, when, how, and even why! The other laws allow unlimited free personal imagination, broad inner vision, but that one allowing no room for freedom itemizes thoroughly everyone and everything, and does not leave the slightest undefined corner."

MOSES raises his arms open palm facing me, in a gesture clearly intended to stop the impetuous flow of my indignant words, while he bursts into an unrestrained loud frank laughter.

Strange master of wisdom, MOSES! Always doing what we least expect of him, sometimes serious and aloof, often hermetic and enigmatic, at times spontaneous and impulsive.

His crisis of hilarity and dance of joy having calmed down, MOSES faces us, looks straight into my eyes and says:

"This law is a play-act, a joke of sort, inducing distraction, fun parenthesis, enjoyable recreation…"

Abashed I am! I look at him, stunned and dismayed. A "joke", the 4th Commandment! MOSES says it's a joke! He who solemnly and publicly declared in his last testament on Mount Nebo that to the Ten Commandments carved in stone we must not add or subtract nothing under penalty of malediction...

I am shivering. The sacred Shabat is a play-act, a joke of sort! I am shaking, my hands wet and freezing.

I almost expect the shock of the first stone a religious fanatic would angrily fling at my face. Over the centuries men and women were considered impious, blasphemers, heretics, and consequently tried then fatally stoned only for having desecrated the Shabat, no attenuating circumstances accepted!

I was so scared, enough to brave the possible wrath of the Master, and confronting MOSES again, I restated his answer as a question:

"The law of Shabat is a joke?"

"NO! NO! MOSES reassures me, in a serious comforting tone. The Shabat day of rest is not a joke. It is the formulation in 41 words which is an ironic play-act of the divine messenger.

There up on Mount Horeb, I made that same remark. I asked: Why so many details to express this simple law? The celestial messenger replied: *"What I say is what I say, you will understand later"*.

"The divine messenger was right! MOSES adds. Forty one words to compose and transmit the law on the compulsory rest day is a "publicity stunt" as you prolix citizens of the 21st century on Earth are now the foremost experts at.

You see, Shimeha, the weekly day of rest is a sanctuary, a capital monument of civilization, it is the open temple, the free initiation center, through which humans access the spiritual dimension of life, on all inhabited planets, in all universes.

Your Earth is still, at your epoch, largely infiltrated by Lucifer,

Satan and legions of human supporters, whose cupidity and materialistic greed are limitless and bottomless. This cupidity coupled with greed already present in my time has extended its empire up to your time.

The predicament is colossal. Those crowds of domineering men, sensual and possessive women, insatiable accumulators of material things and fossilized dogmas, how to effectively persuade them of the necessity to pause, relax, stop pursuing power and material wealth and turn to quietness, calm, silence, to achieve inner peace and hear the celestial music of the spheres?"

Silence.

"And, how to convince that mass of materialistic egoistical greedy individuals, yes, how to convince them especially to give to all beings who depend on them, time to breathe, time for freedom, time to experience transcendent cooperation with the invisible and eventually reveal to oneself the presence of the Divine and his host of celestial beings?

How? By specifying everything down to the smallest detail, by sanctifying the necessity to pause and rest, by ritualizing it outrageously when necessary. Look and see...the old "gimmick" still produces its intended effects. The enslavers complain about it, but they are isolated, powerless to halt the trend of free spiritual time enjoyment. Be the time of rest called Shabat, Sunday, Jameia, weekend, Fourth of July, Labor Day, it delivers its fruits and benefits. Men and women thanks to these times of rest and recreation have the opportunity to explore the celestial roads. Their minds liberated from material worries, men and women may enter their chosen places of worship to sing in harmony with the celestial chorus. Thanks to the 4th Law, rest days have increased in number and this ever-expanding orchard yield fruits more and more delicious...To achieve its mission and provide humans with a regenerative rest, the divine messenger has intentionally over-worded, over-signified the 4th Commandment. That was his purposeful strategy."

Silence.

"In the Sinai desert, during the crucial 40 years gradual preparation of the 12 tribes for their future civilizing mission, I created a recipe of my own to excite the minds and enduringly impress memories. I added spices to the actual facts, adjoining allegoric symbols to the heroic exit from Egypt. I made sure to transform into a legend the experience of an exodus full of obstacles and difficulties to escape from a house of bondage.

Thus it has become the fabled story I engraved in the famous chant of MOSES.[94] My sister, the celebrated Prophetess Myriam sang and taught that epic poem to all women and maidens of the 12 Tribes, dancing to the beat of the "sistra" tambourine.

And now, if individuals or nations want to free themselves from their own greed or that of an enemy, let them intone the potent call of MOSES with a pure and loving heart, and freedom will embrace them, fully, completely, body and soul..."

YELIYAEL has folded the virtual white banner, the Cathedral of Santiago de Compostella, now presents its familiar aspect, high perched statues of saints overlooking the vast paved courtyard, gates wide open to all those who, this Sunday, aspire to enjoy their mind-spirit happiness pursuit.

So, I say to MOSES: "To ensure the days of rest will be respected by the master himself, as well as the women, children and slaves in his house, the celestial messenger emphasized and specified all the requirements. In that regard the message has been well heard and strictly followed in some social quarters…

O MOSES, you are certainly aware of the thousands hours religious dogmatist Jews have been sitting to hyper-codify Shabat with hallucinating pettiness, relentlessly adding the most amazing details to what could be done or should not be done on this day of Shabat, the mandatory day of rest..."

"I know, replies MOSES. And this led to extreme stiffness, senseless ritualizing, boundless bigotry. But it is a small price to pay for such a great masterwork of large-scale liberation..."

SIMHA: "A small price, O MOSES? I remember that in the first century, one had to pay an exorbitant price…"

94 Song of Moses. Exodus 15:1-19

Albert jumps, startled by the boldness of my retort.

Angel YELIYAEL is frolicking on the plaza, listening to the music of the bards playing Keltic bagpipes, little interested in the evocation of human chimeras.

My heart is pounding, pounding. Fortunately we still are in the Corridors of Paradise, 100% Tolerance, Intolerance Zero. I hesitate, barely dare pronounce the unpronounceable. Nevertheless, I concentrate my strength and suddenly let go, precipitously:

"Because he healed a sick man on Shabat day, in Kfar Nahum[95], YEHOSHUA ben Miriam-Jesus was tersely tried by the Sanhedrin's Tzadokits priests and crucified by the Romans..."

"Well, Shimeha, replies MOSES with a slight hint of reproach, do you forget who YEHOSHUA Jesus really is? They who cloak themselves from daylight in the darkness of a cave, can they truthfully claim the Sun is cold?

ALBARDAN: "But, O MOSES, after 2,000 years of post Jesus religious extended practice of Christianity on Earth, Easter Stations of the Cross commemorating the Passion of Christ end at "laying Jesus in the tomb", thereby ignoring the major event, the crucial lesson on the essence of Life, namely the Glorified Resurrection, the negation of Death!"

MOSES: "Have you ever considered a spherical picture broader and brighter than the common flat delusive representations of the trial and crucifixion? Surely the deciphering of the Commandments is propelling your mind and spirit beyond those limited horizons!"

MOSES, extending his arms: "Before we part again, dear Shimeha, Albardan, hold firm my hands, Angel YELIYAEL shall wing us to the far rim of that blue cosmic abyssal cliff, where we shall together greet and admire, from above, the radiant rise of a nascent galaxy…"

---

95 Kfar Nahum, Hebrew name of a small town on the shore of Tiberias Lake, known in the New Testament as Capernaum.

Chapter Eight

The School of Athens

55. Manhattan, April 2001 AD.

THE SAGA OF THE SACRED TEN IS COMPLETED. Back from our expedition in the Corridors of Paradise we quietly regain strength, every day as relaxing and luminous as a Shabat day.

Mission accomplished...Relief and levity. We read, laugh, love, write, talk and spend time on this Earth without skipping a single step, without stealing a single second from eternity. Assiduously we refine the texts of our travel book, analyze sequences, compare our recollections, reliving every facet of our adventures by chiseling each phrase like a precious piece of jewelry, and above all, we dream...

The Ten Sacred Laws have all been explored, scrutinized, investigated, deciphered, unveiled, and we feel at peace...Mission accomplished!..Relief and levity...We just have to leisurely pursue simple goals, more earthy, until the next heavenly storm, the next call to celestial duty.

But last night, as I plunged into the silky stream of a deep sleep...the shiny threads of a dream embroidered clear moving images on the forefront of my unconsciousness...

I saw MOSES smiling mischievously; YELIYAEL's immense eyes blinked three times, casting vibrant yellow and purple sparks in rapid succession; Yohanan BEN ZAKAI pointed at me, a tinge of scolding on his gentle face; LAO TZU gave me a knowing wink; Mother EVE smirked indulgently; BEN FRANKLIN moved his right hand like a musician conducting a waltz; BUDDHA stared at me, re-assuringly, advising me to get rid of anxiety and guilt; Albert was conspicuously counting something with his fingers, gazing at me while frowning...Guilt? Why? What message are my friends trying to send me?

A giant red flash exploded in my foggy mind, illuming my consciousness clouded in sleep. Protected by slumber my dream continued and I saw clearly that the mission of the Sacred Ten was well done, but certainly not complete...Of course, the count is not exact! The Third Commandment, the mystery of the Third Law has not been solved!

And, instantly, the Sacred Ten saga resumed at fast pace:

First Rabbi Yohanan BEN ZAKAI enunciated the Third Commandment in ARCHAE LINGUA.

Then MOSES humorously presented us with the classic translation in English, his accent in every way identical to that of a modern Coptic Egyptian from Alexandria.

LAO TZU undertook the task to pronounce the 3rd Law in French, caressing each sound with the sweet and precious voice of a Chinese mandarin scholar.

Then we initiated together a wonderful philosophical debate, blending poetry, metaphysics and linguistics…

We merrily drew in the huge memory reservoirs of terrestrial historic hidden records, and in the bottomless timeless archangelic archives of the celestial spheres, opening and extricating easily the secret revelations embedded in the 3rd Commandment.

Interested by this open truth-seeking contest many friendly celestials showed up to participate: Socrates disclosed secrets regarding the familiar Genie sitting on his shoulders while he was practicing maieutic in Athens; Rabbi Akiba provided advice on how to reveal Kabalah while avoiding being flayed alive; luminous erudite Beruriah, pioneer of women's liberation, gave us an hilarious speech about much needed male's liberation; indomitably courageous Joan of Arc enlightened the mystery of the Destiny of nations and expounded on the role of Angels in her stunning military victories.

Michelangelo, laughing sarcastically, told us why he had inserted the "pagan" Sybille of Cumes on the ceiling of the Sistine chapel; visionary Leonardo da Vinci dodged a question regarding a certain technical drawing of his resembling a 20th century helicopter, and, to our delight, chose instead to instruct us on how to understand and fluently speak the language of birds.

Albert and I, still imbued with the principle "100% Tolerance-Intolerance Zero", formally invited Adolf Hitler and Tomas de Torquemada to participate…but they were nowhere to be found…

Philosopher Giordano Bruno, brotherly holding Albert's shoulders disclosed "for our eyes only" the source code allowing the deciphering of his essay *De l'Infinito Universo e Mondi* and his unpublished manuscript *The Plurality of Inhabited Worlds*.

Cistercian monk Bernard de Clairvaux revealed three unrecorded events regarding the secret activities of the Knights Templar in Jerusalem…

Also came Victor Hugo, Saint Yves d'Alveydre, Sainte Catherine Labouré, Johan Wolfgang von Goethe, Hypathia of Alexandria, Antoine Fabre d'Olivet, Father Theilhard de Chardin, Arthur Rimbaud, Padre Pio, Eugene Delacroix, Saint Hildegard von Bingen, Wolfgang Amadeus Mozart, Alphonse de Ratisbonne, Winston Churchill…many others showed up and went; several stayed, enjoying the merry vivacious company.

At one time our space patch in the firmament resembled the crowd on Raphael's painting, the School of Athens…

We sat floating in the galactic expanse, comfortably installed on the magnetic currents of energy waves circulating in the intervals of universal matter.

Stars were spinning dizzily, blazing comets danced gracefully, iridescent crystal spheres formed and vanished, approaching and moving away ... the show was grand, majestic!

I woke up suddenly...and as a Mesopotamian scribe would hold a clay tablet or an ancient Egyptian calligrapher a papyrus leaf, I grasped half a ream of white paper and a pen to transcribe in details the words and ideas of this great debate on the Third Commandment, to conclude in complete delight the story of our Quest and investigation on the Ten Sacred laws of MOSES.

My hand strong and flexible, ready for action, lightly resting on the white page, remained motionless. Nothing to say... nothing to write... silence... silence…

And voilà, I had forgotten everything!

I walked out and drifted into the city, turning alternately to the left, right, randomly to North, South, East, West, wandering free and carefree...strangely I felt no sadness or regret…

Back home around noontime I found Albert waiting for me in the foyer. Greeting me with a broad mysterious smile he ceremoniously handed me a letter size piece of paper, folded in three.

"I found this on the floor at the foot of our little fountain. A celestial invitation from YELIYAEL! Addressed to us both. I sense we shall soon take off again on the wings of the Angel!"

I opened the missive and attentively read the angelic message:

From: YELIYAEL
To: SHIMEHA & ALBARDAN
0.1א.2ב.3ג.5ה.8ח.13.21.34.55.89.144.233.377
610.987.1597.2584. 4181.6765.10946
17711.28657.46368.77025.123393.200418
323811.524229.848040.1372269.1541877
2914146.4456023.7370169.11826192.19196361
1.61 0.66666666 + 0.33333333 Call me!

NO END...

APPENDIX
&
BRIEF BIBLIOGRAPHY

APPENDIX 1

Transliteration system used in this book.

Hebrew letters-sounds we have transliterated in English as follows:

B	= בּ	Bet	Â Ô Ê	= ע	Ayin
V	= ב	Vet	P	= פּ	Pe
V	= ו	Vav	F	= פ	Phe
H	= ה	He	PH	= פ	Phe
CH	= ח	Chet	TS	= צ	Tsade
T	= ט	Tet	SH	= ש	Shin
Y	= י	Yod	TH	= ת	Tav
K	= כּ	Kaf			
KH	= כ	Khaf			

All other letters-sounds follow the Latin alphabet:

A	= א	Aleph	M	= מ	Mem
G	= ג	Guimel	N	= נ	Noun
D	= ד	Dalet	S	= ס	Samech
Z	= ז	Zayin	Q	= ק	Koph
L	= ל	Lamed	R	= ר	Resh

APPENDIX 2

Universal Language.

Various common définitions:

1- a hypothetical or historical language spoken and understood by all or most of the world's population.

2- a language said to be understood by all living things, beings, and objects alike.

3- some mythological or religious traditions state that there was once a single universal language among all people, or shared by humans and supernatural beings, however, this is not supported by historical evidence.

The above definitions found on the Internet noticeably acknowledge the existence of the notion of a “Universal Language", while at the same time, belittling terms such as *"hypothetical", "mythological", "said to be"* and the use of past time "*there was once*", definitely induce skepticism in regard with the actual reality of a source Language at present active on Earth and throughout the whole Universe. Furthermore, those definitions point only at the surface of the phenomenon and never even hint at the nature and expression of the "inner" reality of the Universal Language.

Archaeo-Linguistic Analysis & Archae Lingua.

In THE SACRED TEN, the Archaeo-Linguistic Method applied to Biblical Hebrew and modern languages as well, demonstrates the *undeniable* pervasive *presence* of ARCHAE LINGUA, Universal Language ever-springing source of all tongues.

The principles of Archaeo-Linguistic Analysis may also be found in the book "*Angel Signs*", where the authors have endeavored to disclose some wonderful features of the Universal Resonance, revealing the *encrypted core meanings-notions-values* attached to each consonant of the Alphabet.

APPENDIX 3

About Angels

Albeit unbeknownst to many modern men and women, there are millions, even trillions Angels, co-operating in the spiritual realms of the Universe. Knowingly or unknowingly you are benefiting from their presence and assistance.

Evidently, THE SACRED TEN saga has been made possible by Seraph Angels YELIYAEL, YELAZAEL and Archangel GABRIEL.

"Seraphim function as teachers of men by guiding the footsteps of the human personality into paths of new and progressive experience." The Urantia Book.

All Angels have a personal NAME, and, being aware of the powers of ARCHAE LINGUA, the Universal Language common to

Humans and Celestials, you have now the opportunity to establish a direct and conscious connection with one or several celestial Angels.

Learning the exact names of 72 Angels as revealed and decrypted in the book "*Angel Signs*", readers shall become increasingly receptive to the presence of many celestial forces and benefit from their active guidance.

Website http://www.AngelSignsOnline.com

APPENDIX 4

Brief Bibliography

Sepher Torah, Hebrew Version. La Bible édition bilingue, traduction française sous la direction du Grand-Rabbin Zadoc Kahn.
Librairie Colbo 1967 Paris.
The Holy Bible, New King James Version.
The Urantia Book. 1955. The Urantia Foundation.
Fabre D'Olivet, Antoine. Hebraic Tongue Restored. And the True Meaning of the Hebrew Words Re-Established and Proved by The Radical Analysis. Translation by Nyan Louise Redfield, 1921. La Langue Hébraïque Restituée, 1815. Réédition : L'Âge d'homme, Lausanne, 1985.
Saint Yves d'Alveydre Alexandre, L'Archéomètre, Clef de toutes les religions et de toutes les sciences de l'Antiquité by. Edition posthume 1910. Mission des Juifs, 1884 by Alexandre Saint Yves d'Alveydre.
Lao Tzu Tao Te Ching, translation by Stephen Mitchell, Harper Collins 1991.
Lao-Tzeu Tao-Te-king, La Voie et sa vertu, traduit par Francois-Houang et Pierrre Leyris. Editions du Seuil Paris 1979.
Borel Henri. Wu Wei, Etude inspirée par la philosophie de Lao-Tseu. 1931, nouvelle edition 1995, Guy Tredaniel Editeur Paris.
Stewart, Daniel Blair, 1995, Akunathon the Extraterrestrial King.
Plato, Socrates. Cratylus dialogue on Correctness of names.

Haldane, Albert & Seraya, Simha - Angel Signs, A celestial Guide to the Powers of Your Own Guardian Angel, 2002-2011 Manakael.
Foucault, Michel, 1966. Les Mots et les Choses (The Order of Things).
Hegel, G.W.F, La Phenomelogie de l'Esprit, 1807. Traduction Jean Hyppolite, 1939 Aubier, Editons Montaigne, Paris.
Saint Anselme. Œuvres Philosophiques. French translation from Latin by Pierre Rousseau. Aubier.Paris.
Drucker, Johanna. The Alphabetic Labyrinth, 1995 Thames & Hudson
Spinoza, Baruch. The Philosphy of Spinoza by Harry Austryn Wolson. Shocken Books New York.
Bohm, David. Infinite Potential. F.David Peat 1997. Helix.
Wilson, Ian. Before the Flood. 2004 St. Martin Griffin NY.
Schwaller de Lubicz, Isha. Her Bak Egyptian Initiate 1978. Inner Traditions. Also The Opening of the Way, A Practical Guide to the Wisdom Teachings of Ancient Egypt. 1980. Inner Traditions.
Derter, Robert. The Theory of Almost Everything. The Unsung Triumph of Modern Physics. 2006. Plume.
Greene, Brian. The Fabric of the Cosmos. Space, Time and the Structure of Reality.2004. Random House NY.
Poe, Richard. Black Spark White Fire. 1997. Prima.
Spalding, Baird T. Life and Teaching of the Masters of the East. 1924.Devorss Publications.
Lederman, Leon. The God Particle. 2006. Mariner.
Kramer, Samuel Noah. The Sumerians. 1971. University of Chicago Press.
Bottero, Jean. Religion in Ancient Mesopotamia. 2004. University of Chicago Press.
Roux, Georges. Ancient Iraq.1993. Penguin
Cauvin, Jacques. The Birth of the Gods. 2007. Cambridge University.
Lemaire, Andre. Le Monde de La Bible.1998. Gallimard.
Bruno, Giordano. De Gli Heroici Furori. Des Fureurs Heroiques. 1585. Paris. Texte traduit par Paul Henri Michel.1954

ABOUT THE AUTHORS

SIMHA SERAYA, a gifted intuitive, inspirational mentor and angelologist is a Graduate of Paris Sorbonne University, major in Psychology and Sociology. Fluent in English, French, Hebrew and Classical Arabic, she is also a long-time dedicated researcher and discoverer of the fundamental linguistic components and elements constitutive of all languages, ancient and modern. She lives, writes and paints in New York and South Florida.

e-mail: archangel7997@gmail.com

ALBERT HALDANE, is a published cosmic poetry author and philosopher-metaphysician. Continuing his classical education in ancient Greek and Latin, he graduated at Paris Sorbonne University, Master in Hellenistic and Renaissance Philosophy. Assiduous meta-ethicist, hermeneutist and futurologist Albert lives and writes in New York and South Florida.

e-mail: archangel7997@gmail.com

www.ingramcontent.com/pod-product-compliance
Lightning Source LLC
Chambersburg PA
CBHW070857260626
47162CB00007B/2486